RULE OF THE AURORA KING

RULE OF THE AURORA KING

NISHA J. TULI

orbitbooks.net

ORBIT

First published in Great Britain in 2023 by Orbit

1 3 5 7 9 10 8 6 4 2

A CIP catalogue record for this book
is available from the British Library.

ISBN 978-0-356-52338-5

Printed and bound in Great Britain by Clays Ltd, Elcograf, S.p.A.

Papers used by Orbit are from well-managed forests
and other responsible sources.

Orbit
An imprint of
Little, Brown Book Group
Carmelite House
50 Victoria Embankment
London EC4Y 0DZ

An Hachette UK Company
www.hachette.co.uk

www.orbitbooks.net

To every woman who's been told they're too wild. Too impulsive. Too much. May you always stay that way.

CELESTRIA

BELTZA MOUNTAINS

THE MANOR

TOR

NOSTRAZA

SIVA FOREST

ALLUVION

SINEN RIVER

ZELEN
COVE

APHELION

THE SARGA WOODS

OURANOS

Author's Note

Welcome back to the world of Ouranos! I hope you're eager to dive back into Lor's story and find out what happens next.

Expect a lot of angst and pining in this one, and maybe a moment or two when you want to throw the book across the room? I'm sorry, but don't worry, I promise it's all going to be worth it.

Content warnings are pretty much the same as for book 1, but you can find them on my website if you'd like to review them at nishajtuli.com.

Thank you again!

Love,

Nisha

CHAPTER ONE

LOR

PRESENT DAY: THE AURORA

I hurl the vase with all my strength, missing the Aurora Prince's head by just a hair. He lifts his arms to deflect the blow, and it explodes against the wall, peppering him with shards of broken porcelain. I lunge for a nearby table, attempting to snatch up a small crystal dish when he's on me, one large hand snagging my wrist and the other circling my throat. He shoves me flat against the wall with enough force that I grunt at the impact.

"Stop that," he hisses, his face so perilously close to mine I feel the warmth of his breath on my lips. We stand inside my bedroom—no, my *prison*—in a house somewhere in the middle of the Void in the furthest reaches of The Aurora. Outside, there are mountains and an endless stretch of midnight sky littered with rivers of stars and rainbow ribbons of color.

Amya and Mael broke me out of Aphelion almost five weeks ago, and they've kept me here, refusing to let me go. At first, I was convinced they were returning me to Nostraza, but my fate continues to be more complicated than that. Instead, they've stuck me in this opulent room and won't stop asking me questions. I've contemplated the logistics of my escape countless times, but I don't know where I'd go. We're surrounded by nothing but a deadly forest and even deadlier mountains.

"I'm not telling you anything until you bring me Willow and Tristan," I say for the thousandth time, or maybe it's the millionth by now. I lost count weeks ago.

"Not until you answer my questions. I have ways of making you talk, Inmate," Nadir says, baring his teeth, those dark and disconcerting aurora-infused eyes flashing with fury. The colors swirl in his irises, the effect nearly hypnotic. He leans closer, nothing left but a constant wall of ire between us. My skin twitches in response to his closeness, like ribbons are sliding through my blood.

"Then do it," I bite back. He's been threatening me for weeks, and I'm not sure what's keeping him from making good on his promises. So I keep pushing him, trying to make him snap. Wondering how far I can go.

I meant what I said. He *thinks* he knows something and maybe his suspicions are right, but I will confirm nothing until I know my brother and sister are alive.

Even then, this prince is dreaming if he thinks he's getting anything from me.

His jaw clenches, but there's a flicker of hesitation in his eyes, so quick I'm not sure if I imagine it.

"Do it," I taunt as his grip tightens around my throat, the pressure bordering on dangerous.

I stare him down, determined to never let him see my fear.

He will never break me.

"Show me how you're going to make me talk, oh mighty prince. I promise there's nothing you can do I haven't already survived."

"Nadir, stop it," Amya says, entering the room, her disapproving glare taking in the way he has me pinned to the wall. "You can't do that to her."

Nadir turns his furious gaze on his sister, but she doesn't even blink. I'm learning she's mostly immune to her brother's moods and make a mental note to ask her for some pointers.

She's wearing a long black skirt split to reveal legs clad in tight black leather, along with a sleeveless corset, tied with violet laces running up the front. Fingerless lace gloves adorn her hands, and her black hair, streaked with colors, is anchored into two messy buns on either side of her head.

She sits down on a black velvet chair, crossing her legs, completely at ease despite the circumstances of the scene she's just interrupted. Nadir and I glare at each other, the atmosphere sparking as both our chests expand with tight, angry breaths.

"I sent word to Nostraza," she says, drawing both our attentions towards her.

"Amya," he growls, and that strange sensation like cords moving under my skin ripples again.

She holds up a delicate hand. "Don't worry. I was discreet."

"If Father knows she's here—"

"He won't," she says, her own aurora-flecked eyes flashing as her cool composure slips. "I know what's at stake. Don't treat me like a child."

"Are you planning to let me go, or am I to continue standing here with your hand around my throat while you converse in my presence?" I ask.

Nadir looks back at me, indecision warring in his gaze. He wants to do something drastic. He's losing patience, and it's so obvious he's perched on the edge, ready to tip over.

Well, he can keep on waiting. In fact, I'll give him a shove.

When his jaw ticks, our gazes melt into each other and that same feeling, like I'm being touched from under my skin, resurfaces. Though I'd never say it out loud, I can't help but notice it only happens in his presence. I don't want to think about what it might mean. I don't *know* what it means, but I'm sure all it can signal is trouble. He hesitates for another second before he finally lets go of my throat.

"Stop fucking throwing things," he says, his voice low and deadly enough to send a shiver down my spine. "Or I'll chain you up in the basement with my *pets*." The vicious glint in his eyes suggests these *pets* are more monster than friendly companion.

He steps back, watching me like a ravenous predator ready to tear out my throat at the slightest provocation. With my gaze deliberately pinned on him, I step out from his towering shadow and before he can stop me, I reach for the same crystal dish and hurl it against the wall.

It smashes apart with a resounding shatter, and I turn to him with a triumphant smile, flipping a lock of my hair over my shoulder.

I flutter my eyelashes innocently. "You were saying?"

His eyes go so dark they turn completely black, those swirling lights dimming down to nothing but inky pools deep enough to drown in. That pull surges again, like a rabid demon trying to rip straight out of my skin. Why does his anger affect me this way?

Amya covers her mouth, trying to suppress a smile, while I look down my nose at the prince. He growls and stalks over, grabbing my wrist again.

"I warned you," he says, pulling me forward so I nearly trip, my hand slamming into the center of his solid chest to catch myself.

"Wait! I want to hear what she learned from Nostraza. Are Tristan and Willow alive?"

Nadir jerks me around, my back pressing against his chest and his arm banding around my waist before his hand clamps over my mouth.

"Don't tell her anything," Nadir says to his sister, who's clearly about to reply to my question. "I swear to Zerra, Amya. *Don't.*"

Her mouth snaps shut, her lips rolling inwards to the muffled sounds of my protest.

"Let me tell her," she pleads, and the princess climbs a tiny notch in my esteem.

"No," he snarls. "I warned her."

He picks me up by the waist as I flail against the iron band of his arm. After spinning around, he walks me to the door while I attempt to wrestle from his hold, kicking my legs, trying to aim for his shins. Or maybe a far more precious body part.

Of course, he's High Fae and incredibly strong, so I might as well be fighting an iron tree with the personality of a cactus.

We enter the hall to find Mael walking towards my room. At the sight of us, he presses his back and palms against the wall, letting us pass. "Things are going well, I see."

"Shut up," Nadir says as we struggle down the hall and then he stops. I'm still bucking and flailing as he turns around and then around, as if he can't decide where to go.

"Problem?" Mael asks, coming up and folding his arms over his broad chest. He's wearing his usual light leather armor, his black hair cut close and his deep brown skin gleaming under a row of tiny chandeliers suspended the length of the hallway. Amya is behind him with a grin she's obviously trying to contain.

"We don't have a dungeon in this house," Nadir says, as though this is everyone's fault and this salient fact has just occurred to him. So much for the threat of locking me up with his *pets*.

"It's not really that sort of house," Amya says. "That was kind of the point when we built it."

"That was before I realized we'd be harboring a prisoner who behaves like a rabid *child*," he snarls, and I bark out a gleeful laugh that definitely makes him angrier.

The prince practically roars in frustration and then kicks open the door at the end of the hall, carrying me into an enormous bedroom with a huge bed sitting under a long bank of windows, where the northern lights paint the sky in ribbons of color.

As much as Aphelion may have been a court masquerading as a haven of gilded beauty, I miss its bright blue skies like flowers miss the sun. This depressing canvas of grey and more grey is dredging up the painful memories of the twelve years I barely lived under this bleak sky.

Everything in the room is black save for the occasional streaks of color accenting the rugs and furniture—crimson and violet and emerald.

Oh, and the two enormous fluffy white dogs who lie in front of the fireplace, only their heads lifting as we enter, their dark eyes watching us with shrewd curiosity. I think they're dogs—they're big enough to be wolves who feast on small children for supper. Are these the pets he meant? They don't look *that* dangerous. In fact, they're kind of cute if you ignore the fact they could probably take off my head with a single bite.

That's when one of them curls a lip, a low growl rumbling from its throat with its far too intelligent gaze fixed on me.

Okay, never mind. Definitely very dangerous.

Nadir hauls me across the floor as Amya and Mael exchange a careful glance.

"Nadir," Amya says softly.

"Not now," Nadir replies, sharp as a knifepoint. A moment later, ribbons of colorful light peel away from his hands and secure themselves around my wrists. They feel like nothing against my skin, but I can't separate my hands like I've been shackled by tendrils of air.

Mael's dark eyebrow raises, and it's obvious he wants to comment, but he bites his tongue while Nadir binds my wrists to the bedpost with more ribbons of colorful magic. If my primary goal wasn't to rip out his heart and feed it to those dogs, I might admit his power was rather beautiful.

When he's satisfied, he steps back, folding his muscular arms across his chest with a smug smile. He wears his usual uniform of a fitted black shirt and pants, everything tailored to his body with irritating perfection.

"You asshole," I hiss, tugging on my restraints. "Let me out of here."

Nadir crowds me against the bedpost, leaving only a breath of tension separating us. "I told you if you threw anything else, there would be consequences."

I jerk on my restraints with an angry huff, resisting the urge to spit at him. Kick him. Headbutt him. Anything. I'm so frustrated and angry and sick of this shit.

No one will ever let me be free.

"And I told you I won't cooperate with you until you bring my friends here," I snap.

I'm still protecting the secret of our family tie in the hopes I can shield them from what I suspect the prince wants.

"You think you can scare me? I survived twelve years in that fucking prison of yours while you slept in your fancy silk sheets and pranced around in your fancy clothes. Those dogs were probably treated better than I was."

This time I do spit, but somehow he avoids it, my saliva landing on the ground in an unsatisfying drop of nothing.

"You were in that prison because you committed a crime," he says.

"I was a child!" I scream so loud my voice cracks. "I did nothing, you fucking monster!"

"You'll refer to me as 'Your Highness,'" he hisses, swirls of crimson rolling in his eyes.

"You *aren't* my prince." I spit the words, trying to infuse them with the bottomless depth of my hatred.

I will never, ever bow to this pompous Fae asshole.

"*You* are a citizen of The Aurora."

"Go to hell. I am not, and I'll die before I call you that."

His nostrils flare, but he doesn't respond, turning on his heel and gesturing to Amya and Mael to follow. At the door, he stops and looks over his shoulder.

"If you keep this shit up, Morana and Khione won't hesitate to put you back in line."

The two furry monsters in front of the fire perk up at the sound of their names, looking innocent enough with their fluffy coats that look as thick and white as fresh snow. But then they bare their mouthfuls of sharp teeth in a tumble of low growls, reminding me not to be fooled by appearances.

Amya throws me a sympathetic look that I don't return. She slept in silk sheets and wore pretty clothes while we rotted away inside Nostraza, too. She might be the nicer one, whatever that's worth, but she isn't innocent of anything that happened to me and my siblings.

The door closes, and I look around the room. My gaze skates over the dogs whose heads are again resting on their paws, but I'm sure they're acutely aware of my every move. Nadir's black jacket hangs off the back of the chair at a desk in the corner, and the far wall is lined with shelves stuffed full of books.

From the other side of the door, I hear the muffled voices of Mael, Amya, and Nadir arguing about something. Presumably me.

Nadir has been questioning me about who I am and what Atlas wanted from the day I arrived, but I've refused to answer anything. I don't know what he believes, or how close to the truth he is, but I'm not making it that easy for him. Atlas wanted to use me for the power I might hold, and I have to assume this dark prince's ambitions lie in a similar direction.

Tired of standing, I sink to the floor, my magical handcuffs adjusting just enough for me to get somewhat comfortable.

I need to get out of here. Not just this room, but this house. The trouble is I have no idea where I'd go. I have no home and not a penny to my name. And I can't just waltz into Nostraza and claim Willow and Tristan. I don't even know if they're still alive.

The Sun Mirror told me to find the Heart Crown, and I have even less clue about where to start with that. Find it where?

Finally, the door opens and Nadir strides in, tossing me a dark frown before he slams it behind him. Amya and Mael are no longer in tow, and a tiny wisp of fear licks its way up the back of my neck. Suddenly, I'm very aware that I have no idea what this wild Fae prince is capable of. How afraid do I need to be? Will he force me to do the same things as the guards in Nostraza?

My heart rate kicks up, my palms growing damp. I'll die before I suffer anything like that again.

No one here has harmed me physically, but I know I'm walking a razor-thin line with my constant impertinence. But what would be the point in cooperating? I have almost nothing to lose. If he plans to use me like Atlas, then I'm fucked either way. The only power I hold are the secrets locked in my head and the capacity to wield them for Tristan's and Willow's freedom.

Despite the fact he hasn't technically hurt me, it's obvious the prince is lethal and could kill anyone without a thought. He's like a coiled spring ready to strike. He radiates power and menace and an unmistakable aura of darkness. That peculiar feeling under my skin buzzes again, and I inhale a deep breath, trying to suppress it.

Nadir walks over to the fireplace and crouches down in front of his dogs, ruffling their fur while they roll over to bask in his attention. It's clear they hold a special place in his heart, and the scene is so oddly incongruent with his usual behavior that I find myself relaxing a bit. When he's done, he stands, refusing to acknowledge my presence, before he disappears into the bathroom. Then I hear the water running, and I let out a huff, blowing an errant lock of hair out of my eyes.

There's a chill in the air that's the perpetual chill of The Aurora I remember so well. Everything is cold. The air and the sky and their fucking *prince*. I'm wearing a pair of soft leggings and thick socks with a thick black sweater. Thankfully, they're warm and comfortable enough.

The door opens again, and I suck in a sharp breath at Nadir's change of clothing. His top half is bare, and it's virtually impossible not to be taken in by the perfection of his lean, hard physique. The curves and dips of gleaming brown muscle shift and bunch as he walks to his desk, still not looking at me, and shuffles through a stack of papers.

An array of colorful, swirling markings cover his skin, spreading across his chest and the arches of his shoulders. He's wearing a pair of soft black pants that hang off his hips so low it's nearly scandalous. What the fuck. Is this some kind of game to him?

He looks up, our gazes catching, and I quickly look away, mortified I've been spotted staring. I hear him snort out a derisive laugh as he turns down the light on his desk, throwing the room into near darkness, save the lights of the aurora glowing through the window.

"What are you doing?" I ask, peering at him through the dimness. My earlier nervousness about what exactly he plans to do with me alone and tied up in his bedroom cinches my chest tight.

The colors of the Borealis reflect off his skin, his high cheekbones and his strong jaw. He pads along the thick rugs that cover the black marble floor, and there's something awkwardly intimate about the glimpse of his bared feet.

"Going to sleep, Inmate. It's getting late."

"What about me?" I tug on the magic ropes still anchoring me to the bed.

"What about you?"

"You can't just leave me here like this all night."

"Yes. I can. How are you going to stop me?"

I'm definitely not surprised by this answer. I pissed him off earlier and now it's time for his retribution.

"I hate you," I say, dropping my voice to a menacing whisper.

"So you've said, many, many times. As you can see, I'm perfectly at ease with that fact. I plan to sleep like a baby, knowing just how much you *loathe* me."

He walks to the side of the bed, pulls back the sheets, and looks down to where I'm sitting on the floor, a smirk on his face. He slides under the covers and pulls them up, sighing with a groan of satisfaction I assume is meant to rub in how comfortable he is and how uncomfortable I am. It works. I shift on the hard ground, my ass already numb and my arms sore from their restricted movement. Still, it *does* seem like he's planning to, in fact, sleep, rather than exact some depraved brand of revenge.

He lets out a short whistle, and his dogs both stand up and stretch in front of the firelight, the fine hairs on their bodies glowing orange. At first, I think they're headed for me. I swallow a nervous knot in my throat, but they pass by and then leap up onto the bed, settling down next to their master with soft grunts.

Right, even the dogs get better treatment. I should have remembered.

Though I can't see Nadir anymore, only the lump of his blanketed form, I toss him my most withering glare, trying to incinerate him where he lies. As if reading my mind, he lets out another exaggerated sigh, and who would have thought an immortal prince could be so fucking petty?

"Sweet dreams, Inmate," he says, a definite thread of amusement in his voice.

I hold back the snarl perched on the roof of my mouth, refusing to give him even a shred of satisfaction as I stare into the dark and vow to kill him.

Slowly and painfully.

The only thing left to decide is if I'll end the prince or his father first.

CHAPTER TWO

I sleep only in fits and starts, nodding off as my head drops and wakes me with a jolt. Being too uncomfortable to sleep reminds me of those days I spent in the Hollow before Gabriel stole me away. I wonder what my former warder is doing right now. If he knows where I've gone or if he cares at all. He's probably thrilled to be rid of me after all the trouble I caused.

Throughout the night, I listen to the ripple of canine snores mixing with the prince's hushed breaths. I yank on my restraints, wishing I could climb up there to inflict some pain, but he slumbers on, oblivious to my discomfort. Maybe I should start screaming for no other reason than to interrupt his beauty sleep, but decide it's not worth the consequences of what he might do to me then.

Eventually, the sky turns from inky black to somber grey and I scowl, aching for the warmth of proper sunlight and a bright blue sky. Once the aurora lights retreat for the day, leaving behind a depressing slate of emptiness, I wonder again why anyone would choose to live in this place.

I think of the beaches in Aphelion. The heat of the sand and the crash of the water. While things were certainly questionable in the golden palace by the sea, I still crave the luxury of sunshine on my skin.

There's a soft knock at the door before it swings open on silent hinges. A woman in a simple tunic and leggings enters with a silver tray suspended between her hands. I recognize her as one of the manor's staff, because she brings the meals to my room, too. My stomach rumbles with hunger as she casts a furtive glance in my direction.

She evades eye contact as she deposits the tray on a black wooden table situated in front of the windows. She removes a plate of bread, bacon, fruit, and eggs. Cups and silverware and crisp white napkins. A carafe of coffee, its rich aroma permeating the air.

Just like in Aphelion, all the servants are human. I guess Fae are too important to dirty their hands with the menial tasks of cooking and cleaning.

When she's done with the prince's breakfast, she leaves the room and returns a moment later with two giant silver bowls that she places on the floor near the door. Morana and Khione both leap off the bed and pad over to their food, digging in their snouts.

I hear the rustle of shifting bedsheets and watch Nadir sit up, his long hair gloriously tousled from sleep. Last night, I'd tried to stifle my reaction to his bare tattooed torso and gleaming brown skin, but his entire presence fills the room with a sort of barely contained energy. He ignores me as he rises from the bed and strides over to his morning meal.

"Thank you, Brea," he says, his formal tone much nicer than he's ever used with me, before she nods.

"Enjoy." With her hands clasped in front of her, she gives me another surreptitious look and then hustles out of the room. I watch her leave, wanting to call her back. I don't want to remain here alone with the prince. This forced proximity with nothing and no one else acting as a barrier between us unnerves me in ways I don't care to examine.

Now that he's awake, that presence that writhes under my skin stirs again, pulling at my nerves. While he was sleeping, there was a moment of respite, but as he stares at me now, it breathes back into life like a bubble filling with air. I blink, willing it away.

This doesn't mean anything.

He leans in his chair, the muscles in his stomach contracting, while I do my best not to notice the trail of dark hair that disappears into his low waistband. He kicks his feet up on a second chair and pins me with his unsettling gaze as he lifts his coffee cup and takes a loud sip.

Licking my lips involuntarily, I watch his movements, practically tasting the aromatic brew on my tongue.

"Hungry, Inmate?"

My nostrils flare and I give him a hard look. "No."

He smirks as he picks up a triangle of bread and bites into it. I've become somewhat more acquainted with the food in The Aurora over the weeks, but most of it is still unfamiliar. During my time in Aphelion, I experienced so many new things, but every time I turn a corner, I'm struck with yet another deficiency in my upbringing. The mingled aromas of spices I don't recognize linger in the air, making my mouth water.

"Fine, then I won't share."

"Like you were going to, anyway," I retort, and he smirks again, taking another bite and chewing slowly before groaning like it's the best thing he's ever tasted. "So, what do you plan to do with me? Keep me chained here like your pet?"

At the mention of pets, I hear the soft click of paws on the marble floor. They've finished their meals and are trotting over to see their master, their thick white tails swaying back and forth. He gives them each a rub behind the ears, and I notice the way his eyes soften. Can it be this prince has a heart buried somewhere in that chiseled chest?

"Oh, I'm sorry. Even your dogs have the freedom to walk around," I say bitterly.

He meets me with a condescendingly amused look.

"When you can behave as well as they do, Inmate, then I'll consider treating you the same."

"My name is Lor, you asshole," I bite out. "If you want me to act like a human, then stop calling me that."

Nadir takes his feet off the chair and leans forward with his elbows braced on his knees. His dogs turn around to face me, their lips twitching. Something tells me they'd gleefully rip out my spleen at a snap of the prince's fingers.

"But I so enjoy the sound of it, *Inmate*. I don't think I'll be doing that. And it isn't a *human* that I want you to act like."

We both stare at each other, those words hanging in the air like a deadly vow. He keeps digging, trying to force me to reveal my secrets, but I refuse to budge until I get what I want. I will *not* be the one who blinks first.

I lunge for him and snap my teeth. Of course, the effort is entirely wasted since I can't move more than a few inches from where I'm tethered. His dogs' ears perk up, clearly sensing a threat to their master. He makes a shushing noise that settles them both and then he chuckles as he shakes his head. "Atlas thought he was going to bond with you. You would have torn him to shreds."

"At least Atlas didn't chain me to his fucking bed."

Nadir arches a dark eyebrow. "No, he just threw you in his dungeon." I press my lips together, hating that he's right. Why am I defending Atlas? I hate them both. They're both vile, egotistical beasts. "And I'd still like to know why he did that. What did the Mirror say to you?"

"The Mirror rejected me," I say again, which is mostly accurate.

"You're lying."

"I'm not. It told me I wasn't meant to be the queen of Aphelion," I say, the words carefully curving around the truth. It *is* what the Mirror told me, but Nadir will have to torture me before I share the far more noteworthy details it revealed.

Again, I tug on my restraints to no avail. I have to get out of here. I have to find Tristan and Willow and get us all away before we can finally claim our family's legacy.

Nadir peers at me, trying to read the lie in my words.

"Did you hear back from Nostraza?" I ask, and he blinks.

"What?"

"Your sister said she sent a messenger to Nostraza yesterday. Did she hear anything back?"

"I've been in this room with you since last night, Inmate. I have no idea."

I resist the urge to growl at his tone and the way he treats my question as though the answer is of no consequence. Tristan and Willow might be dead, and it clearly doesn't matter to him. While I was off playing future queen, they might have died and I wasn't there. But I also need to acknowledge that this behavior is getting me nowhere. Nadir possesses an uncanny talent for digging under my skin, and I can't keep letting him get to me.

"Can we ask her?" I plead next, trying to make my tone a bit more pleasant even as I'm internally screaming. I hate kowtowing to this asshole.

"When I'm done eating," he says, turning back to his plate and pointedly ignoring me. He *knows* how important this is to me. I haven't been subtle about it.

"Fine." I sit back, leaning against the bedframe as I wait for him to eat, the silence in the room broken only by the clink of his mug and the sounds of his fork scraping the china. The dogs lay down, their heads resting on their paws as they watch me. Probably for any sudden movements. Resting but always alert. I'd do well to remember that Nadir isn't the only animal in this room.

He eats slowly, taking his time, and I know he's doing it just to aggravate me. Nothing about this prince is slow unless it serves his purposes. I suck in a dragged breath, trying to calm my rage and the rapid thud of my heart.

My inability to rein in my temper is one of my greatest weaknesses. One I need to learn to control. After I receive word about my brother and sister, I'll have more options, but right now, I have to pretend I'm willing to cooperate.

Nadir finally finishes eating and pushes his chair from the table, ignoring me as he stalks to the bathroom. At that moment, I'm reminded of the uncomfortable pressure on my bladder. The shower turns on, and I grit my teeth at the sound. How long is he going to take in there?

I squirm on the floor, worried I might wet my pants if I sit here much longer. Maybe I should do it and soil this expensive-looking carpet. We'll see who's the animal, then. But I dismiss the idea, knowing even *I'm* not that insane, trying to focus on something else as I wait.

Finally, the water turns off, and I hear his movements on the other side of the door.

"Hey!" I yell into the empty room, hoping he won't ignore me.

I have no idea what to call him. I've avoided the question for weeks, sidestepping the need to address him directly, but now I'm stuck. Your Highness sounds ridiculous. He isn't my prince, nor will he ever be. And I meant what I said about ever calling him that.

But calling him Nadir feels too intimate—we certainly aren't friends or allies. He's never referred to me as anything but Inmate, so perhaps I can find something equally demeaning. "Hey! I need to pee!"

The door opens a few seconds later, and he's now half dressed in slim black pants that hug his thighs and his hips, along with a crisp black shirt, still unbuttoned so it frames the colorful tattoos that cover his torso. The corner of his mouth hooks up in a wicked smile, his eyes flashing with mirth. "What was that, Inmate?"

"I need to use the bathroom."

He folds his muscular arms over his chest and leans on the doorframe. One ankle crosses over the other as his gaze sweeps over me. "What do you say?"

"Let me use the toilet or I'll pee all over your fucking floor, asshole."

Asshole. Yes, that works, now that I think about it. He shakes his head and runs a hand down his face before he strides over and stops in front of me. I look up, willing my expression into hardness.

"I'll let you go, but don't try anything."

"What would I possibly try? I'm just your poor, helpless prisoner," I say, batting my eyelashes.

He rolls his eyes and tugs at the magical ropes around my wrists. I'm sure he could use magic to do this, but as he unties them, his fingers brush against mine, and that pull inside my veins swells as though my blood is trying desperately to get closer to him.

I yank my hands away, wanting to dispel whatever this is, even if it is completely involuntary. I hate that he makes me feel anything but pure, unfiltered loathing. Once my restraints are off, I rub my wrists and groan as I stand, my body stiff from sitting on the floor all night.

"Bastard," I mutter under my breath as I shake out my legs and then storm towards the bathroom with his dark laughter following in my wake.

His bathroom is magnificent, even if it's smaller than I'd expect. From what I've seen of this house, everything looks expensive and well-made, but it also isn't the Keep. I've inferred the reason I'm being stashed here in the middle of nowhere is because they want to keep my presence a secret from the Aurora King.

Maybe it's because of what they suspect about me. That in the wrong person's hands, I'm capable of wreaking a shit ton of havoc. Well, they're right. Once I figure out how to get out of here and track down that Crown, I have every intention of taking back what's mine.

What I don't understand is why they're keeping me from daddy dearest.

After I go to the bathroom and wash my hands, I stop at the mirror, staring at my reflection. The locket I took from Aphelion still hangs around my neck, and I clasp it with my hand, absorbing the force of the small, chipped jewel inside.

I've filled out in the past months—my face no longer gaunt and hollow, my eyes a little less haunted. There's a roundness to my cheeks that mimics the roundness in my butt and my thighs and my breasts. I look like a woman now and not the feeble girl who was taken from Nostraza. I never expected to be anything but a collection of skin and bones.

A part of me can't believe I ever saw the outside of the prison at all.

Using my reflection to anchor myself, I burrow into the center of my soul, feeling for the magic I know is locked deep within me. Where I've kept it trapped for so many long years. It feels like the jagged edges of two staircases hammered together. Like a puzzle where someone tried to fit a square peg into a round hole before it got stuck.

My eyes flutter shut as I tug at it, attempting to break the two sides apart, but it holds fast. I groan in frustration. All those years ago, I was forced to lock this power away, and now I can't seem to get it back. I've been trying for weeks, because when Amya and Mael "liberated" me from Aphelion, I decided the time had come to release it again. It will be my only line of defense if anyone learns my secrets.

I hear voices on the other side of the door, followed by a knock.

"Did you hit your head in there, Inmate?" Nadir asks with that condescending lilt in his tone. "Please don't tell me I'm going to find you passed out on the floor with your pants around your ankles. How undignified that would be for you."

"Asshole," I mutter under my breath, and I hear his laugh, though there's nothing warm about it. I swing open the door to find him leaning against the wall just outside, his arms folded over his chest, his shirt buttoned and tucked in now.

Our gazes catch and there's another flare of those lines of magic that spark beneath my skin, my nostrils flaring as I attempt to hold it back. Try as I might, I have no control over it.

Amya and Mael are in the room now, both of them watching us with curious expressions.

"Did you hear anything from Nostraza?" I ask Amya, tearing my gaze from Nadir and striding over to where she lounges on a black velvet sofa. Her face softens at my question as she shakes her head.

"Not yet. I promise, as soon as I do, you will know."

I stare at her, not sure what to make of this princess. She was also complicit as I rotted inside Nostraza for over a decade, but unlike Nadir, she actually seems to feel bad about it.

"Thank you," I say, meaning it, because I do believe her on this, whether or not she actually cares. I've made it clear I won't tell them anything until I hear news of my brother and sister, and it's the only reason Nadir feigns interest in the subject at all.

I turn to the prince with a cold glare. "Can I return to my own room now? Or am I still to remain chained to the foot of your bed with less humanity than your beloved *dogs*?"

"Perhaps if you weren't feral," Mael quips, and I pin my glare on him instead. He grins, a dimple popping on his cheek, and I get the sense this High Fae captain could win over the lord of the underworld if he put his mind to it.

"You may return to your room," Nadir says. "But if you behave in such a manner again, your punishment will be far worse than what you experienced last night. That was child's play compared to what I could and *would* do to you."

I notice Amya open her mouth, but Nadir silences her with a look before she snaps it closed again.

With a faux curtsy, I toss him an ingratiating smile. "Of course, *Your Highness*." There. If I say it dripping with sarcasm, then calling him that isn't quite so claustrophobic.

We exchange one more furious look before I spin on my heel and walk away.

Chapter Three

Nadir

Her back is straight, and her shoulders squared as she marches out of the room. She carries herself with a dignity that belies the fact I just made her sleep at the foot of my bed all night. I do my best not to stare at her ass in those leggings, but it doesn't work, my gaze glued to her. When she slams the door, she does it with such force it rattles the pictures on the wall.

After she's gone, I let out a deep sigh and roll my shoulders, trying to put my thoughts back together. Why can't I *think* when she's around me? Everything in my head and my stomach, and for fuck's sake, my pants, becomes muddled and confused, and turns to absolutely excruciating attention.

It's addictive. The way she hates me. The way she burns with that fire that glows so white hot, I ache whenever she looks at me. Like she's always just on the edge of erupting and blowing my entire life to pieces. Not that I've ever been attracted to reserved or docile women, but she isn't just wild, she's practically feral, and I can't stop fucking thinking about her.

Mael's dark snicker draws my attention, rousing me from the snared web of my thoughts. I spin around, my teeth already bared. Gods, I'm constantly on the edge of losing my shit lately.

"What is with you?" he asks, leaning against my desk with his arms folded. "*You* are a complete mess."

He exchanges a knowing glance with Amya, who then turns her concerned gaze on me. She constantly worries, but she doesn't need to. I can take care of myself.

"He's not wrong. You don't seem yourself lately."

"I'm fine. I need a drink." They're both right. I am a mess, and I can put it all down to the woman who just left the room. The prisoner from Nostraza who should mean nothing to me, but who's filled my head and won't let go.

"It's nine in the morning," Mael says.

"So what?" I yank open the glass door on my cabinet that holds a wide variety of spirits. I select a dark green elven wine that feels like a good breakfast liquor. It's not too strong, but should pack enough punch to smooth the edges of my jagged nerves.

I pour a generous portion and then stare at the glass as my thoughts return to *her*.

"I went to the Keep," Amya says, disrupting me from another spiral into my thoughts.

"And?"

She shrugs. "Father seems preoccupied, mostly. When I went to see him, he didn't say much." She plants her elbows on her knees and grins with that mischievous look in her eyes I know so well. "He's *really* not happy you got the entire Aurora court banned from Aphelion."

I snort at that and take a sip of wine, savoring the heated burn down my throat.

"Sorry, I hope you don't mind that I got to tell him."

I shake my head. I definitely don't mind. That's one less conversation with my father.

"I did everyone a favor. No more of Atlas's parties to suffer," I say, dropping on the sofa next to my sister, the ice in my glass clinking. "Where does he think I am?"

"All over. I told him you and D'Arcy hit it off at the ball and you'd gone to visit her for a few days."

I arch an eyebrow at her, wondering if that was really the best lie she could come up with. "And he bought that?"

The ice-cold Star Queen of Celestria isn't exactly my type. Not only because she hates everyone, but because she's already been through seven bonded partners of various genders, all of whom succumbed to "mysterious" circumstances.

No thanks. I want to keep my head where it is.

Amya shrugs. "Like I said, he seemed preoccupied with something."

"How's Mother?" I ask, guilt churning in my gut. I've been away from home for far too long.

Amya shrugs. "She's fine." Her gaze slides away, her shoulders rolling in, but I don't press the matter.

"Did Father ask about the girl?" I inquire instead.

She nods. "He did, and I said you were continuing to search, and that's also why you were still away."

"He doesn't suspect we have her then?"

Though we sit on the very edge of The Aurora in the manor house Amya and I built to get away from the Keep, the king's reach filters into every part of this realm. The property is warded from anyone but us, but I can never shake the urge to sleep with one eye open. Somehow, my father finds a way to ruin everything.

"I don't think so, but I'm not sure how much longer we should keep her here, Nadir. I know you think there's something more to her, but I have to disagree. She seems to be completely human. She doesn't have a drop of magic that I can discern."

I look at Mael. "What more have you heard from Heart?"

"Etienne sent word last night," Mael says, his mouth flattening. "He's been lying low in his usual settlement. I pulled everyone else out to avoid suspicion. Your father's men have been back several times."

"Still searching for something?"

Mael's brows draw together. "Etienne said they gathered up all the women—anyone between the ages of twenty and thirty—and herded them off."

Both Amya and I sit up at that revelation.

"Where?" I ask.

Mael shook his head. "He didn't know yet. He hasn't been able to catch them in the act. Word is they've been doing the same thing in all the settlements."

Amya sucks in a breath. "Father's searching for *someone*, then."

Our gazes all meet as understanding coalesces into something tangible. A truth we've been circling for weeks.

"You don't think..." Amya says. "Then it can't be Lor. There had to be a reason he wasn't that concerned when she went missing. She's just a human, Nadir. Are you sure we don't have this all wrong?"

I shake my head. Amya has a point. None of it makes any sense. If Rion had lost the Primary of Heart, why wasn't he turning over Ouranos looking for her? And why had she been locked up for all those years? He'd *seemed* unconcerned about her disappearance, though I'm still sure he never meant for me to learn of prisoner 3452's existence in the first place.

He'd sent me to look for her as though she were merely a trifling concern, but my father has always been a very good actor and never does anything without a good reason. I can't shake the nagging feeling he sent me to look for her just to throw me off. By pretending it wasn't important, then he'd convince me of the same thing.

I squeeze the glass in my hands, frustrated by this puzzle that reveals a new side every time I blink.

"No, I don't think we have it wrong."

"Why are you so sure of that?" Amya sits forward. "We have no evidence to suggest she isn't just a mortal prisoner who got caught up in something by accident. A case of mistaken identities, perhaps."

One of my ice hounds, Morana, pads over and rests her chin on my knee. I scratch her behind the ear as I contemplate

Amya's questions. Why am I so sure? It's impossible to explain or put into words, but I know. As sure as I know my own name, *I know*.

"Did you tell her the truth about not hearing from Nostraza yet? Is Hylene working on it?" I ask her.

Amya nods. "I told her the truth. But I expect to hear from Hylene soon enough. She'll get them out if they're still alive."

"Do you think this Tristan and Willow are related to Lor?" Mael asks. "She seems awfully possessive of them."

"A brother and sister, maybe?" Amya says. "If she really is High Fae, then they might have magic, too." She doesn't voice what we're all thinking. If *any* of them have magic, then the impossible has happened.

Amya shakes her head. "The baby died. Every story, every account of the war said the queen's baby died with her." Her voice is distant, as if she's recited this in her head a thousand times already.

"Sure," Mael says, moving from where he's standing at the desk and dropping into the chair across from the prince and princess. "But do you really believe three royal Fae would have willingly spent more than a decade inside Nostraza? It makes little sense. And if *they're* the heirs of Heart, then *who* is the king looking for?"

I look at my friend, one of the few people in the world who I trust. We met during the Second Sercen War where we both spent months toiling in a POW camp on the border between Heart and The Woodlands. We became friends immediately, and he's stood by my side through everything. "You're right, it doesn't make any sense, but Atlas knew something about her and I can feel—"

I clip my words off, slicing them down like an enemy intent on spilling out my guts.

"What?" Amya asks, placing her hand on my shoulder. "This girl has you tied up in knots. What is it?"

Mael smirks. "Come now, Amya, you must have noticed our little prisoner is rather lovely to look at. Perhaps our boy is in love."

"Shut up," I growl. "I wouldn't deign to touch Atlas's sloppy seconds with a ten-foot pole. She's a criminal."

The lie sits like a rock in my stomach. I'm not sure why I'm pretending with them—they know so many of my secrets—but she has me questioning everything.

"Touchy," Mael says, rolling his eyes.

"Then what is it?" Amya asks, throwing an incensed glare at Mael.

"My magic feels strained around her," I say. "Like it's trying to come out of my skin. Like it wants to...touch her."

I open my fist, a ball of multi-colored light dancing in my palm. I stare at it, wondering why this part of me that has always been my security net has turned on me, sending me into freefall.

Amya raises her eyebrows, her smooth forehead furrowing. "Have you ever experienced anything like that before?"

I take a swig of my drink, the ball of light flashing out as I shake my head. "Never."

I barely slept last night with her in this room, right at the foot of my bed. My entire body had felt like it was stretching towards her, trying to fold over and around her. My magic had been a tide flowing under my skin, and I had to do everything to pull it back so I wasn't glowing like a fucking star in my bed. I've never had so little control over it.

And her scent. Fuck, it filled every pore of my skin. Every nerve in my body. Every channel in my brain. I was drowning in a sea of it, and if that had been my last night alive on this plane, I would have regretted nothing. I'd been a fool to keep her here all night, but my stupid pride wouldn't let her go.

"That's very strange," Amya says carefully. "But it could mean anything." It's clear even she doesn't believe those words, but I understand why she wants to deny them.

Lor's very existence tears at the fabric of Ouranos, pulling apart its already fraying threads. It's been more than two hundred years since the last Sercen War, and things could only remain stable for so long. Eventually, someone would try to claim the abandoned queendom again, and this had the potential to leave the entire continent a smoldering ruin.

"So I think you're wrong," I finally say. "Despite what she seems, she isn't human. You might not sense any magic in her, but there are oceans of power in her, Amya. I'm sure of it."

Chapter Four

SERCE

S erce scanned the crowd as she anxiously awaited the arrival of the younger Sun Prince and his family. It had been years since she'd seen Atlas—they'd been only children then, causing mischief at some past royal function—but today, they'd start on a path that would bind them forever.

Tonight's party was already in full swing, chatter swelling and the strains of animated music filling the hall. Her mother had gone to great lengths for this one. Roses and swaths of deep red fabric dripped from the walls, making it seem more like they were encased in a flowerpot than the ornate white stone castle that stood at the center of the Queendom of Heart.

While keeping one eye on the door, Serce surveyed the guests with a rising mixture of anticipation and adrenaline. She loved a good party, no matter the reason. Tonight's would be the opening soiree of a two-week-long summit that would hopefully lead to the future protection and prosperity of Ouranos. At the same time, the conditions of Serce's bonding to the Sun Prince would serve as an addendum to the main event.

The first to arrive at the summit had been the Queendom of Tor, led by the Mountain Queen Bronte and her bonded partner, Yael. Tall and muscular with grey feathered wings and long silver hair, they wore the traditional slate-colored warrior garb of their court. With the power of earth and the ability to effortlessly wield boulders the size of elephants, they were both forces to be reckoned with.

Right now they were greeting Serce's mother and father, the Queen and King of Heart, all of their expressions as deadly serious as the circumstances for this summit.

Today marked the first time in history an official alliance would be considered amongst the realms of Ouranos. Not since the Beginning of Days had the rulers of Ouranos united under a singular cause, though this time, they'd be short one member when all was said and done.

Serce's mother, Daedra, had been meticulously orchestrating this scheme with a deft hand for years, and it seemed her wish might finally come to fruition. Though Serce expected some kicking and screaming from the other rulers, first. Even if they were ideologically aligned with the idea, they'd also need at least a few days to beat their chests and air their carefully crafted, but wholly pointless, reservations for everyone to admire.

However, if things went according to plan, Queen Bronte would be just the first to join an agreement with Heart and thus set into motion the preliminary phase of what promised to be a long and bloody battle against the rot that lay to their north. It wasn't lost on Serce that Heart had more to gain from suppressing threats from The Aurora than any other realm, but her mother hoped the implications for all of Ouranos would be enough to sway them to her ends.

Alluvion arrived on the heels of Tor, and Serce noticed the way her mother visibly relaxed when the Ocean King, Cyan, was announced. He had always been aloof and unpredictable, disinclined to get involved in the affairs of the other courts, motivated only by his own needs. Still, even he had to see it was getting harder and harder to ignore the danger that might swallow them all if they didn't act soon. Rion had grown too powerful already, and with his recent bonding to the Aurora Queen, his strength would only grow.

Serce's cousin, Rhiannon, bounced on her toes, also craning her neck as though this bonding would change her life as much as Serce's. In some ways, it would. Once Serce was bonded, Rhiannon's parents would be setting their sights on her to consolidate her future as well. While only Imperial Fae enjoyed the benefit of heightened magic through a bonding, all High Fae were expected to bond at some point—it was simply the natural order of things.

Serce adjusted the neckline of her deep scarlet dress, pushing up her breasts so they were displayed to their full advantage. She didn't see the need to pretend she didn't understand her assets and used them to their potential whenever the need arose.

"Where are they?" she asked Rhiannon, her nerves rippling with anticipation. She wasn't entirely sure how she felt about this arrangement yet. Though she'd lived nearly a hundred years without the constraints of a bonding, she understood that eventually this would be her fate.

She was a queen-in-waiting—without the bond she'd be limited in her magic's potential. She didn't love the idea of being shackled to a single man, especially given the long lifespans of Fae, but she hoped Atlas was liberal in his views. She'd invited more than her fair share of men to her bed, and she intended to keep it that way. There was no single Fae who would ever satisfy all of her needs. Atlas had better know his way around a female's body and not simply rely on his position to dazzle and then entrap his sexual partners.

If he proved worthy, she might even allow him to join her from time to time.

Nevertheless, this was all a small price to pay in the grand scheme of her lofty ambitions. Serce was duty-bound to do right by her queendom, and nothing would deter her from her ascension. She craved the power that awaited her as Imperial Fae more than she had ever craved anything. She was also dying to meet the prince she'd known only as a boy and assess his measure. Who was she being asked to share her magic *and* her bed with?

"Relax. They'll be here soon," Rhiannon said, offering a shy wave to a handsome courtier standing on the side of the room, his glass raised in a toast towards them. Serce knew he'd had his head between Rhiannon's thighs less than two hours ago, and assumed that's where anyone looking for her cousin would find her before this party was over.

"I am relaxed," Serce snapped, rolling the tension from her shoulders. "I think I have every right to be curious about him, don't you?"

Rhiannon said nothing as she returned her attention to Serce and pressed her lips together. "Of course, Serce. Of course you do."

Serce smoothed down her thick black hair, left to hang in its natural loose waves down her back. She fanned herself as a bead of sweat trickled down the line of her throat. It was blazing in here thanks to the dozens and dozens of floor-height candelabras that ran in two lines down the center of the room.

They were completely impractical, but they did give the space a certain sense of atmosphere. Just another touch of flair her mother felt the need to add to everything, as though she were compensating for some deficiency she refused to admit. Not that Serce would ever say that to her mother's face. She was amazed that someone's overwrought gown or intricate hairdo hadn't caught fire yet. Now *that* would liven up this party.

A moment later, heralds flanking the wide doors sounded their horns and Serce winced. More of her mother's theatrics at work—the noise was far too brazen for the cavernous hall.

"Make way for the court of Aphelion and the Sun King," boomed a low fae servant with light blue skin and a thatch of white hair, clothed in the black and red livery of the Heart court. Serce thought he might be some type of elf, though she'd never looked closely enough to understand the differences between the low fae's various species.

The Sun King appeared in the doorway, his hair like spun sunlight. Every member of Aphelion's court was resplendent in gold, fabrics shimmering and buttons winking in the flicker of the candles. She wondered then if the low lighting had been intentional on her mother's part to diminish the Sun King's brilliance. While Daedra might have been seeking allies, the Heart Queen had a petty streak she often failed to restrain.

Serce eyed the retinue as they proceeded down the long central aisle, party guests shuffling left and right, making room for their entrance. She decided the Sun Court was all a little *much*. No one could say the hues of crimson and ebony draped over every inch of the Heart Castle were this ostentatious. They bore a certain quiet dignity and elegance in comparison.

Two handsome princes, walking half a step back, flanked the king. On his left was a young High Fae male with golden blond hair, the spitting image of his father. On the other strode a male with coppery brown hair that fell just past his chin.

Serce straightened her shoulders, scrutinizing the second male intensely. This had to be Atlas. Even after all these years, she remembered that shining hair that seemed painted with fire. By Fae standards, they were young, having lived less than a century. Atlas was nine years her senior, though they both appeared to be in their mid-twenties by mortal years.

The procession stopped at the dais where the Heart Queen's and King's thrones sat. Made of ebony wood, they were polished to a high sheen, and a large red jewel winked in the back of each, reflecting with a million facets. The abundance of candlelight had definitely been designed to highlight their brilliance. Of that, Serce was sure.

Daedra wore the Heart Crown, the silver band marking a striking contrast to the deep midnight hue of her sleek tresses. Serce eyed the Crown, imagining the day when it would finally become hers.

"Your Majesties," the Sun King said in his deep baritone, arms sweeping wide. "It is good to see you after all these years." The low chatter in the room was focused on the newly arrived court with interest. "It is an honor to be here on such an auspicious occasion. One that will see Ouranos find peace as we come together to vanquish our enemies."

Serce held in a snort at the king's ridiculous speech. Vanquish, indeed.

"We welcome you," Daedra said, with a tip of her head, her hands folded in front of her. She was the spitting image of Serce, with brown eyes so dark they were nearly black and light brown skin that gleamed in the room's warm light. "The honor is ours."

She gestured to Serce, waving her over. "And, of course, here is Serce."

Serce stepped between her parents, ever the dutiful daughter, at least on the surface.

Her father dropped a hand on her shoulder, heavy with meaning. While she wished she were bonding with someone she felt a connection to, she understood this alliance was for the good of the continent and her home. They were losing ground to The Aurora, and only a united front would hold Rion back from claiming any more of Ouranos than he'd already taken.

Besides, if Serce agreed to this, her mother would finally choose the descension and retreat into the Evanescence, allowing Serce to step into her destiny as queen. The music blended into the background as Serce inhaled a deep breath to settle her nerves and prepared to welcome the members of Aphelion.

The Sun King, Kyros, stepped forward. "Allow me to introduce my sons. This is Tyr, Aphelion's Primary and the Sun Prince." Tyr also stepped forward and tipped his head. He was everything the Sun Prince should be, golden and bright and gleaming. As the Primary, he would inherit the power of Aphelion once Kyros entered the Evanescence, as well.

"Your Majesties," Tyr said. "It is a pleasure to travel north. I've heard only marvelous tales of your home. I hope to take in some of the sights while we're here."

Daedra nodded. "We welcome you. It's been many years since we've traveled south to see the blue waters of Aphelion. Perhaps there will be more occasions to do so going forward." She eyed Serce and then the younger prince standing on the Sun King's other side, her meaning clear.

"And this is Atlas," Kyros said next, gesturing to the copper-haired Fae, who addressed Serce directly.

"Your Highness," he said, bowing low and looking up at her through a fringe of dark lashes. "The tales of your beauty are no match for the true vision that stands before me now."

Serce controlled the twitch of a muscle in her face as she resisted the urge to raise an imperious eyebrow. Of course, she was beautiful. She didn't need this *male* to validate that. He made it sound like he was doing her a favor by noticing.

Atlas was pleasing enough to look at, but she hoped he wouldn't kick up a fuss when he realized he held the secondary role in this relationship. What she needed was a partner who looked the part but knew when to keep his mouth shut.

"Come," Serce's mother said with a sidelong glance in her direction. "We have a private room where we can discuss the details of our arrangement further."

Daedra gestured for Serce and the Heart King to follow, everyone stepping down from the dais where another low fae servant awaited. They led them, along with Atlas, Tyr, and Kyros, towards an antechamber adjacent to the ballroom. The small room featured an array of black velvet couches with crimson accents and a thick maroon rug that covered a black and white tiled floor.

Everyone chose to stand as they all formed a circle, facing each other like six petals on a flower waiting to be torn away by the wind. The hairs on the back of Serce's neck stood up, hinting at something amiss as she wondered why this discussion was happening in secret.

"We're hoping to have the bonding ceremony before spring, Kyros," the Heart Queen said, and he pressed his lips together in response. "We'll need your army to march on The Aurora before Rion can amass more troops across the Sinen River."

"We'll call for the Trials to commence immediately, but they last eight weeks, so we'll do the best we can."

"Trials?" Serce asked, just as her mother appeared ready to explain why that timeline was unacceptable.

"Yes," said Kyros. "It's how every queen of Aphelion is chosen."

"Serce," her father said, taking her hand in his and squeezing it gently. "You know this."

"Yes, I *know*." She pulled her hand away and faced the Sun King. "But that's if you're bonding to some commoner to put on your throne. I am a Primary and already have a crown of my own to inherit. Besides, I will not be the queen of Aphelion. I will be the queen of Heart and Heart only."

"But should something ever happen to Tyr, it's likely that Atlas would become the Primary, and therefore, you would become queen of Aphelion as well. Thus, the Trials must still take place in the unlikely but still possible event that happens," Kyros said, as though he were speaking to a child who didn't understand a simple arithmetic problem.

Serce scoffed. "I will not enter some contest with a group of simpering women to win *his* hand." She gestured to Atlas, who frowned at her comment, his dark eyebrows drawing together.

"Serce," Daedra said with an edge of warning in her voice.

"No, this is madness. It's insulting. I will not do it."

"It's about the optics," Tyr said, spreading his hands in a placating gesture. "Even if you never rule in Aphelion, we must be prepared. The people would never accept you."

"And you have no issue with your father and brother essentially plotting your death?" she bit back.

"That's not what this is," he said, his posture stiffening while Serce scoffed again. The fool.

"Your Highness," Kyros said. "It is merely a formality. You will win. We will ensure it is so."

"Of course I'd win," she hissed. "*That* isn't what I'm worried about."

She caught the eye of Atlas, whose gaze was darting between his father and her as they volleyed back and forth.

"What do you say about this?" she asked him, challenging him to speak up. If he was to become her bonded partner, then she expected him to support her above everyone in all things. Instead, Atlas just appeared surprised to have been included in this conversation, as though all of this had nothing to do with him. Serce's esteem for both this Fae and this bonding was dropping faster than a boulder rolling down a mountain.

"I think we'll have to keep up appearances," he said, tugging on the hem of his golden jacket. "It will be over quickly."

Serce blinked as something in her chest caved inwards. This fool was to be the Fae she'd spend the rest of her life with? With no backbone and no thoughts of his own? Even worse, he'd take up her father's place as the King of Heart? Her queendom deserved so much better.

"Mother," she said, her voice dropping. "I did not agree to *this*."

"You said you understood the importance of this alliance and that you would concede to a union," Daedra replied, her tone threadbare and her eyes flashing. Serce rarely disobeyed her mother. Few challenged the Heart Queen and lived to tell the tale. "You understand what's at stake."

"I said I'd meet him and I would agree if it felt...right," she said carefully, searching for whatever words would free her from this snare. "I am not competing in some barbaric ritual like a common whore."

There was a collective flinch around the room at her accusation, but Serce didn't care.

Her gaze met with her mother's, and Serce noted the conflict in her expression. Daedra would have never agreed to these terms, either, but she must think like a queen, not a woman with her own personal desires.

Serce was bound by the same chains. If she wanted Daedra to give her the Crown, she'd have to do what was best for Heart, but this felt like too much to ask of her.

"I need some time to think," Serce said to no one in particular, and then spun on her heel to storm out. She entered the ballroom, where the volume of voices and music crescendoed into an incessant buzz as the air grew thick enough to choke her. She put a hand to her forehead, dizzy with anger and frustration and the helpless inevitability that she would have no choice.

Suddenly, she couldn't breathe.

This felt wrong. Everything about this felt off. She didn't want to compete for a partner, and she didn't want to bond to that fool. Surely *she* deserved better than this.

Serce took a sharp right turn and headed for an exit that led into the hallway. Worried someone would try to drag her back to that uncomfortable meeting, she cast a look over her shoulder. Picking up her skirts so she wouldn't trip, she kicked up her pace, trying to distance herself from the threat of her now muddled future.

It was then she careened into a solid object, bouncing back and nearly toppling over when she was saved by a strong arm that circled her waist. Her savior hauled her back to her feet with a gentle but firm tug.

"Whoa," came a deep voice. "Are you okay?"

Serce looked up to find a pair of dark green eyes belonging to a High Fae male—the most beautiful one she'd ever seen—who towered over her. He had tanned golden skin and his long hair was the deepest brown of freshly tilled earth. Braided along the sides of his head, it framed high cheekbones and a strong jaw dusted with a fine layer of dark stubble. He was breathtaking.

"I—" Serce swallowed, at a loss for words for possibly the first time in her life. This stranger mesmerized her, his scent pulling her under. It was warm and earthy, like the sweetness of a million flowers bursting open in spring. With his arm still around her, he steadied Serce and then, as if almost reluctant to do so, pulled away.

"You're Serce," he said. "The Heart Princess?"

She nodded, wondering how he knew. "I am," she said, trying to find her words around a tied tongue. "And you are?"

The corner of his perfect mouth ticked up in a smirk that made her knees go weak. His forest green eyes sparkled as he lifted her hand and pressed his lips to the back.

Serce blinked when her magic responded, as if it had found a mind of its own. It had never done that before. Her crimson lightning sparked through her veins like an oncoming storm, threatening to burst out through her fingertips. As his lips lingered a second longer than was entirely appropriate given her station, a fissure of heat went straight to the carnal place just below her navel.

She let out a small gasp in response, and his eyes darkened, as though he had felt it, too.

"I'm the Woodlands King, Wolf," he said, his voice rumbling and rich. "It's a pleasure to meet you, Serce."

Their gazes met, and Serce felt a tug so profound it seemed to come from the deepest wells of the earth.

It was an irrevocable shift. A moment of reckoning. An unstoppable tide.

As she stared at Wolf, she knew then, with the certainty of the sun that rose over the ocean and the roses that bloomed in the garden, that her life had just changed forever.

Chapter Five

LOR

Present Day: The Aurora

After my crappy night on the floor of Nadir's bedroom, I spend most of the day sleeping. When I'm rested, I continue lying on the bed and stare out the window, allowing a moment to feel sorry for myself. I've been pushing so hard for the past four months, worrying about Willow and Tristan every minute of the day while struggling to decipher some nebulous future I don't know how to articulate.

Letting out a deep sigh, I bury my face in my pillow. I'll give myself this brief pause to wallow and then figure out what comes next. All I know is I can't keep sitting here waiting to find out what Nadir has planned for me. I won't be used like a puppet again. Atlas tricked me into believing all of his lies. I was so starved for comfort, and his pretty words sucked me in, just like he knew they would. I was a battered prisoner who'd forgotten how kindness felt, and I swallowed every one of his fairy tales like sugared berries.

But I can't make that mistake again. I won't.

My thoughts wander to last night and the sight of the prince emerging from his bathroom, wearing practically nothing. I hate that I find him *interesting* to look at, and I really hate that sensation that twitches under my skin whenever he's near.

The way he looks at me feels like he wants to slice me up for dinner. Like I'm the problem. I'm not sure what I ever did to him. He's the one whose father killed my parents and imprisoned me and my siblings for twelve long years.

What an asshole. What right does he have to be angry with me?

There's a soft knock at my door, and I lift my head.

"What?" I say, not really in the mood for politeness. Whoever is standing on the other side comes down to only two options. It could be a servant and they don't really deserve my rudeness, or it could be one of my captors, and they can all fuck themselves.

"Lor?" comes a soft voice and I hold in a groan, recognizing Amya. "Can I come in?"

"Is this about Tristan and Willow?" I call, because that's the only reason she'd be welcome.

"I'm sorry, no," she says through the door. "But I wanted to ask you something."

Rolling back to face the window, I don't respond. There's a long pause, and I listen for the sounds of her walking away, hoping she'll take the hint.

Instead, I hear the crack of the door, and I sigh loudly, resigned to whatever it is she wants. Her light footsteps cross the room as though she thinks she'll be less of a burden if she treads carefully. I want to remind her that isn't how it works. Then I feel the slight shift of the mattress as she sits on the corner of the bed.

"Are you okay?" she asks.

I look over at her. "Did they send you in here to see if you could get anything out of me? Your brother's brute force isn't working, so they send in the *nice* one?"

Amya's smooth cheeks flush and her mouth presses together. "That's not—"

"Save it," I say, turning away. "I'm not going to tell you anything, either."

"That's not why I'm here," she says, and I snort, not believing a word of it.

"Then what do you want?"

I turn to look at her again, and her eyes dart about the room with uncertainty. Pushing myself up, I scoot back and lean on the headboard, stretching out my legs and crossing my ankles as I drag a pillow onto my lap for something to cling to.

"I know Nadir can come off as...abrasive," Amya says. "But it's just because he feels so much. It's hard for him to be casual about anything."

I tilt my head, studying her. "He's an asshole. You all are. You're keeping me against my will, and I want out. Am I still a prisoner of The Aurora?"

"No," Amya says, biting the inside of her lip.

"Then let me go."

"Where would you go?" she asks, a line forming between her brows. "Do you have family out there?" She picks at a loose thread in the duvet and then looks up at me.

I shake my head. "Nice try."

"Lor." Her voice takes on a slight edge of impatience, and I smirk. Do they really think I'm going to be that easy to manipulate? I already fell for that with Atlas, but I'm smarter now. I might have lived most of my life behind bars, but I've always been a quick learner.

"I wanted to ask if you would come down and join us for dinner?"

I frown at her. "Why?"

"Because it's the first time we've all been here since..."

"Since you kidnapped me," I say. "You can say it. There's no point in pretending."

"Fine, since you came here, and we thought it would be nice to eat together." She pauses. "You included."

"So you can ply me for information."

She raises her hands in a placating gesture. "No. I promise I won't let Nadir grill you about anything that happened in Aphelion. At least not for tonight. He won't be deterred forever, though. He always gets what he wants. But at least for this evening, he'll give it a rest."

I smirk at her honesty, and my stomach rumbles, betraying me like a complete jerk. Amya tries to hold in a triumphant smile and mostly succeeds.

"What do you say?" She schools her features into kind patience, and I have no idea if this is all an act. Is she really who she's pretending so hard to be? "Please? I know you don't want to be here, but we don't plan to keep you here forever, and it would be nice to get to know you on a different level."

"You don't?" I ask, snagging on the words in that statement that interest me the most.

She shrugs her shoulders. "Nadir thinks you're important for some reason. And if that's true, then I have a feeling that whatever your role, it's not to stew in this room."

"I don't know what that's supposed to mean," I lie.

Of course, my destiny isn't in this room. The Mirror told me I have to find the Crown. Whatever happens, I have to get out of here. My shoulders roll with the riot of emotions weighing me down.

"Come on, the cook prepared her specialty," Amya says. "I promise it'll be worth tolerating the company."

I roll my eyes and toss the pillow away. "Fine. Let's go."

She stands up with a beaming smile, smoothing down the front of her dress. I study her for a moment, entranced by how elegant and perfect she looks. She's wearing her usual black—a long silk dress that clings to her curves with her colorful streaked hair twisted into a crown on top of her head.

This is what a princess's life is supposed to be like. Full of luxury and pretty things to enjoy. It wasn't supposed to be spent behind the damp walls of the worst prison in Ouranos.

"What is it?" she asks, a line forming between her perfectly arched brows.

"Nothing," I say, tearing myself from my thoughts before I scoot to the edge of the bed. After I stand up, I stuff my feet into a pair of suede slippers trimmed in fur. The floors in this house are freezing.

Amya heads for the door and waits for me to follow. We make our way down the broad staircase that leads to the main level, passing the wide front doors, inset with an intricate pattern of frosted glass. Wishing I could escape, I eye them with a sense of mourning.

Mostly confined to my room, I haven't been through this part of the manor yet. They leave my door unlocked as if to create the illusion I'm not really their captive. But I haven't been in the mood to explore very much, worried I'll run into the prince and have to suffer his presence and his questions.

We pass a hallway lined with both a stocked pantry and a row of boots and cloaks that tunnels into a brightly lit kitchen. I can hear the boisterous voices and laughter of the manor staff as they prepare our dinner.

From the corner of my eye, I note the cloaks all bear a familiar object. An opalescent brooch. The same kind the guards in Nostraza wore to protect them from the Void. The last time I saw one was when I was dragged to the Hollow where Gabriel stole me. Obviously, the prince hasn't trusted me with a pin of my own, nor do I imagine he's going to anytime soon.

"This way," Amya urges, and I turn to follow her, an idea forming that I know I should dismiss. It's an entirely foolish and reckless plan, but it's already solidifying into a shape I can't ignore.

We pass through a large archway and into a cozy room lined with bookshelves and a giant fireplace dominating one wall. Near the fire is a round table surrounded by four chairs, two of which hold a pair of familiar figures. Their conversation stops, both High Fae turning as we enter.

Mael's face stretches into a wide grin. "You came."

I arch an eyebrow. "Were you expecting me not to?"

"I thought you'd toss Amya out on her ass," he says, and I can't help but return his smile. Mael is a disarming mixture of uncultured brute and suave gentlemen, and I get the sense that, unlike Amya, he's shown me exactly who he is.

"She tried," Amya interjects. "Believe me."

I huff out a quiet snort and meet the prince's gaze. He pushes himself up from the table and then pulls out the chair next to him, gesturing for me to take it.

"So glad you could join us, Inmate."

"Nadir!" Amya chides. "Stop calling her that."

The corner of his mouth crooks up in an evil smile as he looks at his sister and then back at me. "Please sit, my *lady*."

"Oh please," I say. "You could barely say that with a straight face."

But I do as he asks, settling into the chair before he picks up a bottle of wine and fills my glass with lavender liquid. I pick it up and sniff, noticing the bubbles that froth to the surface. Everyone else is drinking it, too, so I figure it's safe and take a sip. It's sweet with just a hint of bitterness.

"How's your room?" Mael asks, and his mouth twitches just as Amya kicks him under the table. "Ouch! What the fuck, Amya?"

"She's annoyed you're bringing attention to the fact that my 'room' is a glorified prison," I say pleasantly, taking another sip of my wine.

Mael snorts. "I'm not one for dancing around the truth, darling." He winks and maybe he is a little bit charming if I squint and look at him the right way. He may be friends with these two royal siblings, but he likely couldn't do anything about Nostraza. Perhaps I'll exempt him from the full brunt of my anger.

"My room is fine, in that case. Given the circumstances."

Mael nods and rubs his hands together. "Great, now that we have the pleasantries out of the way, how about you tell us what the Mirror told you before our boy Nadir here jumps out of his skin? The sooner you just give us the truth, the sooner we can let you go."

Mael yelps in pain, leaning down to rub his leg under the table. "Amya. If you fucking do that again, I'm going to dangle you by the ankles from that balcony."

"I told her we wouldn't pester her if she joined us," Amya hisses.

Mael holds up a finger. "Actually. The only one you swore to compliance was your brother. I never agreed to this directly."

Amya closes her eyes, begging for patience. "You know I meant you, too. Now stop it." She grits her teeth and gives him a glare so withering that he holds up his hands in surrender.

"Okay, okay. I'm sorry, Lor. Sheesh. My shins can't take any more abuse."

"Good," Amya says, giving him one more hard look.

Nadir lounges in his chair with an easy decadence, and I'm having a hard time not staring. His gaze catches mine, and I look away, drinking my wine, fighting down that spark under my skin that keeps reaching for him.

"How was your trip into the city today?" Amya asks Mael as a trio of servants arrive, all bearing large trays of food. The smell is amazing, and I perk up, my stomach grumbling. Discovering all these amazing foods over the past many months has been one of the best parts of getting out of prison. Maybe once this is all over, I'll travel to every realm and sample its cuisine.

The servants place copper bowls full of orange and gold sauces in the center of the table. They float with what look like pieces of chicken and fish and vegetables. Another servant holds a platter full of triangular pastries in front of me.

"They're delicious," Amya says. "Filled with spices, peas, and potatoes and then deep-fried. Try them with this." She spoons a generous portion of dark, glossy sauce onto my plate. More food is laden alongside it, including flat discs of fluffy white bread. I watch as Amya tears off a piece and uses it to scoop up some sauce along with a piece of chicken before popping it in her mouth. She moans in appreciation.

I catch the prince watching me, his expression thoughtful instead of devious for once. "Go on," he says. "Eat up."

He pronounces it like an order that I'm to obey without question. A barbed retort sits on the tip of my tongue, but I'm tired and the food looks good, so I swallow it to save for another time.

"The city is in full prep for Frostfire," Mael says. "Your father is really outdoing himself this time."

"I wonder why all the fuss," Amya says, clearly skeptical about something.

Mael shrugs. "Perhaps he's just feeling festive this year."

Nadir lets out a derisive laugh. "That's our father, the life of the party."

"What's Frostfire?" I ask, taking a big bite of my food. The flavors are so astonishing, it's like a flock of Zerra's blessed are working in the kitchen.

"It's to mark the start of winter," Amya says. "It's two weeks of parties and events, leading up to the final night when the Borealis put on their best show of the year. You'll love it, Lor."

My hand pauses mid-air as I'm about to take another bite. "Will I?"

"That is—if you're still here, of course." Amya tosses her brother a worried look. "Sorry. Fuck, this is awkward."

"It is rather strange to be dining with your own captive while pretending we're what, exactly? Friendly? That you aren't keeping me here against my will?"

Amya's shoulders drop as she wrings her napkin in her hands.

"Tell me about Nostraza," Nadir says, and the air vacates my lungs.

"What the fuck, Nadir!" Amya says, slapping down her napkin. "Why are you both behaving like animals?"

"What? We're all done pretending we're having a pleasant evening, so what's the harm? I promised I wouldn't ask about Atlas and what happened in Aphelion, but I didn't say I wouldn't ask about this."

"Why?" I ask, clutching the hem of my sweater like it might shield me from the darkness of my memories.

"Because I want to know."

"So you can nod your head and make sympathetic noises about how terrible it must have been and make yourself feel better about what a good prince you are?"

Nadir snorts. "Hardly."

A soft hand lands on my forearm.

"You don't have to talk about it," Amya says, giving me a gentle look and then shooting an angry glare at her brother.

"What?" he asks. "Are we supposed to pretend that somehow this *human* lasted longer than any mortal is supposed to? And that she has two *friends* inside who've apparently done the same? It's all a little suspicious, don't you think?"

"I should have known this invitation was just a ruse to get information out of me." I shove my chair back, the legs screeching against the hardwood.

"Lor, no," Amya says with another incensed look at her brother. "What is wrong with you? Can't we have one normal dinner without you behaving this way?"

I want to storm out and hide in my room, but the way the prince is looking at me with that smug, knowing expression causes me to snap, all sense of myself exploding from my bottled rage.

"You want to know about Nostraza?" I hiss, stepping closer, my hands balling into fists. "I'll tell you about Nostraza. I was thrown in there when I was twelve years old. I was stripped of everything and made to sleep side by side with the worst kind of monsters you can imagine. Thieves and rapists and murderers who all looked at me and Willow as if we were fucking snacks.

"Tristan spent the better part of those years barely sleeping so he could protect us. I learned to bring down a man twice my size with a single blow to his windpipe, just so I wasn't raped in my own bed every night.

"But never mind the other prisoners, Your *Highness*. What about the guards? The warden? The people who were *supposed* to be keeping some kind of order in that hellhole?"

I move even closer, my entire body shaking so hard my breath rattles in my chest.

"They were even worse because they were supposed to fucking know better. The things they made us do for them. The things the warden demanded of me because I had no other fucking choice. The way I protected Willow by taking it all on myself."

My voice cracks as the warmth of a single traitorous tear slips down my cheek.

"I can still feel the hard stone on my knees and hear the rip of his zipper. The way the other guards would threaten me and torment me because he kept me for himself, all because they wanted a fucking taste, too.

"The beatings I suffered. The torment I endured. Do you know I was in the Hollow when Gabriel found me because I got into a fight over a bar of *soap*? That's how desperate I was for any sliver of comfort in my life. That's what they did to us. Left us out there with no food or water, serving us up as prey for the Void.

"No one, I don't care what they've done, deserves that kind of treatment, oh mighty prince of The Aurora. It nearly broke me into pieces, and it's a miracle that I'm standing here now. Is *that* what you want to know? It's a wonder I'm not more insane than I already am."

Moving right in front of him, I lean forward, placing my hands on both armrests of his chair, our faces inches apart. He doesn't move, his dark gaze boring into me, not a flicker of emotion on his face.

"That's what it was fucking like in Nostraza, you *asshole*."

With that, I push myself up and storm from the room, breaking into a run after I clear the doorway so no one can bear witness to any more of my tears.

CHAPTER SIX

I pace the length of my room, trying to formulate a plan. I have never been so angry or so desperate in my life. Dragging up all those horrible memories cleaved a giant slice through my chest. I *have* to get out of here. I have to get to Nostraza and find Tristan and Willow so we can get far away from these Fae and their dangerous notions of what I can do for them.

Atlas wanted to use me, and I'm sure Nadir brought me here for a similar purpose.

I think again of the Sun Mirror's words when it said this could never happen again. I've surmised it had been referring to the union between me and Atlas, but what did that specifically mean? Did it have something to do with my magic? After learning what a bonding means for an Imperial Fae, I assume Atlas wanted to access the power he believed I possessed.

But *what* couldn't happen again?

When I'd first woken up in Aphelion, I'd been confused and disoriented, overwhelmed by an existence so wholly removed from the one I'd been living. When Atlas told me the Aurora King had chosen me for the trials, it never occurred to me it was Atlas who'd wanted me there all along. What reason did I have to doubt those words?

But he'd lied about everything. *He'd* been the one to take me from Nostraza, and through the snippets of conversation I've gleaned in this house, there is more than one Imperial Fae out there looking for me.

My parents were murdered when I was only a child, and they'd only begun to recount the stories of my heritage. Of the world before my grandmother nearly destroyed it all. I'm not sure what's in store for me. I don't know what happens if I find the Crown, but I can't sit here any longer wondering. My magic is invariably stuck, and I remember all too vividly what happened the last time someone tried to force it out of me.

I clutch the locket hanging around my neck as I pace. The sliver of red jewel is the last thing I have of my mother and the life that was stolen from us. A small piece of the Heart Crown that Willow and I spent over a decade protecting, keeping it out of the guards' reach, sometimes swallowing it so no one could find it.

I stop and stare out the window, studying the scene of snow-capped trees stretching for miles. I know the direction of Nostraza, thanks to the position of the mountains, but I don't know how far away we are. How long could I survive in the Void on my own? I've done it before, but that was under different circumstances.

It's a stupid, reckless plan, but I am under no illusions that Nadir has any intention of ever letting me go. While Amya may seem sympathetic, I still don't trust that she's trying to get my family back. If I want to find Tristan and Willow, I'm going to need to take matters into my own hands.

As night wears on, I listen to the sounds of the manor house settling for the night. There are about ten staff working here and the three Fae who are holding me captive. I've seen no one else during my weeks here, but I'll need to be careful.

Once it's fully dark, I tug on a pair of boots and bundle myself into the warmest clothes I can find. A thick coat and a fur-lined cloak. Gloves and a fur hat to cover my ears. A scarf to protect my chin and cheeks. My first goal is getting one of the opalescent broaches fused with magic that protects their wearers from the creatures in the Void.

It's hard to believe it was barely four months ago that I was in the Hollow for days on end, willing death to deliver me from this life. It's still a miracle none of the forest's monsters got me then, but I can't take that chance again.

I ease open the door to my bedroom and listen for any sounds of life in the hall, hearing nothing but the ambient noises of the manor. Hopefully, the servants have all gone to bed, so I don't have to contend with any witnesses to my escape.

Everything is silent as I peer down the hallway towards Nadir's bedroom. Amya and Mael both have rooms further down, though I've never been inside. With any luck, they left the house after the tirade I unleashed on the prince. They all seem to come and go at will between here, the city, and the Keep, though at least one of them always stays behind to fulfil their role as my jailor. But I also hope that means we aren't too far away from Nostraza.

No one came to try to smooth things over with me tonight. As if that would ever be possible.

Slowly, I creep down the carpeted halls, their plushness muffling my footsteps, and ease down the wide staircase. The carpet is the violet of the aurora; the wood gleaming black. At the foot of the stairs, I step onto a floor made of emerald tiles striated with copper and silver. I'd always believed The Aurora to be nothing but grey and bleakness, but there is a certain quiet elegance in these dark surfaces punctuated with the colors of the sky. I've watched the lights from my bedroom every night, marveling at the way they tug at something deep inside my chest. A memory. A feeling I don't understand.

Keeping aware of my surroundings, I make my way towards the long narrow hallway where the servants' cloaks hang on a row of hooks. On the opposite wall is a shelf stocked with dry goods.

Low chatter between what sounds like two people comes from the kitchen, the firelight from the stone hearth bouncing off the walls as they tend to their duties. I curse their presence and wonder if I should come back later. I don't know how loyal these servants are to their master, or if they'd raise the alarm if they caught me. Though Nadir isn't especially friendly, the people who work here all appear happy enough.

Worried I'll lose my nerve if I don't act now, I approach the closest hook where a long black wool cloak hangs. Heavy boots line the wall, the drips of melted snow leaving small puddles of mud on the floor. Keeping one eye on the end of the hall, I dig through the folds of fabric until I find one of the pins and quickly unhook it.

Petrified I'll be caught, my breath shortens into tight gasps.

After Nadir made me sleep on his floor last night, I shudder to think what he'll do to me if he catches me trying to escape.

There's a break in the chatter as the room falls silent. I go perfectly still. Shit. They heard me. Not daring to breathe, I take a step back, hoping something else caught their attention. One of them snorts and then they both burst into laughter while I exhale the breath trapped in my chest.

While they're still distracted, I grab a loaf of bread from the opposite wall, stuffing it down the front of my coat. Then I turn on my heel and scurry for the front door. Curiously, there are no guards stationed anywhere on the premises. That either means Nadir thinks he's untouchable out here, or he has some other way to keep things out... and in. I'm praying his ego is as massive as it seems, and it's the first option as I turn the door handle and ease the door open.

A cold blast of air ruffles my clothes and my hair, a gust of snow sprinkling the floor with white. With one more glance behind me, I step outside and close the door gently.

The courtyard is covered in a thin layer of snow. It's nearing the end of summer, but we're far enough north that the weather is already turning. South is my destination if there's any chance of survival, which is perfect because that's exactly where I need to go.

A high iron fence surrounds the manor house and I pray it isn't locked. Before I proceed, I pin the stolen broach to my cloak and press the stone in the middle. Mist erupts, surrounding me with the nearly translucent bubble I remember from the last time I was forced into the Void. It feels like a flimsy sort of shield, no more potent than a sneeze, but I hope it's enough to keep me from becoming a meal out in the forest.

The wind gusts against me, and I shiver, pulling my cloak tight. This is stupid. I *know* it's stupid, but I can't sit here anymore waiting to find out if Tristan and Willow are alive. I can't keep waiting here to find out what Nadir plans to do with me or for Atlas to claim the prize he lost. The Sun King isn't finished with me. He worked much too hard to kidnap me, lie to me over and over, and ensure I got to the end of the Trials.

I try not to think too hard about the third potential outcome of this folly. And that's being delivered back into the hands of the Aurora King. I don't know enough about any of these Fae, but I'd bet money he's the absolute worst of the lot.

With a deep breath, I step down the wide stone stairs and down the pathway that leads to the gate. Grasping a bar, I unhook the latch and it opens with a nearly imperceptible squeak before it swings just enough that I can slip through. My breath fogs in the air, and my heart is beating so hard I can feel it in my ears. *Unlocked*. Everything is unlocked. A subconscious warning tells me not to trust any of this, but I've already come this far, and I have to get out of here.

I cast another look at the manor house. Made of black stone and silver mortar, it has a certain quiet elegance. It's made from the same glittering material as the Aurora Keep I looked upon so many times. The same windows that reflect the colors of the aurora. There are intricate carved lattices that frame the edges of the roof and—

Stop stalling, Lor.

With another deep breath, I turn to face the trees, seeing nothing but inky blackness marred by the clouded shield surrounding me. The moon is bright, and I say a silent prayer for that. I'm not sure of where I'm going, only that I need to keep the mountains behind me.

Even from here, I can feel their pull. My brother and sister. The only people I have left in this world. If they're alive, then they're waiting for me.

Snapping a branch off a tree, I brandish it with one hand like a sword, knowing it's a feeble substitute for the real thing, but it's better than nothing. Maybe. With another deep, shaky breath, I place one purposeful foot in front of the other before I take off, vanishing into the darkness of the trees.

CHAPTER SEVEN

For a long time, I half walk, half run down a worn path I pick out through the shadows. Someone has been this way before, and that realization bolsters my courage as I kick up my pace. The wind is mild thanks to the shelter of the trees, and as long as I keep moving, I stay warm enough.

Every so often, I stop and listen to my surroundings, clutching the branch so tightly my fingers ache. It's eerily quiet, like those nights I spent in the Hollow. The most unnerving part had been the silence, knowing the skulking creatures were assessing me. Sizing me up. I wonder what might be out there watching me now, and I shiver.

Don't think about it. Just keep moving. Don't stop until you get to Nostraza.

Sure, I haven't quite worked out how I'll free Tristan and Willow, but that's a future problem to worry about. I've made it this far. I'll think of something.

So lost in my thoughts, I don't notice when the sounds of the forest shift. The wind has picked up and the leaves are rustling, backdropped by a chorus of chittering and chirps. Like the creatures have taken an interest in my arrival and are stirring to life. Shit.

I study the foggy shield surrounding me, hoping it does what it's supposed to as I increase my pace, knowing I couldn't outrun anything that set it sights on me. But my adrenaline is pumping, and it feels better to keep moving.

As my surroundings press in on me, I wonder if I should have stayed at the manor. But that prince was driving me up the fucking wall. If I had to suffer that smug smile one more time, no one could hold me responsible for punching it right off his pretty face. I don't trust any of them, despite Amya and her supposed sympathy. I'm sure she's faking it. Atlas was nice to me, too, and look how that ended up. Pretty words from pretty Fae. They're all liars driven by their own ends.

And their desire for my blood.

A shadow flickers in the corner of my eye, and my throat knots in fear. The shield, I remind myself. The shield will protect me. That's what it does. I look back, searching the darkness and then push forward, still following the path, black trees arching overhead.

Screaming, I skid to a halt when a large shape thumps down in front of me. Something is blocking my path. Something big. Slowly it unfurls its body, its limbs too long for its thin frame and its skin a mottled grey. I remember that shape. It looks like the thing that nearly devoured me before the rain "rescued" me that night in the hole.

It stares at me with matte black eyes that don't reflect the moonlight, which might be one of the most terrifying things I've ever seen.

"Get away," I whisper and point my stick, as if that's going to do a damn thing. I wonder how the shield functions. Will it hurt the monster if it touches it? Can I try to muscle my way past and then run for my life? Its limbs are easily three times as long as mine, though. Something tells me it can move fast.

That thought pulls more knots in my chest as the creature stretches up on its spindly legs. At its full height, it dwarfs me and a horrified scream crowds the back of my throat.

It cocks the head perched on its too-long neck, as if considering me before its face stretches into a macabre grin. It lurches and I stumble, tripping over my feet and landing on my back. The air knocks out of me, and my paltry weapon skitters across the icy ground. The creature leaps, dropping over me, its arms and legs forming a cage made of nightmares. Its leering face peers down at me with the rictus of its smile.

It takes a moment to register that I'm screaming. Over and over. So loud it hurts my own ears, my vocal cords straining like they're being wrenched over a crossbow.

The bubble of the shield is still in place, but that's small consolation right now. Clearly, its effectiveness is limited only to the few inches of space around me, but that's enough. If this thing can't touch me, that means I can try to get away.

Slowly, I back up, sliding out from under the monster as it watches me. A string of saliva drips from its mouth, piercing the shield and landing on my cheek.

"Gah," I gag as I wipe it away with the back of my hand. It stinks like rotten garbage mixed with decaying flesh. Thankfully, it seems harmless.

But why did that get through the barrier?

Zerra, this was so stupid. Why did I do this? I remind myself that I was desperate, and the prince left me no choice. All I had were bad choices, so I picked the one that would take me the closest to what I want. Tristan and Willow. That's logical enough. Sure.

Except right now, with this demon leering over me, I can't help but wish I'd stuck with the choice that kept me somewhat safe in my room. Nadir might be a demon of his own sort, but at least he wouldn't chew me up for dinner. I think. Honestly, I'm not sure. Maybe he was still getting to that part.

I inch back, sliding on the ground underneath the monster, the magic bubble currently the only thing keeping it at bay. The creature inches with me, corralling me between its arms and legs like a bug in a trap. Toying with me.

This isn't going to work—it's just going to keep following me until what? I die and then it can feast on my remains? I wonder if anyone heard my screams. I was counting on Nadir and the others to be blissfully ignorant of my escape until I was too far away for them to do anything about it.

I stop moving and lie perfectly still, staring at the thing above me. It's watching me with that terrible smile still on its face, like it has all the time in the world. I guess it does. It lives out here, and I'll either freeze to death or die of starvation because one loaf of bread won't hold me for long. This thing probably has friends, too, and that idea sets off another wave of panic as my chest constricts.

Sucking in several stilted breaths, I flip over to my stomach and brace my hands and feet against the ground. When I look up at the demon, it's still watching me like I'm a curiosity to be enjoyed for its amusement.

"One," I count under my breath. I'll try to lose it in the forest.

"Two." If I run fast enough, maybe I can make it back to the manor no worse for the wear. No one will even know I was gone. It chafes at me to have to return to my prison, but my desire to circumvent my fate as monster food outweighs my indignation.

"Three." I leap up and start sprinting through the trees as fast as I can, but as soon as I start moving, I already know this is futile. It's right behind me, its long legs easily keeping pace. It's so close I can feel its hot, wet breath on the back of my neck, the smell so strong I retch and nearly stumble.

Thanks to the magical broach, it still can't touch me, so I keep running, pumping my arms and legs. I need to get past the fence that surrounds the manor. Something about it must keep these monsters out. If I can just get through the gate, maybe I'll be safe.

Running, still running, I weave through the trees, my vision blurring with unshed tears when I hear a soft whine and suddenly the shield around me blinks in rapid succession a few times before it winks out completely.

I don't even have the presence of mind to scream as I understand what's just happened.

A large black shadow appears above my head where the monster is now suspended, preparing to devour me whole. And *now* I'm screaming. High-pitched shrieks that tear from the furthest reaches of my soul. I've never been this scared in my life and that's saying something.

The demon arcs as if in slow motion. I can't tear my eyes away as I practically feel the press of air as it descends, claws out, a snarl on its twisted lips. It screeches in ecstasy, the sound echoing across the forest. A fiery streak of tears runs down my face as I scream and scream.

Suddenly, two white shapes burst from the trees, their legs flying against the earth, their howls joining my screams. The demon screeches and, with a burst of speed, I try to swerve out of the path of its trajectory. It lands right behind me with a heavy thud that vibrates the earth as the dogs streak past, barking like they've seen the lord of the underworld himself.

There's a flash of light, and the monster goes flying with an agonized shriek. Its body slams into the side of a tree so hard, the trunk snaps and bows in half, the branches and leaves crashing to the earth.

I'm still screaming as it goes flying into another tree and then into a large boulder half buried in the earth. The sounds of its bones cracking fill the air before its head caves in, and then it stops flailing, its body going limp.

As I collapse to my knees, I press my hands to my chest, my entire body shaking.

"What *the fuck* are you doing out here?" Nadir snarls as he emerges from the shadows, his dark hair hanging in his face and his eyes flashing blue and green and red. "Do you have any idea how close you were to dying?"

He's shouting at me, but I can't form words because my heart is still beating so hard it's making my entire body hurt.

A moment later, I feel a soft touch on my back. "It's okay, you're okay," Amya says softly as she rubs her hand up and down my spine.

"What were you thinking, Inmate?" Nadir is hovering over me now, all towering fury and righteous brimstone. The dogs have returned to his side and are flanking him like a pair of furry sentinels.

"Calm down," Amya says. "Give her a minute. She's obviously traumatized."

Nadir drops into a crouch, meeting me at eye level. "I should think so when you do something as stupid and reckless and... What *the fuck* were you thinking?"

My breath is still coming in short gasps, my limbs trembling from fear and cold and the adrenaline draining from my veins. I was so close to the end right there. I hate this fucking forest and this place and this fucking Fae prince hovering in front of me like he owns the entire fucking world.

"I was thinking," I say, looking up at him furiously, "that you've kept me locked in that house for weeks. You won't let me out, and you won't tell me if my friends are alive! You keep telling me you're trying, but that's clearly a lie!"

When I push up on a knee to stand, I nearly crumple. The shaking in my body has given way to anger instead of fear. How dare he talk to me this way?

Nadir backs up and rises to his full height before I take a step towards him, stopping so close we're practically touching as I look up into his face.

"I was thinking you're never going to let me out of here and that you're planning to use me like Atlas, and I'm not going to survive any of this! So excuse me if I decided to take my chances with the forest!"

I'm screaming so loud now there's little possibility not a single monster in the trees hasn't heard us. I can practically feel their curious stares as they slink closer in the darkness.

It's obvious Nadir and Amya are keeping them at bay somehow, and I wonder how I can get some of that power for myself. As Nadir towers over me, I feel that tug under my skin, like something craving to break loose. That makes me even angrier.

With a curl of my lip, I skirt around him and stomp down the path on the way back towards the manor, taking out my frustrations on the earth beneath my feet.

My escape attempt is aborted for today. But I'm not done yet.

"I don't think so," comes a deep voice behind me, just as a thin tendril of fuchsia light snakes around my waist, while more of them circle my wrists. I don't stop walking until another one wraps around my ankles and yanks tight as I begin to tip. I'm about to crash to the ground when an arm catches me, and Nadir hauls me up over his shoulder.

"Put me down! Why is everyone always doing this to me?!"

"Because you're a menace to yourself," comes the gruff reply. "What did you think was going to happen out here, Inmate? It's miles to Nostraza. You would have frozen to death if that ozziller hadn't gotten you first."

I jerk my body, attempting to dislodge my restraints, but all I'm rewarded with is a low, dark chuckle. I hate this magic of his—it's so fucking inconvenient. Amya follows quietly behind us, her eyes darting between me and the prince. The dogs trot alongside her, their soft white tails held high, and I swear even they watch me with disapproval.

"Are you going to lie to me again about sending a messenger to Nostraza?" I snarl at her, and she has the good grace to look abashed. "You're the fucking prince and princess of The Aurora! You can't get information about a couple of lowly prisoners? Or is it that you won't?"

Amya's dark eyes are concerned as her gaze flicks towards her brother. "It's not that simple," she says so softly that I'm not even sure I hear it.

"Whatever," I mutter as Nadir picks up his pace and then we're flying through the trees at a dizzying speed, the ground whipping beneath my vision. Finally, he slows, and I hear the creak of the gate before it slams. Nadir hauls me off his shoulder and drops me on the ground in a heap, not even attempting to soften my fall.

Our gazes clash as he pins me with a glare. With his eyes never leaving me, he reaches out a hand and sends a twist of blue and green light towards the gate, where it wraps around the bars, sealing it shut.

"Apparently, the threat of the fucking Void isn't enough to keep you inside," he snarls at me. "Do something like that again and I'll—"

"What?" I spit at him. "You keep threatening me, but you aren't brave enough to follow through on any of these empty promises. What are you going to do to me, asshole?"

He bends down, thunder in his expression, and for a moment, a tiny part of me is frightened, sure he could truly make me suffer if he wanted. His hand reaches out and I scramble back, but he catches my cloak in a large fist and yanks me forward, using the other to tear the magical broach from the fabric. It's lost that soft light and is just a dull stone now.

"What happened to it?" I ask.

"It needs to be charged. They only last about an hour."

"Oh," I say, feeling even more stupid than I already do. "I didn't know that."

He arches a dark eyebrow with such condescension that I want to cut it off his face. "Clearly."

I pick myself up off the ground and rise to meet his glare.

"I want to leave. You can't keep me here forever."

"You're not going anywhere until I get what I want."

He steps closer, enough that I have to look up. He's beautiful in the moonlight, its glow glinting off his cheekbones and his strong jaw. His dark hair is a little wild and those eyes that constantly unnerve me feel like they can see right into my very soul. The rush of my blood intensifies as that strange feeling under my skin pulls towards him again. It's driving me insane.

His mouth presses together as if he's also waging some internal battle. Does he feel this too?

"You're not getting anything from me until I know Tristan and Willow are okay," I hiss. "No. Actually, I take that back.

Knowing if they're okay isn't enough anymore. Bring them to me, or you will never get a single word out of me."

"Then I guess we're at an impasse," he says, his hand circling my biceps. I can feel the heat coming off him, his touch sending all of my blood and my trapped magic right to where he holds me in his grip. It's like fire and heat and something else tangled into something I definitely don't understand. "I'm nearly immortal, little girl. I can wait a very, very long time."

He utters those words with a challenge, as if he's testing my reaction.

Does he know my secrets? Did his father tell him anything? About what he did to me? About who I was?

"I have ways of making you talk, Inmate. Cruel, painful ways."

I snort and pin him with a glare. "You think there's anything you can do to me that will hurt enough, oh mighty prince of The Aurora? You think I haven't already been tortured and tormented to the point of breaking?"

Fury coils so tightly in my limbs, I feel like I might snap. "There is *nothing* you can do to me. Bring my friends here, or all of my secrets die with me," I say, fusing as much coldness into my voice as I can. "Until then, I'll be in my room."

I wrench my arm from his grip and spin around. A moment later, I stop and look at him. "And my fucking name is Lor. At least pretend you respect me enough to remember it."

CHAPTER EIGHT

For the next few days, I cloister myself in my room, refusing every advance from Amya and Mael to make amends. Do they think I'm that naïve? They aren't my friends, and they aren't going to trick me into believing they haven't kidnapped and held me against my will.

Nadir doesn't even pretend to be nice, and maybe a part of me respects that. At least he's honest about who he is. Periodically, he bangs on my door and rattles the knob, reminding me he could enter if he wanted. I'm not sure why he doesn't. Maybe I was convincing enough to make him understand I won't share anything against my will.

Regardless, it's his way of reminding me he isn't letting this, or me, go.

At what point will he finally resort to torturing out my secrets? Something tells me the Aurora Prince isn't used to the word "no" and patience clearly isn't one of his virtues.

I won't crack, though. No matter what. I will die before I give him what he wants. In my hubris, I warned him he couldn't break me, but I wonder how true that is. How much longer until he loses his patience and tests that theory? He's got hundreds of years to wait me out, and I'm not sure what I've got.

The golden locket I stole from Aphelion hangs around my throat, and I click it open to reveal the small jewel nestled inside.

The door rattles again.

"Inmate," comes the snarl on the other side.

"Fuck off!" I shout, and I'm rewarded with a low growl before his footsteps retreat once again.

It's late at night when my door cracks open, light filtering across the bed. Blinking awake, I lift up on to my elbow, squinting into the brightness.

"Lor," comes a soft voice. "Wake up, Lor."

Using my hand to shield my eyes, I sit up slowly.

"What is it?" I ask, my voice thick with sleep.

"Come on," Amya says. "There's someone here to see you."

I frown, registering her words as something kicks under my ribcage.

"Who?" I ease up to stand, my heart thrumming with the promise of something I'm too afraid to name.

"You'll see," she says, her eyes sparking with flashes of teal in the darkness. I try not to give weight to my hopes, knowing I won't survive the fallout if I'm wrong.

In my thick wool socks, I pad across the floor to where Amya waits. She's dressed simply for once—in a plain tunic and leggings—though her colorful streaked hair hangs wildly around her shoulders, still giving her an otherworldliness. The lack of her usual dark eye makeup also makes her appear softer and younger.

She beckons me to follow, and we make our way to the wide staircase that descends to the main floor. At the top of the landing, I freeze as a mountain of bricks fills my lungs.

Below, a small group of people stands in the front foyer. The large jewel-toned chandelier throws off plenty of light, so I'm almost sure my eyes aren't deceiving me.

But this can't be real.

I blink hard. And then I blink again, *willing* this to be real. If this is another illusion, I don't know what that will do to me. What if they run away from me again?

"Tris," I whisper, the ground shifting beneath my feet, as everyone below stops and looks up to where I'm standing. "Willow."

It's them.

When they turn to face me, all three of our gazes meet as time stops and thickens with the years and the memories and the infinite hurt of our collective survival. With every bit of love and hope I've held for them all these months.

They're alive.

"Lor!" Willow screams, her voice cracking. "Lor!"

"Willow. Oh Zerra," I breathe as I fly down the stairs, practically tripping over my feet. "Willow! Tristan!"

I've never run so fast in my life. When I make it to the bottom, somehow managing not to slip and break my neck, I throw my arms wide, crying out as I fold them into me. We all collapse to the floor in a weeping tangle of arms and hugs and kisses.

"Lor," Willow is sobbing into my neck. "I thought you were dead. They said you died in the Hollow and I..."

"You're alive," Tristan whispers, his arms around me and his face buried in my hair. "You're alive."

He's shaking and I'm shaking. We're all trembling as we hold on to each other so tight, I fear I might break them. I forgot how thin and frail they both are. Surrounded by wealth and nourished bodies has made me forget what it was like after I got out of Nostraza. Tears flow down my face as we sit on the marble floor, just holding each other.

A piece of me that had been lost finally slides back into place, my heart once again whole.

"Look at you," Willow says, finally pulling away and framing my face with her thin, chapped hands. "Look at you. Zerra, you're so beautiful, Lor. You look so healthy and gorgeous and...gods, I can't believe you're alive." I'm crying so hard that I can't catch my breath, so I squeeze her hand and nod. "But where have you been?"

I open my mouth to speak, but all that comes out is another sob as Tristan grabs and hugs me against him again. His cheek is pressed to my temple, while his hand grips the back of my head. "I thought you were dead. They said the ozziller killed you in the Hollow during the riot." He's speaking as if in a dream, and I agree it feels like none of this can be real.

"I know," I finally manage to choke out. "I know. I'm okay. I was so worried about you." Together, we all stand up, our hands clasped.

Tristan pulls away and looks me over. "I can't believe you're alive."

Like me, my big brother learned to repress any signs of weakness during our years in Nostraza, but tears stream freely down his face as he again wraps me in his fierce hug. Willow circles me from behind, squeezing me tight, and for the first time in months, I can finally breathe.

They're here. They're alive. Everything I did in Aphelion was for them. I want to stand here forever, soaking up the drops of their love as they piece my soul back together.

"Lor," Tristan finally says. "*Where* have you been? Why do you look so..." He stops, his gaze searching my face. I can't imagine how different I must seem from the last time he saw me. My body is so much rounder and healthier. My skin is glowing and my hair is long and shiny. The only physical reminders of my old life are the faded scars on my skin, including the one on my cheek, bisecting my eye and running through my eyebrow.

"That's a very long story," I say, taking Willow's hand and holding it to my heart. "I'll tell you everything."

It's then I finally take notice of the others who wait in the hall. Nadir and Amya watch us, like twin dark pillars, their colorful eyes swirling. They're brighter than normal, shining with silver, as if this reunion has affected them too. Would it be too much to hope the Aurora Prince can feel something deep inside that icy exterior?

"What does this mean?" I ask, my voice hoarse as I scrub a tear from my cheek. "Why are they here? Can they stay?"

Nadir tips his chin. "You laid down your terms, Inmate. They've been released from Nostraza. Their sentences are cleared. You're all free from there. Forever."

Those words plunge through the center of my chest with the weight of a burning coal as I succumb to a fresh wave of tears. Willow starts sobbing again as she leans against me. "Forever? You promise?"

He gives me a curt nod.

"Thank you," I whisper to the prince. "Thank you." He studies me for a moment, his gaze thoughtful, and an uncharacteristic softness flickers across his expression, so brief anyone could have easily missed it.

"You're welcome." He opens his mouth and pauses as though he's hesitating about what he wants to say next. "I should have tried harder from the beginning."

I blink, surprised to hear the admission and a rare show of empathy from this dark, cold Fae.

"I don't understand what's going on," Tristan says, ever the protector. I can sense his mistrust of this entire situation, and he's right to be wary. How am I going to explain everything? "Why is Lor here, and why are you letting us go after all this time?"

"Tris," I say, placing a hand on his arm. "A lot has happened." I give him a significant look that I hope conveys everything I can't reveal in front of the royal siblings. There's a flicker of acknowledgment across his face. They suspect something. About us. About our family. That the secrets we thought had been buried forever have been dug up like withered tulip bulbs and we might be in trouble. "I'll tell you everything."

He nods and looks at Amya and Nadir again.

Another High Fae I didn't notice earlier stands against the far wall. She has long curling hair tied into a high ponytail and is wearing a high collared button up jacket, slim-fitting pants, and tall leather boots. Everything is black, contrasting with the fiery red of her hair. Bright green eyes narrow with suspicion where she stands with her arms folded, one ankle crossed over the other.

"Thank you," Tristan says to the woman. "For bringing us to her."

"Meet Hylene," Nadir says by way of introduction. "A friend." He leaves it at that and then turns back to us.

"They're your brother and sister," Amya says then, her dark gaze flicking between us. "They're not your friends, they're your family."

The three of us all suck in a breath. We'd always kept it a secret, knowing if they ever found one of us out, the other two would be in danger.

"That's why you wanted them so much," Amya continues.

Nadir's shoulders stiffen as the realization sinks in. I see it in the calculation of his expression. He now has three potential weapons at his disposal.

"Yes," I say, knowing there's little use in lying about it anymore. It's obvious to anyone paying attention. No one cared enough in Nostraza or ever looked close enough to notice. But catching me in this lie is only more damning evidence that I'm keeping more secrets.

The prince recovers quickly, his face smoothing into its usual indifference.

"There are rooms ready for your family," he says. "Brea will take them upstairs."

Brea materializes from the sidelines and offers a quick bow to my brother and sister. "Please follow me."

I'm not ready to let them go, but I remind myself they're out. They're here and they're never going back. They're mine.

"I'll be up in a minute," I say. Willow gives me another hug and Tristan glares at Nadir with the same brotherly expression he always reserved for my latest fling in Nostraza. The thought fires a nostalgic ache in my chest. I can't believe they're here and they're alive.

Once they're out of earshot, I turn to the prince.

"Thank you," I say again, and he steps towards me. I ball my hands up as my magic responds, wanting to touch him. "I can't thank you enough."

He says nothing as he studies me before our gazes lock, and something irrevocable shifts between us.

"Please go see your family. Spend time with them tonight," he says. "I'll come and see you tomorrow."

He doesn't need to say what comes next. What he's expecting now. He kept up his end of our bargain, and now it's time to collect his reward.

I just hope the prize I bartered for was worth revealing everything.

CHAPTER NINE

NADIR

I watch Lor go up the stairs and disappear around the corner with a knot burning in my chest.

"So, they're her brother and sister," Hylene says, walking over to stand next to me. She watches the spot where Lor was standing, her brows drawing together. "Did you know that?"

"I suspected it," I reply. "But I wasn't sure."

"This changes things."

Her keen green eyes study me with a mixture of wariness and curiosity. I know she thinks this is all a terrible mistake, and she's probably right. Still, like Amya and Mael, she's willing to support me for now. She's second only to Amya when it comes to questioning my motives. It's been that way since the day we first met at a cabaret in the Crimson District. I needed a chameleon. Someone who could charm her way into any space, especially those where they'd make the mistake of underestimating a beautiful woman.

"I know," I reply.

There isn't just one potential weapon in this house anymore. There are three. Three Fae with the magic of Heart in their veins. I just hope one of them is powerful enough for it to matter.

Amya is now watching the same empty space with her arms folded and her chin jutting out. "They're all mortal, Nadir. There is absolutely no hint any of them are High Fae. I can't detect the slightest scent of magic on them."

I couldn't either, but there has to be an explanation for that. Because I *feel* it.

It's getting stronger the more time I spend around her. That pull that comes from deep within my veins. Like cords trying to explode straight through my skin. My magic becomes wild and untethered every time she walks into the room. I can barely contain it. It wants to reach out and touch her. Caress her. *Do* things to her I'm desperately trying to ignore as I lie awake in bed at night, unable to sleep with the fever that flushes under my skin.

No one has ever left my head so muddled.

I don't know why I can't make myself tell Amya any of this. We share everything. But there's something about this prisoner from Nostraza that tastes like a secret belonging only to me.

There is magic in her. Of that, I'm sure. And mine is trying to get at it.

When she ran off and was nearly attacked by that ozziller, all I could see was a red haze of fury. I didn't need to destroy that monster with as much force as I did, but I wanted to do more than stop it. I wanted it to suffer. For daring to threaten her, I wanted it to feel the excruciating agony of my wrath even after it was dead.

Zerra, I shouldn't have yelled at her like that, but I can't control my emotions around her. I'm dangling off a ledge by my fingertips, my grip so close to slipping.

"So the Primary could be any of them, then?" Mael asks, breaking into my tumultuous thoughts. He eyes me with both concern and amusement, clearly sensing my inner turmoil.

"Why are you so sure it's the girl?" Hylene chimes in.

The circle of my friends faces me. They aren't judging me—just forcing me to consider every angle.

"Because Atlas stole *her*, not her sister or brother, and my father only had the warden watching Lor. He never asked about the other two, which begs the question of whether he knows who they are to her. It can't be a coincidence they've been in there together all this time."

I rub my chin, considering. I need to know what information the king has. My father feigned disinterest in the girl when she disappeared. I remember what he said about her being of no use to him anymore, despite what he'd been hoping. What had he meant by that? And if she *was* the Primary of Heart, why had Rion abandoned her to Nostraza? Why not make use of her? Why is she even alive at all?

I look up to the dark hallway at the top of the stairs again. Though I said I'd give her tonight to reunite with her family, these questions singe the tip of my tongue, leaving a bitter aftertaste. She's been deflecting me for weeks, and I've waited long enough.

Without another word, I bolt up the stairs, taking them two at a time. She can catch up with her siblings tomorrow.

With a fist raised, I stand outside her door, catching the murmur of soft voices on the other side. My hand drops. I should let her have this. When she first saw them, even I had difficulty tamping down a swell of emotions. I'd lay down my life for Amya, so I know what the love of a sibling means. If anything ever happened to my sister...it doesn't even bear thinking about.

But I need answers, and I need them soon. I'm determined to stop my father from his rule of terror, and a secret weapon might be sitting on the other side of the door. Pushing away my reservations, I raise my hand and knock. The voices on the other side cut off, and a moment later, the door swings open.

Lor stands in the doorway with a frown. She's wearing the soft leggings and tunic that she seems to favor, her arms bare and her dark hair piled on top of her head, tendrils framing her neck and face. The fabric clings to her breasts and her hips in a way that makes my cock ache, her scent filling my nostrils—smoke and roses and lightning. That same scent I remember from the Hollow when I'd been searching for clues of her whereabouts.

Somehow, I'd already known it had been her I smelled. It had felt like a shadowed memory, even if that made no sense. I'd never seen her before the night of the Sun Queen ball.

At the sight of her, my magic gives a desperate tug, trying to peel away from my skin, but I leash it down, holding it back with effort.

"Yes?" she asks, casting a worried glance behind me, and now I feel guilty for interrupting. What's wrong with me? I don't care about her convenience.

"I...wanted to see that you'd all settled in okay," I say like the fool I am.

Very smooth, Nadir.

I peer into the room and see her brother and sister both sitting on the violet couch in front of the fire. They're watching me with a combination of fear and curiosity. I can't imagine what a jarring experience it must have been to have been pulled out of Nostraza in the middle of the night and brought to a house at the edge of the Void, only to be confronted by the prince and princess of The Aurora. Do they even understand what's happened?

They're both so thin and sickly, their pallor grey and anemic. That growing shame I feel about the existence of Nostraza expands to fill the space between me and Lor. I was sure neither of her siblings were guilty of the crimes listed in their files. Or if they were, the truth had been twisted to suit my father's purposes.

When Lor had told me what that warden had done, I nearly lost my mind. I'm not sure why I care at all, but he's lucky he's already dead. Otherwise, I would have stormed into that prison and tortured him slowly until he begged me to end him. And I would have enjoyed every fucking second of it. At least I got to watch him die when my father choked him in his study. But that wasn't nearly enough.

As it stands, it's taking all of my willpower not to kill every guard in that prison for even daring to think about touching her. I shake my head, wondering where these thoughts are coming from. Why do I care what happened?

Regardless, my father threw a group of children into Nostraza and left them to rot. If they were the heirs of Heart, then Rion should have just killed them immediately. It would have been the kinder fate. Perhaps that had been the point, though. I wouldn't put it past my father to ensure they suffered for no other reason than because he could.

"We're fine," Lor says, tipping her head and peering at me with a squint. "Are you okay?"

She says it softly, and it occurs to me it's the first time her words aren't coated in barbed wires since I brought her here.

"I'm fine," I say, shaking my head again. I need sleep. And alcohol. Not in that order. "I'll see you in the morning."

We both pause, hesitating as we watch each other and something thrums deep within my chest. A resonance that echoes through my limbs. Before I say something stupid that I can't take back, I give her another once-over and then spin on my heel and stalk away.

CHAPTER TEN

LOR

Stunned, I watch Nadir leave, not sure what to make of that encounter. That was definitely weird. If I didn't know better, I might think he felt bad about interrupting, but that can't be. Courtesy doesn't seem to be a word that exists within his royal vocabulary.

"What was that about? And is that who I think it is?" Tristan asks, stirring me from my reverie.

"*That* is the one and only Aurora Prince." I sit down across from my siblings, who both shoot worried glances at the door. I can hardly blame them. After twelve years in Nostraza, sleeping under the same roof as anyone with ties to the king feels like wearing a shirt that's stretched too tight.

Another knock comes at the door and I get up, wondering if Nadir has changed his mind and is here to exact his price of information. I'll need to hold him off. First, I need to discuss things with Tristan and Willow and decide how much we're willing to share. These secrets don't only belong to me.

It's not Nadir, but Brea, pushing a cart laden with food. My sibling's eyes widen as she places several large platters on the low table in front of the fire. There are thick stacks of fluffy white bread and roasted chicken, stained red with spices. A tray of brightly colored desserts and another with an array of fragrant cheeses from soft and runny to hard and creamy.

My chest twists as I watch my siblings, remembering my bewilderment when I'd finally been fed proper nourishment in Aphelion. I can blame Atlas for so many things, but in a messed-up sort of way, he saved me, too. If it hadn't been for his scheming, I'd have died in that prison, eventually.

Neither of them seems to know where to start, so I sit down and fix a plate for Willow, handing it to her before I make one up for Tristan.

"Go on," I say. "Eat it slowly. It takes a little getting used to."

Willow nods and then studies the plate balanced in her lap as though she's expecting it to dissolve into a puff of smoke. Tristan lays his on the table and sits forward.

"Has he mistreated you?" His dark eyes flash to the doorway where the prince stood moments ago.

I shake my head. "No, he hasn't. Other than keeping me here."

"*Why* is he keeping you here?" Willow asks. Her hair hangs in clumps, still short and brutalized from being shaved off months ago. I touch the ends of my own hair that now hangs to the middle of my back, thinking of Aphelion's-most-coveted-stylist-with-a-very-long-cock, Callias, with an inward smile.

Then I let out a deep sigh before running my hand down my face. "I better start at the beginning."

Over the next hour, I detail as much of my experience in the Sun Palace and the Trials as I can. When I tell them about the final challenge when I thought they had been brought there, a familiar rage flares in my gut at the way we were all manipulated by Atlas. Most of all, I tell them about how I'd spent every single day wondering if they were still alive.

"There was a riot that same night when they said the ozziller killed you," Tristan says. Even with me sitting alive and healthy in front of him, I can tell how much it costs him to say those words. Willow's cheeks are wet with tears, and she scrubs them away with the heel of her hand.

"I'm sorry. I had no way to contact you."

"You have nothing to be sorry for," Willow says. "We just... We nearly broke when they told us."

A tear slides down my own cheek, hearing the anguish in her voice.

"I know," I whisper. "The only thing that kept me going was the hope I'd see you again. That if I won, I'd get you out, and we might be safe and together. That we'd never go hungry or be cold again."

She reaches out a hand and clasps mine. It's so thin and delicate, like she's a baby bird with crystal bones. I hate seeing her this way.

"Gabriel, the warder I told you about," I say, continuing with my story, "told me he had people on the inside who started the riot, creating a diversion. It took me a while to realize that Atlas lied to me about the whole 'tribute from The Aurora' thing."

I think back to when Atlas blurted out he'd *stolen* me from the Aurora King after the last trial. It had been the moment of clarity when it all fell into place and my eyes finally opened. Zerra, I was such a fool.

"So he knows," Willow says, her voice soft, fear filling her dark eyes. "Who you are? What you might be?"

I sigh. "I'm not entirely sure what he knows. When I believed the Aurora King had chosen me for the Trials, I thought it was part of a greater plan I hadn't figured out yet. That he was duping Atlas. It seemed impossible for Atlas to know anything about my past. So I played along, pretending I was exactly who I seemed to be—a human prisoner from Nostraza—and I'm ashamed to say I let myself get swept up in the grandeur of it all.

"Atlas was charming and handsome and told me everything I wanted to hear. I really thought he was being honest about his feelings and after our miserable life—" Tears surface again, threatening to choke me. "I was so stupid. So trusting. I should have known better."

Willow puts down her plate and scoots across the couch before wrapping an arm around my shoulders, where I feel every sharp press of bone against my body. I'm not sure what the future holds for any of us, but I will *never* let her go hungry again.

I hug her as tightly as I dare, tension releasing in my chest. She feels like home and safety and the reminder of everything I thought I'd lost.

"Of course you did, Lor," she says, tucking a lock of hair behind my ear as I wipe away another tear. "I can't imagine what it must have been like to be thrust into all of that. You weren't stupid. You wanted to believe the best of him."

My response is a small smile. Zerra, how I've missed her. I can never do wrong in Willow's eyes. Another sister might resent me for the luxury I've been living in, but not her. She would never begrudge me anything.

"It wasn't until I finished the last challenge and he lost his shit about me standing in front of the mirror that I realized he'd known something all along." I let out a huff of air, my shoulders dropping. "Maybe it was naïve of me not to realize it, but I really thought there were only a handful of people left in all of Ouranos who knew."

"How did he find out?" Tristan asks, running a thumb along his bottom lip. I can hear his wheels churning, already plotting our next move.

"I don't know, but we need to get out of here and go back into hiding."

Tristan looks at the door and then back at me. "Do you really think he's going to let any of us go? Obviously, he suspects something."

I draw my eyebrows together. "No. And I promised I'd give him information if he brought you both to me."

My heart gives another tug at seeing them here, finally. Alive. Thin, beaten, nearly broken, but alive. There's still a chance for us to start over. To claim the life we barely let ourselves dream about.

"I'm not sure I can refuse him now."

"What information?" Tristan asks.

"He wants to know what the Mirror said to me."

"What did it say?" Willow asks.

"It told me I wasn't the rightful queen of Aphelion. That I couldn't be and that this could never happen again. It told me I had to find the Crown." I finger the locket around my neck and then crack it open, showing Willow I still have the jewel my mother entrusted to us all those years ago. Her final words to us had been that we had to keep it safe, no matter what.

"So we aren't going into hiding then," Tristan says.

"We have to, Tris. If Atlas knows, then there might be others who do, too," Willow says, chewing on the ragged tip of her thumbnail.

He stands up and starts pacing, rubbing his chin. "No. The time for hiding is over. Somehow, we survived that place and, by the strangest and most unlikely set of circumstances, we all got out. You can't tell me that Zerra means for us to walk away now."

Willow and I watch him in silence. He keeps pacing, thoughts churning across his face. The weight of our past sits heavy in the room like it's another body thrumming with breath and a heartbeat and the weight of its hopes.

Our parents had only shared pieces of our grandmother's history. Being older, Tristan and Willow always remembered more, though the information was often vague and full of holes. To this day, I'm not sure how much my mother and father really knew and how much they were hiding. Anytime we'd ask, Mother's eyes would fill with tears and she'd be unable to speak. She swore one day she'd tell us everything.

But she never got that chance.

We lived in a house deep in the Violet Forest, bordered by The Woodlands and Heart, where, for years, no one found us. Until that fateful day. Until the Aurora King sent his army to slaughter my parents and steal their children.

Trapped in Nostraza, we continued to live in ignorance about what exactly our grandmother had done, her memory tainted and her name always whispered like a curse. But whatever destroyed our family had sent us into hiding for centuries.

"I don't know yet," I say, responding to Tristan's statement. "First, we need to get out of here. Then we can decide what to do. If we do anything."

Tristan and I share a look before we both turn to Willow. She's always been the cautious one. The voice of reason whenever Tristan and I would get carried away with our plans for vengeance and the reclaiming of our legacy. She's the one to always remind us that none of what we hoped for was ever likely to come to pass.

The truth is that there is no 'if.' There's only 'when' and 'how.' I've waited my entire life for this opportunity, and everything I did to survive in Aphelion was leading me up to this moment. Tristan is right. This has to be destiny.

"Would you support me?" I ask my sister. "You've always thought we should leave this alone. If the chance ever came, I mean."

She takes a deep breath, holding it as I watch her lips moving while she counts to ten, settling whatever emotions she's battling. Finally, she lets out a long drag of air.

"I know I always warned against it," she says, carefully. "I didn't want either of you getting your hopes up, but I also never imagined a moment like this would ever come. I was so sure we'd all die in Nostraza."

Our gazes meet, the three of us coming to a silent but fateful understanding. These two know me better than anyone, and there's no one I'd rather face this uncertainty with. We might lose everything once and for all, or we might achieve the impossible.

"So the first thing is to get us out of here and away from The Aurora," Tristan says.

"And its prince," I add. For now, I keep the strange feelings Nadir stirs within me to myself. Once we're away from here, none of it will matter. I'll be free of it and him.

There's a knock at the door, and Brea pops her head in again. "I'm sorry to disturb you, but the other room is ready for your brother. I'm having another one made up for your sister, but it needs airing out. Would it be okay if she slept with you tonight?"

"Of course," I say, looking at Willow. "Is it okay?"

She looks over at the large, plush bed, her eyes shining, and I know what she's thinking. That bed is so different from the hard cots of Nostraza. I remember the feeling so well, of coasting like you're living in a dream. When something as simple as a comfortable bed is enough to strangle you with longing.

"Yes," she whispers. "Of course it's okay."

Brea smiles and moves to the table where we've been eating, clearing the plates.

"I've also got baths ready for both of you," she says to Tristan and Willow. "And some clean clothes for you to change into."

"Thank you, Brea," I say as she stacks the plates on her cart and then leaves the room with a tip of her head.

Tristan stands from the couch, stretching his arms overhead. I lunge over and wrap my arms around his waist, pressing my cheek to his chest and squeezing. He embraces me tightly.

"I missed you both so much," I say, my voice thick. "I thought about you every day. I did everything I could to get back to you."

He strokes the back of my head. "I know you did, Lor. We missed you, too, and you did it. You got us back. I'm so proud of you, little sister. I still can't believe you're alive."

Willow wraps her arms around me too as the three of us form a pillar of strength. "No one is ever going to tear us apart," she says with determination. "I won't let anyone take you from us again."

We stand together for another moment before we finally break apart. Willow and Tristan head to their respective baths and I dress for bed, sliding under the sheets and waiting for my sister.

When Willow finishes, she emerges wearing a clean set of leggings and a tunic. I can tell she's been crying, but I don't remark on it, sensing she needs time alone with her thoughts. When she slips into the other side of the bed, I take her hand and we fall asleep, clinging to each other like our lives depend on it.

CHAPTER ELEVEN

Warm breath ghosts over my skin, brushing the exposed flesh of my collarbone and my throat, traveling along the line of my jaw, before I feel the softest press of lips in that sensitive spot behind my ear.

The bed dips, and my eyes flutter open on a breathless gasp. There's just enough light to make out the form of a body I know better than I'd like, moving over me. It's strong and big and smells like smoked whisky swirled with a cool arctic breeze.

Nadir whispers something I can't make out, but his rough voice pushes straight through my stomach. My breath catches when the tip of his nose runs along the column of my throat until he reaches my ear. His teeth snag the lobe, scraping gently against the sensitive skin, and I whimper as my hips shift in response.

He drops on top of me, his weight pressing me into the soft mattress, and I moan, delighting in the sensation of his body against mine. It feels like finally releasing a trapped breath I've been holding for much too long. His lips move from my ear, back down my neck, dragging lower as his knee nudges between my thighs. My whole body responds to his touch, that wild feeling under my skin scratching and fighting to be let free. To claim him. To entwine itself with him and hold on tight.

His mouth continues exploring me, skating over the fabric of my thin nightshirt and between my breasts, down my stomach and then up before his mouth closes over a nipple. He sucks on the tip before he nips it with the sharp edges of his teeth, pulling out a strangled sound.

As his thigh presses between my legs, my hips move in response, grinding into it as I desperately seek more friction.

My hands find his hair, fingers sliding through silky locks as he moves to my other nipple, tending to it with all the care of a gardener with his seedlings. His thigh continues its torturous slide as I writhe against it, wanting him to touch me. To taste me. To make me moan louder.

A hand slides up my hip, his fingers teasing the edge of my waistband, and I keep grinding into his leg, wetness soaking the fabric of my leggings. He leans forward so the hard length of his thick cock slides against my stomach, and his hand travels under my tunic, his large palm leaving a trail of my scorched skin in its wake. He cups my breast, rolling the nipple as his mouth continues pressing wet, hot kisses up my throat and collarbone.

I writhe harder, gasping as he moves against me, rubbing his cock between my thighs. His hand dips under my waistband, his fingertips tickling the fevered skin that begs for his touch, making my back arch in response.

"Inmate," he whispers, but his voice is ragged and too distant to be natural.

Suddenly, my eyes fly open.

I'm lying in bed in my darkened bedroom, my chest heaving and my skin burning and flushed. Beside me, Willow sleeps peacefully, her soft breaths dusting the silence.

It takes me a moment to orient myself. To understand it was a dream. That I dreamed about the Aurora Prince coming to my room and dry humping me with his thigh. That I wanted it. And that I absolutely wanted more. Worst of all, that it left me breathless and wet and aching for it to be real.

I smack my forehead with my hand and run it down my face with a groan.

"Fuck," I whisper into the dark.

CHAPTER TWELVE

T he next morning, Nadir is all business again. He bangs on the door and doesn't wait for an invitation before he storms in to find me with Willow and Tristan conversing over breakfast. At the sight of him, my cheeks grow warm. I wonder if he can tell what I dreamed about last night. Do I look more or less guilty if I avoid eye contact?

His gaze catches mine, and he hesitates, his mouth opening and then snapping shut while he helps himself to the chair next to Tristan.

My brother leans back, giving Nadir a once-over full of mistrust, and a knot swells in my throat. Zerra, how I've missed having him around to protect me. Aphelion was so lonely, especially before Halo and Marici deemed me worthy of their friendship.

"It's time to talk," Nadir says, ignoring Tristan, and also lean-ing back in his chair before casually slinging an ankle over his knee. As usual, he's glorious, with his black hair falling in soft waves around his face. His shirt is unbuttoned at the collar just enough to reveal a smooth sliver of skin and the chiseled shape of his chest, along with a hint of his colorful tattoos.

The memory of the way he was lying over me last night caus-es my legs to press together as my stomach dips. His gaze drops to my lap as though he's noticed the movement or is reading my thoughts. Now I worry he can hear what I'm thinking. I don't actually know the capacity of his magic. There's a blaze of color in his eyes—violet and then emerald—before it flickers out, leaving two smooth pits of darkness that feel like they can see everything.

"If you'd like your family to remain here, that is up to you. But you promised me some answers."

There's a soft knock at the door and Amya, Mael, and the red-haired woman I met last night, Hylene, all file into the room.

"What if I don't want *them* here?" I ask, narrowing my eyes.

"That isn't on your list of options," Nadir counters, and I glare at him. "Anything you have to say to me, you can say to them."

"I have nothing to say to you. I think I've made that clear."

Nadir raises a dark eyebrow, studying me. I shift uncomfort-ably, feeling that look straight through the thin fabric of my tunic. "You aren't leaving here until you talk. You're surround-ed by miles of uncrossable forest and mountains and there is nowhere you can run where I won't find you. If you ever hope to earn your freedom, Inmate, you *will* start talking."

Tristan jumps up and plants his feet wide. "How dare you speak to her that way?"

Nadir's response is a lazy, insolent smile, his cool demeanor as constant as a stone wall.

"Tris, it's fine," I say, holding a hand and gesturing for him to find his seat. "I did promise."

"You were under duress," Tristan says, casting a dark look at the prince.

"Nevertheless," I say, attempting to mimic at least a sliver of Nadir's stoic facade.

Amya moves closer and pulls up a chair, forming a circle. Mael stands by the fireplace behind Nadir, one arm propped on the mantel. Hylene leans against the nearby windowsill, her arms folded and one ankle over the other.

"Who are you?" I ask her. While I don't trust any of the others, at least I've become familiar with their presence.

"Hylene is an old friend, and a trusted member of my circle. She takes care of jobs that need doing."

I turn to Nadir. "And is she unable to speak for herself?"

A snort comes from Hylene, her green eyes dancing. "I like her, Nadir."

I can't help but preen at the compliment while Nadir glares at her with the same irascible expression I've become very accustomed to. I wonder what he means by "jobs that need doing," but I'm also not sure I want to hear the answer.

"Can we get on with it?" he growls, tossing her one more irritated look before he returns to me. "Why did Atlas steal you from Nostraza to compete in the Trials?"

I share a look with Willow and Tristan. We agreed last night that I would have to disclose some of the truth, because Nadir already knows something and there's no use pretending it was all a coincidence.

"At first, I thought it was the Aurora King who sent me there," I say, carefully weaving this story with threads of fact and lies by omission. Nadir frowns. "Atlas told me the Final Tribute has always been from The Aurora, and I didn't know enough to question that. He seemed so intent on me winning the Trials, but I assumed he also believed me to be what I appeared—a prisoner from Nostraza who had no chance of surviving."

With my fingers twisted in my lap, I pause, a weight pressing me down.

"I thought perhaps your father was playing some larger game, and I was just a disposable piece on the board. Why send someone who might matter, right?" Bitterness seeps into my voice.

"You hate him," Amya says, her tone soft and her hands pressed between her black-clad thighs. "Every time you mention him, you withdraw into some dark place where no one can reach you. It's about more than just keeping you in that prison."

"I do hate him," I whisper, my voice raw. "He killed my parents. He hunted us down and locked us away inside Nostraza when we were only children. Your father took everything from us." I pin them all with a glare. "And all of you sat by and let it happen."

"We didn't know," Amya says, her face falling.

"You know what that place is. You know what goes on there." Guilt forces her to avert her eyes, but I can't summon an ounce of sympathy.

"Why?" Nadir asks, sitting forward with his elbows planted on his thighs. Apparently, he's brushing aside my accusation like motes of insignificant dust. "Why did my father do all that? Who are you?"

I shake my head, not sure I can force the truth out. I've kept it locked up for so long it's like it's been fossilized in amber, lacking the inertia needed to finally set it free.

Willow scoots closer, taking my hand between hers. The past churns between us as we look at each other. "It's okay," she says. "Mother would have understood that you've been left with no choice. The truth had to catch up to us someday."

I nod then and look at Tristan, who also dips his chin in agreement.

It's then that Nadir suddenly says, "I hate him, too."

Those words land heavy between us like a vulture shot from the sky. I notice Mael straighten by the fireplace, his dark eyebrows rising. Amya stares at her brother and their gazes meet as some kind of secret message passes between them.

"I want to bring him down," Nadir says. I sense those words cost him something. "And I think you might be the key to doing so."

That admission steals my breath.

Other than getting Tristan and Willow back, crushing the Aurora King and everything he holds dear is the only thing I've ever wanted, but I'd be foolish to think I could ever do that alone. Especially with the state I'm trapped in now.

"I'm worried that once you know the truth, you'll try to use me, too," I whisper. "Atlas lied to me. He made me think I was special, but he was just trying to use me. How do I know you won't do the same?"

I rip the words from my spirit, not sure what possesses me to split myself open and lay this confession at Nadir's feet.

He nods, his expression as solemn as my offering. "I can understand that. I give you my word that I'm not here to use you. That I want to join with you. Partner with you. That whatever you're capable of, I'm not here to take it. I want the same thing you want. That's why I'm telling you I hate him with every fiber and breath of my already damned soul. I've spent a lifetime trying to stop him. I can never admit that to anyone outside of this room, but I'm hoping that by telling you this, I might earn a small measure of your trust."

I study him, wanting to believe what he's saying. That feeling under my skin is less insistent right now, though its presence still rolls in waves, reminding me it's always close. I'm not sure how I know, but I'm positive that if Nadir were lying, my magic would warn me. It seems to know and understand him, which is a troubling thought.

"How can I trust you? You stole me from Aphelion and have kept me locked up for weeks. And now you won't let me leave."

Nadir props his chin on his folded hands, his nostrils flaring. "That was...regrettable."

Amya scoffs. "Nadir isn't good at apologies," she says, tossing him a glare that almost makes me smile. The two of them are so much like me and Tristan it makes my chest ache. "What he means to say is he's sorry about that, and it was an error in judgement that his much smarter sister has been telling him was a mistake from the beginning. And if he'd just talked to you like a rational adult, we could have avoided all of this hostility."

"Is that true?" I ask Nadir, who grunts in response. That's a yes, I guess.

I can't trust them.

I don't want to reveal my secrets to them, but I might not have a choice.

We're all dancing around the truth, and while they might not understand the exact shape of what I'm concealing, it's clear they're veering very close to its edge. If I tell them, then at least we've been exposed on our own terms.

Tristan's watching me with a guarded expression that suggests this is my call, but I won't make this decision alone. "If you want to do this, Lor, then we need allies. Even if they're *these* allies," he says, curling his lip.

"Big words for a man who was a helpless prisoner twelve hours ago," Mael says, and Tristan tosses him a glare that causes Mael to grin.

"Both of you stop," I admonish, pinching the bridge of my nose. "Fine. I hope that what you're saying is true. We do need help, but don't think for a moment that I trust any of you." I fix each of them with a penetrating glower.

Amya nods her head sadly, while Mael raises an eyebrow and tips his head. Hylene raises her hands as if to suggest she just got here, and Nadir doesn't even blink as he stares at me. He doesn't really care if I trust him, he just wants to know my secrets.

Inhaling a deep breath, I blow it out slowly and prepare for everything to change.

"My...our grandmother was the Heart Queen who almost broke the world."

Chapter Thirteen

SERCE

"W olf," Serce gasped as he thrust into her, his chiseled bare chest gleaming with a sheen of sweat and his leathery wings stretching like he was about to take flight.

"Oh, Zerra!" He grunted, the tendons in his neck straining as he fucked her so hard the bed creaked while the massive headboard thumped against the wall.

"Serce," he added with a low growl, her name in his mouth like something precious he'd pocketed for safekeeping. She loved the way he said it—like he couldn't get enough of her on his tongue. Which, ironically, was where she'd spent a good deal of the past two weeks—ever since she'd run into him the night she'd turned down the bonding proposal from Aphelion.

Their attraction had been instant. She'd never felt this kind of visceral need to be touched by anyone like this before. Everything about him fired a longing so deep it felt like it had grown roots that tunneled into the center of the earth. It was hard to believe she'd only known him for so short a time. They were so in tune with one another. So aligned in every possible way. It was like Zerra had made them precisely in one another's image.

Destined to be together.

She gripped the thick column of his biceps as he hooked a hand under her knee and drove into her with such ferocity that she cried out with her other hand fisting the blanket for purchase. "Yes," she moaned, her voice and hair as tangled as the sheets. "Oh gods, yes." Her back arched, the tension in her core building and building, before Wolf pressed a rough thumb to her clit, and she blew apart with a scream.

Wolf continued rolling his hips, guiding her through her orgasm before he picked up his pace again, losing control while he pounded harder and harder. She clung to him as he fucked her into the mattress just as she felt a shudder run over his body, his release rocking through his limbs.

His gaze never wavered from hers as his pace ebbed and then slowed until he finally came to a stop. His deep green eyes burned with such heat, Serce was surprised the sheets hadn't lit on fire.

She pulled him down to meet her, their mouths crashing into a kiss that reached straight through her soul.

"Zerra," Wolf rumbled. "I don't know where you came from, Serce, but I'm really fucking glad I accepted your mother's invite to this gathering."

A laugh bubbled out of her throat. "I'm sure Mother's regretting the day she ever sent that letter."

Wolf grinned and rolled off, one arm wrapped around her as he pulled Serce against his chest. She twirled one of his long braids between her fingers as he trailed his hand up and down her side, shivers erupting over her skin.

The past two weeks had been filled with meetings and negotiations and the drawing up and arguing of plans to present a united front against The Aurora. It was now the final night of the summit before the rulers were due back at their own courts, and she'd thwarted every one of her mother's efforts to coerce Serce into accepting the union with Aphelion. Tonight would be a last-ditch attempt to sway her, but her mother was too late. Serce's mind was made up and there would be no changing it. Serce and Wolf hadn't been particularly covert about the time they were spending together, though she was doing her best not to rub it in Atlas's face.

Serce had immersed herself in every detail of the proceedings, hanging on to every word and interjecting with her thoughts, knowing that when the crown passed, she would be taking up her mother's mantle. It had already been decided.

Once the details of the alliance were settled, Daedra would step down in favor of Serce. Rion was too strong and the only way Heart could hope to destroy him would be for Serce to ascend. Even unbonded, she almost outstripped her mother's strength and when she found her match, she'd become unstoppable.

Wolf was watching her thoughtfully, and she smiled, knowing she'd just found the Fae she would bond to. There was no one else she would ever be with again.

"What are you thinking about?" he asked her, tracing the curve of her cheek and the line of her jaw.

She sighed. "Just the ongoing drama of the summit and my mother and her plans."

His expression clouded. "Serce, I don't want to get in the middle of your family matters. If you have to bond with that asshole, I won't stand in your way."

She raised an eyebrow, definitely not appreciating the direction of this conversation. He gripped her hip, pulling her towards him. "Of course, I'd hate every single minute of it, and I have a strong premonition he'd meet with a very unfortunate accident before he could so much as touch a hair on your head."

His voice had dropped to a deadly caress, and she tasted the violence and possessiveness in his words like they were the sweetest wine. She shook her head. Any chance of bonding to Atlas was gone the moment Wolf had walked into her life.

He was hers, and she was his. And nothing would ever change that.

Her smile was feral as she tugged his forehead to hers. "Then Atlas should be grateful I'm refusing him. I'm basically doing him a favor."

Wolf growled and then rolled on top of her, pressing her into the mattress as he bestowed her with another bone-deep kiss.

A knock on the door drew both their attentions just as it swung open.

"Serce," her mother said before Daedra stopped dead in her tracks, her dark eyes blinking furiously. Wolf remained in his position without a shred of self-consciousness, despite the fact he was completely naked and lying on top of the queen's daughter.

"You got the knocking part," he said with a wicked smile, his wings twitching. "But you might consider waiting for the part where you have permission to enter. Your Majesty."

His grin turned positively gleeful as Daedra's cheeks flushed while she attempted to stifle her chagrin.

"Serce, I need to speak with you," she said, pointedly looking away from Wolf.

"As you can see, I'm busy right now."

The tips of her mother's pointed ears turned even redder, and Serce wasn't sure if it was because of her fury or the embarrassment of catching her daughter in a state of post-coital bliss. She was having a hard time caring either way, knowing Daedra was here just to lecture her about Atlas again. "I'll see you at dinner."

There was no mistaking the dismissal in Serce's voice, and it was obvious her mother wanted to refuse, but they were all painfully aware of the naked male lying on top of Serce, his cock still hard against her stomach.

"Fine, but I would speak to you *alone* tonight," she said, pinning Serce with a dark look and then turning around and slamming the door.

Wolf collapsed on top of Serce, his face burying into the curve of her throat where she felt the vibrations of his laughter.

"It's not funny," she said, smacking him on the shoulder, but she also couldn't contain her giggles, even if she was slightly mortified. He was still chuckling as he kissed her and, regrettably, rolled off.

"I guess we should get ready. I don't need any more reasons for your mother to hate me."

He winked and scooted off the bed, going in search of his clothes as she admired the roundness of his perfect ass and his thick thighs. He was the most beautiful man she'd ever seen, and every time she looked at him, it stole another drop of her breath away. Any longer and it would be like she was permanently living underwater—but she certainly didn't mind.

"Keep looking at me like that, and we will be late," he growled, and her gaze fell to his stiff cock before she slowly licked her lips in challenge. He shook his head and ran his hand down his face.

"You're going to be the death of me, Serce."

He said it with fondness, though, and then stepped into his pants and buttoned them up with a flourish.

She blinked up at him with an innocent smile.

"I'm counting on it," she said, returning his wink.

A short while later, they left her room and made their way to the dining hall for dinner, where she was preparing for another ambush from her mother. They'd made sure to arrive fashionably late, so there was little opportunity for undesirable conversations. The room would already be filled with nosy guests, dying to hear an argument between the Heart Queen and her Primary.

Even Daedra wouldn't scold her in front of the entire delegation of Ouranos.

She hoped.

But when they entered the room, Serce realized her mother had chosen to fight dirty tonight as she noted the seating arrangements.

The Heart Queen eyed her with cool detachment and a knowing smirk from where she sat at the head with the king to one side and an empty seat for Serce on the other. Wolf's spot was reserved at the furthest end of the table with the lesser nobles.

It was an outrageous affront to have the king of The Woodlands so far from the other rulers. Serce stiffened as her mother tossed her a look that said this was in retaliation for her earlier behavior.

Was Daedra so intent on joining with Aphelion that she'd risk the centuries-old alliance with The Woodlands? Wolf noticed the slight at the same moment, and Serce was about to protest when he grabbed her hand and squeezed it, tugging her towards him.

"Don't," he said. "It's fine."

"It's an insult," she hissed in his ear as the chatter continued while a few curious glances stole their way.

"I can handle one dinner. It's not worth making a scene. Soon we'll be away from here."

His voice rumbled low in her ear, and it wasn't lost on her that they stood whispering like conferring lovers. Well, that's exactly what they were. The look on her mother's face was black as ink as she glared at Serce, who rewarded her mother with a smug smile.

Wolf squeezed Serce's hand one more time and was about to make his way to his seat when she held him back, wrapping an arm around his neck and pulling him in for a long, deep kiss. Wolf didn't miss a beat, his hands cupping her ass as everyone around the table burst into hushed, scandalized twitters.

When they broke apart, Serce stared up at him with her swollen lips parted. She desperately wanted to drag him from this room and demand he fuck her against a wall some place where it wouldn't matter how loud they were. But there would be time for that later. As if he were reading her thoughts, he gave her a sly look and then turned to find his seat, shaking hands and greeting other guests on his way to the far end of the room.

Picking up the hem of her bright red gown, Serce strode over to the head of the table, pretending nothing was amiss. She dropped into her seat, where naturally, Atlas was already waiting to her left.

"Good evening," she said to him pleasantly, noting the hardness in his jaw. His gaze flicked to Wolf, who was still engaged in conversation, before it landed on her again.

"Am I really so objectionable?" Atlas asked, the soft words spoken only for her ears. The hurt in his voice almost made her feel guilty about rejecting him in such a public way. But it had been his choice not to defend her when she'd refused to participate in the Sun Queen Trials. If he'd done so then, she would have agreed to the union during that meeting, and she would have honored that.

But he was a spineless fool, and so she'd met Wolf, and that had changed everything.

None of this was her fault.

"It has nothing to do with you," she said, as a low fae pixie with pale green skin and bright pink hair filled up her wine.

It was partly the truth. It had almost nothing to do with him.

The Sun King, Kyros, and his son Tyr also sat near the table's end. She couldn't help but feel like she'd been surrounded by a brigade intent on dousing her in oil and burning her on a stake.

"You're late," her mother hissed, her brown eyes flashing. So much for not being scolded in front of a room full of people.

Serce looked about, feigning innocence before directing a pointed look at her empty plate. "It appears that I'm exactly on time, Mother."

Daedra glared at her daughter as the food started to come out. The conversation between Serce, her parents, and the royals of Aphelion came to a halt as they began their meals, all of them eating in awkward silence.

Serce had little appetite anyway and nibbled at her food while her mother continued to shoot her a series of angry glares. As the meal wore on, Serce's patience wore thinner and thinner. She was a grown Fae and had the right to make her own fucking choices.

Finally, she couldn't take it any longer. She dropped her fork on the plate with a loud clatter and slapped her hand on the table, several guests jumping at the disruption.

"Out with it, Mother," she snapped, sitting up straight and pressing her lips into a thin line. "Say whatever it is you want to say. We're here with our *allies*, are we not?"

The room had gone silent, everyone around the table peering at the princess with glee and curiosity. Serce was giving them a show tonight and tongues would wag all over Ouranos about this.

Daedra's face had turned red, her eyes narrowing into knife-sharp slits. "Serce," she said, and it was laced with so much venom Serce actually flinched. "Stop acting like a spoiled child and do your duty."

"Daedra," the Heart King said, laying a soft hand on her mother's arm.

"No," the Heart Queen replied. "She wants to make a scene, then let's make a fucking scene."

Serce had never seen her mother lose her cool in public like this before. Daedra was normally a pillar of stoicism.

"I'm not bonding to Atlas," Serce said, though by now she was sure this was obvious.

"We need their armies to stop Rion."

"Why can't they offer them without a bonding?" she countered, turning her glare to Kyros, who blinked at the accusation. "If they're allies like you claim, why can't they offer their aid regardless of a bonding? What kind of allies are they that they'd demand this price? What's to say they won't turn at the first hint of a better offer if their loyalty is so fickle?"

Serce had clearly caught the Sun King off-guard, and he shifted in his chair. She offered him a smug smile, sure she'd just poked a sore spot. Atlas cleared his throat, and she wheeled her frustration on him.

"And what about you? If you were a king, would you behave the same?" She addressed Tyr next. "And what about you? Is this the kind of king you plan to be?"

"Serce!" her mother barked. "You go too far."

She let out a derisive huff. "You're all just a bunch of cowards who only act when it suits your purposes. You have the alliance of The Woodlands, Celestria, Tor, and Alluvion, Mother. Let that be enough. If Aphelion's loyalty is so capricious and they want to bury their heads in the sand, then let them. Once I'm queen, we won't need their pathetic army, anyway."

Her mother shoved back her chair and rose while Serce did the same.

"You overestimate what you're capable of," Daedra said, and Serce chose not to acknowledge the slight to her abilities. Mother and daughter stood off against one another. Crimson lightning sparked along Daedra's skin in a flashy show of power Serce knew was an attempt to intimidate her.

Daedra might be stronger right now, but Serce was already twice as powerful as her mother at the same age. When Serce took the Crown, her mother's magic would be a mere shadow of what she could do.

A fact for which her mother had never forgiven her.

From the corner of her eye, Serce saw Wolf approaching. His large hands were loose at his sides, and as he came to stand behind her, she understood something about him. Something that made him so different from men like Atlas. He'd come to back her up but not take over, proving he would be there for her no matter the cost.

What they had was about so much more than lust. Though that part was pretty fantastic.

"You," her mother hissed, pointing a finger at Wolf.

"Don't," Serce said, stepping in front of him as his hands landed on her waist, and he squeezed her hips in a gesture of solidarity. "Don't finish that thought, Mother, lest you lose the only allies you have left. I have answered the question of my bonding with Atlas. This discussion is over. If you can't convince them to offer their help without me, then that isn't my problem. Descend, give me the Crown, and their armies won't matter."

"You aren't ready yet," her mother said.

Serce shook her head before she stepped back, taking Wolf's hand.

"It's you who isn't ready. While you come to your senses, I'll be in The Woodlands."

That information loosened her mother's tongue.

"You wouldn't dare leave," she said, crimson lightning sparking in the surrounding air. Serce reigned in her own destructive magic that begged to be released. It was a calculated move intended to show Daedra that Serce had more control over her magic. A fact her mother didn't miss as her eyes blazed with fury.

With a detached tip of her chin, Serce replied, "I'll be back in a few months."

Then she tugged on Wolf's hand before they both marched out of the room in the wake of a silence so profound you could hear the drop of a single grain of sand.

CHAPTER FOURTEEN

LOR

PRESENT DAY: THE AURORA

It's as though every molecule of air in the room freezes into hard pellets as Nadir, Amya, Mael, and Hylene stare at me like they've seen a ghost rise from a pile of ashes. I suppose in a way it has.

"How? How can you be Serce's grandchildren?" Hylene asks. "Your mother or father are supposed to be dead."

I flinch at her frank words, and she has the grace to look abashed at her insensitive comment. "Sorry."

"Our mother. She is," I say. "Thanks to your king. She's been dead since I was twelve."

"But the baby died during the war," Amya says. "The history books say Serce's only child died with her."

Tristan tips his head, arching a sardonic eyebrow. "Try to keep up, Princess. Obviously, it was a lie intended to protect the royal line from retribution for our grandmother's mistakes."

Amya presses her lips together and shoots my brother a dark look.

"When the war started going in The Aurora's favor, our grandparents worried for the safety of their child and thus made arrangements to have her hidden, just in case," Willow says. "Obviously our mother didn't know all the details, but she was actually born just before Serce died and grew up deep in the Violet Forest of The Woodlands. She was the only direct family member left after our grandmother destroyed the entire queendom. It was imperative to our legacy that she survive."

She falls silent as the prince and his companions all look on with shellshocked expressions.

"Someone had to have known," Nadir says. "Who took care of her?"

"Our great-uncle saw she was watched over."

"Cedar," Nadir breathes. "All this time, he knew?"

I nod, remembering The Woodlands King sitting with his bonded partner at the Tribute ball, so wholly in love with her. I'd felt nothing for the great-uncle I'd never spoken to, knowing he had abandoned us to the Aurora King. Clearly, we had meant nothing to him, and he had simply acted out of loyalty to his brother. He'd probably been relieved to get rid of us, no longer tasked with bearing this secret.

A memory ticks as I recall Atlas declaring he and Cedar were friends. Could it have been Cedar who betrayed us? But to what end? And why, after all these years? Holding on to that thought for now, I store it away to discuss with Tristan and Willow when we're alone.

It's Tristan's turn to pick up the story that both my brother and sister recall with more clarity than I do. "Our mother said she never saw him. That a woman had been assigned to care for her until she was old enough to live on her own. Being human, the woman died long before any of us were born."

Tristan meets my gaze, and my hand encloses the locket around my neck. We've already agreed that even if we revealed the truth about who we were, the red jewel I held in my possession would remain our secret from the Aurora Prince and his circle for now.

"Eventually, our mother grew up and met another Fae from The Woodlands. They fell in love and he moved to the forest with her, where they gave life to three children. She said they tried to have as many as they could to boost the Heart family line, but after complications with Lor's birth, they were unable to conceive any more."

"This is unbelievable," Hylene says. "How was this kept a secret?"

"Apparently it wasn't, though it took the Aurora King over two hundred years to find us," I say, my voice wooden as I remember that day. How my parents had known something was wrong the moment we saw a string of torchlights weaving through the forest. Tristan had been exploring in the woods as he often did, and my father had secreted me and Willow into an underground bunker in the backyard.

I hadn't known it had been there until that moment, but it was obvious they had planned for that day all along. My mother handed me and Willow the necklace with the jewel and told us to keep it safe, no matter what happened. It wasn't until Atlas told me about the Artefacts and the red stone in the Heart Crown that I suspected what it was. When the Sun Mirror told me to find the Crown, I was sure.

Then my parents closed the door on me and Willow and told us not to leave until my father returned.

Only he never did.

I can still hear their screams as they died. I still see that male that leered over us when that trapdoor opened, his face spattered with my mother's blood.

Over the years, Willow and I took turns keeping the jewel safe, finding ever more creative places to hide it on or inside our bodies.

"So your mother had magic," Nadir asks.

I nod my head. "Quite a bit of it."

Nadir blows out a breath and runs a hand through his hair.

"What?" I ask, sensing there's something he isn't saying.

"You understand that the magic of Heart is gone?"

I blink and shake my head. "No. What does that mean?"

"When the Heart Queen nearly broke the world, she took the magic of Ouranos with her. For decades, not a single person on the continent could channel even a drop of it."

My eyes widen at that. "Why not?"

Nadir shakes his head. "No one is completely sure, but there are many theories. Mostly that she tried to touch forbidden magic, and it backfired dramatically. Eventually the magic came back, slowly at first, like whatever was blocking it had sprung a leak until everyone eventually regained their strength. Everyone but the citizens of Heart, that is. No one has been able to wield its power in almost three hundred years. Or so we thought."

I allow that information to sink in, reeling in the enormity of his words. We know so little about where we truly came from and what our grandmother's actions had wrought. Our mother had been separated from any family or knowledge and had almost nothing to pass on. Just a stone she knew nothing about and a legacy that had to be kept hidden.

Trapped inside Nostraza, we weren't in any position to learn much more.

"That's why everyone speaks of her that way," I say. "Like she's a curse."

Nadir dips his chin with his mouth pressed into a line. "You can imagine how much havoc it wreaked when everyone lost their magic, and how scared they are at the idea of it ever happening again."

Willow, Tristan, and I share a look. This is the history we come from? Do we really want any part of this? *Forbidden magic.*

"And you three?" Nadir looks us over one by one.

"But you're all *human*," Amya interjects. "None of this can be true. You aren't glamoured. I would have sensed something."

"No, we're not glamoured—you're right," Tristan says. "This is one of the gifts of Heart. The ability to 'fold' into yourself and become human. We aren't really, of course, but for all intents and purposes, no one could ever tell the difference. The drawback is that you have no access to your magic or any other Fae gifts."

"Fascinating," Amya breathes, studying us again as if we're windows she can peer into.

"As I was asking before I was interrupted," Nadir says, glaring at his sister. "What about you three?"

"I have almost no magic," Willow says. "Really, just enough to do this." She gestures to her human form.

"I've got a little more," Tristan says and then folds his mouth together, having no desire to reveal his entire truth. No one presses him further, but that's when every set of eyes in the room falls to me. I swallow the knot of tension growing in my chest as Nadir tips his head and arches an eyebrow.

"And you?"

"I have magic," I say, carefully. "More than a little, though I haven't touched it since I was a small child."

"Our mother always wore her disguise and insisted we do the same, terrified someone might learn of our secret," Willow says. "We've all been in these forms for a long time."

"Can you get out of them?" Amya asks.

"Of course," Tristan says. "It's just been so long, I can't even imagine what it would feel like."

"Do it," Nadir says, and Tristan shoots him a dirty look, but Nadir says nothing as he stares at my brother. Tristan then looks at me and Willow, and we both nod. After all these years of hiding, it's time to let go. That the prince knows even this much signals a bell that can no longer be unrung.

Tristan closes his eyes as he rolls his shoulders, then concentrates on pulling apart the threads that keep his human form together. It takes only a few seconds before it sloughs away, and my brother sits before me, transformed.

His ears are pointed, and his eyes are brighter. He's still my brother, but he's just a little more. I notice the other four Fae in the room sniff the air as they register the change.

"That's amazing," Amya says. "I didn't even know that was possible."

"I suspect it's the kind of thing any court would want to keep secret," Tristan says, his voice suggesting that she had better keep it as well.

Tristan nods at Willow. She returns it and then she, too, transforms into a version of my sister I don't remember. I didn't think it was possible for her to be more beautiful than she is, even with the way Nostraza ravaged her, but she's so radiant there's a collective intake of breath around the room.

My heart is pounding against my ribs, knowing what comes next as every eye in the room again swings to me. The weight of Nadir's stare is like a finger running down the center of my chest. I think of the dream I had last night and shiver. His eyes darken at the same moment, and I wonder what he can sense in me.

"I can't," I say, shaking my head, tears building in my eyes. "I've been trying since the lot of you kidnapped me and..." Willow takes my hand, squeezing it, and I hold on to her, letting her ground me. "And I'm stuck."

"I don't understand," Nadir says. "What do you mean, you're stuck?"

I try to explain what's happening. It's like a wall of interlocking bricks I need to pull apart from the inside, but I can't get a hold of an edge, like trying to pry a splinter loose from your finger by your nails. Nadir's eyebrows draw together as I talk, and I can't help feeling like I'm letting him down.

"I don't know what to do," I say after I finish.

The room falls silent as we each retreat into our thoughts. I look out the window, the sky a pale wash of grey. Snow is falling gently, sparkling in whatever source of light exists outside.

"The Crown," Tristan says and my gaze snaps to him as I pin him with a *why are you bringing that up?* look. Last night, I'd explained to them what I knew of the Artefacts, and Tristan had been particularly fascinated by the existence of the Crown. His expression remains guarded, but he presses on. "Maybe it could help you release your magic."

"That...is not the worst idea," I say. "But it's missing. No one knows where it is. The Sun Mirror told me it had been lost to time and that it didn't know if it still existed."

"Right," Tristan says. "That's the flaw in this plan." He winks at me and I can't help the smile that crosses my face.

"You didn't tell me that," Nadir accuses. "You said the Mirror only rejected you."

I arch an eyebrow. "I'm well aware I didn't tell you that. I'm telling you now. But only because I agreed to a bargain in exchange for the safety of my brother and sister. The Mirror told me the Crown was lost, and that I needed to find it. There. You've been told."

I decide that bit of information is harmless enough given what they already know, and maybe, by some miracle, they can help us find it. I keep the part about returning to the Mirror when I do and give Tristan a look that tells him to shut up about it, too.

"Do you think it's possible Father knows?" Amya says, sitting up straight in her seat. "Somehow, he found out about the three of you. What if he knows where the Crown is, too?"

Nadir is giving her a thoughtful look, his thumb running over his bottom lip. I stare at his mouth, thinking of the way it felt when he dragged it over my skin last night.

No, it wasn't him, I remind myself.

That was just a dream, and why am I still thinking about it?

"It's possible," he says, before he looks at me. "As the Primary, you might be able to feel it."

"The what?" I ask.

"The Primary. Every Artefact denotes a Primary when they ascend a new king or queen. They become the heir when the current ruler either dies or chooses the Evanescence. Typically, it's the one with the strongest magic in every realm and often follows through family bloodlines, though not always."

"Oh," I say, several things clicking together. "How do you know I'm the Primary?"

"Because it was you my father and Atlas were both interested in. Somehow, they must have known. And if you think you have more magic than either your brother or sister, then it has to be you."

I go silent, considering his words.

"How old are you?" he asks.

"I'm twenty-four. I'll be twenty-five in a couple of months."

He nods. "So you'll come into your true power soon. You had strong magic as a child?"

"From what I can remember."

"Then you're definitely powerful," he says with such certainty that it makes my insides glow. I'm powerful. I'm strong. If I could just get myself unlocked.

"What's the Evanescence?" Tristan asks, picking up on Nadir's earlier words.

"It's a sort of death, but not quite," he replies. "There can only be two Imperial Fae alive at any time in a realm. The Primary and whoever they choose to bond with. For the next Primary to ascend, the current Primary must either pass on or choose the descension and travel to the Evanescence. No one knows exactly what it is, but it's a state of existence between life and death."

"That sounds awful," Willow says. "Why would anyone choose that?"

Nadir shrugs. "Fae live a long time, and ruling for centuries can become wearisome. Many choose it once they feel certain their Primary would make a fit ruler. And the legends say the Evanescence is actually paradise."

Willow scoffs at that. "Sounds like convenient propaganda to fool people into giving up their lives."

Nadir offers her a soft smile, the expression transforming his face in a way I've never seen before. It does something weird to my chest. "Perhaps."

"Who's the Primary for The Aurora?" I ask.

"I am," Nadir says matter-of-factly, and why doesn't that surprise me at all?

"Figures," I say, and I swear I see the ghost of a smile cross his lips. "What do you mean when you say I can sense the Crown?"

"I mean that you should be able to feel its presence when you're near it. If my father has it, then the Keep is the most likely spot."

"I can't go in there," I say, horrified at the thought of entering that building that towered over me in the throes of my worst misery. Of entering that narrow back door that became the source of my darkest hell.

"I didn't take you for a coward, Inmate," he says, and I'm about to protest that he has no idea what he's talking about, but I sense he's testing me. Goading me into proving him wrong.

"Fuck you," I say instead, and this time I'm rewarded with a smug smile. "How would you get me in there?"

He shrugs. "The twelve nights of Frostfire start in a few days. I need to return to the Keep then, anyway. You can come with me."

I narrow my gaze at him. "And who will I say I am? Your father is still looking for me, is he not?"

He leans back in his chair and crosses his legs. "You'll be there as my female *companion* for the duration of the festival. We can search for it then."

I snort at that. "Absolutely not."

Nadir's mouth stretches into a slow smile. "Afraid you'll like it?"

"Hardly. I'm not sure how I could possibly stomach it. He'll see right through the green pallor of my skin."

"Do you have a better plan, Inmate?"

"Stop calling me that," I hiss, leaning forward.

Mael unfolds himself from his position at the fireplace. "If you two could stop flirting, maybe we can get on with it? You'll argue and bicker in your fucked up little version of foreplay and then you'll agree, Lor. This is the only way."

I glare at him, and he offers me a cocky grin.

"Why do you want to help us?" Tristan asks. "What's in this for you? You aren't doing this out of the goodness of your heart."

Nadir blows out a breath, leaning forward. A lock of his dark hair falls over his forehead, and my hands twitch at the intense desire to tuck it back. What is wrong with me?

"I told you I want the same thing you do," he says.

"And what's that exactly?" Tristan asks.

"To take down the Aurora King."

My stomach clenches. "Because you hate him," I say.

"That, and because The Aurora deserves better than him."

"And that's you?" I ask, my voice incredulous. He gives me a dark look.

"Why can't you get rid of him on your own?" Tristan asks. "Why do you need Lor?"

Nadir holds us with his unsettling gaze, flashes of emerald swirling in his eyes. "This can never leave this room."

Tristan offers his own serious gaze. "You know our secret, and it's a pretty big fucking secret. It seems only fair you share something else in return."

Nadir tips his head. "Fair point."

"I need you for two reasons," he says, making eye contact with me. "First, my father is bonded and, therefore, more powerful than I am. It would be exceedingly difficult for me to kill him. But the second is that even if I did manage to do that, I would lose my position as the Primary."

"Keep explaining," Tristan says.

"There is a condition of the Artefact's magic that if the Primary heir kills the king or queen in power, then they'll lose their magic and a new Primary will be named. But not just a new Primary. The power of the royal family would transfer elsewhere."

"Where?" I ask and Nadir shakes his head.

"I don't know. But it's not a risk I'm willing to take."

"And I'm guessing dear old dad isn't planning to choose the Evanescence anytime soon?" Tristan asks.

"No," Nadir says, his tone dry. "None of the other rulers in Ouranos have my father's kind of power either, and even if they did, I'd have a hard time convincing any of them to kill him for my sake." He's staring at me as he speaks. "But your grandmother was powerful beyond all reason. She's the strongest Primary to ever exist, if the history books are to be believed. And if you have any of that, then *you* might be stronger than the Aurora King."

The room goes utterly silent as that declaration settles over us like a giant life-sucking parachute.

"Stronger than the Aurora King," I whisper, my entire body thrumming with a feeling of limitless potential. One that speaks to every wish and dream I whispered into the darkness, night after night that I wasted away inside his prison.

Nadir nods. "You might have the ability to take him down. And you also have the necessary motivation."

I let out a shaky breath.

I knew the legacy of my grandmother was important, but I never dreamed it could be this big.

"So, there you have it. My biggest secret. If anyone ever knew what I was planning, I'd be tried for treason and executed without mercy."

Our gazes meet, and that magic that lives under my skin gives a sharp and insistent tug.

There is something important about this moment. Something indelible about the promise I'm about to make. For me and for Tristan and Willow. For my mother and father, who gave their lives for us.

"You have my secret and I have yours," Nadir says. "I hope that means that we can trust one another for as long as it takes to find the Crown and restore your magic. You want him gone as much as I do. Maybe more." I nod as he continues. "So come with me to the Keep and search for it."

"As your pretend plaything."

The corner of his mouth kicks up into a smile that, unfortunately, makes my knees go weak. "That's just an added bonus. It's a win-win literally every way you look at it."

"Fine. I'll do it," I say, not sure I like this, but understanding this is my only option. While I expect Nadir to be satisfied he's won, something troubled crosses his face. There for a moment and then gone.

"Good, then it's settled," he says, standing up. "You'll need some proper clothes to wear." He addresses Amya. "Get her measurements, and tell Cora to have some things sent to my wing in the Keep."

Amya rolls her eyes as she stands, looking us all over one more time as if she still can't believe we're real. "I'll send someone in to see you, Lor."

Nadir is almost out of the room already, but he turns one last time to glance at me, an inscrutable look on his face before everyone else follows in his wake.

When I'm alone again with Tristan and Willow, we share a collective breath.

"Do you think we can trust them?" Willow asks, and I shake my head.

"No. But I'm not sure what other choice we have."

"I guess we're doing this, then," Tristan says, running a hand through his hair.

The tangled web of secrets we've kept for so long hangs between us like either a noose or a lifeline.

Only time will tell which.

I nod slowly. "Yes. I guess we are."

CHAPTER FIFTEEN

A few days later, I converse with Willow and Tristan over
breakfast in my room. We've spent as much time together
as possible, catching up and soaking in each other's presence.
I'm still so grateful they're alive and that they've been returned
to me that I keep expecting to wake up and find out none of it
was real.

Thankfully, my nights have been free of filthy dreams featur-
ing the Aurora Prince.

I'm not disappointed about it. I'm definitely not. That isn't a
headache I need right now.

"I can't believe I have to leave so soon after getting you back,"
I say before I take a big sip of coffee and then a bite from a scone
dotted with berries.

Willow's eyebrows draw together. "I know. But hopefully, it won't take long to find out if the Crown is in the Keep."

"I don't want to go back there." My voice is wooden with the memories of that past.

"I hate that you have to," Tristan says, his jaw clenching. He keeps tossing looks to the door as if waiting for some threat to come barging in.

"Tris," I say. "Promise me you'll relax. You've spent twelve years looking out for us, but here, you're safe. At least until I get back. Take some time to just rest, okay?"

Tristan scans me slowly from head to toe, and I know how hard it is for him to do what I'm asking. The things he did to protect us both haunt him, and I worry they're stains he'll never be able to wash away. His nod is slow even as his shoulders remain tight.

"Try," I say. "Just try."

"I will. Thank you. For getting us out."

"Don't thank me. You two were the only thing that kept me going through everything that happened with the Trials. I tried to be strong for you."

"We're so proud of you, Lor," Willow says. "Mother and Father would have been so proud of you."

I give her a sad smile. "Even if I spilled all our secrets?"

"It was a necessary move. We couldn't contain them any longer. It wasn't a burden that should ever have been placed on us, and I suspect there are many things we have yet to learn before this is over."

I nod. "I think you might be right."

"Are you going to be okay with...him?" Tristan asks, his eyes once again flicking to the door.

I nod. "I think so. He may be a bastard, but I don't think he's *that* kind of asshole. He's never made me feel threatened. Not really."

Tristan arches a skeptical eyebrow.

"I'll be fine," I say quickly, not wanting to delve into the complicated feelings I have about the Aurora Prince. "And what other choice do we have?"

"Just be careful."

"You know me," I reply with a wink. "Careful is my middle name."

Tristan groans and rubs a hand down his face.

"Tris, she's survived a whole lot on her own already. I'm sure she can handle this. Our little sister isn't so little anymore."

My heart squeezes in my chest as I smile at her. "I love you, Willow."

"I love you too, Lor. But *do* be careful, okay? We have so much lost time to recover, and I want to see you again soon."

"I promise," I say when a knock comes at the door and Amya pokes her head in.

"It's time to go."

I hug Tristan and Willow goodbye, hanging on to them for a few extra seconds, trying to convey that I'd walk through fire barefoot over hot coals for them.

They hold on, too, our connection binding us into something so much more than just family or friends. We've spent half our lives united by our collective grief and a resolute will to just *survive.* But now, everything is changing and we've been offered a glimpse of a life that we could barely imagine.

Our mother often mused about a queen rising in Heart again, and once upon a time, that idea was a fantasy we used to comfort ourselves when the world felt like too much. But as we stand together in this manor house on the edge of The Aurora, possibility weaves us a shiny new string from the frayed threads we've clung to for so long.

"Eat up," I say, my voice thick as we pull apart. "Get some meat on those bones. You have some catching up to do." They agree as I turn and follow Amya out of the room.

After I close the door behind me, I stop.

"What is it?" Amya asks.

"You promise they're safe here? No harm will come to them?"

Amya presses her mouth together and dips her head. "I swear it, Lor. I won't let anything happen. Someone will always be around. I'll have to come and go between the manor and the Keep during the festival, but when I'm not here, Hylene or Mael will watch over them. We will guard them with our lives."

I step closer to her. "I'm holding you to that."

"I know. I would expect nothing less."

Our gazes hold for a moment, and I try to understand what I see in her expression. Sorrow. Hope. Sadness. Regret? While this is a new beginning for me and my family, I sense there is something important happening here for these royal siblings as well.

"Fine. Then I should go. Hopefully, we won't be long."

Outside, Nadir waits in the courtyard, wearing thin leather armor that clings to the shape of his broad frame. I try not to notice the swell of his thighs or the way his shoulders fill out his jacket. His long hair is tied back in a knot, highlighting the lines of his face where the dim morning light glints off his angled cheekbones and a strong jaw.

His dogs wait obediently on their hind legs, their tongues lolling out, but the glint in their eyes speaks of something wild.

Impatience laces Nadir's frown as I emerge from the house and pull my wool coat tight, lifting up the wide fur collar so it covers my cheeks. The hour is early, and it's chillier than I'm accustomed to. While I'd grown used to the cold while living in Nostraza, my weeks in Aphelion have thinned my tolerance for these inhuman sub-zero temperatures.

Amya told me Frostfire celebrates the dwindling days of autumn before we descend into the eternal chill of The Aurora's winter, but this is a sorry excuse for the end of fall. I shiver, hoping that I'll have found my way out of here with Tristan and Willow long before then. Once again, I long for the sunshine and warmth of Aphelion as a gust of bitter wind knifes straight through my coat.

"I called for you an hour ago," Nadir says, his eyes sparking, the colors entrancing me as they swirl in his gaze. I wonder if I'll ever get used to the feeling of being pulled under whenever he's around. Or better yet—how do I make this stop?

"I was saying goodbye to my brother and sister, who I haven't seen in months and who thought I was dead until a few days ago," I snap. "It's six in the morning. Why do we need to leave so early?"

"Because I want to get to the Keep before other guests start arriving. If you're already there, then there will be no one to notice your arrival and fewer questions." His lip curls with a sardonic smile. "Unless you want the entire nobility of The Aurora to know the Heart Queen is alive and loose?"

I narrow my gaze. "I'm not the Heart Queen."

Yet.

The warmth of the locket around my neck pulses against my skin as though it's alive, pulling me toward a destiny that's becoming both more and less murky with each passing day.

"Fine," I say, rubbing my hands up my arms as I scan the courtyard.

"Only one horse? I'm not riding with you."

Nadir faces me with one elbow casually resting on his horse's saddle. "Do you know how to ride? I don't imagine you had too many lessons in Nostraza."

I shake my head. "Zerra, you are such an asshole."

His answer is a dark chuckle before he hops onto the saddle. "You can ride with me or you can walk."

I fold my arms and give him a smug look. "You can't leave me alone out there, and if I choose to walk, you'll have to go just as slow."

Unfortunately, the smugness of his answering smile does an annoyingly good job of eclipsing mine. "I've got centuries, Inmate. I'm in no rush."

"I thought you wanted to get there before everyone else arrived?"

"I thought *you* wanted to find the Heart Crown and reclaim your magic?"

Fuck. Of course he's right and the longer we argue about nothing, the longer it will be before I find the Crown and take back what's mine.

"I hate you," is all I say as I approach the horse, wondering how I'm supposed to get on. We rarely left our house in the woods when we were children, and I had no reason to learn how to ride. While my parents were able, any time we traveled to the village markets, me and my siblings would ride in a cart.

"Is it safe?" I ask, peering into the gloom of the Void. I've spent my entire life trained to fear this forest, and the few times I found myself within its depths didn't work out so well for me.

"You'll be fine. The ice hounds will keep the things that go bump in the night away."

"What if the thing that goes bump in the night is sitting on the horse with me?"

He doesn't respond to that, but the gleam in his eyes suggests my question isn't far off the mark. I look at the two dogs, still sitting at attention.

"Is that what they're for?"

"Among other things," he replies. "Now quit stalling. Let's go."

Nadir holds out his hand with his palm facing up. I look at it and back to him. He doesn't move, an imperious tilt to his chin as he waits for me to decide. With a snarl, I finally grab it and choke on a sharp inhale as our skin collides, that feeling I can't shake ready to burst out in a shower of sparks.

Recently, I've realized I started feeling this the night of the Tribute ball when I danced with Nadir. The shift was so slight, I didn't think to note it, but in hindsight it's been getting stronger and no more so than when I'm in his presence. It's not enough to actually free my magic, though.

I catch his blink and the slight flare of his nostrils, but otherwise Nadir seems unmoved as he hauls me up on the horse behind him. Suddenly, I'm not sure what to do with my hands, and I hold them up awkwardly as he casts a look over his shoulder.

"Ready?"

"I think so," I say, worried about his wicked smile.

"You might want to hold on."

Before I can respond, he turns and kicks the horse into motion so abruptly I nearly topple off the back. I reach out for him, grabbing his waist with one hand and then the other, feeling the hardness of muscle flexing beneath the leather. The horse picks up its pace, galloping towards the still-locked gates. Nadir flicks a hand, and they swing open just as we fly through. The dogs chase alongside us, racing along the ground with such speed they become two white streaks blurring against the gloom.

They both let out a rolling howl that echoes through the Void and makes the hairs on my neck rise to attention.

The horse is also picking up speed, and I'm forced to wrap my arms around Nadir's waist as I cast a look back at the manor, hoping Tristan and Willow are going to be okay without me. We keep flying faster, and this doesn't even seem natural. Should a horse be able to move like this?

"Can we slow down?" I shout as I feel myself slipping back.

Holding on tighter to Nadir, I try not to think about how strong he feels or the way he smells—like the fresh, clean sting of a winter breeze. I remember that scent from my time living in Nostraza. On those rare winter nights when I found myself outside alone and the prison had quieted down. It was a rare instant of peace when I could take a breath and try to remember what it felt like to be alive.

His scent reminds me so much of the place that was once my prison and my home for so long.

He ignores me, snapping the reins, the scene becoming a smear of black leaves and trees. I cling tightly to Nadir, my face pressed against his back, noting the twitch of the muscles in his chest and stomach as he navigates us left and right. The air is cold against my cheeks and my fingers are going numb. I left my gloves in my pockets, but we're traveling so fast I don't dare let go to reach for them.

Nadir bends forward as he steers us at a dizzying pace. I flex my hands, balling them into fists, trying to warm them up, but it's no use. A moment later, I feel warm skin against mine, Nadir's hand big enough to clasp both of my hands in his. He squeezes them as a trickle of heat seeps across my fingers and then travels up my wrists and my arms, before it washes over me like I'm being dipped headfirst into a bathtub of steaming water.

I've spent little time around magic despite my heritage, and it's still catching me off-guard. It seems natural that a Fae from such a cold place would have the ability to generate warmth. I presume now that's why he's dressed so lightly. Maybe he doesn't feel the cold. His magic continues to filter over me, and my own responds, apparently soothed by this act. Instead of trying to tug through my skin, it moves slowly, slipping through my limbs like delicate, floating tendrils of seaweed.

A sigh falls from my lips, and my eyes close as I sink into the sensation, the ripples of our magic gliding against each other. I don't understand what this means, but right now I'm just glad to be warmer.

We ride in silence, but for the periodic howling of the ice hounds, for what feels like a very long time. Zerra, it really was stupid to think I could have made it to Nostraza on my own.

With my thighs against Nadir's and our bodies compressed together, it's hard not to keep thinking about my dream. Truthfully, I can't stop thinking about it. I'm grateful he can't see the blush that creeps to my cheeks. Even if he could, I'd just blame it on the cold.

Finally, the horse slows, and I lift my head up from where it's pressed against Nadir's shoulder. The Aurora Keep looms in the distance, a dark blot against a grey sky. It's exactly as I remember, that black stone inexplicably glittering despite the absence of sunlight. I cast about for a view of Nostraza, but the Void's thicket of trees hides the squat buildings of the compound. It's just as well. With Tristan and Willow finally free of its chains, I have no use for that place ever again.

Nadir slows us to a trot as we near the Keep, and I swallow the anxiety climbing up my throat. I remember its bleak interior in flashes. The nights I was brought here so many years ago. Where was Nadir then? I'm not sure how old he is—he appears only a few years older than me, but I know better than to trust that when it comes to the Fae.

Does the prince I'm clinging to know what the king did to me? They're memories I've buried so deep to protect myself, and I'm not prepared to face the king again. In Aphelion, I'd been ready to see him at the ball, but now that I'm here, back at the Keep, I'm not so sure.

Here, everything feels more raw and exposed.

We're on a battleground, and this is the Aurora King's territory.

We ride through the walled city that surrounds the castle, and I take it all in with wonder. Buildings made of the same glittering stone line dark cobbled roads, everything more warm and quaint than I expected thanks to the stained glass windows and colorful jeweled adornments everywhere I look.

There's a sense of strained merriment as we walk through the streets that I can't parse out. Like they're all putting on a show with a cheerful story line, but everyone knows this play actually has a tragic ending. But then I wonder if I'm just imagining things as we pass vendors selling exquisite handmade jewelry, bolts of brightly colored fabric lined up like drops of candy, and steaming mugs of melted chocolate with tiny pastries dusted with icing sugar that smell absolutely decadent even from several feet away.

What surprises me the most is the city isn't composed of only humans and High Fae. There are also other beings, most of whom look human or Fae in shape, but have skin in colors like blue and green and purple and hair in a rainbow of vibrant shades. Some of them have claws and sharp teeth, while others sprout wings from their backs like dragonflies or birds.

"Who are they?" I whisper into Nadir's ear, and I swear I feel him shiver.

"Low fae," he says, his voice tight as his gaze scans the crowd milling below.

I nod, not really understanding what that means, but vowing to ask more questions later.

I've never seen the city, and I want to ask Nadir to stop so I can explore, but I'm sure he won't agree since apparently we're in a rush. Maybe there will be time for that later. As we pass through the crowds, everyone nods and bows their heads to the prince with respect. The children's eyes light up at the sight of the ice hounds while they squeal in delight. The dogs stop, dropping onto their hindquarters and allowing the kids to stroke their fur with patience before they trot after us again, the line of children snaking behind them.

We make our way closer to the Keep before Nadir takes us through the gates with a nod to the guards flanking each side. He brings the horse to a stop and then hops off before he circles his hands around my waist and pulls me down. I'm too surprised to protest, but the unmistakable feel of his touch lingers even after he lets go.

"Come," Nadir says with the jerk of his head. He holds out his hand to me, and I frown before he steps closer and whispers in my ear. "You're here as my plaything, Inmate. At least pretend you can stand to touch me." My eyes close as my body reacts to his nearness and his throaty growl. Why does that sound ricochet through my bones?

"Then maybe you should stop calling me Inmate," I whisper in a hiss, and he crooks up the corner of his mouth.

"Maybe." He holds out his elbow this time, and I take it, deciding this is a little less intimate and at least our skin won't be touching. "Put up your hood. Just in case."

I do as he says, covering my ice-crusted hair before we stride up a wide set of stairs and through a large arched door, servants bowing and murmuring greetings as we pass. There are more of the low fae here, dressed in royal livery with the crest of The Aurora embroidered on their chests.

Pressing my shoulder with my free hand, I think of the same black symbol branded onto my skin. Nadir's gaze flicks to where I'm touching, our eyes meeting for a heavy second, before he looks straight ahead and then directs me around corners and down several halls. The Keep is more luxurious than I remember. Or perhaps I was just never taken to the places where the civilized members of this court lived.

Gleaming black marble striated with the colors of the aurora stretches under our feet. The same hues are woven into thick tapestries and plush velvet furniture dotted throughout the halls.

"Your Highness," a human woman says to us, dropping into a curtsy. She's dressed also in servant's livery and is maybe a few years older than I am. "Welcome back."

"Have my things arrived?" Nadir asks, and the woman nods, clasping her hands and bowing her head.

"Your lady's things, too, Your Highness."

"Good. Thank you." Nadir gives my arm a small tug, and we continue down the wide hall.

We finally stop at a set of doors with sentries posted outside. Nadir acknowledges them with a curt nod and then ushers me through the black wooden doors carved with an array of intricate patterns. I don't have time to wonder at their beauty as I'm steered into a palatial bedroom. It's at least twice the size of Nadir's room in the manor and also features a long bank of windows that looks out to the sky.

I survey the room, noting the massive four-poster bed covered in luxurious black sheets. The room also includes a complete set of plush furniture arranged in front of a large fireplace, along with rows and rows of bookshelves, stuffed full of leather-bound volumes.

I let out a low whistle just to be a pain in the ass. "So this is how the prince sleeps while the inmates lie on the cold, hard ground. Do you know they fed us so little, sometimes there were days I could barely get up?"

I whip around to face him, my cloak flaring. He stands at the door with his dark brows drawn together.

"How do you expect us to treat criminals, Inmate?"

"I wasn't a criminal." I say the words softly, but I swear he flinches as though I walked up and shouted them in his face. It's there for a moment and then gone as a temporary shadow falls over his eyes.

"That wasn't my doing."

He stalks into the room, unbuttoning his jacket as he walks towards a door that must lead to a bathroom. I intercept his escape, maneuvering in front of him. He nearly bowls me over, stopping so short that he has to grab onto my shoulders for balance lest we both topple over. I try to control the squeak of my breath that his touch awakens before meeting his gaze.

"You let it happen," I say, willing him to feel the shame of knowing that place exists as he stands by and does nothing.

"I didn't know you were in there," he snarls, leaning closer, towering over me like an angry mountain.

"You didn't care to know. Didn't bother to see who was behind those walls. There are plenty of others who don't belong there, either."

He narrows his gaze. "If you're trying to invoke some kind of remorse in me, it won't happen. Nostraza exists for a reason and even if there are a few who've slipped through the cracks, it's a small price to pay for the thieves and murderers and rapists who *do* belong there."

He glares at me one more time and then steps around me to stomp to the bathroom, slamming the door behind him.

Zerra, what a dick.

CHAPTER SIXTEEN

NADIR

I slam the door so hard I'm surprised it doesn't pop off the hinges. Then I strip off my jacket and my shirt, nearly tearing the buttons in my haste. My skin is boiling, heat coursing over me in suffocating waves.

When I'm around her, I can't breathe. I can't *think*. I'm tongue-tied and can barely speak when she looks at me with that accusing stare and that mixture of raw vulnerability and fierce defiance in her eyes.

Why is she the most breathtaking thing I've ever seen?

And it's not just a physical attraction. Though yes, I want to touch her so badly my hands ache, but I've never met anyone who was so fucking *sure* of herself.

How can this woman have spent half her life in Nostraza and turn out like that? It should have broken her. It should have left her as a shell. But somehow, she survived both that *and* Atlas's Trials and came out on the other end in a blazing ball of confident fire that threatens to burn me up every time she walks into the room.

It's as though her spirit has always understood her legacy and her purpose.

She behaves exactly like a queen. A slightly wild one with a short fuse, but a queen nonetheless. Gods, when she scolds me like that, I want to kiss her. Partly to shut her up, but mostly to feel those lips against mine and bask in that savage *anger* as I tear off her clothes and fuck her so hard she sees stars.

I made a grave error in suggesting she ride with me today. I thought I could handle it and with my ice hounds in tow, it was the fastest way to get here. But I'd ridden that horse like the lord of the underworld had been on our tails.

I storm over to the shower and flip it on, leaving the temperature icy cold. I strip out of my pants and step under the stream, shuddering in relief as the chilled water tempers my fevered skin. My head bent, I let it run over my hair and down my back, dousing me in an arctic chill. It does nothing to push away the memories of Lor hanging on to me, her thighs pressed against mine and her warm breath on the back of my neck.

She smells like every fantasy I've ever had. Like the roots growing in the earth and the hearts of blooming roses. Like lightning and smoke and pure untamed flames.

It's all I can do to focus when she gets too close. My cock stirs for the hundredth time today, and finally, alone in the shower,

I allow myself the luxury of indulging in my needs. I grip it in my hand, stroking myself slowly as I think of the way she smiles when she doesn't notice I'm looking. Of the way she holds herself like a queen in a way she has no right to yet.

Gripping my cock tighter, I think of her full lips and those round breasts and the way she leaned against my back on the horse. The way she whispered in my ear, having no idea how much I wanted to throw her off, pin her to the ground, and bury my head between her thighs.

I need to get this under control. I'm going to be around her day and night for however long it takes to find that Crown. The Keep is huge, and it's going to take us probably the entire festival to search it from top to bottom.

And that dream. Fuck. That dream had nearly undone me the other night. It had taken every ounce of my willpower not to throw off my bedcovers and march into her room to continue exactly what my thoughts had started.

I can still hear her breathy pants and her moans every time I close my eyes. I can't stop thinking about what she'll really sound like when I do that to her, because I've decided no matter how much she hates me, I have to have her. One way or another, I won't be able to live with myself if I don't make her moan like that outside of my dreams.

I start moving my hand faster, holding myself so tight it hurts as my stomach tenses. I'm so worked up, this won't take long. A moment later, my cock twitches and then I release against the glass wall with a groan. I probably shouldn't have just left her alone in my room. I wonder if she can hear what I'm doing, but then I shove that thought away, because the very idea of *that* makes me want to get myself off all over again.

Forcing myself to focus on the moment at hand, I wash my hair and body and then step out of the water, finally feeling like I can face her again. At least for a little while.

Shutting off the faucet, I grab a thick black towel from the rack and dry myself off before wrapping it around my waist. After swinging open the door, I scan the room to find Lor elbow-deep in a black trunk sitting in the center of the room.

She's pulling out a myriad of clothing and draping items on the sofa that sits in front of my fireplace. Dresses and tunics and leggings, along with boots and shoes, everything in inky fabrics highlighted with the occasional flashes of crimson and emerald and violet. There are lace and silk stockings, leather pants and corsets, floaty black skirts and dresses, and I realize my sister has decided to dress up Lor in her favorite outfits. I run a hand down my face.

Lor pauses what she's doing, looking up at me with her mouth slightly parted in the most delicious way, her lips so pink and plump, I want nothing more than to bite down on them until I draw blood. Her cheeks flush as her eyes drift over my body and that look goes straight to my chest. Did I come out here like this on purpose? Maybe.

I pretend not to notice her reaction as my dick stirs under my towel again. It would be so easy to pull it off, wrap her hair around my hand, and press my cock between her lips. A shiver travels over my skin that has nothing to do with my cold shower as I walk to my closet and throw open the door.

I can feel her eyes on me, something I have no interest in dissuading. I pick out a pair of clean black pants and a black shirt and then reach for the edge of my towel.

"Stop. What the fuck are you doing?" Lor asks before I peer over my shoulder at her.

"I'm getting dressed," I reply, issuing a challenge with my tone.

Her eyes narrow. "I don't think so. Not like that you're not."

She drops the items she's holding and stretches up to her full height, defiance in her stance. She's a good deal shorter than me, and I want to pick her up and toss her over my shoulder and do all kinds of things to her. Things I shouldn't be thinking about.

She holds out a hand to stop me from approaching as I saunter over. "Go into the bathroom and change. Do I really need to share this room with you? This place is huge. Can't I have my own room?"

Her pull draws me closer. I know I should resist. I know I shouldn't give in to this, but I can't seem to stop myself. Just being around her makes the entire surface of my skin release from the tension I'm constantly holding.

"You're here to play the role of my sexual plaything," I say in a low voice, and she bristles at that statement. I resist a smile, loving the way her cheeks flush and her eyes sparkle when she's pissed off. "If anyone caught wind of you sleeping in another room, then it would blow your entire cover, *Inmate*."

I hiss out the last word with venom and watch the rage flare in her eyes again. Fuck, why is making her angry so hot? I don't care if she hates me when I fuck her, though I wonder if all this baiting is any way to convince her she needs it, too. Maybe she's into the idea of a good hate fuck, though. That thought has my cock stirring again.

"And just for good measure, it's probably best if it sounds like you're having a very, very good time while you're in here. I do have a reputation, after all. No one is going to buy this if they don't hear you screaming my name in ecstasy every night." I arch a dark eyebrow and she scoffs, folding her arms over her chest.

"You've got to be kidding me."

With a smirk, I toss my clothing on the sofa. "And this is my room. I'm doing you a favor, remember? If you don't like it, you can go to the bathroom."

She returns my comment with an arched brow of her own, her gaze drifting to the towel that hangs low on my hips before she yanks it back up, an irresistible blush of color highlighting her cheeks.

"Fine," she says, picking up the small pile of clothing she's set aside, crushing it to her chest, and storming past me. It's her turn to slam the door, which she does with a resounding thud.

As soon as she's gone, I drop onto the sofa, running a hand down my face and along the back of my neck.

Zerra, she is going to be the death of me.

CHAPTER SEVENTEEN

LOR

Clutching the new clothes to my chest, I knock the bathroom door closed with my hip and press my back against it. What the fuck was that? He was about to strip down in front of me? Does he have so little regard for my existence that he barely sees me as a person sharing his room? A veritable stranger who he was about to get naked in front of like I wasn't even there?

I toss the clothes on the counter, trying to sort through the conflict of my thoughts. One that's appalled he was about to drop his towel in front of me and one that sort of wanted to see what was under there.

No. Stop it, Lor. He's a monster. It doesn't matter what's under there.

I take a furious shower, scrubbing myself clean with vigor as I marvel at the vast array of soaps and shampoos lined up on the shelf and smirk. No wonder the prince's hair is so shiny.

Lost in my thoughts, I go through the motions of cleaning myself, careful to keep my hair out of the stream, not wanting to get it wet. Once I've calmed down from my encounter with Nadir, I turn off the water and find a large towel to dry off before I dress in the clothing Amya picked out for me.

After sliding on a pair of sheer black stockings, I step into a black skirt that stops mid-thigh and flares out in a cloud of black tulle and chiffon. My top is a fitted dark grey sweater that plunges into a vee and skims over my body, showing off my breasts and waist. I tie my hair into a high ponytail to get it out of my face.

When I'm done, I cautiously ease the door open, half expecting to find Nadir lying on the bed wearing nothing but a confident smile.

When I see he's fully clothed, sitting in front of the fireplace, reading a book, I let out a breath of relief tinged with a traitorous pang of disappointment. He looks up as I exit the bathroom and go to retrieve a short pair of black leather boots sitting at the base of the trunk.

The weight of his stare drifts slowly over my body as I sit down, pulling them on and noticing how his gaze lingers on my legs before it snaps back to mine, the colors in his irises swirling. The magic under my skin is an ever-present buzz, constantly wanting to leap from my skin and *get* to him. There's no denying it's him it wants—I only wish I understood why.

"So what now?" I ask. "Where do we start?"

Nadir snaps his book closed and sets it on the table. "I thought we could start down in the vaults. There are dozens of them underground, where my family's wealth is kept. A relic such as the Crown might blend in just enough to go unnoticed, and it would be a safe place to store it."

I slap my knees and stand up. "Then what are we waiting for? Let's go."

I want to get this over with as quickly as possible. As soon as I find that Crown, I can unlock my magic and get me and my siblings as far from The Aurora as possible. I don't care what Nadir wants from me. I don't trust him and if he really thinks I could be stronger than the Aurora King, then I don't need him. I'll take care of that monster on my own.

He's giving me a strange look from across the low table separating us.

"What?"

He shakes his head, his brow furrowing.

"You'll need to be inconspicuous. There would be nothing amiss about someone finding me down there, but it's not a spot I usually bring my sexual conquests."

My smile is purposely obnoxious. "Maybe your usual conquests are boring."

There is a pause that lasts for a heartbeat before he says, "Maybe." He stands up and drops his arrogant expression on me. "Can you put on something more...subtle?"

I look down at myself. "What's wrong with this? Your sister chose these clothes."

Nadir rolls his shoulders. "I am aware, which means you won't blend in like that."

I blink slowly, once and then another time.

"First off, *you* don't get to tell me what I can and cannot wear, and second, I'll hide if someone comes. Aren't you the prince of this drafty tomb? Just tell them to mind their own business."

His jaw clenches as his eyes drift over me again, and I can't figure out what his problem is. Does he really think I'm going to change my clothing just to make him happy? It's not like I'm wearing a flashing red light strapped to my forehead.

I fold my arms over my chest and tap my foot. He steps closer to me, leaving only a tiny gap between us. My heartbeat kicks up when his eyes fall to my mouth and then back up. A shiver makes the hairs on my arms perk up, and I do my best to conceal it. Zerra, why am I reacting like this? Sure, he's attractive in an objective way, but he's the *Aurora Prince*. He represents every layer and locked chamber of my deepest loathing.

"Are we just going to stand here all day while you stare at me?" I mean the question to come out with dry impatience, but it sounds more like I can't catch my breath.

"No," he says, stepping back, his expression hard. Then he strides for the door and turns to look at me just before opening it. "Coming, Inmate?"

For the next few hours, we wander through a maze of stone corridors that remind me far too much of my former prison. I do my best to spool in my panic as we travel through a series of small rooms fortified with bars and iron doors. I imagine I can almost hear the endless screams and anguished moans that make up the bleak symphony of Nostraza.

"Go slowly," he instructs me, "try to feel for a tug or a call to your magic. You'll know it when you feel it. For me, it's like a fishhook pulling in my gut."

"Do you think it'll work with my magic stuck the way it is?" I ask, walking slowly past a glass cabinet filled with crowns of various styles, grandeur, and complexity. I run my hand along the glass, trying to feel something beyond the tug of my magic towards Nadir. I'm worried I won't be able to tell the difference between the Crown's presence and the way my body keeps reacting to him. But I definitely can't share those concerns out loud.

"I'm not sure," he says. "Can you feel your magic at all right now?"

"A little," I say, providing some version of the truth. "It feels like ribbons moving under my skin."

He nods as he follows behind me, and I suppress the urge to snap at him to back off. He's muddling my thoughts with his proximity.

"That means it's there, so that has to be a good sign. Hopefully, it's enough for you to feel the Crown."

I nod as I keep walking, taking in the piles and shelves and rooms stuffed with gold and jewels and treasure.

"Does The Aurora have a slum like The Umbra?" I ask, thinking of the way the Sun Palace had been gilded from top to bottom while there were hungry people just blocks away.

"In a manner of speaking," Nadir says, keeping a few steps behind me.

"Why?" I ask, spinning around to face him and planting my hands on my hips. Atlas had seemed so comfortable with The Umbra's existence. Are all royal Fae impervious to the shame of such disparity? "How can we be standing in this vault filled with dusty jewels if there are people out there starving?"

"I am not the king of The Aurora," he says, his tone as icy as a mountain wind.

My gaze narrows. "That sounds an awful lot like an excuse."

"I've done what I can," he says, surprising me with the answer. "Set up programs to help the children, at least, and provide comfort where possible."

"Oh," I say, dropping my hands. "That's...commendable."

He snorts and picks up a jeweled dagger, tossing it in the air and catching it by the handle with ease. "Don't think it was out of the goodness of my heart, Inmate. A well-fed populace is one that's less likely to rebel or cause trouble. It's only to try to keep some of the peace."

My eyebrows draw together. "Really?"

"Yes."

"Then why not help everyone?"

"Because my father doesn't agree with me. His style is more about fear and intimidation. The withholding of basic needs. After all, if everyone is too happy, how would he control them? There are constant rumors of rebellion throughout the realm, but instead of addressing their concerns, he chooses force and steel."

My chest tightens at those words. Of course, none of that surprises me. "That's why you want to take over?"

He gives a casual shrug. "Partly." I turn around and continue scanning the room, walking slowly past the piles of treasure. Maybe this prince is more than I've given him credit for.

"Why are you asking me this?" he asks after a moment. I stop and turn around to face him again.

"There was a thief I was close with in Nostraza. Willow told me he's still in there," I say, noticing Nadir's eyes darken at that comment. "He stole because he had nothing else to live for."

Nadir tips his head. "That seems likely, yes."

I say nothing at that, considering everything he's just shared. It's not exactly the benevolence I'd hope for, but it's not a complete disregard for the plight of the less fortunate, either.

Atlas had absolutely no clue. At least Nadir is aware.

Does it matter *why* he wants to feed everyone? Is it just enough that he does?

We continue through several more rooms, still coming upon nothing. My feet are aching, and I stop to lean against a wall, picking up my foot and rotating my ankle.

"I think we should stop for today," Nadir says. "It's getting late. We can resume this tomorrow."

I nod gratefully, wanting to get off my feet. We walk in silence back to his room, where dinner waits for us on the low table in front of the fire. My stomach rumbles, and I drop onto the sofa and pile some food on my plate.

Nadir does the same while I stare out the large windows, noting the hints of the bright lights starting to ripple in the sky. His gaze follows my own as he watches them, and I wonder how they affect him. His magic resembles the lights so much. Is it tied to them, as well? I want to ask, but something about the question feels too intimate. I'm not here to get to know him. He's merely a means to an end.

Nadir's sharp gaze lands on me a moment later, and the heaviness of that look throbs through my entire body as the insides of my thighs tighten. Zerra, I wish I'd stop reacting like this.

"The first Frostfire party is in an hour. You'll need to change into something more..." He waves a hand in my direction. "Something else."

"A party?"

He nods and stands up, smoothing his palms on his thighs. "Everyone will be there."

I shake out the sudden numbness in my fingers. "What about the king?"

"Of course him," Nadir says, missing the flavor of my distress. "But don't worry, with me by your side, he won't bother looking twice at you." There's a bitterness buried in that comment, and I wonder why Nadir hates his father so much. What did the king do to him? Is this simply about how he chooses to rule? "It looks like Amya sent some dresses. Pick one."

"Can't I stay here? You go without me."

Nadir is now rummaging in his closet and looks over a broad shoulder. "If you're here as my companion, it would be highly suspicious if I didn't bring you to the opening gala to show you off, Inmate. Get. Dressed."

An order. I bristle at his tone, but also realize what he's saying makes sense. Getting up, I dig into the trunk again, locating a dress and then heading for the bathroom.

The dress is long and black with a silk bodysuit layered under a sheer skirt and sleeves made of flowery lace. The effect is both understated and risqué all at once. When I pull it up over my hips and let the thin fabric skim along my curves, I feel like a queen.

I love the way I've filled out since those first days in Aphelion when I resembled an angry skeleton. It's a wonder to behold myself like this—healthy and vibrant. Like I was meant to be. Like I've lived a life that was fed by more than just the scraps of wishes and broken dreams.

Amya also supplied a makeup bag, and I dig into it, opting for a smear of dark red lipstick the color of black cherries and thick black lines around my eyes. I leave my hair loose, shaking it out of its tie and letting it settle around my shoulders in gentle waves.

When I'm satisfied, I head back into the room in search of shoes to go with my ensemble. I find a pair of black heels with ankle straps that I slide on.

Nadir has changed into a crisp black shirt, covered with a fitted vest with laces up the back that forms to him like a glove. His midnight hair is partially tied back, strands framing his face. I hate how my stomach tumbles when he gives me an assessing sweep. A hand drifts to his chin, and he rubs it before he takes a deep breath. I wish I could hear what he's thinking. What's going on behind that burning gaze that's practically peeling me apart?

"How do I look?" I ask.

He tips his head and swallows. "Have you been trying to unlock your Fae form?"

Did he just deflect my question? Do I look terrible?

"Of course I have," I say, looking down at myself. I haven't stopped trying, not for a moment.

The look he gives me suggests that maybe I'm not trying hard enough, and I resist the urge to walk over and wrap my hands around his throat.

"Is there something wrong with the way I'm dressed?" I ask again.

"No," he replies, the word clipped. "You look fine."

"Oh," I say, trying not to let that answer bother me. I thought I looked rather nice, but I suppose he doesn't care. To him, I'm just a tool. Just a criminal from Nostraza he's using to get what he wants. Why am I concerned with what he thinks, anyway?

Gods Lor. Get your shit together.

"Ready?" His voice is rough, and I give an uncertain nod, not actually ready, but knowing I have little choice in this. I'm here to put on an act so I can claim the ultimate prize. He doesn't give me any more time to think about it because he holds out an elbow, intending for me to take it.

There's almost a flash of apology in his expression as I hesitate.

"For appearances," he says, something strangled in the sound, but I think he's misconstruing the reason for my indecision. It's not that I don't want to touch him. It's that I'm afraid of the way I react every time I do. Nevertheless, I will myself to loop my arm through his, the shock of his touch splitting through me like lightning.

We both exhale together, twin gusts blowing out.

Without another word, Nadir guides me from the room and through the shiny hallways of the Keep. They're filled with people, all of whom tip their heads at Nadir in acknowledgment as we pass. He returns their nods, forgoing any attempts at conversation. For my own part, it's like I'm a specimen on display, as I'm met with an equal mixture of curiosity and disdain.

We pass several more low fae with their unusual coloring and features.

"What are low fae?" I ask, and Nadir's jaw tightens.

"They work in the castle, amongst other things."

"I've never seen one before. Do they only live here? I didn't see any in Aphelion."

He gives me a dark look. "That's because low fae are considered the lowest form of citizen. In Aphelion, they all live in The Umbra. Atlas can't bear to have them anywhere near him."

I inhale sharply at those words. "Why?"

"Prejudice. They can also perform magic and High Fae don't like the idea of anyone else being able to use it. So, they decided a long time ago to treat low fae like scum, so they'd stay in their *place*."

This is monstrous. I hate the sound of all of this.

"But your father doesn't mind having them around?" I ask, carefully, already knowing I'm not going to like the answer as my rage for the king and his son builds. Just when I thought Nadir might not be quite as awful.

Nadir snorts. "Here in The Aurora they are slaves. Instead of shunning them, my father uses them for indentured labor."

"How can you do that?" I ask, my voice rising as several people peer our way.

"Calm down," Nadir hisses.

"I will not. This is terrible!"

A low fae with pink skin, purple hair, and a pair of shimmering butterfly wings glides past us, balancing a tray of drinks in her hand. Her expression is one of uncertainty and fear before she scurries off.

Nadir pulls me into a room and slams the door, crowding me against the surface.

"I *know* it's terrible," he says, seething, his black eyes swirling with color. "I didn't say I agreed with it."

My shoulders drop. "You don't?"

"No. I don't. I disagree with the practice entirely."

"Oh. Is this something you'd change when—"

He clamps a hand over my mouth.

"Don't. Be careful what you say when we're anywhere outside of my wing."

Right. Of course. Nadir is planning to commit treason. I nod and he eases his hand away. I've left a deep red print from my lipstick on his palm. We both stare at it for a moment and then our eyes meet, and it suddenly occurs to me how close he is, causing my neck to flush with heat.

He clears his throat and grabs my hand before he wrenches the door open. "Let's go."

We enter the hallway again, and a few knowing smirks are tossed our way. I glare at them before Nadir tugs me towards him and wraps an arm around my waist.

"Try to look like you're having fun," he whispers. "Maybe like you were just thoroughly fucked in that room and enjoyed it."

I purse my mouth into an irritated frown. "This is my *'I was just fucked in that room by an asshole'* face." To my surprise, Nadir barks out a laugh before directing me down the corridor, his arm still around me.

Finally, we approach a tall set of black wooden doors where people are streaming in and out of a large room draped with miles of purple velvet. I come to a halt as we're about to enter, suddenly overwhelmed at the idea of seeing Nadir's father in the flesh after all these years.

Nadir raises his brows. "Ready, Inmate?"

With my hand pressed to my stomach, I take a deep, cleansing breath that does nothing to calm my nerves. I've never been less ready for anything than I am at this moment. I've faced down the worst sorts of monsters in my life, but nothing eclipses the one that rules this Keep.

"As I'll ever be," I say softly and then square my shoulders as I prepare to face the Aurora King.

CHAPTER EIGHTEEN

O ur entrance is anti-climactic. There are so many bodies pressing into the space, I can barely see past them. Nadir firms his arm around my waist, and I allow him to lead me through the crowd.

When I'm nearly knocked over by a giant High Fae, Nadir holds on to me tightly.

"Watch where you're going," the prince snarls and the male blanches visibly.

"Apologies, Your Highness." He bows low to the prince.

"It isn't me you need to apologize to."

The Fae drops his gaze on me, disdain etched on his face. Here I am, a human woman on the arm of the prince. His whore for the night. I don't deserve his respect. He sniffs and casts a surreptitious look at the prince, clearly feeling slighted.

"It's fine," I say, but Nadir grips me tighter.

"It's not fine." He doesn't look at me as he stares at the offending Fae. "You are my guest, and Virgil here is going to apologize for his carelessness." Though he doesn't outright say it, the threat is unmistakable.

"You don—"

He silences my protest with a look, and my mouth snaps shut before he glares at Virgil again.

"Of course," Virgil finally stammers, turning his bow to me. "I apologize for my clumsiness, my lady. I hope you'll forgive me."

"It's fine. Really," I say, and before the male can reply, we're moving again.

Nadir draws me away and we continue through the crowd, emerging into an open area where Fae loiter on an array of velvet divans, most of them with cut crystal glasses suspended in their hands. Nadir finally lets go of my waist, opting to take my hand. I want to pull away, but I remind myself that this, too, is part of the act.

"You didn't have to do that," I say. "I was fine."

"Virgil is a disrespectful fuck," Nadir says, the lines around his mouth tight. He pins me with a look. "And I did have to do that."

I furrow my brow and bite my bottom lip. "Okay. Thanks, I guess." He nods, his shoulders stiffening as he looks away.

"Nadir!" comes a breathy voice, and we stop as a gorgeous Fae approaches, dark blonde hair falling in silken waves around her shoulders. Her emerald-green dress is the perfect contrast to her olive skin and is cut so scandalously, I can't figure out what's holding it up. It exposes her taut stomach and her lean thighs, along with an impressive pair of breasts that are spilling out over the top. She's breathtaking and completely intimidating.

"Where have you been?" she coos, flattening her entire body against Nadir as she kisses one cheek and then the other, leaving a bright pink smear of lipstick. Seeing that mark on his skin makes my stomach twist, but then I remember my lip print still on his palm.

I got here first.

I blink. Where did that thought come from? Why do I care whose lips are on him?

"The Keep is such a bore when you're not here," she continues, still pressed against him with her hands on his waist. She hasn't glanced at me even once, despite the fact he's still holding my hand.

"Vivianna," Nadir says with a tipped smile. "Things have kept me away. You look delicious." I bristle in irritation at those words. He told me I looked *fine*, and this female gets "delicious?" Nadir's gaze flicks momentarily towards me and then to our clasped hands, and it's then I realize I'm squeezing his fingers so hard my knuckles have gone white.

As I force my grip to loosen, he returns his attention to Vivianna, whose plump lips are turned down in a pout. "Will you come see me later?" she asks as she drags a possessive hand down his arm.

He gives her a sly smile, and I try to yank my hand from his. I can't believe they're acting like I'm not standing right here. Nadir hangs on tight, his hand crushing mine, making it impossible to pull from his hold. What the fuck is he doing?

"As much as I'd love to, I'm afraid I'm not available tonight," Nadir says, apology in his tone as he tips his chin to me. Why does that answer annoy me so much? He'd love to? It sounds like the only reason he isn't already cock-deep inside her is because he's stuck here babysitting me.

It's then Vivianna finally deigns to notice my presence as she draws away from Nadir, careful to keep her hand planted in the center of his chest. "Oh." Her green eyes sweep over me in a way that reminds me all too much of the way everyone treated me in Aphelion, and I tamp down the snarl in my throat. "I see. A human, Nadir?"

He smirks and tips his head. "You know I like to try everything."

Vivianna sniffs and I want to punch her in her pouty pink mouth. I'm squeezing Nadir's hand again with so much force, I swear I feel his bones creak.

"Some other time," he says to her. "I promise."

She's somewhat mollified by that vow, her gaze sliding to me for a heartbeat.

"I'm going to hold you to that," she warns.

"I'm counting on it."

Zerra, I hate this bastard. How dare he flirt with her right in front of me? He's practically undressing her with his eyes. This time I do yank my hand from his, and storm off, having no clue where I'm going, but wanting to distance myself from Nadir. I stop and look around. I need a drink. There's clearly plenty of alcohol here.

A moment later, I feel a warm arm circle my waist, followed by the prince's low voice in my ear. "What's the matter?"

"Nothing," I say, trying to extract myself from his grasp, but he hangs on tight.

"Are you jealous?" He directs me towards a small divan clearly meant for two.

"Don't be ridiculous. Why would I care who you fuck?"

Dropping into the seat, he pulls me down next to him. I keep my body stiff and my arms folded. If anyone were looking, it would be glaringly obvious that I hate the Fae next to me.

"Of course. I must've been mistaken," he says. "You nearly ripped my hand off, but that must have been for some totally unrelated reason."

I glare at him. "Shut up."

He lets out a low chuckle that suddenly cuts off. I follow his gaze to see what's drawn his attention and then I go even stiffer.

It's him.

The Aurora King glides towards us like he's walking on satin. He's the spitting image of Nadir, only a little broader and maybe a few years older. While Fae are basically immortal, they still do age slowly once they reach adulthood. The difference in their ages is almost noticeable due to the finest of lines around the king's mouth, but he's exactly as I remember him. That harsh face and those cruel eyes that follow me into my nightmares.

The king strides to where we're seated, and I brace myself, unsure of what to expect. I needn't be worried because, just like Vivianna, Nadir's father doesn't even glance at me. It's like I'm not even here. Is it because I'm human or because I've been branded as Nadir's toy for the week?

"Finally, you're back," the king says. "I need to speak with you."

"I'm busy," Nadir says, leaning back and throwing an arm over my shoulder. I'm about to throw him a dirty look when a sharp pinch to my upper arm makes me flinch. Right. I'm supposed to be playing a part. Awkwardly, I try to soften my posture and lean into the prince.

"Now," the king says, his tone leaving no room for dissent. Nadir sighs and removes his arm before he sits forward.

"Fine." He stands and looks down at me. "I'll be back in a few minutes. Try not to get into any trouble, In—" He stops and runs a hand through his hair, clearly flustered by his near fumble. "I'll be back in a moment," he says again and then walks past the king before the two of them melt into the crowd.

It's not until the king is out of sight that I realize I'm trembling. Partly with fear and partly with rage that after everything, he didn't even deign to notice me. He doesn't even recognize me. I remind myself that's for the best. It's paramount to my safety that the king thinks I'm dead and harmless, but that doesn't stop me from feeling as insignificant as a mote of dust.

A low fae servant bearing a tray full of drinks passes, and I signal for one. He hands me a glass, and I down its contents, trying to settle my nerves. With my hand pressed to my heart, I force steady breaths through my mouth and nose as I search for a second drink.

Someone thrusts a glass into my view and then a High Fae drops onto the divan next to me. He gives me a dazzling smile that nearly outshines his mane of glorious silver hair.

His brown skin is gold dusted and his eyes are the same deep amethyst as his brocade jacket.

"You looked like you could use this," he says, holding out the glass to me. "Being the prince's *objet du jour* not all it's cracked up to be?"

I don't ask how he knows who I am, or rather the role I'm playing, but I presume gossip travels like a match to a dry book around here. Ignoring his question, I accept the glass and take a long, fortifying sip.

The Fae chuckles, his smile full of bright white teeth. I wonder if any of the Fae are just a little bit ordinary. Surely, there must be someone amongst them who doesn't look like they were pieced together to perfection.

"I'm Tharos," he says, holding out a hand. I take it, giving it a shake.

"Nice to meet you," I say, wondering why he's decided to talk to me. "I'm Lor." Then I wince, realizing that giving my real name might not be prudent, but Nadir and I never discussed what I should call myself. What reason would this Fae have to know who I am, anyway? If Tharos notices or makes any connection, he gives no sign, instead bringing my hand he's still holding up to his mouth and pressing his lips to the back of it.

"The pleasure is mine, Lady Lor."

I pull my hand away and give him a cautious smile.

"I've never seen you around here before. Where did Nadir find you? Are you new to The Aurora?"

Why is Tharos asking me this? Is he digging or just being polite? Knowing I can't give a straight answer, I instead offer a suggestive wink before I take another drink.

"I can't give away the prince's secrets," I say with a coy lilt, causing Tharos's grin to stretch before he belts out a hearty laugh.

"Fair enough, my lady."

"This is my first Frostfire, though," I say, deciding that nugget of information is safe enough. "At least my first time seeing it from inside the Keep."

Tharos's eyes sparkle at that. "Well, then let me fill you in on all the gossip."

He scoots in closer, draping an arm along the back of the divan while his thigh presses against mine. Uncomfortable with his familiarity, I shift my leg away, but he doesn't seem to notice. A servant offers him a cocktail from a silver tray, and he takes one before he sits back and points to someone in the crowd.

"That there is Lady Wensel and her husband Archibald." He then swings the glass to the other side of the room, where a handsome Fae is watching them with a desperate look on his face. "And *that* is her fuck boy." I sputter out a giggle, slapping my hand over my mouth. I shouldn't laugh, but after being in the Sun Palace, I discovered how idle and useless most of these nobles are.

For the next few minutes, Tharos continues to regale me with stories of who betrayed who and who's screwing each other and who knows about what. I listen intently, partly out of fascination but also because if I'm truly destined to take the Heart throne, then every other realm in Ouranos is a potential ally or enemy. The prince may be helping me now, but that means nothing when it comes to the future.

Tharos leans in close as he talks, speaking in my ear lest he be overheard. As he regales me with his stories, I grow more comfortable with his presence. He seems to be simply enjoying himself without needing anything more. He's so much lighter and carefree compared to Nadir, and I find myself enjoying a respite from the prince's intensity.

I catch sight of Amya across the room, dressed in a magnificent gown of black satin. She gives me a subtle tip of her chin both in acknowledgement and confirmation that my brother and sister are safe.

I'm not sure how long me and Tharos keep talking, but after another drink and some more gossip, I'm far less tense after both the encounter with the king and watching Nadir flirt with Vivianna. He makes a joke, and I let out a genuine laugh for the first time in ages, my head throwing back.

That's when a shadow falls over me, and I look up to find the prince of eternal darkness glaring at Tharos like he's about to reach into his chest and pull out his beating heart.

"Get away from her," Nadir says, his voice so low and dangerous I swear every light in the room flickers in response.

"Nadir," Tharos drawls, all smiles. "I was just keeping your friend here company while you attended to your important royal matters." He waves a hand and Nadir snatches it, twisting Tharos's wrist until there's the unmistakable snap of bone. Both me and the silver-haired Fae gasp as his glass falls from his hand. "I said, get away from her."

We're suddenly the center of attention, dozens of curious stares pointing our way.

Tharos's face has gone pale, and he's clutching his wrist, his eyes watering with pain. "I meant no harm, Your Highness."

Nadir's fury could melt iron. This is getting awkward. What is he so pissed off about? Tharos lurches up to stand as Nadir crowds his space, his posture curved with aggression. Both Fae are nearly matched in size, but somehow Nadir manages to come off like a giant. For his part, Tharos looks like he's about to vomit, and I can't figure out what's going on. I stand up, too, afraid this is about to get even more violent, and grab Nadir's arm.

"It's fine," I hiss. "He was just keeping me company and telling me about everyone at court. Nothing more. Will you stop acting like an animal?" I wonder if this is about his pride. I suppose there must be some kind of unwritten rule about touching the prince's plaything, but this all seems a little over the top. Nadir shutters his angry gaze on me, but a moment later, something snuffs out the deepest edge of his wrath.

He turns back to Tharos. "If I catch you anywhere near her again, I'll tear out your throat. This is your only warning." Still clutching his wrist to his chest, Tharos swallows and then nods. "Get out of here."

Tharos doesn't wait for another order before he scurries off like his pants are on fire.

When he's gone, Nadir takes my arm and directs me back to the divan.

"I want to leave," I tell him, pulling my arm away, but he catches it and tugs me towards him so my body is flush against his. His arm snakes around my waist and he levels his mouth to my ear.

"Stay." A ripple shudders over my skin at the way his low whisper taps at some secret place deep inside me. "Please."

I'm so surprised by the "please" that I blink. There is something pained in it, like he's barely grasping its tattered edges. He pulls back, his dark gaze sinking into mine, and I find myself nodding.

"Okay."

He doesn't exactly smile, but there is a light of muted triumph in his expression as he leads me to the divan and then pulls me onto his lap. Immediately, I try to get up, but a large hand clamps down on my hip. "Remember the role you're playing, Inmate." He whispers it again, and I despair at how my body reacts. It's like being seduced by a rumbling volcano that's close to erupting and burning me to a crisp.

A passing High Fae stops and glances down at us. He's got a shock of brown hair and twinkling blue eyes. "Inmate? That's a fun pet name, Nadir. Who's this, then?"

Nadir smiles and pulls me in closer with one arm while he reaches up to shake the hand of the male. "Just a little role-playing," he replies, dodging the question about who I am. "She likes it when I chain her up." He squeezes my thigh and winks at me. "Don't you, sweetheart?"

I glare at him, considering whether I'll gouge out his eyes with a spoon or a knife. He's doing this just to get a rise out of me, and he squeezes my leg again, with a reminder.

"I just love it," I say, my teeth grinding together.

The Fae chuckles and claps Nadir on the shoulder.

"Lucky bastard. Enjoy Frostfire, my lady." He tips a bow to me and walks away, still laughing to himself.

"I'm going to kill you," I whisper, and again I try to get up, but Nadir holds me against him, thwarting my attempt. We're nearly eye level for a change. He tips his head as though waiting to see what I'll do next, but I know he's right. I'm here to play a part, and storming out of here doesn't fit that role.

"I can't wait until you try," he says in a thick voice that makes my insides twist with a delicious thrill. His hand slides up my back, his warm palm skating over my exposed skin. He pauses ever so briefly, his fingers flexing against the scars I know are there. Then he pulls me in closer, and I do my best to pretend this is what I want, while also making it seem like I'm not enjoying it at all.

As I lean in, his hand slides higher, cupping the back of my neck, his fingertips pressing into the tendons when my thighs flex in response. What is happening to me? Why am I having such strong physical reactions to him? I need to be careful.

I wanted to trust Atlas so badly that I lost sight of what was right in front of me. I'd spent so much of my life living with the worst kinds of beasts that any warm attention was hard to resist. I know Nadir's just playing his part, too, but he's proving far more adept at it.

Gently, he tips me closer, his hand still on the back of my neck. Nadir surveys the room, and I follow his gaze, noting the surreptitious glances cast in our direction.

His fingers are absentmindedly tracing a pattern on my hip that also sends a tremble over my skin. My magic is soothed the closer he is, and right now it's a silken slide moving through my blood. I can tell it still wants more, though. But more of what?

"Can I place my hand on your knee?" he asks in that barely re-strained way. "It would be expected that I'd be a little more...affectionate with my publicly declared Frostfire companion."

Casting a look about the room, it's obvious what Nadir means. The partygoers are getting bolder and looser as the night goes on, the divans scattered around the room hosting more than one subtle but carnal encounter. It reminds me of the parties in Aphelion, and I remember what Callias told me about Fae and their primal urges.

"We can leave soon," he promises in a tone softer than I'd expect. "But to make this seem real, we really should stay a while longer."

I nod, not taking my eyes from the rest of the room.

Nadir's other hand lands on my knee, bared by the slit in my skirt, and my stomach leaps. My gaze finds his in a rush and then neither of us seems to be able to look away.

"You might want to put your arm around me, too," he suggests, and I nod again, my words lodged somewhere in the back of my throat. I do as he asks, curling my arm behind his shoulders, which means more of me pressing against him.

"Are you okay?" he asks, and I'm again caught off-guard by the concern in his voice. He seems so different from before, and I don't know what to make of it.

"I'm okay," I say, not entirely sure if that's true. When I feel his hand slide up the side of my thigh, my breath hitches, my bottom lip catching between my teeth. His eyes go dark, absent of those swirling colors, while he continues the slow progression of his large warm palm along my leg.

My stomach gives a conflicted flip as his hand slides higher, the tips of his fingers brushing the edge of the bodysuit I'm wearing at my hip. The room falls away, and the only thing I notice is the background hush of the music and chatter and soft moans filling the air. Nadir's fingers slide inward along that edge of the fabric, so close and yet so far from the flutter between my thighs. Is this real? Or part of the show? What do I want? My mind says one thing, but my body is saying something else entirely.

But it's just this room and the sounds and the scent of sex hanging in the air. Nadir is handsome, and I'm having a purely physical reaction. This is no different from Atlas. I was using him and I'm using Nadir, too, but as the prince's hand does another sweep, his fingertips skating just along the hem of the fabric again, I know I'm kidding myself. This is nothing like Atlas at all.

Suddenly, the room becomes stifling. This moment becomes too much. I need to get out of here.

"I can't—" I shake my head and push myself away, sliding off his lap. "I'm sorry," I whisper before I spin around and bolt for the exit.

CHAPTER NINETEEN

Somehow, I navigate my way back to Nadir's room after asking at least a dozen servants for directions. They all give me wary glances as I fly through the halls like I'm being chased by a demon.

When I see the familiar doors of Nadir's wing, I throw myself inside and race to his bedroom, wishing there were somewhere else I could retreat, but I don't dare wander the Keep on my own.

Digging into the trunk Amya sent, I find a pair of soft leggings and a tunic. Quickly, I strip out of my dress, sighing in relief at the soft and far more comfortable clothing. Thankfully, there's a bar cart near the window, so I stride over and pick up a decanter of dark red liquid.

Not caring what it is, I fill up a glass and chug the entire contents back, definitely starting to notice the woozy effects of consuming too much alcohol. But it isn't enough to dull the tremors of seeing the Aurora King, nor the ache below my stomach when I reacted to Nadir's touch. I don't *want* to feel any of these things. He may not have been directly responsible for my imprisonment, but he knows what goes on inside Nostraza. How can I ever forgive him for that?

There are parts of my life I've yet to come to terms with. The worst moments that I've shoved down in the depths of my soul. What the warden made me do. What the king did during those nights in the Keep. The scars that still linger on my skin and the ones that live below the surface that will never fully heal. The constant reminders of everything I've already lost and everything I still might lose. I didn't get the chance to process any of it while I was in Aphelion as I kept fighting for my life, but I can't keep ignoring it forever.

My glass is empty again, so I pour another one and drain it, too. Then I pick up the bottle and drop onto the sofa, kicking my socked feet on the table while I pour myself another.

The fire is lit, the flames warming the cold room. Morana and Khione lie on the hearth, studying me with their postures relaxed. I wonder how they can stand the heat with all that fur. Despite that, a chill seeps in from the large bank of windows. How can this be a pleasant place to sleep?

I eye the enormous bed, supposing I'll find out soon enough. I hope Nadir isn't seriously thinking we're going to both sleep there, though. The only other option would be this sofa, which would be comfortable enough for me, though I suspect it would be too small for his large frame.

I sigh. There's no way he's giving up that luxurious bed for my benefit. Still, this sofa is a thousand steps of improvement over the bed I had in Nostraza.

The door opens and I refuse to look over as Nadir enters the room, bracing myself for the inevitable lecture about abandoning the party without his permission or whatever he decides to scold me about today.

He walks over, his steps muffled by the thick carpets, and undoes his vest, tossing it on the chair before he opens his cuffs and rolls up his sleeves to his elbows, revealing a pair of thick veined forearms. I watch all of this from the corner of my eye as I sip on my drink, my head starting to spin. I really should stop drinking, but it's the only thing taking the edge off my corkscrew of emotions.

Nadir settles onto the sofa and reaches over to pick up the bottle that is decidedly less full than when I started. He tips it, checking the contents and raises an eyebrow, but says nothing as he returns it to the table. His arm stretches along the back of the sofa as his knee brushes against mine.

"The king wanted to know about you," he says. I sit up, my senses firing in warning. "Don't worry, I don't mean the version of you that was sitting in that room, but the escaped prisoner 3452."

"What did you tell him?" I ask, shooting a look at the door, sure the king is about to burst into the bedroom with an accusing finger before he drags me to that wretched place deep in the bowels of the Keep.

"That I found your body washed up on the shores of Alluvion."

"He thinks I'm dead." The pressure in my chest releases.

"He does. So for now, you're safe." Nadir stops, exhaling a small breath that somehow manages to curl and wrap around my body.

"You were shaking when he came to talk to me," he says, once again throwing me off. I wouldn't have thought he'd noticed. I meet his dark gaze, willing defiance into my expression.

"He killed my family. Shouldn't I shake when I see him?"

Nadir nods slowly, as though he suspects I'm not being entirely truthful. I'm not sure why I'm keeping this from him. Why I can't give voice to the torture I suffered at his father's hands. Maybe if I hold on to the memories tightly enough, they can't come apart and strangle me.

"Is that the only reason?" he asks.

"That's not a good enough one for you?"

"No, it is. I understand why you'd hate him for that, but it feels like there's something you're not telling me."

I take another sip from my glass, avoiding his gaze.

"There's nothing."

He doesn't press me any further, and we both fall into silence.

"Who was that female?" I ask, holding my hands up in front of me to mimic a large pair of breasts. Zerra, I'm definitely drunk.

Nadirs snorts. "You mean Vivianna?"

I scowl. Even her name is more interesting and luscious than mine.

"She's an old friend."

"Have you fucked her?" The question slips out of its own volition, and I wish I could take it back.

"Why do you care?"

"I don't."

"Sure seems like you do."

I definitely don't respond to that and take another swig of my drink.

Of course I don't care.

I stare at the fire, and he does the same as we sit in silence for several long minutes. Despite everything, it's strangely comfortable, not tense or awkward. The room is absolutely spinning now, and I drop my head back, staring at the ceiling rotating above me as I groan.

"Perhaps you've had enough of that." Nadir takes the glass from my hand and places it on the table. I clap my hand over my eyes—my head pounding and my stomach churning.

Suddenly, I bolt upright, leap off the sofa and trip over Nadir as I scramble past his long legs.

"What are you—" he asks as I stumble for the bathroom, slam open the door and practically skid on my knees along the smooth tiled floor. I lift the toilet lid and promptly hurl up the contents of my stomach as sweat beads on my brow.

Breathing heavily, I will the world to stop spinning before registering the soft click of footsteps and then a pair of gentle hands in my hair. Nadir gathers it up, pulling it away from my face as I vomit again, retching over and over. I'm not sure how long it takes, but he crouches behind me, never letting go of my hair and rubbing my back as another wave of nausea hits, followed by another.

When I think I'm finally done, I slide to the floor and press my cheek against the cool tile. My skin is clammy and my mouth tastes like the bottom of a sewer, but at least my headache has subsided to a dull ache.

Nadir stands and walks to the sink, where he pours out a glass of water and then brings it over. Holding the glass to my mouth, he lifts my head just enough that I can take a sip before it drops back to the floor with an agonized moan. Zerra, I feel like shit.

He gives me a moment and then makes me drink some more water before he returns the glass to the counter. My eyelids are so heavy I can't keep them open. They drift shut, and I shudder through a wave of lingering nausea.

A moment later, strong arms scoop me up, and I'm lifted in the crook of the prince's hold. That scent—the one that reminds me of cold winter breezes and the first dusts of snow—fills my nose. I breathe out an instinctive sigh. Why does it feel like a memory I can't touch?

He carries me out of the bathroom and gently lays me on his massive bed. The sheets are cool and silky and feel amazing against my clammy skin. I sigh again as I cocoon into the mattress while Nadir lays a blanket on top of me.

Gentle fingers brush a tendril of hair from my face and tuck it behind my ear. I'm just coherent enough to register this show of tenderness that is so wholly incongruent with the male I've come to know these past few weeks.

The back of his hand brushes my forehead and travels down my cheek with the lightest of touches.

"Tomorrow, we'll search in the east wing near my father's apartments," Nadir says softly. "Providing you're in any state to do so."

There's another pause and then the lightest stroke of fingers along my jawbone.

"I don't know what that bastard did to you, but I'm going to help you get your crown, Heart Queen, and I'm going to make him pay. For all of it."

With that chilling declaration echoing in my head, I drift off to sleep.

CHAPTER TWENTY

SERCE

286 YEARS AGO: THE WOODLANDS

"It's so nice to see you again," Serce said, tipping her head towards Rion and then his bonded partner, Meora. She bounced a baby with a head of thick black hair on her hip. "I see you've brought your son. How...nice."

She gave the child an awkward smile and swore its squished expression turned skeptical. Was it possible for a baby to raise an eyebrow? She'd never really understood children. They made her vaguely uncomfortable, like animals who might bite, or worse, cry when they got spooked. The baby cooed at her and then reached for her face. Serce stepped back with a jolt, quickly smoothing back her hair.

"Sorry about that," Meora said with a sheepish smile. "Nadir's a little grabby. Aren't you, sweetheart?" She regarded the boy with such affection, Serce *almost* felt something twist in her chest. Or perhaps it was just indigestion.

Wolf, on the other hand, had no such compunctions around babies. His face split into a wide grin as he grabbed Nadir from his mother and swung him around. "What a sweet little Faeling," he said. Serce had to admit that watching him holding a child like that, with so much love and tender enthusiasm, was rather beguiling.

The baby laughed at Wolf with a boisterous and joyous sound that filled the room with lightness. Wolf wrapped the baby in his arms and tossed Serce a grin before he winked at her.

Her hands drifted to her stomach. Though he hadn't outright said it, he'd hinted more than once that he couldn't wait to be a father someday. If Serce were being honest, the thought had rarely crossed her mind until she'd met him. She knew eventually she would need to produce an heir or risk the magic of Heart being transferred to another bloodline, but she recoiled at the thought. Why were only those burdened with a womb the ones saddled with this sticky task?

As Wolf touched his nose to the little boy's, the child broke into a huge toothless smile. Serce thought *maybe* she could see herself being a mother with Wolf at her side. But whatever joy the baby had manifested in Wolf seemed to have the opposite effect on the Aurora King. Rion glared at them both, saying nothing as he settled into one of the opulent green sofas arranged in the center of the spacious sitting room.

They were in the heart of the Woodlands Fort, surrounded by curved walls that made it feel like they were inside a hollowed-out tree. Hardwood floors polished to a high shine were covered with an array of thick green rugs trimmed in gold.

"Can I offer you something to drink?" Serce asked, gesturing to one of the liveried servants waiting at the side of the room. Meora settled in next to her partner, and Serce noted the imperceptible shift in the Aurora King's posture, as though he were trying to distance himself from her.

Rion arched a dark eyebrow, scanning the space before his gaze touched Wolf, who was now seated next to Serce, the baby still on his lap.

"Isn't it wonderful to see the two of you playing house so nicely? What does your mother think of this little arrangement? I heard there was quite the scene at the summit last month. I suppose my invitation was lost in the mail."

Serce tried not to let her anger show at his condescending tone. She wondered for the thousandth time if it was a mistake to invite him here. But she'd sent countless messages to her mother, trying to make amends, and they'd all gone unanswered. Serce was starting to panic. Her spies had reported Daedra had been overheard saying she wouldn't move towards the descension after all, now that Serce had spurned the bonding with Atlas.

Serce remembered her mother's last words about not being ready that night at dinner. She couldn't believe her mother could really be *this* petty. They both understood how important it was for Heart to be at its strongest. Serce couldn't let that happen. The only thing she'd ever wanted, before she'd met Wolf, was to get her hands on the Heart Crown.

Meora saved Serce from having to answer Rion's question as she placed a hand on his arm. She didn't glance his way as he threw her a dark look. "I'll have a glass of Varmique Annata. I hear the vintage is especially good this year."

Serce nodded and gestured to one of the servants to give Meora a glass of the famed Woodlands wine.

"Rion?" she asked, and he tipped his chin. While the servant poured out the drinks, the baby cooed in Wolf's lap as he lifted the boy into the air. The baby giggled, and Wolf's answering grin could have lit up the sky.

"I can take him," Meora said, sounding apologetic, and reaching for the child. "If it's too much trouble." Wolf waved her off, tucking the baby against his side again.

"Not a chance. I think he likes me." The baby looked up at Wolf, his tiny face bunching into a toothless smile. Heat flushed up Serce's neck. Why did Wolf look so appealing like this? The provider. The protector. She'd never known she wanted that in a partner, but it was suddenly very sexy.

Meora gave Wolf a tight smile and settled back against the sofa, clearly relieved to be getting a break from the child. Serce wondered why the queen didn't have a nanny helping her.

"So," Rion drawled, taking a sip of his wine. "*Why* have you invited us here, Serce?"

She twisted her hands in her lap. She was wearing a green, floor-length gown made of soft flowing fabric that fell around her like spring leaves.

"My mother plans to keep the Heart Crown from me," she said, knowing there was no point in dancing around the truth. "She was supposed to descend next year, but rumors say she's changed her mind."

She conveniently didn't add the salient point about it being a strategy to best Rion's strength, of course. The true depth of her power was a secret they'd kept for reasons exactly like this. Serce said a silent thank-you for her mother's foresight.

Rion appreciated directness, though, and Serce could tell she'd intrigued him when a light sparked in his eyes. He let out a low whistle. "I knew your mother had a temper, but that is quite the change of heart. What could you have done to anger her so?"

She exchanged a quick glance with Wolf, who silently urged her to answer. "I was to bond to the youngest Sun Prince, but I refused."

Guilt spiraled around her throat. Not only was she bartering with the enemy, she was revealing her mother's plans to move against Rion. But she reasoned she had a higher purpose. Heart could not fall to The Aurora because of her mother's short-sightedness.

"Is that so?" Rion asked. "And why was that? Were the armies they promised not to your liking, Princess?"

Serce bit the inside of her lip. Of course. If he already knew about the summit, then he likely knew the reason for it.

"He was going to make me compete in those barbaric Trials. I refused."

Rion's gaze skirted to Wolf. "And?"

"And then I ran into Wolf, and fate has a way of leading us on the path we're meant to follow."

Rion's answering laugh was laced with poison. "I see. So all this is because you fell in *love*." The inflection on the word 'love' was scathing. Serce noticed Meora visibly flinch before she caught herself and then held completely still, as if pretending it hadn't happened.

Serce's gaze caught Wolf's and there was no question about it. They'd only known each other for a few months, but she'd already fallen so deeply in love with him, it was like she'd plunged into a well with no bottom.

"So what if we did?" Serce said, keeping yet another truth from Rion.

From the moment she'd met Wolf, she'd understood this was more than *just* love. The way her magic and her body responded to his presence was reverent. Something powerful and sacred. It had been a few weeks after their first encounter that they'd confirmed what they already knew in their hearts. They were mates—a hallowed bond so rare between High Fae as to be practically a legend. Serce had never heard of it happening in her lifetime, nor had Wolf. They both cherished this fact and this secret, holding it close to be savored only by them until the time was right to reveal it.

Rion scoffed and sipped his drink. "Then you're both bigger fools than I ever gave you credit for."

Serce rolled her neck, ignoring the insult. Rion had always been a cold-hearted bastard, and she'd expected nothing less from him. The way he pulled away from Meora like he couldn't

stand to be in her presence told Serce he would never understand her feelings, anyway.

"Be that as it may, I called you here to form our own alliance."

The barest raise of his eyebrows was the only outward show
of surprise, and Serce was sure she'd just thrown him off-guard.
She twisted down her smirk of triumph as his gaze once again
slid to Wolf.

"An alliance with The Woodlands? After all this time?"

Wolf nodded. "Serce cannot lose her crown. I won't let it
happen."

Her heart swelled at the raw passion in his voice. If they
hadn't been sitting here with somewhat polite company, they'd
already be fucking like animals on the floor. As if hearing her
thoughts, Wolf threw her a feral smile with a promise in his
eyes. Gooseflesh erupted over her skin. She had never thought
it was possible to feel this way about anyone.

"And what would an alliance mean?" Rion asked, once again
turning his dark swirling gaze to Serce.

"The Woodlands armies, of course."

"Your armies are less than half the size of mine," Rion said,
addressing Wolf now. "That's no incentive."

"Help me get the Crown from my mother," Serce said, and
Rion sat up.

"And how should I do that?" Rion asked, an eyebrow raised.

"Let's not play games, Your Majesty." The words hung in the
air between them. An accusation. A gauntlet set ablaze and
slapped down on a field of dead grass.

There were plenty of rumors about how the previous Aurora
King had been forced to descend into the Evanescence, though

it was never spoken of out loud. To even suggest such a thing was the height of taboo. But if anyone knew how to make it happen, Serce had a hunch it was the ruthless Imperial Fae seated before her.

Rion said nothing to that, only tipping his head and waiting for whatever she could offer him next.

Serce then took a deep breath, forging on, knowing that what she was about to say next would cross a bridge that would crumble to dust behind her, never to be resurrected. "And then you'll have the armies of Heart at your disposal, as well. We'll help you take over the rest of Ouranos. Together, we'd be unstoppable. You know it's true."

As her voice fell silent, the fuse she had just lit crackled between them.

"You would do that? Give Ouranos to me?"

"As long as you leave Heart and The Woodlands to us," she said quickly. "They belong to us and us alone."

"Why?"

"Because I want my crown, and I will do anything to get it." She said it simply, knowing that a male like Rion would understand this raw call to power for power's sake alone.

Rion rubbed his chin, considering her offer.

"That seems fair enough," he said slowly, as if testing the words and deciding if he really meant them. "I'll consider it."

Serce dipped her head. "That's all I ask," she said, feigning subservience, hoping to appeal to his ego.

A shrewd look narrowed his gaze as he studied her and then Wolf, who was still bouncing the baby on his knee as it cooed and gurgled.

"As you think on it, please remain as our guests for a few days," Wolf said. "The Sage Pear Grove is spectacular at this time of year, and I'd love to take you for a tour."

Rion stood, buttoning up his jacket and tipping his chin. Meora followed his lead and crossed the space, taking the baby from Wolf and hitching him to her hip.

"Thank you," Serce said, approaching Rion, who gave her another once-over.

"We'll talk again, Serce. It's clear we have similar interests. Perhaps there are many things we can do together."

She nodded with a strained smile. She didn't trust him for a moment, but she needed him to consider her proposal and, hopefully, agree. For now, she would pretend they had aligned interests.

Because Serce wasn't to be trusted, either.

"Do you think he'll say yes?" she asked Wolf as they retired to his bedchamber later that evening. Rion and Meora had declined to join them for dinner, claiming they were tired from travel and that they would see Wolf and Serce tomorrow.

A relief, really. They had called off the planned formal affair and had instead eaten a casual supper in the same sitting room where they'd received the Aurora King and Queen earlier.

"I think he will," Wolf said. "You've offered him more than half of Ouranos. His own ambition has always blinded him and he won't turn that chance down. He just wants to let you stew a bit."

Wolf dropped on the brown leather sofa that sat under a large window and pulled Serce onto his lap.

"You seemed quite taken with the baby," she said carefully, as his arms wrapped around her.

"I love children. You know that."

She swallowed and nodded. "I do. You've never said you wanted children. With me, I mean."

Wolf grinned, his beautiful face transforming and his deep green eyes sparkling.

"Serce, you are the only woman I have met in this life or any life who I'd want to have children with. You're mine now and forever. I only worried it was too early to say such things, and you haven't shown much interest in a child."

She looped her arms around his neck. "Perhaps I could be persuaded. The boy was rather...cute." She wrinkled her nose, and Wolf barked out a hearty laugh. He cupped the back of her neck, and bent her down for a kiss.

"Do you have any idea how beautiful you are?" he asked, and she smiled.

"Do you have any idea how sexy it was watching you care for that child? There was something so...paternal about you."

She ground her hips into his lap, and he groaned as his hand clamped down on her waist.

"If I'd known that, I would've invited every child in the kingdom to visit."

She snorted out a laugh. "Don't you dare."

He chuckled before he kissed her again.

"We'll need to send for the High Priestess soon," she said next, starting to pull at the laces of his shirt, exposing a taut sliver of his bronzed skin. She slid her hands under the fabric, savoring the hard and unyielding flesh of his refined body.

"I'll send a messenger first thing in the morning," he replied, nuzzling her throat, his hand sliding into the slit in her robe, where he found her bare skin. "What exactly did she tell you in her letter?"

"She said it's possible for two Primaries to join their Artefacts, though it's never been done in living memory as far as she was aware. But she recalled reading about it in the Book of Night. She promised to look for the reference, and then hopefully the details on how we might accomplish it."

His hand slid higher, tugging open the tie holding her robe together, the silken fabric revealing the scraps of her lacy underwear. Wolf made a low sound in his throat as he licked her neck and slid his hand along her stomach.

"And then what?" he asked, nipping the space behind her ear. She gasped as his hand slid lower, teasing the inside of her thigh.

"And then our magic will join, similar to when a Primary bonds to a High Fae or a human, but she believes bonding two Primaries will have a tenfold effect on our magic."

Wolf slipped his hand between her legs, teasing her through the already soaked fabric of her underwear. She parted her legs and tilted her hips as he pushed aside the silk and slipped his thick finger through her wetness.

"What else, Serce?" His voice was husky, the tone rough.

"Then you and I will become the two most powerful rulers in Ouranos." His finger pushed inside her and she cried out as his thumb circled her clit. "And...we'll...crush Rion. And conquer...every...corner...of...the...continent."

Her words came out clipped as Wolf used his other hand to pull at the lace covering her breasts and sucked on a nipple, his tongue teasing it before he bit down with a sharp flash of pain that made her whimper.

He continued to pump his hand in and out of her, and she rode it with abandon, seeking her release that wound tighter and tighter.

"*You* will be the most powerful, Serce," he said, his words low and dangerous. "And I will stand beside you—my queen, my heart, my *mate*—and help you take it all."

CHAPTER TWENTY-ONE

LOR

PRESENT DAY: THE AURORA

Even the dim absence of light in The Aurora is an assault on my senses as my eyes crack open the next morning. A whiff of food turns my stomach, and I squeeze my eyes closed, willing my nausea to settle. I hear the clink of utensils and the sound of liquid being poured into a cup.

A warm body presses against me, and I reach for it, realizing it's covered with thick, soft fur. One of the prince's ice hounds—I can't tell which one—lifts her head and looks at me before lying back down and closing her eyes. Should I be worried she's about to bite off my face? She seems to be half asleep, though.

A moment later, a shadow falls over me, and Nadir stands there, looking down with a white mug cradled in his hand. "How are you feeling, Inmate?" There's an amused gleam in his eyes and a smug smile on his face that I want to slap right off. Except I'm not sure I can do so without puking all over him. "You made quite the spectacle of yourself last night."

I narrow my gaze and then wince, because holy shit, even that hurts right now. Thinking of last night, I remember the way he held my hair back and then carried me to bed. There isn't a single drop of that tenderness left in his demeanor. Did I imagine him doing all that? Maybe it was a drunken haze and just another dream. But I ended up in this bed somehow.

"I want to die," I say, rubbing my temple, trying to coax out a sliver of relief. Nadir's chuckle borders on evil as he takes a sip of his coffee. Slowly, so slowly, I sit up, the entire room rolling. The second ice hound is snuggled at my feet, and I wonder why the change of heart when I was sure they both wanted to eat me.

But I'm in too much pain to really care.

Groaning, I slide my legs to the floor, putting my head between my knees as I fight down another wave of dizziness.

"These should help," Nadir says, picking up a bottle from the nightstand and handing it to me. It's filled with small white pills. "Take two and come and have breakfast. We have a lot of ground to cover today."

"What happened to 'if I was in any state to do so?'" I ask, recalling some of his words from last night.

"You do the crime, then you suffer the punishment."

"Do you have that motto tattooed on your ass?" I ask, tipping two pills into my hand and snapping the lid back on the bottle. We both know I'm talking about Nostraza, but he doesn't seem affected by my question. He sinks into his seat and then tears into a strip of bacon.

"Thinking about my ass, Inmate?"

I gag on the bile that climbs up my throat and turn away, incensed at his attitude and wildly disappointed I *did* imagine those gentle but vengeful words he uttered last night. I swallow the pills, followed by the entire glass of water standing on the nightstand, and sit with my eyes closed for several minutes, focusing on the currently staggering effort of not throwing up.

The pills take effect quickly, dulling the throb in my head and settling the roil in my stomach. When I feel somewhat normal again, I let out a sigh of relief and ease myself up. The dogs finally rouse from their positions and jump to the floor before they pad over to their bowls to eat their own breakfasts.

After looking across the large bed, I frown.

"Where did you sleep last night?" I turn to Nadir, who is now watching me from under a pair of thick, dark lashes.

"In my bed."

"But I was in your bed."

"I am aware of that," he says with disdain. "It was hard to miss the smell of your vomit all night." He pauses with his fork poised in midair and wrinkles his nose before adding, "And right now."

I look down at myself, smoothing my rumpled tunic and wincing at the crusty evidence of his words. "Sorry," I say, realizing he let me sleep in his bed like this. I should be thanking him.

"And don't worry," he adds next, "there was nothing I was remotely interested in." He waves a hand as if to suggest my complete and total lack of desirability before he resumes eating.

"You remind me of Gabriel," I mumble under my breath, finally standing up and walking over to pick up a dry piece of toast to nibble on the corner.

"What was that?"

"Nothing. Just someone else who knew the right way to flatter me."

Nadir smirks and sips his coffee, his eyes never leaving me. I sit in the seat across from him, heaping sliced plums on my plate.

"We'll search in the east wing today. It's near my father's apartments. If he has it there, then maybe you'll feel it if we're close enough. I'd prefer not to enter his study or bedroom unless we're absolutely sure we need to," Nadir says next. "Though we'll still want to keep you out of sight. It's one thing for me to be wandering in the east wing, but another to bring my pet there."

I ignore the pet comment, knowing he's just trying to get under my skin. I'm too tired and hungover to be a pain in his ass right now. Instead, I nod in agreement and take another bite of my toast. My stomach gurgles angrily, but I force it down, knowing I'll be lightheaded if I don't get something in.

"Coffee?" he asks, holding up the carafe. I nod and hold out my cup before he fills it. After I add a generous amount of cream,

I take a deep sip and sigh as the caffeine perks up my sagging corners.

"I'm still worried I won't be able to sense it," I say, voicing the concern that's been on my mind since we hatched this tenuous plan.

Nadir regards me carefully. "It is a possibility, but we won't know for sure unless we try. Being unable to access it doesn't negate its existence. While I can't be one hundred percent certain, I'm confident you'll still be able to feel it."

I let out a frustrated huff.

"You've been trying to unlock it?"

"Yes," I say. "I'm trying." Even as I think about it, I go inside myself, reaching for that place I can't pull apart. It's like teasing a loose thread that's too small to grasp with your fingers, constantly slipping from your grip.

"May I?" Nadir asks.

"May you what?"

"Use my own magic to see if I can help. If you're the Primary, it should be strong enough for me to touch it."

I don't hesitate at the offer. I want to figure this out so badly I can taste it. I want to be free of this cage. None of my goals or dreams are possible as long as I'm trapped this way. "Yes. Please."

Nadir sends out a tendril of translucent violet light. It circles around my shoulders, and I watch it like it's a snake poised for attack. Maybe I shouldn't have agreed to this after all, but if he really wanted to kill me, he could have done so many times already. My eyes track the ribbon of light wrapping around my torso, and my own magic responds, soothed by his presence.

It rolls in soft gentle waves, thrumming under my skin with languid grace like frigid syrup.

"Neat trick," I say as more ribbons of light surround me. "What else can you do with this?"

His expression turns sly. "All kinds of interesting things, Inmate. Things that would make your toes curl."

There is a definite hint of suggestion in his words and when I realize what he means, my lips part and then snap shut.

"You're a pig."

His laughter is low as his magic twirls around me tighter and sinks into my skin like water absorbing into parched sand, followed by another sensation, something closer and deeper to my heart. I gasp before it strengthens and tightens against my organs.

"Can you lead me to where you feel the block?" Nadir asks, all business now.

"How?"

"You can feel my magic in you?" I nod with a shiver. "Close your eyes and imagine you're holding on to it, like a piece of ribbon or string. Pull on it."

I do as he asks, and the softness of his light twists through me, entwining with the power trapped under my skin. The two threads of magic slide together and suddenly I'm seized with flutters of slippery wet heat, and my mouth parts as my thighs clench together. I clear my throat, trying to recover my focus as the sensation roots deep into my core, winding tighter as I try to lead his magic to the trapdoor right in the center of my chest.

When I think I've directed him to the proper location, I open my eyes to find him staring at me with such a sense of open rawness, my breath hitches. This feels so wildly intimate. It's like I've stripped naked and draped myself over the table for his perusal. His magic twists inside my chest and then I feel it trying to pry at that locked gate that refuses to budge.

He spends a few minutes doing all the same things I've tried over and over, to no avail. His face is a mask of concentration as he focuses on the task, and I take this moment of quiet to watch him, tracing the lines of his nose and jaw and cheekbones. He's really quite beautiful, in a cold and savage sort of way. When he's not snarling at me, anyway. One might not call him handsome in the traditional sense, but there's something far more magnetic about him than could ever be captured with such banal sentiments.

As if sensing my careful perusal, his eyes flick to mine and our gazes hold as I feel his magic pull away from the center of my chest and then slide through my limbs, spiraling through my arms and legs like our two halves are dancing to a lilting tune only we can hear.

We're both caught in a trance, our breaths the only sounds in the room. But I've never felt more at peace than I do right now. I've never felt so comfortable in my own body. There's a disconcerting sense that I've found something I've lost. Like I've come home.

I blink and look away, severing the connection, trying to dispel this strange rush. This feels too much like a complication I can't afford right now. Clearing my throat, I push my chair back a few inches, as though that will make the slightest bit of difference.

"See? Locked tighter than an underwater vault." My voice is raw and shaky, and I wish I understood why he's affecting me this way.

Nadir says nothing for a moment, the colors in his eyes swirling faster than normal. "I see," he finally says and then he sits back, shredding the last thread holding the tension in the room together. "We might be able to work on it."

I swallow and nod, thinking about doing that with him again. Whatever *that* was. I might be in way over my head here.

After two more pieces of toast, a strip of bacon, and a mountain of plums, I'm feeling much better. The pills are mostly working, leaving only a small throb in my temple I can manage.

Nadir waits for me to shower and get dressed. I move quickly, though he doesn't seem impatient. I feel his gaze as I go about the room and, for some reason, I can't seem to make my limbs work properly. I keep dropping things and fumbling everything I try to pick up. His presence is a constant force pushing in on me. Thank Zerra I was completely passed out last night. I shudder to think of the dreams I might have had with him lying right next to me had I been coherent.

After finding a clean pair of leggings and a fitted black top with sleeves that fall past my wrists with loops for my thumbs, I stuff my feet into a pair of soft black boots. My hair is still damp from the shower, so I leave it down, but I clip in some of the fake colorful hair pieces Amya provided. They look just like the ones in her hair, though I think hers might be natural. I wonder if the people of The Aurora buy these imitations to look like their princess. I'm not sure why that thought makes me smile.

"Okay, I'm ready," I declare, feeling much better than I did an hour ago.

Nadir is giving me an odd look with his mouth flattened into a line.

"What?" I ask, looking down at myself. Have I been found wanting yet again?

His nostrils flare, and then he looks away. "Nothing. Let's go."

We exit the room and he leads me through the winding hallways. We come to a halt just as we're about to turn a corner. "There will be guards stationed at the entrance. It would be better for them not to see you. I can shield you for a short time. They won't notice you as we pass through, but you'll need to stay close."

"It won't be like what we did...in there?" I gesture vaguely in the direction we just came, both terrified and thrilled at the idea of his magic touching mine again.

"No," he replies, shaking his head. "This won't be like...that."

"Okay."

"Put your arms around my waist. The more of you touching me, the better."

I raise an eyebrow at that, but don't comment as I obey his request.

"Good girl," he says and then gives me a surprised look, as though he hadn't meant to say that. The words feel foreign and yet familiar in a way I can't quite place. But I reason it's a step up from "Inmate."

After another moment, the swirl of his magic blooms around me in ribbons of bright light. It's so beautiful I'm caught up in the way it moves like streamers waving in the breeze. They pull in, wrapping around me, and then sink into the weave of my clothing.

Nothing else seems different as I look around, but Nadir ushers me forward confidently now. I shuffle along, trying not to make any noise as I cling to his waist, feeling rather foolish and trying not to let my hands wander along the taut planes of his stomach and chest.

He nods to the two guards flanking both sides of a large archway. They're both low fae, with pale green skin, wearing the black soldier's uniform of The Aurora. One of them is bald with large pointed ears, and the other has a thin line of black hair running down the center of his skull.

"Your Highness," the hairless one says, his tone deferential. "What is your business in the east wing?"

"I'm headed to the library," Nadir says before handing a piece of paper over to the guards. The guard frowns at it and scratches a spot on his cheek before he hands it to the other one. I look up at Nadir, who's pretending I'm not there. Just the prince out for a visit to the library all on his own while I hang invisibly off him. This is so awkward.

They exchange a few more words, and the guards reluctantly stand aside. I don't know why I'm surprised the king wouldn't even let his own son anywhere near his rooms, but I shouldn't be. It seems he treats everyone with the same level of disdain.

We breeze past the low fae and enter a wide, quiet hallway. Nadir directs me into an alcove and then pulls his magic back, the same ribbons of color spreading out and then dissipating in the air.

"Keep an eye out for more guards," Nadir says. "I can only hold the glamour for so long at a time and we might have to do that again if anyone approaches. It takes a few seconds for it to fully render, so we may not get enough notice. In that case, hide yourself as quickly as you can."

Not waiting for me to reply, he grabs my hand and pulls me down an empty hallway. I try not to acknowledge the warmth of his hand and the sick little thrill I get when he squeezes it. That thing we did with our magic earlier has thrown me off, making me react in unwelcome ways. I hate this asshole.

Nadir leads me through several hallways and into numerous rooms that all blur together. We stand in each of them, waiting for something to trigger, but it's an empty stretch of nothing. With every room we check off, I grow more and more dejected.

What if the Crown isn't even here? What if it's hidden somewhere else in Ouranos? We could be searching forever. Even worse, what if it doesn't exist anymore?

I clutch the locket around my neck and squeeze it, thinking of the tiny shard of red stone nestled inside. This came from somewhere, though, and that Crown has to exist.

Everything depends on it.

As we snake through hallways, we encounter the occasional guard or maid or servant, but manage to avoid their attention. It seems Nadir has plenty of practice making his way around the Keep without being noticed. Would anyone be foolish enough to challenge the king within these walls, anyway? Maybe not. But I will. I don't care what happens to me. I will take him apart bit by excruciating bit as soon as I get the chance.

We turn another corner, and Nadir quickly backs up, bumping into me and stepping on my foot.

"Ow!"

"Shut up," he hisses, pushing me back.

"What—"

A deep voice floats from around the corner and I seize up. I know that voice like I know my own heartbeat. I hear it in my nightmares and the swirling void of my very worst memories.

Nadir spins around and scans the space as the king and whoever he's speaking with move closer. Nadir drags me towards a narrow door and shoves me inside. He slams it shut, engulfing us in complete darkness. The space is so tight that my back is crushed to the wall and Nadir is pressed at my front. I can barely move.

He covers my mouth with a hand, and I shake my head, but he doesn't relent, pressing harder. I go still as I hear the king's voice again. He seems to have stopped and is now conversing right outside, the door muffling his words. All I know is the king is just a few feet away, and I have no idea what he'd do if he caught us here.

Nadir drops his hand, satisfied that I appreciate the need to be quiet. We both wait in tense silence as I try to control my breathing and my pounding heart. A small light flares, illuminating the outlines of Nadir's face thanks to the dim aura that surrounds him.

He's leaning on his forearms against the wall, caging me in. In another reminder, he presses a finger to his lips, and I nod, my hair rustling against the wall behind me.

The voices outside continue as I become increasingly conscious of the prince's body flattened against me. Heat prickles up the back of my neck and my cheeks warm as he looks down, the strong lines of his face arranged into a mask of intensity.

I'm not sure if I imagine the way he leans in even closer, but my skin is buzzing in every place he's touching. Even fully clothed, the sensation is so heady it's like we're completely naked.

No, not *quite* that. I have a feeling that would feel very different.

My dream from two nights earlier surfaces, and the space between my thighs gives a noticeable throb. What would it be like to be taken by this wild and fearsome prince? Atlas had been enthusiastic, but gentle. Something tells me there's no place in his life where Nadir feels the need to be gentle about anything.

My breath becomes tighter. The space feels smaller and smaller as the thrum pounding low in my stomach takes up all the room in the closet. Eventually, the voices outside start to dissipate, dropping away as the sound of their footsteps retreat into the distance. When it seems like they're gone, neither one of us moves.

Nadir's face is so close to mine I can feel the softness of his breath against my lips. I want to inhale his crisp arctic smell and lose myself in it. His face moves closer, and my entire world shrinks down to this moment and the prince. The feel of his strong body against mine and the way his arms are caging me in. His mouth looks good enough to eat, and I want him to devour me whole.

"Lor," he whispers. His voice is soft, but there's something as jagged as torn iron buried in that single syllable. He said my name. My actual name and I've never loved the sound of it more than I do at this moment. That simple, nothing name that was given to me to keep me as anonymous and unremarkable as possible. Somehow, he makes it sound like it's a name forged in fire and created for a queen.

"Nadir," I whisper back, wanting to feel his name on my tongue, too. To feel those clipped parts I've wondered about ever since I heard it. Why did his parents choose to mark him with a word that means rock bottom?

He's holding so still, it's like he's made of glass, and I'm so hot I want to explode into a million shards. Then he drops his head and runs his nose along the curve of my throat, taking a long, luxurious inhale as my head tips to the side. I grip the wall behind me, worried I'm about to collapse under the weight of my desire.

Slowly, he drags it up until he comes to the sensitive spot right behind my ear and lets out a ragged breath that envelops me from every side. I don't move, not entirely sure where I want this to go. Rationally, I regard him as one step down from his father. He's the son of my enemy. But physically, I can't stop reacting to him in a way that leaves me nearly shattered and breathless with wanting.

I feel the nip of his teeth against my skin and then the crawl of his warm mouth as he makes his way back down the column of my throat. My hips move of their own accord, arching into his and he responds, grinding his body against me. The rock-hard evidence of how this is affecting him sends a whole new wave of ripples down my spine.

He pulls his head up and meets my eyes, those swirling colors visible in the closet's dimness. There is so much written in the way they move I can't believe I've never realized how tied to his emotions those lights are. There's conflict in them. And a desire so visceral, my core melts into liquid heat.

But then a second later, they go dim, turning into a midnight sky, his fists clenching against the wall before he looks away with such force it's like he's breaking out of concrete.

"Let's go," he says, his voice rough. "We need to get out of here before my father finds us."

"What?" I ask, bewildered at his sudden shift in mood.

He pulls away and wraps me in his glamour. This time he doesn't invite me to touch him, and I wonder if I've done something wrong. Then he opens the door before slipping out and gesturing for me to come along.

I do as he says, following in his hurried footsteps, confused about what's just happened.

CHAPTER TWENTY-TWO

"**S**o, what exactly did my grandmother do? How did she cut off everyone's magic?" I ask, flipping through the book in my lap. I've spent the last two days combing through Nadir's library, delving further into the history of my grandmother, trying to seal up the gaps in my education.

Was it because my parents didn't know the truth or because they were keeping things from me? I hope it was because of ignorance and not because they wanted to hide it. I'd have a hard time understanding how they could leave me to face everything without giving me this knowledge I need so desperately. They had to know I might end up on my own someday.

Nadir looks up from the book he's reading, seated on the sofa across from me. We're in his room, the incident in the closet sitting between us like a boulder. Neither of us has acknowledged it with words, but it's been hanging there in every look and accidental touch since then. At night, when we lie on opposite sides of that big bed, you could practically scoop the tension up with a shovel. I'm just grateful I haven't had more dirty dreams because then I wouldn't be able to look at him ever again.

As we dance around the elephant in the room, we've spent two more days combing the Keep, but we've only come upon silent dead ends.

"No one really knows," Nadir replies, closing his book and leaning back before he crosses an ankle over his knee. His dark hair is loose and inexplicably wind-tossed, even though I'm sure he hasn't left the Keep all day. "When your grandparents tried to take over Ouranos, rumor suggests they were working with one of Zerra's High Priestesses, but they all died before anyone could figure out how or why. There's no one left alive who was there at the end. The main clue that suggests they were working with powerful magic was the Woodlands Staff was found amongst the wreckage, miraculously unharmed."

"Just the Staff?" I ask. "Not the Crown?"

"Just the Staff."

I flip the page and then back again.

"How exactly does High Fae magic work? What does Imperial magic mean?"

Nadir sits forward, bracing his elbows on his knees. "There are two types of High Fae power," he says. "There's the regular line of magic that can belong to any Fae. Some have it and some don't, and some have it both in varying degrees of strength and affinity."

"I'm not sure I understand."

"It's like a human who is a gifted painter. They may have training from a teacher, but ultimately, some will be better at it than others, no matter what. And that same Fae might have a terrible singing voice. It's the same with magic."

"There was a hair stylist I met who said he was adept at beauty magic."

"There's an example," Nadir replies. "That was his affinity and likely a skill he's cultivated."

"And Imperial magic?"

"That is the magic sourced from every realm. It is the lifeblood and the thread that holds the land and its people together. When the magic disappeared, we all felt it. The earth began to crumble, lakes and rivers drying up, sickness plaguing the animals, humans, and Fae. Some areas of Ouranos still haven't recovered. Imperial magic is strongest in anyone who belongs the royal family, particularly those of the direct line."

"Like you and Amya."

"Yes. Or you and your siblings."

"But they don't have much."

He nods. "I've considered that. I've been wondering if it's a side effect of the same affliction that cursed everyone's magic."

"So you think they could have more?"

"Perhaps."

I reflect on those words, wondering how Tristan and Willow would feel about that. They've never suggested they resent their lack of power, but I can't help but think about how they could better protect themselves if they were stronger.

"Did the Mirror reveal anything to you at all about your magic?" Nadir asks, and I shake my head, being truthful this time.

"It told me this was forbidden." I'm not sure why I decide to reveal this now, but the words have been weighing heavy on my conscience. Were they related to my grandmother, too?

Nadir arches an eyebrow. "What was?"

"I don't know. It said this could never happen again, and I could only assume it meant the bonding between me and Atlas. Do you know why?"

Nadir shakes his head before a thoughtful expression crosses his face. "It's odd."

"What is?"

"I've never heard of anyone who isn't ascended speaking with the Artefacts like that."

It's my turn to arch my brow. "You haven't?"

He shakes his head. I open my mouth to protest, but he silences me with the wave of his hand. "I'm not saying I don't believe you. Just that it's peculiar."

I slump back against the sofa. "I can't believe my grandmother allied with your father," I mutter, flipping another page angrily. Nadir's dark chuckle has me looking his way.

"It seems history is repeating itself. Does that bother you, Inmate?"

"Yes," I snap, turning back to the book.

"Well, don't worry. It was his word against a dead queen. I'm sure there's more to the story than he ever let on. Anything he said was undoubtedly manipulated to make him look like the hero."

Silence fills the room with a weighted tension, and I look back at Nadir, who's studying me carefully. "What?"

He leans forward, uncrossing his legs and bracing his elbows on his knees. "What did he do to you? I know he's responsible for your parents' deaths—"

"He murdered them," I interrupt. "In cold blood."

Nadir drops his head and then looks up. "Yes, he murdered them. But that doesn't entirely explain the haunted look in your eyes every time I mention him. What else happened?" He cants his head, and it feels like he's looking straight into my soul where the rotting carcass of my secrets lie.

"Nothing," I say.

"I don't believe you."

I glare at him, pressing my lips together. "Too bad."

"Are we going to talk about what happened in the closet?" I ask and wince. I wanted to change the subject, but this topic is mired in just as many pitfalls as the previous one.

Nadir's jaw clenches and his shoulders tighten. "Happened?"

My gaze flicks upward in irritation.

"Don't fucking pretend you don't know what I'm talking about." Pushing myself up from the sofa, I slap the book on the cushion and storm to the window. There's nowhere for me to go in this place, and I'm going crazy, always trapped here in this room with him.

A moment later, I sense his presence behind me. His hands plant themselves on the glass on either side of my head. He's leaning so close that I go completely still.

"What are you doing?"

"Let's talk about what *happened*, Inmate."

"Don't call me that," I hiss, looking over my shoulder at his smirk. I want to punch that face, but I also really want something else. *I think.* I shake my head. *Fuck.*

"Let's talk about how you pressed yourself against me. I could smell how wet you were in that closet."

I fold my arms tighter, letting out an indignant sound and refusing to look at him. "I did no such thing. You pressed yourself against me." We've both moved closer, only the barest whisper of space between us. "Just like you're doing right now."

He pushes in closer, and I don't resist. I don't move away. Instead, I lean into him, enjoying the way he feels against me far too much. "So you don't deny how wet you were?"

"I felt you, too," I say. "I wasn't the only one affected in there."

"You weren't." His voice drops to a rasp and his lips brush against my ear. "I feel it every time you're in the room. You make me so fucking hard I can't think straight. I've jerked off in the shower every day, thinking about you. Thinking about how much you hate me."

My breath lodges in my chest like wet sand.

Oh Zerra, what is going on here?

I should walk away right now. I should nail this asshole in the balls.

"I *do* hate you," I say, more breathlessly than I intend.

He drops a hand from the window and picks up a thick lock of my hair, pressing it to his nose and inhaling with a groan. I should be appalled by that—I'm not some beast to be sniffed. But I'm not. Zerra, why is that making my cheeks burn?

"I hate everything about you and your wretched family and this horrible place. Once I leave here, it'll be too soon if I ever see The Aurora again."

"I know that. *And* you hate how much you want me." He presses in closer so his body is now flush with mine and every curve and arc of his hard frame is shredding my paper-thin resolve.

"You're delusional," I say, hoping my lie isn't as transparent as it feels. "I want nothing to do with you. I'm only here to get my Crown."

His chuckle is low and dark. He drops my hair and then his hand slides across my stomach before he yanks me towards him, my ass meeting the hard length of his cock. I almost allow a groan to slip from my mouth as he rotates our hips together in a listless circle.

"I know that, too, Inmate. That doesn't stop me from wanting to strip off these clothes and fuck you so hard the bed collapses."

"I... You... This is highly inappropriate." I will myself to pull from his grasp, but I can't seem to make myself move.

"Spend one night with me. I'll break you into pieces. I'll fuck your mouth and your pussy with my tongue and my cock and my fingers and make you come so many times you lose count. I'll make you beg for it again and again."

My legs press together, and I attempt to swallow the thick knot caught in my throat. My nerves are firing with heat and the longing to let him do every single one of those things.

"I had a dream about you," I say, wondering why the fuck I'm telling him this. He goes still.

"What happened?"

I hesitate before his grip against my stomach tightens.

"Tell me."

"It was in the manor house. You came into my room and laid on top of me and..."

He lets out a whoosh of air, snipped into ragged pieces. "I had the same dream."

Something foreign but distantly familiar flutters in my chest.

"It felt...so real," I say softly, staring at the expanse of sky outside where night is descending, the barest whisper of the northern lights appearing.

"It did," he agrees, his slow movements starting up again. He slides a hand under my sweater, his palm resting on my stomach, scorching a line of heat that radiates out through my limbs. "It felt *so* real."

Somehow, he manages to move even closer. Like he wants to pull me right inside.

"Say yes," he says. "One night. One long, endless night where I promise you more pleasure than you ever thought possible."

My mouth opens and then closes. A pathetic part of me wants to say yes, but I nearly fell for one royal Fae who was only after one thing.

"How can I trust you?" I hate how small and uncertain I sound. Atlas didn't break my heart—I know now that I didn't love him—but he broke something. For one fleeting moment, I'd believed someone had wanted me for me, but I'd been so blind and foolish. I should have learned the only people in this world I can trust are Willow and Tristan.

"This isn't about anything but fucking," he says, and I should be appalled by *that*, too, but something about his bold honesty kindles a fire low in my stomach. "This isn't about anything more than skin and heat and my cock driving into you until your mind turns to jelly."

I spin around and back up. The cold window presses against my back and Nadir shifts another inch, his heat boiling my skin.

"I....don't think that would be a good idea."

There is not one believable shred in the tone of my voice, and he smiles.

It's not a warm smile. It's slow and seductive and hooks between my legs with a stubbornness I'm trying to resist. No, it's definitely not warm, because it practically lights me on fire.

"Think about it," he says. "Don't say no, yet."

I shake my head, but it feels like I'm moving through cold tree sap. It's so hard to find the momentum to refuse him outright. "I can't."

"Why not?"

"I don't know."

The corner of his mouth ticks up. "Promise me you'll consider it."

I find myself nodding before I know what I'm doing. I'm *already* considering it, but this would be a terrible mistake. He leans in closer and I push back against the unyielding glass. He's not touching me, but all it would take is a deep breath to bridge the distance.

His head drops next to my ear with a gentle brush of lips. "Understand I'll be ready at any moment you're ready to say yes."

Finally, I force my sluggish limbs to respond, my knees bending to slip under his arm that's caging me against the glass.

"That isn't going to happen," I say, trying to sound confident, but it comes out shaky and not even I believe it.

Nadir turns, folding his arms over his chest and tipping his head. "We'll see about that, Inmate."

"Yah," is the most articulate response I can summon as I spin around and bolt for the bathroom. It has a lock on the door, and it's the only place I can run.

CHAPTER TWENTY-THREE

NADIR

I crouch down in front of the female, who stares out the window, her dark eyes blank and devoid of emotion or consciousness.

"Mother," I say softly, laying my hand on hers. Her skin is cold and dry. Thin, like old parchment that would rip with the slightest bit of pressure. I can't remember the last time she's been outside, and I'm long past hoping she'll ever do so again.

"How are you?"

I don't know why I always ask. I never get an answer. Sometimes she'll blink in response. If she's having a good day, I might note the pressing of her lips and the briefest flicker of awareness in her expression. But never anything more. Still, I try, hoping that if I keep asking, she knows I'm here for her and that I forgive her for everything.

Amya perches on the bed, one arm wrapped around the bedpost with her temple tipped against it. Her eyes are dark and flat as she watches me.

"Do you want to talk to her?" I ask my sister.

She shakes her head, leaning away. "Not today."

"You never want to."

Amya stands up and walks around to the other side of the bed. "Because I don't know what to say."

"Tell her about yourself."

"She's not listening, Nadir."

"You don't know that."

Amya scrunches her eyes together and rubs her face with both her hands. "I don't want to fight about this, okay? I come to see her when I can, but I never knew her, Nadir."

I stand up and kiss my mother on her brow before I smooth down her black hair. She's beautiful—Amya looks so much like her—but she's a shell of the mother I once knew.

"I'll be back tomorrow," I promise, just like I do every day, and I try to keep it as often as I can.

Then I whirl on Amya.

"She's still your mother," I growl, pushing her out of the room and closing the door softly behind me.

"I know! You think I don't know? I want to love her, but I never got the chance. How am I supposed to feel anything when this is the only way I've ever known her?"

Tears fill her eyes, and my anger softens. She's right. It isn't her fault. Amya never experienced her light and kindness, so why should she feel the same way I do?

"I'm sorry," I reply. "I just get so—"

"I know," she says softly, taking my hand. "I know."

We leave my mother's wing and head through the Keep, making our way towards Amya's rooms.

"Have you received any news from Aphelion?" I ask as we enter her bedroom. It resembles mine in shape and size, but it's far more colorful. Crimson, violet, teal, and fuchsia are splashed through the sheets, furniture, rugs, and pillows.

"Atlas is looking for her," she says as she heads for her dressing table while I pace the length of the room, running a hand through my hair. "He's been sending out secret search parties to every realm."

"Does he suspect us?"

She shakes her head, looking at me through the mirror as she runs a brush through her hair. "I'm not sure. Either he knows and is assuming we wouldn't hide her in the most obvious spot, or he's hedging his bets and investigating every ruler. If he found out her secret, it's entirely possible others know, too."

"That's information we need," I say, and she nods.

"I know. My people are doing what they can."

"Good." I turn and pace in the other direction, considering everything Amya just said, wondering how Atlas knew who Lor was and what he specifically planned to do with her. I've known Atlas a long time, and I've never gotten the sense he's capable of such ruthlessness, but maybe I've read him all wrong.

Amya continues, still facing the mirror as she lines her eyes with a black pencil. "Rumors are saying he's refusing to set a date for the bonding ceremony with the winner of the Trials."

I say nothing to that, thoughts running through my head.

"What else is bothering you?" she asks, coating her lips with a thick smear of deep purple lipstick.

"Nothing," I say too quickly. What *is* the matter, exactly? There are so many things crowding for my attention, I can't decide which is the most aggravating.

Lor. That's what's most aggravating. The way I can't get her out of my head and the way she keeps looking at me, like I'm going to bite out a piece of her. I want to. Zerra, how I want to sink my teeth into her warm flesh. I shouldn't have said those things in my room. I should have kept on pretending she had no effect on me, but that's never been my style. But now she's acting like a frightened rabbit, and I worry I've pushed her away.

Clicking the cap back onto the golden tube, Amya places it on her vanity and spins around. "Sure. Sounds believable."

I glare at her and pace to the other end of the room.

"Any luck with the Crown yet?"

"No," I say, dropping into a plush violet armchair arranged around a low coffee table near the foot of her bed. "We searched the vaults, and most of the east and west wings, but she says she feels nothing. I'm worried that whatever is blocking her ability to touch her magic is preventing her from sensing it."

"Or it's just not here."

Amya sits across from me. She's wearing a short dress made of frothy layers of tulle, her legs bare and her feet adorned with a pair of black heels that lace up her calves.

"Or it's just not here," I agree, not willing to accept that fact. "And if that's the case, then it could be literally anywhere in Ouranos."

Amya nods, picking up the bottle of wine on the table next to her and pouring herself a glass of the blood red liquid. She takes a sip and then presses her lips together.

"But you have some idea."

"Am I that obvious?"

"Only to me, big brother."

I smirk and lean back in my chair. "If it's not here, then wouldn't it make sense that it's closest to where it was last seen?"

Amya blinks at that. "You'd take her into Heart?"

"If I have to."

"That area has already been searched thoroughly. Many times. For years."

"But none of them had the Primary," I counter, and her shoulders slump.

"Nadir...what are you planning? If you find it there, you might not be able to control her."

I scoff. "I'm not worried about that."

"Why not?"

"She may be strong, but she has no idea how to use her magic, and she isn't bonded yet. Besides, I'm sure I'm stronger."

Amya tips her head. "How can you be so positive of that?"

I arch an eyebrow at her, and she rolls her eyes. "Oh, to have the confidence of a male born to privilege."

I shake my head, leaning forward and clasping my hands between my knees. "I don't think she *needs* controlling. She wants to end Father as badly as we do. Sometimes I think her loathing of him runs even deeper than mine."

Amya snorts. "That doesn't seem possible."

"She gets that haunted look any time he's mentioned. When she saw him at the event the other night, she was shaking so hard her teeth were chattering."

Amya frowns, her glass pausing in mid-air. "He did something to her."

My jaw clenches. I know Lor's keeping something from me about my father. "It's the only explanation."

"But she was a child." Our eyes meet and Amya's breath hitches. "He wouldn't hurt a child."

She says it in a way that makes it sound like a wish she knows will never be granted. Amya wants to believe he's more than he seems. She still clings to a feeble shred of hope that there's goodness somewhere in him.

"He threw her in prison. All three of them."

She nods, releasing a tense breath.

"Does it make you reconsider everything?" Amya asks, tipping her head.

"What do you mean?"

"About this place we call home? Three innocent children were tossed inside Nostraza for over a decade and we had no idea."

"How were we to know?"

"We had no idea," she follows up, "because we never bothered to care. We didn't know because we assumed we understood the kinds of people that are in there. What if there are others who don't belong there?"

My stomach drops, remembering the same words Lor hurled at me.

"Don't be soft, Amya. What are we going to do? Let them all go?"

"What about what she told us, Nadir? About what happened to her?"

The blood in my veins simmers, thinking about the warden. Zerra, how I wish I could have torn out his heart and shown it to him. As for my father, it's everything I can do not to march through these halls and tear him limb from limb, damn everything that happens to me as result. He might not have held the knife that carved those scars all over her body, but he's responsible for them all the same.

Of *course* it's made me think differently about everything. My only concern has ever been about keeping the peace in The Aurora, and that's where my involvement with Nostraza ended. I never gave another thought to who found themselves behind those bars.

There comes a knock at the door, and we both look over as Mael enters.

"How are Willow and Tristan?" Amya asks as Mael drops into another vacant chair. I give my sister a curious look, wondering why she's so concerned.

"They're fine. Hylene will keep an eye on them for the next few days."

Amya sits back and nods, apparently satisfied with that answer.

"Have you heard anything more from Etienne?" I ask Mael as he pours himself a glass of wine.

"Just more of the same. Your father's men have gone through most of the settlements and rounded up all the women. Etienne's working with the resistance to hide as many as they can, but the ones your father's soldiers find are taken into a large tent, where they're doing tests on them."

"What kinds of tests?" Amya asks, leaning forward.

"He thinks they're testing them for magic. There's a lot of screaming."

Both my sister and I frown.

"He's searching for the Primary," I say. "It's the only thing that makes sense."

"Of Heart?" Mael asks.

"Where else?"

"But we have the Primary?" Amya asks. "Don't we?"

I nod my head. "Yes."

Mael leans back and gives me a skeptical look. "Are you sure? Maybe your sweet little prisoner is lying to all of us."

"She's not."

"I'm really going to need you to start thinking with your head, not your cock," Mael drawls.

"Fuck off," I reply, my voice dropping. "I *am* thinking with my head."

Zerra, I hope I am. Lor has my thoughts so tangled up, I'm not sure what I'm doing half the time anymore.

Mael snorts and takes a sip of his wine. "Sure you are."

After another pause, he continues. "I've been doing some digging, and the vote is currently sitting at five to three in favor."

Amya sits up. "What vote?"

I give her a grim look. "I haven't had the chance to fill you in yet, but the other night, Father said he was tabling a bill to amend the mining labor laws."

Amya narrows her eyes. "The low fae."

I nod. "He wants to do away with the clause that prevents their conscription before they reach the age of maturity."

"So he'd have children working there," Mael adds, as though we don't understand the implications of such a change.

Something dark flashes in Amya's expression. I know it's the death of that last bit of hope. Our father is a tyrant, and it's the only way he knows. His continued oppression of the low fae has been a point of contention during his rule. There are some who don't agree with his methods, but the prejudices against the low fae run deep, and most are content to let the pot sit unstirred. I've tried to convince my father slavery isn't necessary, but unsurprisingly, he isn't moved by my words.

The accords put in place when the low fae were indentured decreed that any decision made regarding their servitude had to be voted on unanimously by the council. The king's power is absolute, but not quite. A fact for which I'm forever grateful.

"He wants *me* to help convince everyone to vote in his favor," I say, shaking my head. When he ordered me to do his bidding at the Frostfire party on opening night, it took all of my willpower not to smash in his head. Maybe it was part of the reason I'd gotten so angry when I'd seen Tharos with Lor. But maybe not. When I saw him touching her, I officially lost my shit.

My father knows I don't support the enslavement of the low fae, but he delights in forcing me to do things against my will. It's always been that way, and he'll do whatever's necessary to bend me to his wishes.

I can't fucking wait to wipe that smug grin off his face.

"Anyway, I am doing everything I can to ensure they don't vote in favor," I say.

"He's going to know," Amya says, quietly.

"I'll deal with the consequences later. The bigger goal is to get rid of him. Then I'll have the power to stop all of it."

Mael gives me a sidelong glance. They're both worried about me, and I know I'm getting reckless, but I'm also getting desperate. We're at a tipping point, though I'm not sure what the implications are yet. All I know is something is shifting, and I need to seize this chance while I can.

We share a grim look when yet another knock sounds at the door.

"Enter," Amya calls before a servant appears.

"Your Highnesses," he says, bowing to us all before addressing me. "You asked that the lady be brought to you when she was ready for the party."

Lor appears through the door, and my heart nearly stops. She's breathtaking in a black gown with a deep neckline and adorned with violet lace. The slinky skirt slits high up her hip and shows off the curves of her leg. Her light brown skin gleams like it's been dusted with silver. Our eyes meet and everything, *everything* stirs within me. My worries about the kingdom are pushed away as she stands there watching us with that open gaze that makes my chest hurt.

When I propositioned her a few days ago, it had taken every ounce of my strength not to press her to that window and kiss her until she forgot her own name. I want her like I want air and the magic that flows in my veins. Why is her draw so powerful?

An awkward silence hangs in the room as Lor's eyes shift between us, finding me and holding my stare. I'm completely caught up, and I'm not sure what to do about that. I've never felt this way about anyone, much less for someone I barely know.

A squeal blasts through my thoughts as my sister leaps up and runs over to Lor.

"I knew this would be perfect on you," she says, taking Lor's hand and admiring her. "Isn't she perfect?" She looks at me, her face shining and a knowing glint in her eye.

"Yes," I say, my voice rough. "Perfect."

Absolutely fucking perfect.

Lor is watching me and, for the first time in days, she doesn't look like she wants to turn around and hide. Instead, there's a curiosity that lights up her eyes. Something that speaks of anticipation rather than dread.

It's hard not to hope she's considered my words and changed her mind. Maybe I was too blunt and honest. I know what happened to her in Nostraza, and maybe she's never been with a man who didn't force her.

Fuck. And I came on to her like an animal. Guilt twists in my chest. No wonder she can't look at me.

I stand up and approach as her head tips up before her delicious lips part and her tongue nips out to lick them. How I wish with every shred of my soul I could take it between my teeth and...

And it's then I notice how silent the room has gone. Amya, Mael, and even the servant that delivered Lor here, are all staring at the two of us—Amya with a bright knowing look in her eyes and Mael with a smirk.

I shake it off, pretending nothing is amiss.

"We should get going," I say, holding out my elbow. Lor looks at it and hesitates before I dip my head. "We must continue to keep up appearances."

"Right, of course." She loops her arm through mine and looks up at me with such a raw mix of innocence and cunning it makes my dick stir.

I vow then to show her how sex can be with someone who doesn't force her into it. I may be a lot of things, but I am not *that* kind of male. I will wait until she asks. Until she's clear that she wants it. Then I'll show her how it can be with someone who worships every inch of her body from their knees.

I just hope I don't lose my mind before then.

CHAPTER TWENTY-FOUR

LOR

Tonight's party is in an area of the castle I recognize from our searching, but it's been transformed, decorated with candles and luxurious draped fabrics for Frostfire. I walk in with Nadir, Amya, and Mael, taking in the lushness of my surroundings. The Keep isn't anything like I expected. It's far more beautiful than when I looked upon it during those miserable nights in the Hollow.

"How are my brother and sister?" I ask Amya with my arm looped through Nadir's.

My limbs are still shaky from earlier. I hadn't been able to catch my breath when I'd walked into her room. Nadir had been so striking in his perfect black suit, cut to fit the lines of his body like the fabric had created an entire religion just to revere him.

"They're fine. I promise," Amya says. "They miss you, though."

I nod, pressing my lips together, hating that we'd only been reunited a few days before I had to leave them again.

"They insisted on helping, so I've got them doing a little research, looking for any obscure references that might help us find the Crown."

"Oh, that's a good idea," I reply, reminding myself that this is why I had to abandon them for now.

After that little speech in Nadir's room a few days ago, I've started to wonder if he's intentionally distracting me from my purpose. Is there some larger plan I'm not seeing? Did he mean what he said, or is he trying to throw me off? And what do I want the answer to be?

But he's also been helping me during every free hour of the day and seems wholly intent on finding the Crown. But is this all a ruse? I don't trust anyone. I *can't* trust them.

His words have cycled through my head on a loop, and it's practically all I've been able to think about. I need to stay focused.

"Thank you for watching over them," I say, returning to the present and Amya smiles.

"It's my pleasure."

I nod and turn away, discomfited by the princess. She seems so desperate to be my friend, but I blame her as much as I do Nadir and the king for what happened to the three of us. She isn't absolved from allowing Nostraza to exist in the state it does.

We sweep our way into a wide hallway decorated with hundreds and hundreds of candles interspersed at random heights along the walls. Musicians play string instruments as guests in their finery amble down the center towards an enormous arch that opens to the outside.

We pass under it, but when we cross the threshold, I realize we're actually under a massive clear dome. It's filled with sleek jewel-toned sofas, the floors covered in thick rugs. Waiters snake through the space with trays in their hands bearing small bites and cocktails.

Looking up, I understand why the dome is clear. The northern lights are out and they're even more breathtaking than usual. I'm transfixed by the slow ribbons that drift across the sky.

"They're at their best during Frostfire," Nadir says, his voice low in my ear.

I let out a puff of air through my nose. "When I was locked away, the rare nights I saw them, it was like a tiny, wasted part of me came back to life. It always felt like a reminder there was the possibility of an existence beyond those walls if only I could hold on for one more day."

My mouth snaps shut. I didn't mean to say all that. Nadir's watching me with something inscrutable in his expression. It seems to straddle a line between conflicted and apologetic right before he blinks it away.

"I've felt the same sometimes," he replies. "About how they restore a piece of you, of course. Not...the other part."

I scan our surroundings, noting the fine clothing and jewels, the chatter and laughter. I'd always been so sure nothing worth living for could exist inside the Keep during all those nights I dreamed of the day I'd storm its walls. But this is beautiful. It's full of life and laughter, and I can't decide if that makes me feel hopeful or even more resentful about everything.

I don't want to feel sorry for myself. The circumstances of my heritage always meant my destiny would never be normal or safe. I understand that. But it's hard not to wish things had turned out differently for my grandmother, so that me and my siblings could have had the life meant for us. Instead, we're going to have to fight for it and take it back.

But maybe that's better. Maybe it will mean more when we do.

"Shall we?" Nadir asks, taking my hand and leading me to an arrangement of sofas in the center of the room. My breath hitches when I see the Aurora King, one leg crossed over the other, an arm stretched along the back and a drink in his other. He's speaking with a stunning High Fae. Her long red hair is twisted in a thick braid that falls over her shoulder, and she presses her ample cleavage against him.

I stop and then Nadir does, too, and we both stare. Catching his expression from the corner of my eye, I understand that we're looking upon this scene through entirely different contexts. His hand tightens around mine, and I realize I have no idea if there's an Aurora Queen. I've never heard one mentioned, and I think I understand what might be bothering Nadir as the king shamelessly flirts with the Fae at his side.

But the edge of Nadir's anger steadies me. It's like he needs me, and I can't be the one who falls apart right now. With a slight headshake, I wonder where that thought came from.

Why does it matter if he needs me? And why would I think he's my responsibility in any way?

Amya has swept past us and is kissing cheeks with partygoers, lounging in what is clearly a place of honor.

Finally, Nadir comes back to himself and tugs me along. As we enter the circle, the king's eyes fall on his son, skating over me as though I'm no more important than the tall flowerpots forming the perimeter. I stare at the king, waiting for some flicker of recognition, but he looks right through me like I'm nothing.

I'm pulled towards a seat where I settle between Amya and Nadir. Mael doesn't sit, instead stalking the boundary of our nook, surveying the guests.

"Is that really necessary in here?" I ask, pointing to the captain.

"Do you take my safety so lightly?" Nadir asks, his tone almost teasing. It's a side of him I've yet to see, and it almost makes me smile. "Mael takes his job very seriously."

"Except when he doesn't," Amya adds as she accepts a pale blue cocktail. Mael, clearly overhearing us, looks at me and winks. Their ease with one another reminds me so much of me and Willow and Tristan that I sigh, wishing they were here.

Nadir slides his arm along the back of the sofa before his finger starts tracing gentle circles on my shoulder. Sliding into my role, I sink into his side, trying not to notice how nice he feels or the scent of his skin. The words he uttered are ever at the front of my mind, coated in a forbidden darkness that's calling to let it take me over.

Amya is speaking with someone on her left, and it feels like Nadir and I have been absorbed into a bubble where only the two of us exist. His other hand lands on my bared knee and I meet his gaze, wondering if this is the show we're putting on or if the real show was the one in his room when he said he wanted me?

"I'm sorry if I frightened you. The other day," he says.

"You didn't," I say, meaning it. Frightened isn't what I felt, though I couldn't name the specific emotion if I tried. "I was just surprised."

He leans in closer, like a lover whispering sweet nothings in my ear. But he isn't my lover and there was nothing *sweet* about what he said.

"You look breathtaking, I—" He breaks off and seems to be collecting himself.

"Why do you want me?" I ask softly, not wanting anyone to overhear our conversation. "Is this about what I can do? Atlas said some very similar things, but all he was doing was using me."

"It's not. It has nothing to do with that," he says, and there's something open in his expression. Like he's a page in a book where I can read every word, but I only know some of the language.

"I still don't understand."

The hand on my knee tightens.

"Dance with me," he says, standing up and pulling me with him.

I follow along with the wide breadth of his shoulders leading me through the crowd until we find the dance floor, where the lights are dimmed low as couples sway together.

"I've never been one to keep my attraction to a woman a secret," he says, his mouth close to my ear. "I understand he broke your trust, but I'm not promising you anything. This is just sex, Inmate."

I admit, hearing him say that makes this feel safer. Like it really is what he says. I think of my old friend in Nostraza, Aero. How our relationship had been much the same. We'd been drawn together by our circumstances and the need for one another. And not much more.

Living inside the prison, I had no reason to ever hope or dream of something more. That, too, was just sex, and I enjoyed it. More than enjoyed it. Even if I don't understand why, I can't deny the pull I feel for Nadir.

I should hate him. I *do* hate him. For so many things. But I also want him to keep touching me.

"I know your past is...complicated when it comes to matters like this," he says, almost in hesitation, and I raise an eyebrow. I could dig in the knife and tell him it's his fault, or at least the fault of the king sitting a few feet away, but I don't. For once, I hold my tongue.

"I'm fine," I say. I will not show any weakness in front of him. He understands nothing about what I went through, and I'm not willing to crack myself open so he can root through the deepest of my vulnerabilities.

"I should have been more mindful of that before I spoke."

"I said it's fine."

"Have you ever been with someone of your own choosing?" he asks carefully, and I can't decide what he wants to hear. What is the purpose of this line of questioning? Does he care about my feelings?

"Of course I have. And I don't need your pity." I pin him with a fierce look, and he nods.

"I'm drawn to you," he says next. "I don't want you for your power—I have enough of my own, but you must feel what I do. When our magic touches? What we both felt when I went inside you?"

Ignoring the way his voice drops when he growls the words "inside you," I swallow and nod. His hand slides lower, resting on the curve of my back, pressing me closer.

It's impossible to deny I'm experiencing the same things he's feeling. I've been doing a pretty inadequate job of pretending.

"What do you think it means that you had the same dream I did?" I ask.

He pulls up to look at me, a wicked smile on his face. "That the universe wants us to fuck, too."

I huff out a mortified laugh.

"Only if we take this slowly," I say, unable to stop the words as they slip out. He arches one of his dark eyebrows.

"So it's to be torture, then?" His smile stretches into one that reminds me of what an arrogant lion must look like when it knows it's cornered its prey. "I'll take you however you'll have me, Inmate."

"Stop calling me that," I counter.

"Absolutely not."

"I hate you," I say, meaning it, too.

"I know," he replies. "It's why I want to break you so fucking much."

"What if I say no? Now and tomorrow and every day after that? Will you still help me?"

"Yes," he says without hesitation. "That isn't what this is about. My promise to you has nothing to do with this." Nothing wavers in his fierce expression, and I want to believe him.

"Zerra. I'm going to regret this."

But the needy ache builds in the space below my navel, demanding that I give it what it wants.

"What if I said I wanted you to touch me?" I ask, not really sure what I want the answer to be. Except, I do know, I'm just too much of a coward to admit it.

"Then I'd tell you to spread your legs," he says, his voice working its way through every cell of my body.

"What? Here?"

"Why not?"

I glance about the room. It's filled with people eating, drinking, and talking, and engaging in lustful acts of their own. Not a soul is paying the slightest bit of attention to us.

"What if someone sees?"

The corner of his mouth tips up. "Are you shy?"

"Don't look at me like that. Like you're so goddam superior. Of course I'm fucking shy. Don't tell me you'd want a roomful of people watching."

Somehow, he pulls me closer. "Look around you. You're amongst the Fae and no one would care. If you asked me, I'd spread you out in the middle of the room and feast on you for everyone to see. The only reason I'm glad you won't is because I want you all to myself."

His words are spiced air and dark tendrils of smoke winding themselves around my thighs and deep, deep into the quivering place where I *want* him to touch me.

"If it makes you feel better, I won't let anyone see. It will be our little secret."

He maneuvers me to the edge of the dance floor, where the light cloaks us in shadow. It doesn't hide us exactly, but it offers a thin blanket of security. His hand slides down my hip, gripping it with a possession that makes heat flare between my thighs. He's stirred me into such arousal with just his words, I'm worried I'll melt into an actual puddle on the floor if I allow him to proceed. What else can I do but test that?

"Okay," I say, my voice shaky, as I fist the fabric of his jacket, already feeling like I'm a pebble kicked off a cliff.

He lifts a hand and skates it along the side of my hair, his eyes bright with swirling tendrils of blue.

"Be a good girl," he purrs in my ear and my heart kicks in my chest. "Spread your legs." His hand drops lower, landing on my exposed thigh. "You are so fucking sexy in this dress. I just about passed out when you walked into the room."

"Who are you?" I ask, looking up at him, completely overwhelmed.

"I am your worst nightmare, Inmate. But right now, I'm going to make you come so hard, you're not going to care."

His hand slips further, finding its way beneath my skirt, a finger brushing against the front of my underwear. He presses, rubbing me through the thin fabric, and I gasp.

"Part of the fun is to make sure you keep quiet. Do you think you can do that?" His finger slips under the edge, sliding through my wetness, and I groan softly.

"I don't know," I say.

He brushes his lips against my ear, nipping at my neck, teeth sinking into my flesh hard enough to make me squeak. As his finger presses my clit, my entire body goes soft and stretched all at the same time.

I shouldn't be doing this. I shouldn't be *letting* him do this.

I already allowed myself to get swept up in one Fae royal who promised me the world.

This has to be another mistake.

"No," I say, pushing away suddenly. This is all too much. "I'm sorry. I shouldn't have done this."

As I spin around, I don't wait for him to reply. I'm ditching another party, and he's going to be furious with me. He let it go last time, but it probably doesn't look great for his plaything to be leaving again. But I'm too distraught to care.

What was I thinking? I can't let my guard down again.

I stomp through the room, bursting into the hallway where a few guests mingle, and I suck in a deep breath. My skin is electric, my entire body flushed with arousal and confusion and the shame that I've let myself get carried away.

"Lor, come back. It's okay." His hand circles my biceps, and he draws me to a stop, pulling me in close. "We don't have to do anything you don't want." He takes my hand and leads me through a door that opens to a small stone balcony. Inhaling a deep breath of cool air, I lean against the wall and press my hand to my chest, closing my eyes.

When I feel his presence, I open them. He stands in front of me and puts his hands on the wall on either side of my head. "Are you okay? I didn't mean to make you feel uncomfortable."

"You didn't. I'm sorry. I just..."

"Atlas betrayed your trust. I understand."

I bite my lip, looking up at him. "Do you?"

"Yes. But I'm being honest with you. I know I've given you no reason to believe me yet, but I'm not trying to take anything from you. Not anything you aren't choosing to give freely. I won't touch you again, Lor. Not unless you ask me to." He tips his head. "Except to keep up appearances, of course." He flicks his eyes in the party's direction and then back to me.

"For appearances?" I ask, raising an eyebrow and he shrugs. "That sounds like a loophole."

"A necessary one. And one I might take advantage of." He winks, but I don't believe that lie anymore. While this Fae definitely has some questionable morals, forcing himself on me isn't one of them. Of that I'm sure. That reminder helps settle my nerves, my shoulders releasing.

"Kiss me," I say, and his forehead furrows in surprise before his eyes turn dark.

"You're sure?"

I nod, my mouth suddenly dry and my stomach flipping in a pleasant, if terrifying, way. I don't know if I *should* believe him when he says he's not planning to take anything from me, but I *do*. With Atlas, I wanted to believe him so much that I convinced myself his lies were the truth.

But that's not what this feels like. This time, I do trust his words. Maybe it's foolish, and maybe I haven't lived enough to understand who's really out to deceive me, but something in his expression tells me to have faith in him, at least on this point.

"Yes, I'm sure."

He wastes no more time as his mouth crashes into mine. There's nothing gentle or tender about this kiss, not that I expected there to be. It's raw and fierce and full of that same intensity he brings to everything. His tongue drives into my mouth, slicking against mine, and I moan before I throw my arms around his neck. He shifts closer, his strong body flattening me to the stone wall against my back.

This is electric. Every hair on my body stands up and my magic, my magic is alive like it's never been before. It dances and sparks under my skin. But it's not trying to break free, it's spinning and moving like its arms are thrown wide, and it's celebrating under a shower of falling stars. I feel it slide against his as his hips drive into mine, his hard, thick cock pressing into my stomach. He deepens the kiss, his mouth devouring me. His hands are still dutifully planted on the wall, and I remember he said he wouldn't touch me unless I asked.

"Finish what you were doing in there." I say, breaking away for a moment. "Put your hands on me. Touch me again."

He lets out a groan. "Here?"

"Yes. Right here."

"Fuck," he says as his mouth devours mine again, and his hands land on my hips, his grip firm and possessive. "Fuck, you taste so good." We kiss some more, the hunger between us swelling and my thighs growing damp from my wet and throbbing core.

"Please," I say, my words ragged.

"As you wish, Heart Queen."

His mouth moves to my throat, where he places a trail of hot, wet kisses down my collarbone, moving lower. His hand cups my breast, his fingers rolling my nipple into a tender point through the fabric. "I'm going to do more than that, though."

"What?" I say, opening my eyes to see him fall to his knees before he runs his hands up my thighs. Reaching up, he kisses my stomach as his fingers hook into the waistband of my underwear. He stops, peering up at me, asking for permission, and I nod with my heart lodged in my throat and the ache between my thighs bordering on pain.

He drags my underwear down, lifting one foot and then the other as he feeds my shoe through the opening. When he's taken them off, he stuffs them into his jacket pocket and graces me with a villainous smile I know I'll see every time I close my eyes from now until the day I die.

One half of me is panting in anticipation while the other is terrified that I'm getting myself in too deep with this Fae who could eat me for dinner and then casually pick his teeth with my bones.

His hand slides up my calf, his grip firm on my skin. He lifts my leg and runs his nose along the inside of my thigh, biting the soft skin hard enough to make me gasp while my standing leg nearly buckles. As an aching thrill shoots to where he's nipping my skin, my head drops against the wall.

Nadir leans closer, hooking my knee over his shoulder before he presses his face between my legs and inhales deeply. "Fuck, you smell good, too."

I'm dimly aware of the sounds of the party not far away, but we're concealed here on this terrace. It's enough to make me feel both safe and exposed in the most exhilarating way. I grip one hand against the wall and then the other lands on top of Nadir's head where I grab on to his hair just as he drags the flat of his tongue up my soaked center in a long, filthy slide.

"Oh, Zerra," I cry out, gripping his hair tighter, loving the way it feels between my fingers. I've wanted to touch it for so long. He circles the tip of his tongue against my clit in strong, slow circles. My hips thrust, but he uses his arm to pin me against the wall.

"Don't move," he orders. "I plan to take my time, Inmate."

My knees already feel like jelly, and I'm not sure how I'm going to keep myself standing much longer. He does as he promises, tasting and nipping and sucking, bringing me so close to the edge I can barely stand it.

He slides a finger into me and then another, pumping them in and out as his tongue makes rough circles against my clit. My hips jerk, and he lets me go so I can ride his face while he lets out a deep moan of satisfaction.

"Such a good girl," he purrs, fucking me with his hand as he peers up at me. "I'm going to make you fall apart." As promised, he returns to what he was doing, his fingers curling inside me and his mouth sucking and licking.

I whimper as the tension low in my stomach winds tighter and tighter. "Oh gods. I'm going to come."

I'm rewarded with another hum of satisfaction before he sucks my clit between his lips, and I fly into pieces with a ragged cry, waves of pleasure twisting through my limbs. My back arches and my head scrapes down the hard stone wall as I cling to the edge of the release towing me under.

Zerra, I have never felt anything like that.

When I finally stop shuddering, Nadir climbs his way up my body. His large hand circles the back of my neck and he crushes his mouth to mine, his tongue driving into my mouth where I taste myself. His kiss devours me, claims me, making my knees go weak again. There is such ferocity behind it, it almost feels like he's telling me something. Trying to write a message I have yet to decode.

Finally, he pulls away, our eyes meeting as we both let out quick breaths, our chests heaving with effort. "It's a good thing we came out here, because you definitely aren't quiet."

My cheeks heat, but I roll my eyes and flip my hair back, trying to look like I'm in control. "Yes. Well...that was all right I guess."

He smirks, clearly seeing right through me. "I can't wait to make you moan like that again. And again. And again."

He punctuates his words with another fierce kiss and then pulls away. "We should go back to the party."

"What about you?" I ask.

"What about me?"

"Don't you want..."

He smirks. "I very much do, but you wanted to take it slowly and I'm trying to earn your trust."

I cock my head. "By giving me orgasms?"

He grins, and the smile transforms his face. I didn't even know he was capable of such a boyish smile. "I figure it can't hurt."

I huff out a laugh and then frown.

"That didn't leave you frustrated?" I ask, wondering if this is really all a game. Is he just trying to distract me? Is this Atlas all over again? He grabs my hand and presses it to the front of his pants, where I feel his thick, hard cock under my palm.

"Does this seem to you like I wasn't affected?" he growls. "It's taking every shred of my willpower not to throw you over my shoulder, take you to my room, and fuck you senseless."

My stomach flips at his words, and I wobble a strange line between thinking this is all the worst idea ever and very much wanting him to do exactly as he says. He drags a finger down my cheek.

"If you don't mind though, I should play my part as dutiful heir, and it would make me look a little less pathetic if my date didn't abandon me at every event?" He tips his head, and I understand this for the question it is. He's asking me and giving me the choice to say no.

"Okay," I say. "I can do that. And I'll try not to run away this time."

He smiles and then pushes himself away. "Thank you."

Heading for the door, he holds it open and I slip through. We start walking when I stop and grab his arm. "Wait. You still have my underwear."

He pats his jacket pocket with a feral smile. "It's mine now." Then he winks and starts walking again, leaving me to scurry after him with the tips of my ears burning.

I catch up to Nadir, just as we enter the room, wholly conscious of the slickness between my thighs and how exposed I feel, not wearing any underwear in a crowd of so many people.

"I need a drink," I say, and I've never meant those words more in my life.

Nadir turns to me with that wicked grin, pressing a hand to the small of my back.

"You said no touching unless I said so," I say, straightening.

"I said when we're alone. Right now, you're still playing the part of my toy. Loopholes, remember?"

"I remember," I say, before I lean into his touch. I shouldn't love the way his hand feels against the bared skin of my back. But I guess I've already leaped off that bridge and plunged into the churning waters below.

This is just physical. He's gorgeous. He's got a filthy mouth and his attention feels good. But the attention from Atlas felt good, too, and look where that got me. Nadir has shared his truths, and I might be a fool to believe that he wants nothing else from me.

He steers me towards a bar where they're mixing an array of colorful cocktails in the hues of the aurora lights. As we approach, a handsome bartender looks up and winks. The hand on my back tightens as a low growl comes from Nadir.

"What can I get you, beautiful?" the bartender asks with a slant of his head. His smile is bright and his eyes are playful.

"She'll have a—"

"Excuse me." I cut Nadir off. "I can order my own drink."

The bartender is looking a little less relaxed now as Nadir stares him down.

"Then this idiot should keep his flirting to a minimum."

I push Nadir back and step up to the bar, rolling my eyes. Nadir and I both order a cocktail before I peer over my shoulder and narrow my gaze at him. "I don't belong to you, Aurora Prince. There's no need for this act."

No, I don't belong to Nadir, but there's a definite surge of butterflies in my stomach at his obvious jealousy.

He leans in, whispering in my ear. "I just had my tongue inside you, Inmate. Didn't you know that Fae are very territorial?"

I scoff, but his hand wraps around my hip, pulling me towards him.

"I'm just having a drink," I say, my tone dry.

His hand slides across my stomach, and despite the fact I had the most toe-numbing orgasm less than ten minutes ago, I feel a spike of renewed desire. My magic coils under my skin. Instead of its usual threaded slide, it's more like thousands of springs trying to bounce free.

"He knows better than to touch the prince's plaything."

I glare at him, his mouth stretching into a grin that is nothing less than savage.

"Are you my plaything, too, then?" I press a hand to his chest and slide it down, savoring the feel of his body under his shirt.

"I'm whatever you want me to be."

Our eyes meet, and I resist the urge to look away.

The bartender finishes with our orders, sliding two short crystal glasses across the bar. Apparently, he's feeling bold, because he tips a smile my way. We both take our glasses and then turn away, weaving through the crowd.

"I think I'll have him killed." Nadir takes a casual sip of his drink, and I choke on mine.

"Why?"

"I don't like the way he was looking at you. He was watching your ass as you walked away."

I blow out a breath, puffing a lock of hair out of my eyes. "Is this what you're going to be like now?"

"This is how I always was. I'm just not hiding it anymore."

I stare at him, wondering if I'm going to regret what I've just gotten myself into. I'm sure this was a mistake, but there's something about it that feels like it was inevitable. I could have kept fighting it, but eventually, no matter what I did, I would've ended up here, anyway. I'm definitely not sure why that is.

Still, I can't shake the feeling that he's going to ruin me. Maybe not in the same way Atlas nearly did, but ruin me all the same, perhaps with much more permanent consequences.

"You're going to ruin me, too, Inmate," he says softly, making me realize I just said at least part of that out loud. "Lucky for you, we'll go down in the blaze together."

Chapter Twenty-five

We spend the next two days scouring every wing and room of the Keep, hoping I'll feel something as we delve into each dark corner. The tone of our interactions has shifted significantly. Nadir has made no advances, holding to his promise that he wouldn't touch me unless I asked him. I need more time to think before I pursue this any further.

I have a lot of trauma to unpack that goes beyond just what happened with Atlas. Spending years compartmentalizing my torture and my abuse allows me to function in a somewhat normal way, but I'm not foolish enough to think it means I won't have to face it, eventually. But that's a luxury I don't have time for right now. One day in the future, when I've ensured Tristan and Willow are relatively safe, when I've secured a stable future for us, then maybe I'll have that freedom. For now, I do what I must to survive.

"Let's go down to the catacombs," Nadir says after another fruitless afternoon of searching.

"What's that?"

"An abandoned area of the Keep. I don't think it's been used for anything in centuries, but now that I think about it, it might be an ideal place to hide something of value."

His expression is thoughtful as he directs me through the wide hallways. As we clatter down a narrow stone staircase, I go quiet. They say smell can be one of the strongest triggers of memory, and it's at that moment that I'm assaulted by a barrage of buried recollections. The crisp scent of magic. The odors of sweat and blood and vomit. The taste of dusty, forgotten corners and the stench of despair.

As we near the bottom, I stumble on the stone steps, pitching forward and crashing into Nadir. He swings around to catch me by the waist before I topple down the rest of the way. My breath is coming in quick gasps, and I clutch at my chest as my heart thrashes against my ribs.

"What's wrong?" he asks, picking me up and descending the remaining few steps before placing me on the ground. The surrounding hallway sharpens into agonizing clarity. I know those archways and those doors and the dark places they lead. Screams, ones I've long since repressed, echo in my ears. My body tenses and my limbs tremble.

"You're shaking. What's the matter?" he asks, his tone fierce and his eyes blazing. "Tell me what's wrong."

"I can't." I shake my head, tears burning my eyes. "I can't..." I don't know what I'm trying to say. I can't tell him. The words won't come out. I can't be here. I need to get away. "Please."

Finally, he understands what I'm unable to voice because he scoops me into his arms and flies back up the stairs. He doesn't pause as we return to the main level, and he delivers me straight back to his room.

When we get inside, he sits me on the sofa, draping my shoulders in a blanket. He then heads to the fireplace, where he stokes the logs, coaxing out a roaring flame. I can't stop shaking. My clothing sticks to my skin under a thin sheen of sweat.

His eyes keep returning to me as he next heads to the bar, pours out a generous portion of whisky, and then sits down before he places the glass on the table. A moment later, he hauls me on to his lap and wraps me in his arms.

Instantly, I sink into him, pressing my head to his shoulder while his chin rests against my forehead. We say nothing for several long minutes as he holds still and waits for me to process what I'm going through.

After a few minutes, he asks softly, "What just happened?" I let out a deep, shaky breath. "Does this have to do with my father?"

"How did you know?" I ask, looking at him.

He tips his head with an uncertain pull on his mouth. "Call it a lucky guess."

I bite my bottom lip, the words hanging on the roof of my mouth. The only people who know what happened are Tristan and Willow, and they've tried for years to get me to talk about it, but I've always refused. Partly because I didn't want them to feel any guilt for what I suffered, and partly because revisiting those moments only dredged up the pain.

"Tell me," he says. The words are soft, but there is a command in his tone. "I want to know what he did to you. Please."

Nadir is watching me with a mixture of ferocity and stoic understanding. I remember his words about his father. When he told me he hated him, too. There was a brutality in that statement, like a wound that had been ripped open and left to fester. This Fae, who has turned me into a complete mess, might be the only other person in the world who truly understands my loathing for the king.

Taking a deep breath, I slide off his lap, not because I don't want him to touch me, but because everything about him overwhelms me, and I need the clarity of distance. Sliding the blanket off, I sit on the table so I can face him and pick up the glass of whisky. I will my nerves to settle as I take a deep, long sip.

"When your father's soldiers found us in the woods, they killed my parents," I say softly, the words coalescing around me with a starkness like it was yesterday. "They found me and Willow in an underground cellar where my father hid us. I didn't even know it existed until that day, but clearly my parents had built it, expecting something like that to happen."

My voice feels like a wooden puppet, the words hollow and yet pulsing with the lives that were taken. Nadir's hand lands on my knee, his large palm warm, but there is nothing suggestive in the touch. He's only trying to offer comfort.

"You can tell me," he says. "There is nothing you can say that will shock me when it comes to my father."

I nod and continue. "They found Tristan hiding in the woods, and he fought like a wildcat. Killed three of your father's soldiers before they could restrain him. I was so proud of him." I smile at the memory, even if it's a gruesome one. "My brother is the bravest man I know.

"We were tossed into a locked cart and taken to The Aurora. I don't know how long it took, but we were barely fed and were forced to go to the bathroom in our clothing. They refused to let us out. We slept like that for days. It was awful." Nadir's hand tightens on my knee, his dark eyes burning with fury.

"Eventually we arrived at Nostraza. I remember how big your father seemed. He was like a giant. He told us we were to forget who we were. To never mention it to anyone. If we did, he would ensure that two of us died while the third one watched. Which one was to be a surprise. But he didn't just forget us there. At least not right away."

I swallow as the memories churn closer to the surface before I take another sip of alcohol. "We were all locked in our human forms, as my mother had instructed us, but somehow, your father knew it was hiding our High Fae forms. He started with Tristan and Willow and easily forced them to shift so he could test the levels of their magic. As they told you, they both had little and allowed him to see it."

I take a deep breath, looking at my hands as my fingers grip the glass.

"Then he focused on me. At the time, I didn't know why he was so intent on finding my magic, but when you told me what a Primary is when we were at the manor house, I knew. That's what he had been searching for. But even without knowing that, some instinct told me it would be dangerous if he knew what I was capable of. I may have been a child, but I understood that powerful magic was a gift to be coveted.

"So I told him I had no magic. That I was as powerless as Willow, and the only thing I could do was slide into my human form. I don't know why he didn't believe me. Maybe he knew something already. Whatever it was, he was determined to prove me wrong.

"For months, for years, he brought me into the Keep regularly—to the catacombs, as you called them. There, he tried everything he could to get my magic out of me. He tortured me and tormented me with his power."

I look up at Nadir to see a myriad of emotions reflected in his eyes. Anger. Pain. Rage.

"But I was stronger. I held out." Then I let out a breath. "But his magic wasn't like yours. It looked different. It felt different. It was darker and smokier. It bore the scent of death. He dug and dug into my heart and my mind and my bones, searching for it. After enough time, I knew that if he discovered it, my life was over. Either he'd kill me or find some way to use me. And so I hung on. I locked it away.

"I endured the beatings when he'd get so frustrated that he'd resort to thrashing me with his fists. I endured it all until, finally, one day, he stopped. I'll never forget the last time he tossed me back into Nostraza, and I never heard from or saw him again."

My breath is in shreds, and my chest is heaving as though I've just run a great distance. I've never spoken those words aloud to anyone, and I feel both lighter and as heavy as a block of iron. When I look at Nadir, there is so much dark wrath in his expression, I blink and lean back.

He shakes his head and then closes his eyes, taking in a long, slow breath. His hands are trembling, as though he's trying very hard to restrain himself.

"So he doesn't think you're the Primary," Nadir says slowly. "This makes so much more sense."

"I don't know what he believed in the end, but he gave up. What makes sense?"

"That he let you go so easily. When we found out you'd been taken, he sent me to look for you, but he never seemed all that concerned. I thought he was pretending to throw me off the trail, but he also told me that while he hoped you'd once prove useful to him, you no longer were. Why didn't he just kill you three and get it over with?"

I flinch at his words, and his shoulders drop before he rubs a hand down his face. "I'm sorry. I didn't mean it like that."

"I think it was insurance. Just in case we turned out to prove useful. But as we all matured into adults, I think he realized that wasn't going to happen. Maybe he just forgot we were there."

"Maybe," he says. "What does your magic do? Can you remember?"

I nod before taking another sip, planning to hold these cards close to my chest. "I remember a little. Lightning. It's red and it can destroy practically anything. And I can heal people, but I can also tear them apart. Make them bleed out from the inside. Those are the most noticeable gifts."

"When was the last time you used it?"

"It's been over a decade. I was about ten when my mother insisted I stop. She lived in fear of our discovery and was sure it would draw unwanted attention. Of course, now I know why."

Nadir's jaw flexes. "What about your brother?"

"You'll have to ask him. Those are his secrets to tell," I say, knowing Tristan wouldn't want me to share this without his knowledge. Nadir gives me a hard look. "Don't worry, next time I see him, I'll put in a good word for you."

The corner of his mouth ticks up for a fraction of a second. Then he peers at me and tips his head. His hand rests on my knee again and it tightens. "I know the memories are hard, but do you think you can try to search the catacombs with me?"

I inhale a deep breath, placing the glass on the table and pressing my hands under my legs. Nadir shifts so his knees sit sandwiched on the outsides of mine. His knuckles brush along my calves, and I am painfully aware of his touch and his presence. He's breaking his rule about not touching me, but I don't mind. A gesture of comfort isn't what I meant when I laid down those terms.

"I'll try," I whisper. "I want to find it, too. I don't want to stay like this anymore."

"I'm sorry," he says, and I frown. "I'm sorry that I sat by and let that all happen. I didn't know, but if—"

He doesn't finish the thought, and our gazes meet, a moment flickering between us. I look away, picking up the whisky and taking another sip. It burns down my throat, warming my stomach.

"Does that help?" he asks, his hands still cupped around my knees, and I shrug.

"They healed most of them in Aphelion, but I used to be covered in scars," I say, and his eyes darken with more smoldering fury. He reaches out, his thumb gently brushing my cheek, where I know the bottom tip of my scar sits.

"It's ugly, I know. But it's a reminder," I say, waiting for him to grimace or make a scathing remark.

"It's not ugly at all. It's noble."

I let out a small huff. "Noble?"

"It speaks to something important about your character that you wear it so proudly. I've never, for one moment, thought it was ugly. I remember the first time I saw you at the ball, how beautiful you were."

I take another sip of my drink just so I can look away, because I'm on the verge of cracking.

"I'm going to make him regret it all," Nadir says, a deadly edge to his words. "I'm going to take him apart piece by piece. It's always been my deepest desire, but now, it's a need more violent than the need to draw air from the bottom of a lake. I'll make him hurt."

There is such raw certainty in that statement that my stomach clenches.

"I want him dead," I say. "It's one of the few things that has kept me going through all this. The drive to make sure he pays."

Nadir nods, those swirling eyes burning with colors as he stares at me. "Drink some more."

"Why do you hate him?" I ask, wanting to understand more about this dark prince. "Your feelings for him are more complex than just the things he's done on the surface. Why do *you* hate him so much, prince of The Aurora?"

I whisper the words, but they echo in the quiet room. The fire crackles and pops, and Nadir seems to weigh something in his mind.

"You trusted me with another of your truths," Nadir says. "Don't think I take that lightly. So instead of telling you, I'll show you."

CHAPTER TWENTY-SIX

N adir and I walk through an area that's unfamiliar to me.

"We haven't searched here," I remark.

"No. I doubt my father would store anything of importance in this wing. Keep your senses open just in case, though."

I nod and do as he asks as we continue our march through the halls. He's quiet and tense, his expression growing harder the further we go.

Finally, we arrive at a set of wide black doors, and he grasps the handle before easing it open. I get the sense he's about to entrust me with a secret he shares with very few people.

"Come on," he says, and I follow him into a large bedroom decorated in silver and cobalt. It has the same black floors and one of those long windows that looks outside, but it's like someone attempted to make this room cozier and more homey than the rest of the Keep. Soft lighting casts shadows across the room, and a fire crackles merrily in the hearth.

Nadir looks at me with his jaw tensed, and my senses flare in alert.

Finally, I notice the chair that faces the window standing next to the bed. There's a figure sitting in it, so still it's easy to miss anyone is there. Nadir holds out his hand for me and, without thinking, I slip mine into it. His warmth carries up my arm and disperses through my pores, my magic purring like a cat luxuriating in a sunbeam.

He leads me towards the figure in the chair. It's a Fae with dark hair and eyes the color of amethysts. She looks just like Nadir and Amya, and there's absolutely no doubt in my mind that this must be the Aurora Queen.

"This is why I hate him. Or at least why I hate him the most," Nadir says softly. He lets go of my hand and drops into a crouch in front of the queen. She continues to stare out the window. I realize she has no idea we're here as I watch her unblinking stare and the way she sits like she's carved from granite.

"What happened to her?" I ask, sinking to my knees next to him. I don't know why, but I want to be on the same level right now.

"My father, that's what."

I sink further, sitting on the carpet and leaning against the window, my legs bent and my arms wrapped around them as I stare up at her. "She's beautiful."

Nadir nods from his crouch before he slides over to sit next to me. We're just barely touching, and I resist the urge to lean closer.

"She was. She still is. But she's not who she once was."

He takes a deep breath, and I wait for him to gather himself, sensing he needs a moment before he unburdens his mind with the demons that plague him.

"When my parents were young—when my father was still the Aurora Prince—he met my mother at a party. Her name is Meora. It was actually during Frostfire. They had a little too much to drink. One thing led to another, and they ended up sleeping together.

"My father wasn't interested in her, though. He'd just been using my mother to make the female he loved jealous. And it worked. So he rejected my mother and sent her away, planning to bond with the Fae he loved."

My lip curls in disdain. Why does none of this surprise me so far?

Nadir stretches out a long leg and hooks his arm over his knee, keeping his gaze on his mother.

"But then a few months later, my mother showed up, pregnant with me. At first, my father tried to get rid of her, but as soon as she was sent away, the Aurora Torch went haywire."

"What do you mean?" I ask.

"It lit up, sparking colorful flames that nearly burned down the throne room when they caught the curtains. No one had ever seen it do that before. It wasn't until my mother was called back that it finally settled down, and then they all knew. My mother was carrying the future Aurora Primary in her womb. That day, all our fates were sealed."

Nadir meets my gaze, and I read the pain in his eyes.

"My father had no choice but to bond with my mother and ascend with her to become king and queen. I don't know what ever became of the Fae my father loved. If she ever returned, I never saw her."

Nadir's head tips back, thunking as it hits the window. "My father was furious. Blamed my mother for entrapping him and tricking him into having sex with her." Nadir snorts. "As if his cock just accidentally fell into her."

I frown at the bitterness in his voice, itching to reach out to him. It's clear how much this is affecting him, and a part of me wants to offer comfort, but it doesn't feel like this is where our relationship is just yet. Whatever a relationship between us means.

"He never forgave her. And consequently, never forgave me for being the child that kept him from the Fae he loved. My mother sheltered me by her side at every moment because she didn't trust what he might do. She refused to allow a nanny or anyone else to help her, worried one of them might have been working for him.

"He was a monster to her every day of her life, except for a brief interlude around my fiftieth year. I don't know why, but they were happy for a short time. I'll never forget it. That's when Amya was born, and I thought my father finally saw in her the life he had imagined for himself. Even if he still hated me, I didn't care, as long as he loved my mother and my sister."

I turn to face him, resting my head on the window as I stare. The cold glass is soothing against my cheek.

"But Amya chose me over him. Even as a toddler, she was so enamored with me, she'd follow me everywhere. Maybe she sensed the cruelty in our father. Maybe she knew how much he would eventually hurt and disappoint her, in the end. Whatever it was, she chose me in a battle I didn't even know I was fighting.

"That brief respite of temporary joy she'd brought to my father evaporated when he understood he came second to me in her eyes. And that was it. He shut out my mother for good. It was around then she just stopped...existing. I think she'd been so hopeful things were finally changing that when she realized they hadn't, it simply broke what was left of her heart. I don't know if she loved him, but I know she wanted to try. She retired to this room and stopped speaking.

"Another reason I want my father gone is to free her from this. Anyone bonded to a Primary can't die on their own. As long as he keeps living, she'll do the same, no matter what happens to her. As much as I want her to get better, I don't think she ever will. She's lived this way for more than two hundred years, and I think what she craves most now is the promised peace of the Evanescence."

I frown at that. "Wouldn't he be there, too?"

"He would, but if it's paradise like they claim, then I'd hope she could find some joy far, far away from him. As it stands, she's trapped here."

"How does it work?"

"The ascension bond is truly binding. They can feel each other's emotions, and they can't ever be too far apart. The pain becomes terrible, or so I'm told. When you're bonded to someone who hates you, then it's truly a sort of prison."

"Wow," I say, at a loss for words. *That's* what Atlas wanted to do to me. Bind me to him forever, never able to have a life of my own.

Nadir lets out a drawn-out sigh.

"Amya blames herself. She doesn't admit it to me, but I know she thinks if she'd just chosen our father, then our mother wouldn't have broken."

"She was a child," I say, leaping to the defense of the princess. "She didn't know. Of course she went with the person she felt safer with."

Nadir's face is grim. "That's what I tell her, too, and she says she accepts that, but I can tell by the way she avoids coming here that the guilt eats at her. If anyone is to blame, it's me."

"Why do you say that?"

"If I'd been better about protecting her, maybe he wouldn't have turned her into this." Nadir looks at his mother with a longing I never imagined I'd see from him. Something twists deep in my chest. I know there's no point in telling him this wasn't his fault. I can see that he's wearing that shame like a shield. It's a feeling I understand all too well, and that it's something only he can work through.

I huff out a breath. "Poor Amya." And then I look at him. "And you, too. It kind of explains a few things."

Nadir raises a brow. "What things?"

"Nothing. Never mind." I'm not about to explain that maybe his asshole tendencies are a direct result of how he's been treated by his father. The dark chuckle that follows tells me that maybe he understands what I'm not saying.

"Do you come here often?" I ask.

"Every day that I'm in the Keep. I try to never be away for too long."

"I don't understand you," I say as he looks at me with an expectant expression. "You don't seem to care about anyone other than your sister and Mael, and yet, you do things like this or try to clean up the slums and feed people. You don't make sense."

His mouth crooks into a wry grimace. "I don't take pleasure in other's suffering simply for the sake of it." His jaw tightens and we both know who he's alluding to. "I don't want to rule by fear or by the will of my hand. That doesn't breed loyalty or devotion. Someone very wise told me a long time ago that a kingdom with happy subjects will always be the most prosperous one. That's what The Aurora deserves. Not to have the threat of everything taken from them if they put a toe out of line."

"Why do you have such a blind spot when it comes to Nostraza, then?" I ask. "Why allow that to exist?"

He shakes his head. "Because I believed some people, no matter what they're given, are irredeemable. That everyone who was there deserved to be."

"And now?"

"And now I'm a little less sure about that."

It's not much, but it's a definite shift from my first weeks back in The Aurora, when he kept me trapped in the manor.

"Why are there only humans in Nostraza? Are there other prisons for High Fae? Or low fae?" It's something I've wondered ever since I learned of the low fae's existence.

He shakes his head. "No. Low fae who are accused of crimes are executed without a thought. There is no trial and no questions are asked." My jaw drops open. "And High Fae don't go to prison. They pay a fine or if their crime is bad enough, they might be subjected to a few weeks of house arrest. But that's about the extent of it."

I blow out a breath, understanding that this prince and this kingdom, and this battle I'm waging, have so many more layers than just what's at stake for me and my family.

Then he lifts his head as he pins me with a dark look.

"Despite everything I just said, make no mistake, Inmate. If anyone or anything gets in the way of what I want, I will stop at nothing to destroy them."

His words sound like a vow, and I believe them with my entire heart.

"And what is it you want, oh prince of The Aurora?"

"In the immediate an end to my father's rule. And the rest...I'm still deciding on that. I've found my earlier priorities might be shifting."

"And what is it you *really* want from me?"

His grin is wicked, the suggestion in his eyes obvious. "I think I've made that clear."

"That's it?"

"I want your help in deposing my father, but beyond that...no." The last word comes out strangled, like it isn't entirely the truth. "And you're wrong. There's one other person I care about."

"Who?" I ask.

"You."

I scoff. "You didn't care about me when I was rotting away in Nostraza."

"A mistake."

"I'm not sure I believe that."

"Perhaps I'll yet prove it to you." It feels like a promise, and the idea makes me nervous, my insides squirming with discomfort. I want nothing from the Aurora Prince.

I want to get my Crown, and I want to get as far away from here as possible.

I blink at him and say, "Perhaps."

CHAPTER TWENTY-SEVEN

We continue sitting in silence for several more minutes. The Aurora Queen stares unblinking out the window, and I wonder what's going on in her head. This is no way to live, and my hatred for the king coalesces into something even more sharp and jagged. I don't know this queen and she means nothing to me, but the way Nadir just spoke slices a piece of me away.

I think about what he said. About how the Torch started acting strangely when she'd been carrying him in her womb.

"Do you think," I start carefully, "the Aurora Torch would talk to me, too?"

Nadir's gaze snaps to mine, the colors in his eyes swirling. He blinks. "Why the fuck didn't I think of that?"

"You think it could work?"

"There's only one way to find out." Nadir stands and holds out a hand to me. I take it and he pulls me up. We're standing so close I have to crane my neck to look up at him, and this entire exchange seems to have shifted the fabric between us.

His eyes drop to my mouth, and I feel that slight movement arrow straight through my torso where my thighs tighten. He had his tongue inside me a few days ago, but that was just base desire and need. An itch we were both scratching. The look in his eyes right now feels like something different, and I don't know how to reconcile that. Nadir still represents every minute of misery I lived through for twelve long years.

Clearing my throat, I step back and smooth down my sweater. He snaps out of whatever spell was pulling us under and turns to his mother. Bending over, he presses his mouth to her forehead, lingering for a long second before he pulls away. When he looks at me, his usual fierce expression is in place.

"Let's go see if the Torch will speak to you, Inmate."

Once again, we're on the move, winding through the halls as we make our way to the heart of the Keep. The corridors are quiet, everyone resting after all the late-night parties.

We traipse down a wide hall, the occasional guard eyeing us as we pass. Nadir grabs my hand, then wraps his arms around my shoulders.

"It's *really* big, sweetheart," he says. "You'll love it. You know what they say about the size of a prince's Torch?" And then he winks and I roll my eyes. I guess I'm supposed to pretend I'm his plaything, and he's trying to impress me.

At the end of the hall is a wide set of doors that stretch way above our heads. Two guards flank them, one nodding to Nadir as he grasps the large iron ring that serves as a handle and hauls it open on silent hinges.

I marvel as we enter the enormous space, reminded of the day I woke up in Aphelion and was taken to the Sun Palace throne room to meet Atlas. But where Aphelion's throne room had been bright and gleaming, The Aurora's exists in direct contrast, with shiny black floors and glittering black walls that sparkle with flashes of colors. Just like in Aphelion, the ceiling is a curved glass dome, this one opening to the grey Aurora sky.

Our footsteps click as we enter, the sound echoing off the room's high corners. Ahead sit two massive black thrones, carved from more of that glittering stone I've become so familiar with. On the wall behind them is a mural of sorts, but this is no simple painting. Ribbons of color move and slide against each other, creating a slow, mesmerizing dance, just like the real lights in the sky. For a moment, I lose myself in its hypnotizing waves.

Nadir is still holding my hand, and he squeezes it, bringing me back to the present. It's a direct contrast to the Sun Palace, but there is also something monumental about this place. Something profound in the absence of light. With a strange lurch in my stomach, I look at the Fae standing next to me, so perfectly bred to fit into this room, with that dark hair and those swirling eyes. I get the strangest sense I'm looking into a future yet to happen.

"Are you okay?" he asks, and I shake my head before he tugs on my hand and we make our way to the front of the room.

Suspended between the two thrones is a bracer, and in it sits a large black torch, a warm flame flickering in its mouth. We stop in front of it, and I'm again struck by the most profound sense of destiny. Like every moment of the past twenty-four years have schemed and plotted to bring me to this place.

"It's not that big," I joke, trying to dispel the tension creeping up my back, and Nadir snorts.

"Wait until you see it up close," he replies, and I'm pretty sure we're not talking about the Torch anymore.

"What do I do? How do I talk to it?"

I feel him shake his head next to me. "Try lifting it up. That's how the ascension happens." I swallow and stare at it, wondering if this is ridiculous. Why did the Mirror talk to me? What if I just imagined the whole thing?

Letting go of Nadir's hand, I step forward. Then I turn back to look at him where he now stands with his hands stuffed into his pockets. He tips his head but doesn't rush me as I brace myself for what might come next.

Then I reach out and grasp the Torch. It's carved from a dark material I don't recognize and is cool to the touch. I lift it out of its brackets, surprised to find it's fairly light. For a moment, nothing happens, the bright orange flame continuing to flicker, but then it begins to turn colors, flashing from violet to crimson to emerald.

A moment later, Nadir moves next to me, his forehead creased.

"Is it supposed to do that?"

He shakes his head. "Sure, but usually only for the ascended." He looks down at me, a line between his brows. "Who *are* you, Heart Queen?"

I open my mouth and then close it, not entirely sure how to answer that.

Ah, what do we have here?

The voice pops into my head, and the room around me melts away. I'm standing in another room now, the torch no longer in my hands. The floors are covered in rainbow glass, and there don't seem to be any walls. Just stretches of blurred color that fling out into the distance.

Well, well, well. You've come to see me, Your Majesty? I heard a rumor that you were out and about.

"Do you know who I am?"

Of course I know. I remember you. All those years you've spent so close to me. Nearly within my reach.

The voice moves around me as though it's a person circling me slowly, assessing me from every side.

So you're what has the prince in such knots lately. I've never felt his turmoil so acutely, Heart Queen. What is it about you that is affecting him so strongly?

I swallow, unsure of how to answer.

"I'm looking for the Heart Crown. Do you know where it is?"

There is a pause of silence, and I think it won't answer.

It isn't in the place you're looking.

"It's not in the Keep? Or in The Aurora?"

That I can't answer for sure. But I don't feel it anywhere near me.

"Can you feel the Artefacts?"

Sometimes I can. That doesn't mean it's not near, but it's far enough away that I cannot feel it.

"That doesn't make any sense."

I'm sorry, but it's the best I can do, Heart Queen.

"You knew who I was all along? Why did you never tell the Aurora King?"

My loyalty is first to Ouranos and to my goddess Zerra, Your Majesty. Then to my king. But his heart is dark, and Ouranos would have only stood to lose if he had known. It would have only suffered.

"But the prince knows. Is that not dangerous?"

The torch pauses again and I wait, spinning around in the strange void, not sure where I'm supposed to be looking. The feeling is entirely disorienting.

No. I do not think it is. The prince wants something from you, but it is not your power.

I inhale a deep breath, feeling a strange shift behind my heart.

But...that way lies only heartbreak, Your Majesty. That way lies only ruin.

I blink. *"What do you mean?"*

It says nothing and I wait.

"What do you mean by that? Please tell me."

Still, it says nothing, and I squeeze my hands into fists.

"Hello? Answer me!"

Suddenly my hands turn scalding hot, and I scream as I'm hurled back to the throne room, nearly dropping the Torch.

Nadir catches it from my fumble and then moves to replace it in the brackets before he turns to me. I shake out my hands, staring at them, but the skin is unblemished.

"What happened?"

"It spoke to me," I say in a whisper, and he lets out a deep breath.

"Why do the Artefacts talk to you? You aren't ascended yet."

"I don't know." I shake my head and rub my arms, chilled in a way that has nothing to do with being cold.

"What did it say?"

I look up at him, still trying to rub the feeling back into my hands, something bottoming out of my stomach. The torch said I was safe with Nadir. That he wanted something from me, but it wasn't my power.

But it could only end in heartbreak and ruin.

Why does it suddenly feel like I've lost something I never had to begin with?

"What did it say? Did you ask about the Crown?"

I shake my head. "Yes. It said it didn't think it was close by."

"What do you mean? In the Keep or in The Aurora?"

"I asked the same thing, and it wasn't sure. It just said that it couldn't feel it."

Nadir runs a hand through his hair and lets out a frustrated noise. "But that means it still exists, at least."

I nod, slowly. "Yes, I suppose it does."

"Well, that's something." Nadir paces a few steps and then turns back to me. "What is it?"

I realize I'm staring at him, still thinking about what the Torch said. How will this Fae break my heart? How will he ruin me?

"Nothing. That was just a little disconcerting. I'm fine."

Nadir gives me a slow nod. "Then we still need to check the catacombs, just to be sure. After that, I think we can safely say it's not in the Keep. Do you think you can do that? What if we give it a day or two?"

I nod. "Okay. I can try. What if I don't feel anything there?"

Nadir runs a hand along the back of his neck, his dark eyes swirling with crimson ribbons of light.

"Then we have to decide our next move."

CHAPTER TWENY-EIGHT

After we leave the throne room, we head back to Nadir's wing of the Keep. Unable to get warm, I decide to take a hot bath. I need some space to think. There are so many things to consider—the lack of any more news about the Crown and the fact the Torch always knew who I was as I rotted away inside Nostraza.

And, of course, what it said about Nadir.

That I tied him into knots and that he was after something else from me. Nadir said he wants me physically, and that's all it is, and I'm trying to believe him. But sometimes when I catch him studying me, it feels like there's something he isn't saying. I shake my head. This is silly. He's a prince, and I'm a prisoner from Nostraza. I want nothing from this Fae.

But what had the Torch meant about heartbreak? That *Nadir* would break my heart? He can't do that if I don't give it to him. That's something he'll never have from me. I nearly lost it to Atlas, and I won't make that mistake again.

The problem is, I haven't been able to stop thinking about the party when he kissed me and touched me and tasted me. It's stirred me into a constant state of restlessness. I don't know where to put my hands or where to look when I'm around him. I can't keep pretending that I don't want him to kiss me again or make good on everything he promised.

The water goes cold while I stew about the prince, undoing the entire purpose of this relaxing hot bath. Resigned to shivering for the night, I finally drag myself out, putting on a lacy black bra and underwear and tying on a silky magenta robe.

When I emerge from the bathroom, the room is warm, and the fireplace is blazing, where Nadir's ice hounds lie with their eyes closed. They've become decidedly less hostile around me in the past week, which allows me to ease into my place here a little.

He sits on a plush chair, staring at the fire, his gaze flicking up. There's something luxurious and rumpled about him, the top buttons of his shirt undone and his hair loose around his shoulders. A glass balances on his thigh, filled with the whisky he's so fond of, his large hand cupping the top.

He's beautiful, but I steel myself against those thoughts. He is my enemy. The Fae Prince that sat in this luxurious Keep while I lived with less than nothing.

This dark prince will *never* have my heart.

The Torch did me a favor today, reminding me to remain focused on what matters. The Crown. Willow and Tristan. Our family legacy.

No, he will never have my heart, but after what he did at the party the other night, I need to even the score. I refuse to owe the Aurora Prince anything. Sex has never been about love for me. It's been about survival, and often, pleasure.

Tonight, it will straddle the line of both.

Slowly, I approach, the silk of my robe tickling my ankles, deciding I'm just the right amount of naked for the plan that has suddenly taken root in my head.

His eyes never leave me as I draw near. They're full of hungry calm. Like an eagle about to swoop in on a mouse. I say nothing as I take the glass from his hand and set it on the table. Then I lift a knee and straddle his lap, his breath responding with a sharp incline. The robe still covers me, the fabric bunching around my hips. But all it would take is one pull on the tie for it to fall open. Clearly, we're both thinking about it as we both look down and then back up.

I lick my lips before I say, "You said you wouldn't touch me unless I asked?"

He nods, his eyes scanning me.

"You let me hold your hand today," he says.

"That's true. But you know I didn't mean that kind of touch."

He smirks, the corner of his mouth tipping up to reveal a dimple in his cheek that practically shreds my heart.

"Can I touch *you*?" I ask with a tilt of my head.

"You can do whatever you fucking want to me." His voice is rough, like a file dragging along a stone, and it makes my stomach tighten. He leans in. "The dirtier the better."

I place my hands on his shoulders and slide them down the planes of his chest, feeling the ridges and dips of his muscle through the fabric of his shirt.

His hands come to my hips, his fingers digging in. It sets off a wave of longing I barely recognize before I wrap my fingers around his wrists and place his hands back on the chair's arm-rests.

"Ah-ah, I didn't say you could touch me."

His eyes light up, emerald flecks sparking. "So you can touch me, but I can't touch you?"

I tip my head. "Does that change your previous answer?"

"Fuck no."

I clamp down on the smile that threatens to surface at the earnestness in his tone before I return my hands to his chest and continue my exploration. He holds still and seems to be simultaneously trying not to breathe while fighting for air like he's drowning.

I reach for the button of his shirt and open it, followed by the next, spreading the fabric wide.

"What are you doing?" he asks with that barely restrained edge in his voice. I open another button and then another, baring smooth brown skin and the swirls of those colorful markings that flow over his chest.

"I like looking at you," I whisper, having trouble breathing myself. I press my hand flat to his skin where I can feel the rapid pounding of his heart.

"I like looking at you, too. Very much."

In response to that, I offer him a coy smile. Standing up from the chair, I back up and pull on the tie of my robe, letting it slide from my shoulders and drop to the ground.

"Fuck," he says with a breathless sigh before he rubs a hand down his face. There is such raw hunger in his eyes that I feel a warm throb below my navel. "I'd like to look at even more of you." His eyebrows raise at the hopeful suggestion.

I snort a laugh. "That's not happening."

"Then what, Heart Queen?"

Zerra, why does he have to call me that? I should tell him to stop, but I love the way he makes it sound. Like it's always been waiting for me and all I have to do is walk up and take it.

I slide my knee back onto the chair and then return to my previous position, feeling the telltale evidence of how this is affecting him press against the thin fabric of my underwear. When I roll my hips, we both moan. This feels better than it should. Maybe this is a bad idea, but I can't seem to stop myself, either.

As much as I hate him, I also can't stop wanting to touch him. It's become a fundamental need as important as water and air.

His hands clench on the armrests, his body a tightly coiled spring. "Let me touch you," he says, with a command that nearly makes me relent, but I shake my head instead.

"Then touch yourself for me. Squeeze your breasts."

I raise an eyebrow, thrilling at the order in a way that surprises me. But I do as he asks, cupping my hands around them and pushing them together while he lets out a shuddering breath as his cock grows stiffer.

"Touch your pussy," he says with a growl. "Take off your underwear. Let me see how wet and pink you are."

I want to do it. Every part of me wonders what it might feel like to have him watching me. But I won't give him what he wants. This moment is about what *I* want. About taking back a semblance of the control I've allowed to slip away.

Ignoring his request, I tease my nipples through the lace of my bra. His eyes never leave me. Then I grab his shoulders before I roll my hips again, rubbing his thick length along my now wet and aching core.

The chair creaks, because he's gripping the armrests so tight I think he's close to tearing them right off. I swivel my hips another time, letting out a gasp as his head drops back, and he groans. "You're fucking killing me."

I finish what I started with his shirt, opening it the rest of the way and baring his stomach. I decide I want to lick it, so I roll my hips one more time—this one's for me—before I slide off his lap and fall to my knees.

"What are you doing?"

I place a kiss to the center of his chest and then drag my mouth along his taut stomach, licking and nipping the skin as his muscles tense.

"Please," he begs. "I need to touch you."

I peer up at him through my lashes, giving him my best evil smile as I reach for the button of his pants and flick it open.

"Fuck," he says again as he realizes what I intend. I run my hands up the insides of his thighs as they clamp against me, and then I lean forward and press my mouth to the fabric straining against his swollen cock.

There is only a moment of hesitation on my part. The last time I did this was inside Nostraza, when I'd been forced to do it to survive. When it was the only thing I had to offer. When it wasn't my choice.

But like with Atlas, it had been my choice then, and it's my choice now. I won't give him my heart, but I will give him this. I'm not too blind to understand that while I can never forgive his role in my torture, he's also softened some locked-up place deep inside me I'd thought would be calcified into stone forever.

The look of reverence on his face tells me this is the right choice. I want to undo him the way he keeps undoing me.

Easing his zipper down, I tug on the fabric of his underwear and inhale a sharp breath as his thick, swollen cock pops out.

"Oh. My," I say, noting how large he is and would that even fit?

"I told you it was better close up," he says, and I look up to catch his smirk. It's definitely time to wipe that smug look off his face.

"Zerra," Nadir moans as I wrap him in my hand and stroke him, while the tendons in his neck strain. "I'm going to die if I can't touch you. Literally fucking die in this chair." The desperation in his voice makes me smile, speaking to a sadistic part of me that's enjoying making him suffer even if he's about to get a reward.

Ignoring this plea, too, I stroke him with my hand gripped tight and then lean over to suck on the swollen head, running my tongue along the slit and tasting the salty hit of his arousal.

His hips jerk and I take more of him into my mouth, using my hand to keep pumping. His groan shudders right through me, finding the wet throbbing place between my thighs. This act has never felt like this before, and I'm as turned on by it as he is.

I peer up at him, and he's watching me with an unguarded look, his cheeks flushed and his mouth parted.

"Zerra, you are so fucking beautiful," he says. "You look so perfect with my cock in your mouth."

I shouldn't enjoy those words as much as I do, but they send a fresh wave of arousal straight to my clit. I continue my movements, taking more and more of him in my mouth as his hips start moving. Eventually, I stop trying to control it as I grip his legs and let him thrust in and out, his cock hitting the back of my throat.

Nadir is groaning, the sound so raw it's animalistic. "Fuck, that's a good girl. You feel so fucking good," he says, his hands still obediently gripped on the armrests, and the sounds of snapping wood and tearing fabric mixing with his moans.

"I'm going to come," he breathes and a moment later, I feel him thicken before a hot wet spurt fills my mouth. I do my best to swallow it all until it seems he's wrung out. I wipe my chin and look up at him. The look in his eyes is a combination of hazed lust, smug satisfaction, and, if I'm not imagining things, a hint of bewilderment. I don't think much befuddles the Aurora Prince, but I hope I just turned his entire world upside down.

The leather of the armrest creaks and we both eye the deep tears in the fabric, stuffing spilling out and the wood splintered to nothing but toothpicks. He pins me with a dark look. "Take off your clothes. It's your turn."

The guttural snarl in his voice makes my core clench. I'm aching desperately, and I want to run to the bathroom to relieve myself, or better yet, let him do it. The way he made me come on that terrace the other night makes my knees go weak whenever I think about it. Which has been more times than I care to admit.

But I resist the urge to cave into his demands. I will not give him back the upper hand. This was my move, and I'm keeping the ball in my court. Smoothly, I get to my feet, looking down at him.

"I have to go meet your sister. We're going shopping. She's going to show me the Violet District."

Nadir is up in an instant. He strides over to where I pick up my robe, tucking himself in his pants. "Like hell you are." He reaches for me and then closes his fist, vibrating with frustration. "Inmate."

"Oh, I'm Inmate again? I was a good girl a minute ago." He snarls and a thrill washes through me. Zerra, it feels good to rile him up like this. "Now we're even." I shove my arms into my robe and tie it up.

"Even? Is that what this is about?" Nadir steps closer, and I feel the towering weight of his presence. He doesn't touch me, but he's so close there is nothing but tension and a thick fog of lust between us. "We are not *even*. We're not even until I make you come at least five times to my one. Spread your thighs, and I'll make you come so hard and so often you won't remember your name."

My heart skips in my chest. Why does he have to say things like that? And why do I like it?

"One to one, Prince," I say, trying to sound like I mean it. "And it's only you who has trouble remembering my name."

I pat him on the cheek with a patronizing smile as his pupils blow into black pools of nothing.

"Lor," he calls as I scoot past him and head for my trunk to pick out some clothes.

"Oh, so you do remember it," I say idly as I select a pair of leather pants and a thin black long-sleeved shirt. I hope he doesn't notice the shiver that traveled over my skin when he growled my name.

"Get back here, so help me Zerra, I will..."

I spin and stick him with a look. "You'll what? You promised not to touch me that way unless I asked."

His hands fist at his sides, and he looks like he wants to punch a hole in the wall. Or through something much thicker and harder. I gather my clothing and pad across the room, doing my best not to break into a run as I feel his eyes burning holes into my back. When I get to the bathroom, I rush inside and slam the door with my heart thundering in my ears.

CHAPTER TWENTY-NINE

NADIR

After Lor slams the door, I stare at it, my teeth grinding so hard they're about to turn to dust. My blood is boiling, and I can't get enough air, still reeling from how hard I just came. I've ruined that chair, but I'd buy every single one in the fucking kingdom to experience that again.

As I hear her moving around on the other side of the door, all I can see is the way she looked when she dropped her robe. Every curve and line and all that soft skin, and fuck, I'm never ever getting that out of my head for as long as I live.

Pacing the floor, I wait, wondering what she'll do when she emerges. I'm like a dragon protecting its horde. She's mine now, whether or not she knows it yet. I can't believe she sucked my cock and then walked away. What game is she playing? Did that not affect her? Was that just a transaction? Tit for tat?

If she thinks this is the end of it, she's never been more wrong about anything in her life.

The door clicks, and she opens it, inhaling a sharp breath as she catches sight of me. My shirt still hangs open, and I'm sure my eyes must be alive with color right now. They're always their brightest when my emotions are high. My father knows how to control them, but I've never been able to manage it with the same proficiency.

She quickly looks away, refusing to meet my gaze, and moves across the room, picking up a pair of boots. She's almost as stunning in clothes as she is out of them. Black leather pants and a form-fitted top offer a tantalizing hint of what's underneath. This is almost better. Now that I know what's there, she's like a present waiting to be unwrapped. By me. And only me.

Still not looking my way, she sits on the trunk at the foot of my bed, and I watch her, trying to gauge her thoughts. Her hands are shaking, but is it because she's been left in a state of abandoned arousal, or is it because I'm making her nervous?

When her boots are on, she flips her hair over her shoulder and does a quick check in the mirror before striding towards the door.

She's going to leave without saying anything, so I head her off, blocking the way. She comes to a halt and looks up, somehow managing to look down her nose despite the fact she's nearly a foot shorter.

"Move," she demands.

"No."

Her jaw clenches, and there's a turmoil of conflict in her deep brown eyes.

"Move," she says again, this time with more force. "I'm late to meet your sister."

"She'll get over it. Stay here with me."

She shakes her head. "No, I need to leave."

What does she mean by that? She isn't saying she doesn't want to stay, just that she needs to leave.

She glares at me, fierce defiance in her expression. This is when she's her most radiant. When I'd gladly fall to my knees and destroy entire continents if she asked. Even if she didn't.

"We aren't done here," I say.

"We are for now. Get out of my way. Are you going to make me a prisoner again, too?"

Her words are pointed, and they have the intended effect, landing with a sharp jab and exploding in the middle of my chest. When she told me the story about her magic and what my father had done, it had taken every ounce of my willpower not to storm through the Keep and rip off his head.

"Don't compare me to him," I snarl, my fists balling at my sides.

"Then let me leave."

I have no choice. Of course, I won't keep her here against her will.

Finally, I step aside, and she doesn't look at me as she reaches for the door handle. I force myself not to react. Not to reach out and pull her against me like I desperately want. If she's going to be mine, then I need to take this slowly. However strong she seems, the life she's lived means earning her trust won't be simple.

"We aren't done here," I say again. I think I catch the merest twitch of her shoulders, but otherwise she doesn't react as she steps out and slams the door behind her.

Running a hand through my hair, I drop on the trunk at the foot of my bed and then groan as I remember the way she looked on her knees. Zerra, I've never felt like this. Like I'm going to come out of my skin if I don't get more of her soon. She's baiting me. Holding me at a distance. And it's driving me insane.

I drop my face in my hands, thinking again about my father and his actions. I knew she'd lived through hell inside Nostraza, but I've been trying to convince myself I wasn't responsible.

But I can't keep pretending anymore. I let her rot there, just as my father had. And I'd stood by while she'd been tortured by that monster. I could have done something. I've always known what Nostraza was, but I turned a blind eye, too focused on my own ambitions and oblivious to my blind spots. The guilt is eating me alive.

I'm already moving towards the door before I truly understand what I'm doing. Buttoning up my clothing as I walk, I storm through the Keep, my footsteps forceful enough to practically vibrate the floors. A red haze of anger blinds me to my surroundings, my chest tight and my throat tighter.

"Nadir!" comes a soft feminine voice that brings me up short.

Vivianna saunters towards me, all tits and skin, wearing a clinging teal dress that would normally have my cock stirring. Today, it just leaves me cold.

"I've barely seen you this week!" she says, her bottom lip thrusting out. "Where have you been?"

"Busy," I say, about to continue walking, but she steps in front of me.

"What? With that *human*?" Her nose wrinkles, and that makes red bleed into my vision. "I'm lonely. Come to my room. I can satisfy you so much better than she can."

She drags a single finger down my chest. The same spot where Lor just kissed me and then licked me, and my entire body shivers at the memory. I *do* need a good fuck. I'm so wound up, I need to release this tension, and while I wouldn't normally hesitate at Vivianna's invitation, the idea makes my stomach churn.

"No, thank you," I say, again attempting to keep walking, but she presses her hand flat to my chest and then grabs me between my legs.

"Nadir," she whines. "You can't leave me empty. Don't deny me. You're already hard." She strokes my cock through my pants, and my wire-tight tension snaps. I grab her wrist and press it against her chest.

"Don't touch me. I said no," I snarl, and at that, she finally blinks. Message received. "And that isn't because of *you*."

I drop her wrist and she steps back, her blood-red mouth formed into a perfect 'O'. I've never turned her down before, and as I toss her one last look, something tells me I'll never touch her again.

Once more, I'm on the move as I approach my father's study. The guards stationed outside try to step in front of me, but I'm not in the mood. I shoot out a hand, colored ribbons of light dispersing into the air. They wrap around the guards' throats, silencing them before they collapse to the floor. They'll recover eventually. I think. Honestly, I don't care. Add it to the list of my sins.

After that, no one else bothers me as I storm to my father's study and slam open the door. The king sits at his desk with a blonde High Fae in his lap, their noses touching. Both their heads swing my way as I burst into the room.

When I find yet another thing to piss me off, my furious gaze falls on the female, who visibly pales. I shouldn't make this her fault, but still I hate her for being here when my mother sits on the other side of the Keep withering away to nothing.

"Yes?" my father asks, his tone imperious, as if my finding him here with someone who isn't his bonded is of no consequence. I know Fae aren't known for being loyal lovers, but after everything he's done to her, every transgression is too much. My fists clench as I resist the urge to leap over the desk and wring this asshole's neck.

It never ends. Everything Rion does is carefully designed to suit his pleasure and desires. I can hear Lor's screams ringing in my head, imagining her tears, but always with that proud look on her face. He'd tried to break her and failed. Anyone could see that.

My mouth opens as I'm about to loose a tirade on this bastard who's hurt almost everyone I love every day of his miserable life. But then I stop, remembering what's at stake for Lor. How she needs to remain anonymous for now. I'm going to help, and it's not just for my own ends, but because I want this for her.

When did I start to care about this woman who should mean nothing to me?

The moment I laid eyes on her, that's when. Fuck.

"Get out," I snarl at the Fae on my father's lap, and she looks to my father for confirmation. He nods, and she stands, smoothing down her skirts and tipping a curtsy at us before she scurries out of the room.

After she leaves, I whirl back on my father. "You know, your *queen* still hasn't said a word in years."

Rion flicks his eyes skywards, leaning back in his chair. "This old song, Nadir?"

My teeth grind again as a dull ache throbs in my temple.

"What do you want?" my father asks, and I roll my neck, trying to calm myself. I can't punish him for what he did to Lor. At least, not yet.

"What are you searching for in the Heart settlements?" I ask instead.

The king's eyebrows rise. "Spying on me, are you?"

Ignoring the question, I plant my fists on his desk. "Why are you rounding up the women?"

The king might think he's untouchable, but I'm here to remind him I can play these games, too.

He flattens his mouth. "That is none of your concern."

"Why are you testing them for magic?"

My father stands, pressing his hands to the desk, his eyes going black. "If I catch wind of that little weasel Etienne anywhere near my soldiers—"

"Don't finish that thought," I growl. "Do *not* threaten any of my friends."

Rion narrows his eyes before he rounds the desk to stand in front of me. He's broader than I am, but a few inches shorter. He tugs the hem of his jacket, the only tell that he's been thrown off by this conversation.

"Friends," he scoffs. "*Friends* are only a weakness. Surely you know that by now."

"Spoken like someone who's never had a genuine one in his life."

He ignores my comment and strides over to the window, looking out with his hands laced behind his back. "What I'm searching for is none of your concern at this time. When I have need of you, I'll be sure to let you know."

It's an obvious dismissal, and I narrow my gaze. Zerra, how I wish I could read his mind. He's obviously lying about searching for the Primary, but why is he looking for her now? Why did he try so hard to get Lor's magic out of her? He can't bond to her like Atlas planned. Is there some other way he might use her power? I'm missing something vital about this entire situation.

I watch him, his back straight, and his chin lifted, and I'm sure I can taste the lie in all of his words.

As I hesitate for another moment, he looks over his shoulder again.

"Have you secured the necessary votes from Amber and Violet? I'm told Jessamine is holding out on us. I'd like to have this bill passed before the end of Frostfire." He swivels to face me with his hands still behind his back and his shoulders squared. He's referring to the mining labor laws he wants to alter.

Animosity hangs between us like a black cloud in the air. I want to tell him there's no "us." I want to walk over there and rip out his heart. Does he really think I'm going to support this *and* try to win others over to his cause? He already knows my feelings about the low fae.

Will he resort to his usual threats to bring me in line?

An acerbic retort sits on the tip of my tongue, but I remind myself that Lor needs me. Keeping my father distracted with this nonsense might help give us enough time to find the Crown before he does. And discover what his greater plans are. So, I tip my head, the effort so stilted it's like I'm made of rusted parts.

"I'm working on Jessamine," I say, hoping I sound at least a little like I'm telling the truth. Partially, I am. I will go and work on her, but only to convince her how bad of an idea this would be for The Aurora.

"Good," Rion says. "Don't let me down, Nadir."

He doesn't add the word "again," but it still rings as clear as a crystal bell.

CHAPTER THIRTY

LOR

"Try it on," Amya says, holding up a silver necklace set with amethyst stones that twinkle in the light. The shop where we stand is busy with dozens of customers picking out trinkets to wear for various Frostfire activities. Amya tells me that while the parties continue in the Keep, the citizens of The Aurora hold their own nightly celebrations in the city, as well.

I take the necklace from her and secure it around my throat, letting it drape over my gold locket. I won't take it off under any circumstances.

"What is that you're always wearing there?" Amya asks with her eyes on the necklace I stole from Aphelion. I clasp it in my hand.

"It's the last thing I have from my mother," I say, and her eyes turn shadowed.

"Oh. I'm sorry."

I shake my head, then check myself in the mirror, admiring the ornate necklace.

"Nadir loves violet," Amya says casually, picking up a ring and admiring it on her finger.

"And?" I give her a skeptical look.

"Nothing," she says with a shrug. "Just thought you might like to know."

I pin her with a glare, and she tosses me an innocent smile full of bright white teeth.

"Your brother is..."

"I know." Amya picks up my sentence, apparently understanding exactly what I'm about to say. "But I promise he's not all bad once you get to know him. He just has a rough exterior."

I think of all the days we've spent together. I don't really know how I was going to finish that sentence. He's confusing? He leaves me feeling all kinds of things I shouldn't? Things I don't want to feel? We've shared so much in such a short time. So many truths and so many secrets.

My knees are still rubbery and my cheeks flushed from what I did in his room this afternoon. I smile to myself, remembering the look on his face when I left him standing there. Getting one up on him feels better than it should. I wonder what he did after I left?

"Yah, I'm seeing that," I say, and Amya gives me a knowing look that I choose to ignore.

The Aurora Prince is still the reminder of everything I've lost. How can I ever look at him and not see the past? The deaths of my parents? My imprisonment over twelve long, miserable years? The ominous words of the Torch ring in my head like a drum beating on a constant wind.

Heartbreak.

Ruin.

The Aurora Prince will *not* have my heart.

"Come on," Amya says. "Let's go find you a dress for tomorrow." She gestures to the shopkeeper. "She'll take this one. And I'll have those." Amya points to a pile of jewelry gathered on the counter.

The shopkeeper bows his head. "I'll have them sent to the Keep, Your Highness."

"Amya, you don't have to keep buying me things, and I already have plenty of dresses."

Amya rolls her eyes. "Please. There's no such thing as enough dresses."

I can't help the grin that surfaces. I have to admit, I do love all the lace and silk that Amya chooses. After wearing only drab grey tunics for most of my life, these beautiful clothes make me feel like an entirely different person. In Aphelion, I could never settle into the golden dresses. They always felt wrong, like they were made for someone else. But here, the clothes fit me with more ease.

We enter a quiet dress shop with only a handful of customers. Seated on plush chairs, they sip on glasses of champagne as the staff cart out an array of dresses for them to examine.

When I see the price tag on the one nearest to me, I understand why it's not very busy in here.

"Amya," I say, feeling strange about taking her money. "I don't know about this." I'm not here as her guest or her friend. I'm here to destroy her father and upset the very fabric of Ouranos.

"It's fine! Cora!" Amya apparently doesn't see it that way, because she takes my hand and drags me through the store to where the shopkeeper, a High Fae with sparkling silver hair, waits for us with a patient smile. I suppose the princess of The Aurora gets top-notch service wherever she goes.

"Your Highness," Cora says with a deferential tip of her head. "We've set aside some things we think you'll like. And your companion?"

Amya pulls me forward. "Help Lor find something perfect for tomorrow's Frostfire party." She then bounds into a changing room and lets out an exclamation of joy from the other side of the curtain. "This is gorgeous!"

Cora smiles and scans me from head to toe.

"You are the prince's guest?" She tilts her head and I blink, surprised that she knows, but there's no judgement in her expression, only professional curiosity. I nod and she points to a corner of the store.

"The black dresses are over here, then."

"Do I have to wear black?" I ask, and she hesitates, her eyes flicking to the closed curtain, where I can hear Amya changing.

"Generally, the prince's companions do."

I narrow my eyes at her. "How many "companions" have you dressed?"

Cora's cheeks color, and she opens and then closes her mouth. "A few, my lady."

I don't know why that hits me so hard. Of course, Nadir has been with other women and brought them to the Keep. Still, the thought sits like a stone in my stomach. I glance at the shopkeeper, but this isn't her fault.

"Okay, show me."

Her shoulders sag in relief before she leads me to a display of glittering black dresses highlighted with flashes of aurora colors. I finger the soft materials, wondering which one I should try.

"I will say, though, my lady," Cora says softly, standing behind me. "You are the first to arrive with the princess. And all those clothes I sent up were for you?" I nod. "He's never done that before."

She gives me a small smile with her hands clasped in front of her. Those words loosen something else inside me I can't quite parse out. Does that matter? Do I care?

It's then my eyes alight on the most stunning dress I've ever seen. The material is bright red, the neckline low, with a bodice that laces up the back. I circle the mannequin, admiring the fall of the long red skirt, and I think of the stone encased in the locket around my neck.

Red.

The color of home.

Of the legacy that was taken.

Of the rivers of blood that will run from the Aurora King when I finally get my revenge.

"This one," I say. "I want this one."

Cora nods her head, though I can tell she's wary about my choice. She takes it off the mannequin and then leads me to a dressing room where I slip into the garment.

It fits me perfectly, skimming over my hips and falling to the ground like scattered rose petals.

"Let's see," Amya calls from the other side. I tug back the curtain and step out, and Amya's jaw drops.

The royal family wears black. Nadir's companions wear black.

But I am not his conquest. I am not his to claim.

I'm not part of their royal line.

I have my own family.

And I am my own fucking castle.

Our gazes meet, and I can see Amya understands what this means to me.

"It's perfect," she says. "We'll take it."

A short while later, we head through the Violet District in search of something to eat. I'm told The Aurora comprises eight districts, named for the colors of the lights in the sky. Each one is famed for some form of craft or resource. Violet is jewels and textiles.

Amya leads us towards a cozy-looking pub with long wooden tables arranged out front. We drop into one, sitting across from one another.

"Well, that was a productive day," Amya says, wiping her brow as though we've put in a great amount of effort. I give her a small smile. It was fun, I won't deny it, but it's hard to settle into the idea of fun when I've never had this luxury before, nor when there's so much at stake.

A moment later, Amya leaps up. "They're here!"

I turn around, and my heart squeezes. Tristan and Willow are walking down the street, flanked by Mael and Nadir. I jump up and run over, wrapping them both in a hug.

We head for the table. "Why are you here?"

"I thought maybe you could use a little pick-me-up," Amya says to all of us. "It's not safe for them at the Keep, but I thought we could sneak them into the city for dinner."

Tears bite the backs of my eyes as I wrap Tristan in a big hug, the leaded air in my chest already more buoyant.

"Thank you," I say to Amya, suddenly realizing just how much I've been missing them both. Willow slides in next to Amya, and Tristan sits next to me.

"Where's Hylene?" Nadir asks Amya.

"She's waiting for a message from Etienne," Amya says, and some secret exchange flickers between brother and sister.

"Who's Etienne?" I ask, but Amya shakes her head.

"Just a friend." She takes a sip of her drink, and I'm sure she's keeping something from me.

"How are things going?" Willow asks me, and I look around, conscious of anyone hearing us. Amya waves a hand, dispensing some invisible form of protective magic.

"No one can hear you now," she says. "Talk freely."

"No luck," I say. "We haven't found a trace of the Crown." I swallow as everyone leans in closer. "I held the Aurora Torch. It spoke to me."

Amya's eyes go wide, and she looks at her brother. "You did what?"

"We thought since the Mirror spoke to me that maybe the Torch would, too."

"What did it say?" Amya asks.

"It told me the Crown wasn't near enough for it to feel it."

"What does that mean?" Tristan asks.

"I don't know. We've got a few more places to look in the Keep and then..."

"What?" Willow asks, her eyebrows drawing together.

"The prince said we'd have to figure out where to search next." I let out a deep breath. That Crown could be anywhere. Ouranos is huge and I know so little about anything.

"We've been searching through past accounts and records of the Sercen Wars," Willow says. "There are mentions of it here and there, but it's hard to know if they're just red herrings. Amya says there have been many supposed sightings over the years, but it's never resurfaced."

My shoulders fall, and she takes my hand across the table. "We'll keep looking. Don't worry. We're going to find it."

Tristan wraps an arm around my shoulders and draws me closer, planting a kiss on my head. "You're not doing this alone, Lor. We're going to be with you every step of the way."

"She won't be alone." We all look up to find Nadir standing over us, his arms folded. My cheeks flush when I notice he's staring at me. "I'll keep searching with her."

Tristan visibly bristles at that. "She needs her family. People she can *trust*."

"She can trust me." He says it with such certainty my stomach flips.

"Both of you stop it," I say.

Tristan ignores me. "I don't like it. I don't like you being away from us, and I don't like you being alone with him."

"Tristan, enough. He's only been helping me."

Nadir smirks at my brother and then moves around the table to plant himself on my other side.

"Hey," I say, suddenly feeling shy in his presence, relieved he doesn't seem angry about the way I left him. This afternoon brought out something in me I hadn't known was there, but now that we're no longer alone, a small flicker of uncertainty passes over me.

"Hey," he says. He's straddling the bench, facing me so that I'm in between his legs. "Did you have a fun afternoon?"

He arches a dark brow, and I can practically read the words on his face. Did I have fun abandoning him when he'd offered me some very specific entertainment?

"I did," I say, not taking the bait and deciding to lob some dynamite of my own. "I met Cora, the shopkeeper who told me about the *parade* of the prince's companions who've bought dresses from her."

Nadir leans closer as the rest of the table continues chatting away, ignoring the two of us. "Should I pretend you're the first woman I've been with?" he says quietly into my ear.

"No, I..."

"I'm not the first man you've been with."

"Of course you aren't."

His eyes darken at that. "I know I can't be angry that you've fucked others before me, but it doesn't make me any less inclined to rip out their throats."

I snort. "Technically, I haven't fucked you," I say, lightly.

"Yet," he says, and I give him a sidelong glance. "What I did with my tongue was fucking, Inmate. And what you did this afternoon…"

He trails off, and I look over my shoulder. Thankfully, everyone else is too engrossed in their own conversations to pay us any attention.

He leans in closer, his mouth right against my ear again. "Fuck, that was the hottest blow job I've ever gotten. I'm going to be thinking about that for a very, very long time, Heart Queen."

A shiver consumes me, and a smile creeps to my face at the gravity in his tone. I love how unguarded he seems ever since he told me about his attraction. Like he's holding nothing back.

"You're welcome," I say, and his answering laughter is dark and low.

"I told you the Fae are territorial, and I have no interest in anyone else. As long as there's the slightest chance you'll let me touch you again, I have eyes only for you."

"And if there isn't a chance? What if I say that was it and I'm done?"

His shoulders lift, the light in his eyes sparking.

No one has ever said "no" to him, that much is obvious.

"Then I'm going to work very, very hard to convince you otherwise."

I let out a shaky breath.

Fuck, this prince really is going to be the death of me.

The sky darkens as we finish our meal and the Borealis starts to streak across the sky. Willow and Amya have moved to a nearby table and are deep in conversation. Clearly, they've been getting to know one another while I've been at the Keep. I hope Willow is being careful and not falling for any of Amya's lies. I still can't fully trust her.

But then who am I to talk? Mael and Nadir are conversing at the far end of the table, and I take a moment to study Nadir, appreciating the curves of his broad shoulders and the way his biceps strain against the fabric of his shirt. Why did Zerra make this Fae, the son of my sworn enemy, so beautiful?

I mean, they're all beautiful in the way of High Fae, but around Nadir, I can never catch my breath. My magic slips under my skin, reminding me of what it wants. It's only when he's touching me that it finally curls into satisfaction.

"He's been treating you properly?" Tristan asks, catching the direction of my stare and leaning down to speak to me in a quiet voice. "Because if he does anything to hurt you, I'll tear off his limbs and beat him senseless. That prince is way too in love with himself for his own good."

I smile at Tristan, touching his cheek.

"What was that for?"

"I love you, big brother. You've been watching over me our whole lives, but we're out of Nostraza. I don't need you to fight my battles for me anymore."

Tristan snorts and pops a spiced peanut into his mouth, crunching down on it. "I haven't fought your battles for you since you learned how to throw a punch and nail a guy in the balls so hard he cries."

"Yah, but who taught me to do that?"

Tristan looks at me, concern in his expression. "I'm always going to look out for you, Lor. I'm your brother. That's my job. No matter how powerful you become. Even after we find that Crown and you're sitting on that throne where you belong, I'm still going to look out for you."

I lean against him, resting my head on his shoulder.

"Do you think that's where this all ends? Do you think that after everything, the three of us will get the chance to just be happy?"

He pops another peanut in his mouth and tips his cheek so it's resting on my head.

"I don't know, but I'm going to do everything I can to make it happen."

I peer back up at him. "You know what, Tris? There are days when I want to scream and rage about how unfair this all was. How none of it should have happened this way. We should have grown up safe and content with our parents, but then I realize how much worse it could have been if the two of you hadn't been by my side, and that makes me feel like the luckiest person in the world."

Tristan frowns, his eyebrows drawing together.

"What? Why are you looking at me like that?"

"You've changed so much. I'm just so fucking proud of you."

My cheeks heat at his words. Maybe I have changed. Maybe this is who I was all along, but I'd never gotten the chance to be myself. Everything I am was buried under a thick cloak of pain.

He huffs out another laugh. "To think the last time I saw you, you nearly killed a woman for taking your soap."

I shake my head. "I was a little...wild. I still am. It's just easier to control myself when I'm not starving and cold all the time."

He gives me a sad and serious look. "I understand what you mean. These last few weeks have been..."

"I know." I lay a hand on his arm. "I know."

"But that slightly unhinged spirit makes you kind of loveable," he smirks and knocks his shoulder against mine. "You're going to make an amazing queen."

"I still have a long way to go, but thank you. I wouldn't be any part of who I am without you in my life."

Tristan wraps an arm around my shoulder and pulls me into him, holding me close. We sit in silence for a moment, listening to the sounds of the city and people bustling around us. It feels so peculiar to exist in something as normal as a busy evening.

"What's with those two?" I ask, gesturing with my chin to Willow and Amya.

Tristan blows out a sigh. "Yah, that. Apparently they're 'friends' now."

"How come you're not glaring at Amya like you do at the prince?"

Tristan raises an eyebrow. "You really want me to answer that?"

"I know she might seem like the nice one, but—"

"But what?"

"Nothing," I say. "I think she really might be the nice one."

Tristan smirks and takes a long sip from his drink.

"Keep an eye on her, okay?" I say to him and he squeezes me tighter.

"You're supposed to be the baby sister."

"We both know the order of our birth has never had anything to do with the roles we play, Tris."

"Yah," he says, softly.

Chapter Thirty-one

A few hours later, when the sun has set and the city is bursting with the sounds of the night, Tristan and Willow bid their goodbyes. We hug each other tight, hoping we'll see each other soon.

We only have the catacombs left to search, and Frostfire is nearly at an end. After that, I'm not sure where my path takes me. I just know it will be with them by my side. Thinking about those dark bowels of the castle makes heat prick at the back of my neck. Nadir said he'd give me a few days, but sooner or later, I'm going to have to face those dark corridors.

After Mael and Amya escort my family back to the manor, only Nadir and I remain behind. He holds out an elbow, and I thread my arm through his before we stroll through the streets.

"It's hard to believe this all exists," I say. "That there are happy, healthy people living here so close to the prison."

I look at Nadir, who's watching me with wariness. "Don't worry, I'm not going to lecture you about Nostraza tonight. It's just a wonder to behold this all. I've never really been inside a proper city. We lived so deep in the woods that we rarely saw many people. In Aphelion, I never left the palace except for the Trials. I've read books and stories about places like this, but they never fully conveyed the energy of a city teeming with life."

Nadir looks around us, a thoughtful expression on his face. "When you're used to something, it's hard to appreciate it for its beauty," he says. "I forget how alive this place feels. This area used to be what you would compare to The Umbra."

"Really?" I look around at the stone buildings, each one tidy and neat. They rise around us, their square windows lined with curtains and flower boxes. The streets are paved with wide grey stones, and there is no doubt these people are cared for. Emotion sticks in my chest. "I always thought The Aurora must be such a miserable place. That there couldn't possibly be any happiness here."

Nadir tugs his arm, so it pulls me closer. I'm not sure if the move is intentional or not, but I wrap my hand around his biceps to steady myself. "I can understand why you might have thought that." He stops and shakes his head. "But it's tenuous. Always on the brink of collapsing because of my father."

He breaks off, his mouth pressing into a thin line.

"What?" I ask, sensing he has something else to share with me.

"After what you told me about my father, I went to find him this afternoon to rip out his throat."

I tighten my grip on his arm. "Why?"

"Because I was so fucking furious with him. I wanted to hurt him for hurting you."

We've stopped walking, and the surge of the crowd moves around us, everything but the two of us melting away.

"Please tell me you didn't," I say, confused by his reaction.

"I stopped myself. I knew that wouldn't do you any favors."

"Good," I reply, pulling him by the arm. "The thought was nice, I guess. Even if it's a little murderous."

He lets out a low, dark laugh. "Don't pretend you don't like it, Inmate."

I don't answer that, but maybe I do. My life has been filled with so much violence, and I'm tired of it, but I also know it's the only way through.

We keep walking in silence until we happen upon a large square where music is playing and couples are swaying to the sounds. Amongst the noise, children scream in delight and laughter fills the air. Overhead, the lights are flowing across the sky in rippling ribbons of color.

"It's so beautiful," I say.

"It is," Nadir agrees, but when I look at him, he's staring intently at me. I look away, overwhelmed by the tangle of feelings in my chest.

"Do you want to dance?" he asks, tipping his head in the direction of the swirling couples. There are a few faces turning our way as they recognize their prince standing in their midst.

I shake my head. "I don't know how."

"You danced with me in Aphelion."

"Terribly," I say with a laugh, which elicits a smile.

"I didn't notice."

The meaning in his voice is clear, and I swallow a knot of nerves.

"Come on." He takes my hand. "You don't need to do anything but let me lead."

He pulls me through the crowd, coming to a stop in the middle where he draws me closer, an arm wrapping around my waist.

"Let you lead?" I joke as he laces his fingers through mine. "I don't know about that."

"Just for the dance. I promise." I let him do as he says, guiding me through a series of simple steps as we twirl with the music. The lights streak overhead, painting everyone with illuminated rainbows. When I look at Nadir, colors swirl in his irises, pink and blue and violet. His expression is soft, the lines of his face different from what I'm used to.

"What's on your mind?" he asks.

"I'm not sure how to act around you."

His face tips into that cocky smile as he pulls me closer so our bodies are flush. "Why not?"

I roll my eyes. "Don't pretend you don't know what I'm talking about. What is this? You and me?"

His hand slides up the back of my skull before he grabs on to my hair and gently bends my head up. Our lips are so close, I can practically taste his breath on my tongue. "I told you already, we're just enjoying each other's company. I want you and I know you want me."

He presses me against him, cutting off a scoff of feigned laughter. "Admit it."

"I admit nothing," I say, and he smirks.

"Fine. Keep lying to yourself. I promised I wouldn't do anything you don't want. You're the one in charge of how fast this goes."

Zerra, I know I shouldn't trust him. I know I shouldn't believe him. I can't let myself get swept up in the smooth words of a royal Fae ever again, but I fear I've already let this go too far. His expression is so earnest, and his words feel like a truth ripped from his soul. They make me feel confident and safe, but I can't keep ignoring the warning voice in my head.

"So, do we keep sharing the bed?" I ask.

"Is that what you're worried about?"

"I'm not worried. I've just never done this sort of thing before."

"Done what?"

"I don't know. Had a relationship like this. When I was in Nostraza, there was never anything beyond tomorrow. It was just...it was different."

His grip tightens on me. "Good. I want this to be different."

He spins me around, and I laugh as he lifts me off my feet, twirling me in a circle. I'm having fun. I don't remember a day when I genuinely had fun in so many years. Right now, everything that's at stake seems far away and distant and, for the first time in a long time, I allow myself to breathe.

Tears build in my eyes, and I blink them back. This is what I'm fighting for. This is the hope I held on to every day I lived inside

Nostraza. Everything I fought for during the Trials. For me and for Tristan and Willow, who had all of this taken away.

I think of the people living in the Heart settlements waiting for their queen. They also lost everything the day my grandmother destroyed their home.

Tomorrow, I'll face down those dark hallways of the Keep, pushing away the memories of what the king did. Finding the Crown is the most important thing. It's the only way I can save us all.

"Where are you?" comes a soft voice, and I blink, looking up at Nadir, who's still swaying us to the beat of the music. "You aren't *that* perplexed about the bed?"

I huff out a laugh and shake my head. "No. I was just thinking that I'm ready to search the catacombs. Thank you for giving me time. You must think I'm being dramatic."

He tips his chin towards me. "Absolutely not. I think you're very brave."

My cheeks warm, and I look away, the intensity of his gaze starting to undo me. He leans in close, his cheek resting against my forehead as he twirls me again. "As for the bed, we can keep sharing it. There's plenty of room, and you have nothing to fear from me."

There's more he's not saying buried in those words. A brilliant flash of light streaks overhead, and the music swells to a joyful beat.

I nod slowly, looking into his eyes, and whisper, "I know."

CHAPTER THIRTY-TWO

SERCE

"Guess who?" Serce asked, covering Wolf's eyes from behind. He sat cross-legged on the floor, and his arms snaked behind, wrapping her against him.

"Hmm? The love of my life? My mate? The most beautiful and fearless queen to walk this plane?"

Serce laughed and then looped her arms around his neck, kissing him behind the ear. "Were you always this smooth with the women?"

He looked over his shoulder and winked. "It never mattered before, and now it never will again."

"Well, I should hope not," she joked before he put a hand behind her head and pulled her in for a deep kiss. After they broke apart, she asked, "What are you doing?"

Before him sat what looked like a chessboard covered in an array of carved figures. He had another block of wood in his hand that he was whittling with a small knife. The figures were beautifully intricate, made to look like The Woodlands sprites and elves that inhabited the realm's forests.

He shrugged his wide shoulders. "Just making a little something in case Zerra sees fit to grant us an heir. I want to teach them how to play. My father taught me. It's a bit of a family tradition."

Serce said nothing as he dug the tip of his knife into the soft wood, prying out a sliver. He cast a look over his shoulder. "I hope that's okay for me to say."

She smiled. "Of course it is. We talked about it, and I'm open to having a family. You know that. We need an heir, regardless."

His forehead furrowed. "Aye, but you're not entirely comfortable with the idea yet. You can't pretend with me."

She let out a shaky breath. "I'll get there. The idea is still new. I really hadn't given it much thought until I met you. I love you, Wolf, and if this makes you happy, then I want to give that to you."

"Your happiness matters, too," he said. "I don't want you to feel trapped."

"I know," she said softly as she buried her chin in the crook of his neck, watching him work. "And that's why I don't feel trapped. Because you're giving me the choice. Besides, you know no one could make me do something I didn't really want."

He chuckled, the sound as warm as an open flame.

"Yes, I do know that."

At that moment, there came a firm knock at the door.

"Come in," Serce called before one of her lady's maids swung it open.

"Your Highness," she said, dropping into a quick curtsy. "The High Priestess has arrived."

Serce let go of her hold on Wolf and pushed herself up, her hands pressed to his shoulders.

"Excellent. Where is she?"

"In the salon, Your Highness."

"Thank you, Stiora. We'll be there in a moment."

Stiora curtsied again and closed the door as Wolf dusted wood shavings from his brown leather breeches before standing up. He picked up the chessboard and placed it on the table, along with his knife. He pulled Serce close, wrapping his arms around her waist. She stared into his bright green eyes that sparkled with mischief.

"You ready?"

"As I'll ever be," she replied.

He grinned and took her hand as they made their way to the salon to meet with Cloris Payne. As promised, she was waiting in the Oak Tree Room, perched on the edge of an upholstered green chair with a tea service placed on the table in front of her, her hands clasping and unclasping in her lap.

At their entrance, she stood and bowed. "Your Majesty," she said, addressing Wolf before she turned to Serce. "Your Highness."

"Thank you for coming," Serce said. "We've been eagerly awaiting your arrival."

The priestess dipped her head, her silver hair spilling over her shoulders. Half if it hung to the middle of her back, while the rest was braided and then coiled into an elegant knot at the back of her head. She wore a simple black dress that managed to look both humble and regal on her angular frame.

The priestesses were High Fae who swore their lives to Zerra, acting as her emissaries here on the corporeal plane. They were said to possess a specific strain of magic, the details of which were conveniently known only to them.

"When one receives a summons from the Woodlands King and the Primary of Heart, one doesn't linger."

Serce offered a smile that didn't reach her eyes. This was the second time she'd met with Cloris, and something about the priestess made her uneasy. "Please sit."

"I'd prefer if we moved to the floor," Cloris said. "In front of the fire. It's where I'm most comfortable."

"Of course," she replied, unfazed by the unusual request. She'd heard that priestesses derived their power from fire.

Wolf grabbed several of the sofa cushions and arranged them in front of the massive hearth. Cloris sank to her knees on one while Serce did the same. Wolf opted for the floor, one knee propped up with his arm slung over it. He wore his usual green tunic, the thin material straining against his thick muscles.

"Thank you," Cloris said. Her face belied her age. It was also said the priestesses' life spans moved differently than other High Fae, and it was hard to tell if Cloris was twenty or two thousand, despite the fine lines framing her eyes and the sweep of her long grey hair. There was an agelessness about her that was hard to pinpoint.

"I've been doing some reading, as I promised," she said, digging into the bag slung over her shoulder. She pulled out a slim book with a faded cover. "There are so many competing history books in Ouranos, it's difficult to parse which ones are real. I suppose, in a way, they all are. It's a challenge when we enjoy such long life spans. History isn't exactly history when those who lived through it are still amongst us."

She settled down, collapsing on one hip and opening the book. "I've come across only a few passing references to Primaries who've ascended with one another's Artefacts. You understand it's been thousands of years since anyone attempted it?"

She peered at Serce. There was no judgement in her expression, only the curiosity of a professional interested in seeing what was possible. Serce knew when she'd met Cloris, she'd be the perfect Fae to execute her plans. The priestess was known for toeing the lines of magic and challenging boundaries. Serce exchanged a look with Wolf, but his confidence had never wavered. He believed in this as much as she did.

"Why?" Serce asked.

Cloris shook her head. "Primaries aren't normally eager to share their power with someone who matches their strength. The bonding has always favored one side and was never meant to be a union of equals. Besides, the process is difficult from what I've gleaned. The nearest I can determine is that when two Primaries bond, their magic can become erratic unless both are powerful enough to control it. We'll need to implement some safeguards. Adding to that, a Primary bond can only be achieved using a willing vessel of the goddess's magic, which of course is rare to come by."

Serce considered that. She knew she was powerful—possibly the most powerful Primary to ever exist. If anyone could control it, she could. And she had no reservations about sharing her power with Wolf. She eyed the priestess shrewdly with a nagging feeling that Cloris wasn't being entirely forthright about everything. Goddess's magic, indeed.

"Have there been no other Primaries who were drawn to one another?" Serce asked. "Or possibly mates, even?" She kept her question casual, not wanting to reveal anything to Zerra's disciple.

Cloris shrugged her narrow shoulders. "I've never heard of a case with mates, though it seems unlikely there haven't been Primaries who held a more than friendly interest in one another. I suppose they might have entered relationships without the bond, content to keep their magic separate."

Serce shook her head vehemently. Not only was there the question of using the bond to increase her power, she *had* to bond with Wolf. It was said that mates who didn't bond would eventually succumb to permanent death. They'd bypass the Evanescence and simply cease to exist. To lose a love like theirs would fail to honor the sacred gift Zerra had bestowed upon them. There was no question that it had to be done.

"No, that's not good enough."

"I understand, Your Highness." The corner of Cloris's lip turned up in a way that suggested she already knew Serce and

Wolf were mates and was simply humoring them by pretending otherwise.

"What would have happened if I'd bonded to Atlas and Tyr had died? Wouldn't we have become two bonded Primaries then?" Serce asked, wanting to understand all the possible loopholes and pitfalls of this magic.

Cloris waved a dismissive hand. "Oh, the younger Sun Prince is not the next Primary. It wouldn't have been an issue."

Serce frowned at that. "He's not? Then why did they want me to compete in the Trials in the event something happened to his brother?"

"Well, *they* don't know he isn't," Cloris said with a sly glint. "They are simply assuming. I understand why, given he is closest to the Sun King and Tyr, but the Artefacts make their choices based on many factors."

"But you do know?"

"I am a conduit of Zerra, Your Highness. I know many of her secrets."

"Should you be telling us this?"

Cloris tipped her pointed chin. "We are allies, are we not?" She blinked her wide eyes and Serce nodded, definitely on her guard. What game was this priestess playing?

"Of course."

"But it *can* be done? Between me and Serce?" Wolf asked.

Cloris nodded, flipping through the book. "It does seem that way. But you'll need both Artefacts." She looked at both Serce and Wolf with the question in her eyes.

"I'll get it," Serce said. "That won't be a problem."

"And the issue of your mother descending?" There was a note of condescension laced with that question Serce didn't care for, but she tried not to let her irritation show.

"Just leave that to me," she replied.

Cloris nodded. "Good. Then I shall pray to Zerra for her guidance. May she look favorably on this union." She snapped the book shut and tipped her chin towards Serce. "How far along are you?"

"Excuse me?"

She gestured to Serce's midsection. "You're pregnant, aren't you?"

Serce felt the shift of Wolf perking up next to her, his hand coming to the small of her back. She pressed her own hands to her stomach and looked at him. There was so much hope and love in his eyes that her heart missed a beat.

"Serce?"

She opened her mouth, nearly at a loss for words. "I guess I've been feeling a little off lately. I thought I was just tired from all the stress."

Wolf broke into a huge grin and pulled Serce towards him, wrapping her into an enormous hug before he buried his face into her hair. "I love you," he whispered, his voice cracking. She wrapped her arms around him, too, clinging to him, feeling the weight of this moment on her shoulders. A mother. Could she do this?

He pulled away, brushing a lock of hair from her face. "Tell me you're okay with this, Serce. I want you to want this, too."

She swallowed and touched his cheek, his rough stubble pricking her fingers. He was so beautiful it made her heart squeeze every time she looked at him. "I want it, Wolf. With you, I want it."

He smiled again, pulling her close and clutching her tight. "You've made me so fucking happy."

As if finally remembering someone else was there, they both turned to Cloris, who was watching with a patient smile.

"May I?" she asked, holding her hands towards Serce. She nodded and Cloris gently placed them on her stomach, her eyes drifting shut. Serce held still as the priestess's eyelids fluttered.

Wolf moved in closer, a line of concern forming between his thick brows. Serce gave him a look of reassurance, and then Cloris opened her eyes and smiled. "I'd guess about three, maybe four, months."

Serce blew out a long breath and ran her hands over her stomach. "Are you sure?"

"Give or take a week," Cloris answered.

If that was true, then she'd gotten pregnant while they'd still been in Heart during the summit. Knowing this life had started in her home made her feel like this was indeed her destiny. This was how it was all supposed to happen. She'd never been more sure of her purpose.

Wolf's eyes were flushed with love and a look of wonder.

"Serce," he whispered. "Can it really be?"

A grin bloomed on her face. She *was* happy about this. Seeing him so happy made her happy, too. "I think so." He flung his arms around her, tears staining his cheeks. They hugged for a long while, when once again, they remembered they had an audience.

"Sorry," he said to Cloris, who shook her head.

"Not at all. It's a momentous occasion. You should be celebrating."

"Does this change anything?" Serce asked. "Regarding our plans?"

Cloris shook her head, clasping her hands together. "I don't think so. Since it's highly likely you're carrying another Primary, I think this can only work in your favor."

Wolf clasped Serce's hand and kissed the back of it, his eyes shining.

"So what do we do once we have both Artefacts?" Serce asked, returning to business.

Cloris held up the book in her hand. "There is a ritual of sorts that's outlined in here. It's not quite like the ascension, but it's similar. I'll need to study the details a bit more. When do you think you can get the Crown?"

Serce bit her lip, thinking about their next course of action. She'd have to be careful about how she approached this. No one could know what they were planning. Mother had been poisoning the ears of the rulers of Ouranos about her for months, and convincing Daedra to descend was growing more difficult by the day.

Serce looked to Wolf. "We'll have to go for a visit soon."

He nodded sagely. "I'll get everything ready."

"Good." She turned back to Cloris. "I can't thank you enough for everything. For this knowledge and this gift." She pointed to her stomach, running her hands along it.

"I had nothing to do with that," she said with a coy smile. "As for the knowledge, I do expect the compensation we discussed."

"Of course," she replied. "The Ark of the Coeur will be yours once this is over. I swear it."

"Wonderful." Cloris clapped her hands together.

"Won't you stay the night?" Serce asked. "Tomorrow is the new moon, and a feast is being prepared. You must celebrate with us."

Cloris smiled before tucking her book into her bag. "I should be getting back home, but one night can't hurt."

"Perfect," Serce replied with a smile. Wolf stood and helped her stand, his arm wrapping around her waist. She called for one of the servants just beyond the door.

"Yes, Your Highness?"

"Please escort the High Priestess to one of the guest rooms. And send some refreshments up. I'm sure she's famished."

"Thank you, both of you," Cloris said before bowing and then following the servant out of the room. When she was out of earshot, Serce strode to the door and addressed one of Wolf's guards.

"See that Cloris doesn't leave her room. She is hereby a prisoner of Heart and The Woodlands."

The guard dipped his head and scurried off to do her bidding. Wolf wrapped her in his arms from behind as she shut the door and spun to face him.

"She'll come with us to Heart. We can perform the ritual there. It'll be easier than bringing the Crown all the way back here. Fewer moving parts."

"I'll get my army ready for travel," Wolf said, his eyes flicking to the door Cloris had just exited. "She won't be happy about this."

"It can't be helped. No one can know of our plans, and she's now a loose end. Once we're done with her, then she'll need to be eliminated. I don't know what she wants with one of my family's oldest heirlooms, but I have no intention of giving it to her."

Wolf nodded and brushed her bottom lip with his thumb. Their gazes met, and they both looked down at her stomach before looking up again. Wolf broke into a glorious smile.

"You've made me so happy, Serce. You'll get your crown and then we'll claim all of Ouranos and start our family together. Soon, we're going to have everything we've ever wanted."

Chapter Thirty-three

LOR

Present Day: The Aurora

The morning after our dinner in the Violet District, I make good on my vow and allow Nadir to lead me back to the catacombs. As we descend into the arched stone corridors, the aroma that sent me into a tailspin last time drifts up, nearly knocking me over.

Swaying where I stand, I close my eyes and will my thrumming heartbeat to settle. Nadir lingers close to me, quietly waiting as I collect myself. When I feel ready, I peel my eyes open and peer into the gloom.

Grounded with the knowledge this is another step on a path to happiness for me and my siblings, I'm trying to approach this grim task with courage. The Aurora King can only keep hurting me if I let him. I'll do this for Tristan and Willow. For every citizen of Heart who lost their home, too.

"Are you okay?" Nadir asks, and I nod.

"Let's get this over with."

His jaw turns hard before he takes my hand, and we start walking. The boundaries between us have been slowly crumbling, and this simple action feels natural in a way I would never have expected when we set out with this plan two short weeks ago.We move swiftly, trying to cover ground as quickly as possible. I look straight ahead, blocking out the sight of anything that might feel too familiar.

Holding my breath, I try my best to concentrate on whatever it is I'm supposed to notice if the Crown is near. Frustratingly, there's nothing. No change. No discernible difference. The only thing I feel is the tug of my magic and its only interest is Nadir. I've stopped fighting it as much as before, and it responds by purring softly like a newborn kitten, especially when he's touching me.

"I think that's enough," he says eventually. "It's clearly not here." He touches my cheek and gives me a soft smile. "Are you okay? I'm so proud of you for doing this."

"I'm okay," I reply. A little shaky, but having him here with me made it all a little less terrifying. "But what are we going to do now?"

He winks. "I've always got one more idea. Let's go."

When we ascend into the regular part of the castle, I finally release the tense breath I'm holding as we hurry through the halls and back to Nadir's wing. A tray of food has been left out for us—nuts, cheese, slices of soft bread, and crackers—along with a bottle of wine. I pour myself a glass and take a long gulp.

"So what's your idea?" I ask as Nadir sits down next to me.

"My father doesn't really have friends, but I learned this morning that Vale, the closest thing he has to one, just arrived at the Keep this morning."

"Why does that matter?"

"Because it's strange for him to have missed almost all of Frostfire. I wonder if perhaps my father sent him out on an errand that could prove useful for us to know about."

"Do you think he would tell you?"

Nadir shrugs. "Vale loves to hear himself talk. Especially when he's got a few drinks in him. And for some reason, he's always liked me."

"Well, in that case, I'm not sure I can trust anything he says."

Nadir's face breaks into a wry smile before he drops his voice and fixes me with a dark look. "You're going to pay for that later, Inmate."

"Only if I let you," I counter, and he smirks as a knot ties in my stomach.

In spite of everything, his presence feels too easy. Too comfortable. The way he held my hand the entire time today was the only thing keeping me from falling apart. Why is he so far under my skin? It's both thrilling and terrifying.

"I'll make sure of it," he promises.

Trying to break the tension and dispel the constant ache in my chest, I stand up abruptly. "Then I should go get ready."

Nadir nods as I head for my closet and pull out a dress before I go into the bathroom to change.

Several minutes later, I'm putting on a pair of earrings when there's a soft knock.

"Come in," I say as the door swings open and Nadir walks in, tugging on the cuff of his fitted black dress shirt. He's wearing a black jacket that molds to his broad chest and tapered waist in a way that makes my breath catch.

"Dear Zerra," I say, the words slipping out. His dark hair hangs loose around his shoulders, and I can still feel those silky strands running through my fingers. Finished with my jewelry, I clench my hands, willing them to behave.

Nadir's gaze sweeps me from head to toe, his eyes darkening.

"Gods," he says, the word strangled from his throat. "You look good enough to eat."

As I apply my lipstick, Nadir comes to stand behind me. I straighten up as we both watch each other in the reflection. My magic thrums under my skin, always trying to reach for him.

"Why don't we skip the party and stay here?" he says, his voice silky.

"And do what?" I bat my eyes at him in the mirror and he smirks.

"I can think of a few things." His mouth is so close to my ear, his breath snakes down the front of my dress, causing an eruption of goosebumps. A warm knuckle travels the length of my bared back, slowly dragging along my skin. Magic courses to that tiny point of contact, swirling around every bone of my spine.

"What happened to the red dress I saw in the closet?" he asks.

"Aren't I supposed to wear black?"

"Why would I care about that?"

"Doesn't black tell everyone I belong to you?" I say with a roll of my eyes.

"I don't need a dress for anyone to see that."

I huff out a laugh and shake my head.

"Amya bought it for me on a whim, but I didn't want to draw too much attention to myself with it."

"Maybe you can model it for me later."

"We have to go. We need to talk to Vale."

"I know, but you have no idea how much I want to rip this dress off and fuck you on this counter."

My breath is shaky, and I hope he doesn't notice the way my hands tremble as I cap the lipstick and place it on the counter in question.

"I'll show you the fun things I can do with my magic," he adds with such suggestion in his voice that my core pools with liquid heat.

Gathering myself, I meet his dark eyes in the mirror. "Play your cards right, prince of The Aurora, and maybe you'll get it all tonight."

Nadir's nostrils flare, and I sense him trying to collect himself, too. I turn around, my breasts brushing against him. "Shall we go?"

He grabs my arm, pulling me back.

"Let me taste you again," he says, his voice rough. "Before we go downstairs."

My throat goes tight. "You'll mess up my hair. And my make-up," I say, grasping at any straw I can. Everything in me wants to say yes, but still I hesitate.

"I promise I won't," he says, stepping closer, his mouth brushing my ear. "You'll just sit there like a queen while I worship you from my knees."

Our gazes meet and my stomach sinks as his hand slides along my hip and up my ribs. I feel myself nod, and his mouth tips up into a smile. He takes my hand and slowly draws me into the bedroom, standing me in front of the trunk at the foot of his bed.

He drops to his knees and slides his hands under my skirt, hooking into the waistband of my underwear. With his eyes never leaving mine, he drags them down my legs and helps me step out of them as I balance a hand on his shoulder. My breath is shallow, and my heart is pounding hard enough to feel right to my toes.

When he's taken them off, he tosses them to the side and stands up. I look up at him, his eyes swirling with magenta and teal and violet.

"Sit down," he commands, and I'm helpless to resist as I drop onto the trunk, suddenly wanting to obey his every whim. He drags a finger across my cheek and hooks his thumb into my mouth. I bite down on it and he groans, the colors in his eyes moving faster.

"Zerra, you're going to destroy me, aren't you, Heart Queen?"

He once again falls to his knees and presses his palms to the insides of my thighs, spreading my legs apart.

"Lean back," he says, and I do as he asks while he slides up my skirt, baring me to him. For a moment, he doesn't move. He just stares before he grips my knees and then looks up with a grin that lights up his entire face. The sight of it makes my heart twist.

"Don't you dare close your legs. I want to get a look at how beautiful you are." Then he leans down and runs his nose through my wetness, inhaling deeply with a moan. Moving in closer, he lifts up one of my legs and drapes it over his shoulder just as he licks me with a long, luxurious sweep of his tongue.

My hips buck, and I cry out as one of my hands threads into his hair while I use the other to balance myself. He licks me again, the tip of his tongue circling my clit as my entire back bows in response.

"Zerra, you are better than fine wine and thousand-year-old whisky," he groans as he drags my hips forward. He feasts on me, fucking me with his tongue as he laps me up like he's lost in the desert and looking for water.

"Nadir," I gasp, gripping the strands of his thick, dark hair, my head tipping back. "Oh gods, don't stop."

He doubles his efforts at that, the stubble on his chin offering delicious friction as I grind my hips into his face. "Yes," I pant, sure the makeup he promised he wouldn't ruin must be melting off.

I feel the tip of his finger dip inside me, and I look down. He's observing me with an intense expression as he slowly eases it in. We both watch where he fucks me with his hand before he adds another finger and then leans in again, the tip of his tongue roughly circling my clit.

My release is right there, but I resist it, wanting to prolong this just for a little longer. Right now might be the freest I've ever felt. In this Keep that once haunted my dreams with this dark prince at my feet, I feel more powerful than I ever have in my life. There are still so many things to overcome, but possibility—pure bright unfiltered possibility—looms before me with the promise of the future I was denied.

"Lor," Nadir growls as he thrusts his fingers into me and then curls them, "come for me." And then I do, letting out a cry as a wave of sensation rocks through me, shuddering through my limbs and toes and fingers. I keep on coming, the surge cresting over me for what feels like forever before I finally catch my breath.

Nadir remains on the floor, watching me with a sort of reverence I can't interpret. His face shines with the evidence of my release, and he gives me a dark smile before he reaches up and kisses my neck, sucking gently on the skin.

"You see, Heart Queen?" he whispers. "Like I promised, there isn't a hair out of place."

CHAPTER THIRTY-FOUR

When my breathing finally returns to normal, Nadir rises and draws me up to stand, kissing the back of my hand.

"We should go," he says, his voice thick. "We'll finish this after the party."

I nod with my heart caught in my throat, both disappointed we have to leave but also relieved I have a bit of time to contemplate the idea of losing myself completely to him. It's getting harder to separate my emotions from my desires, and if we continue in this manner, I might lose myself to a point I swore I wouldn't.

He won't have my heart.

At least for now, this gives me some time to get my head on straight and remind myself this is only physical. He gives me another once-over that I feel with a throb low in my stomach, and then he steps back, holding out his elbow for me.

"Let's go, Heart Queen."

"Am I getting my underwear back this time?"

He gives me a predatory grin. "Definitely not."

I sigh, pretending to be put out, and take his arm.

We make our way through the Keep, following the trickle of guests also decked out for an evening of entertainment, just as we arrive at yet another large room designated for tonight's party. The space is lined with fur rugs and wooden benches covered with thick blankets. The ceiling is open to the night sky, and a massive bonfire burns in the center of the room, flames leaping and sparking in the air. I see Amya holding court with a circle of admiring Fae, her smile bright as they all laugh at something she's just said.

Nadir takes my hand and winds us through the crowd. By now, the elite of The Aurora have become accustomed to my presence and know who I am. Or at least they know the story we've been telling.

"Nadir," comes a cold voice, and we both come to a halt in front of his father. Nadir's hand tightens against mine before he draws me closer.

"Father," he says, his tone equally chilly. The king peers around Nadir, and for the first time in years, his eyes land on me.

"You haven't introduced me to this lovely young woman who's been occupying all your time. How insufferably rude."

Nadir tenses and my own breath kicks in my chest. Does he suspect something? Why is he suddenly noticing me now?

However, the king's gaze is fused with mild boredom and mostly disdain. He's only asking to get under Nadir's skin, not because he really cares who I am. Nevertheless, something fiery licks in my chest. How can this monster stand a foot in front of me and have no idea who I am? I meant so little to him that he can't even be bothered to remember my face?

Sure, I was younger and was a very different version of myself, but hatred so pure and white burns straight to my fingertips, forcing them to curl against the fabric of my skirt. I used to think Nadir was cold and unfeeling, but he's a raging inferno of passion compared to the king, whose entire demeanor speaks to the indifference of a windswept tundra. Lonely, barren, and dead.

Nadir tugs me back, stepping ever so slightly in front of me. I know it's to protect me, but I refused to be dismissed.

"It's a pleasure to meet you," I say, holding out a hand to the king, leaving it poised in midair. My jaw hardens as I note the indecision in his face before he finally deigns to take it and then tips his chin. I conceal the shudder that runs down my back as he drops my hand, his lip curling.

"The pleasure is mine," he says evenly, his eyes sweeping over me again with cool apathy. It's so patently obvious he thinks I'm beneath him.

"Nadir," the king says, dismissing me again. "I need you to speak to Karlo when he arrives. He's keen on my proposal, and I know you two go way back."

I resist the urge to scream at the king as he pretends I don't exist. To shake him and confront him with what he did. Nadir tugs my hand softly, just enough that I snap out of my trance.

I will get my opportunity, I remind myself. I just need to be patient.

"Why do you need me?" Nadir asks.

The king pelts him with a hard look. "Are you not the heir to this kingdom? At least pretend to show some interest in running it."

It's my turn to squeeze Nadir's hand as his jaw clenches. He drops his head forward. "Of course, Father. I'll do what I can," he bites out, and Rion arches a dark brow before he nods curtly and turns away. When he's disappeared into the masses, Nadir swings to me.

"What the fuck did you do that for?"

I shake my head. "I'm sorry. It's just when he looks through me like that..." I trail off, staring at the space where the king disappeared, my heart thudding in my chest. "Sometimes I don't think. He barely noticed me, anyway."

Tristan can say whatever he wants about how I've grown, but it's moments like this when I'm reminded of how far I still have to go. One day I'll learn to control the impulsiveness and wildness that got me into trouble so many times in Nostraza.

The look on Nadir's face when I turn back to him clenches something in my chest. "I...get it," he says softly. Still holding my hand, he draws me closer, his finger coming under my chin to tip my face up. "I get it. But you need to be careful."

His face is so close to mine that the noise and the surrounding chaos dims to a hushed murmur. Why do I go breathless every time he looks at me like that? *Why* does he keep looking at me like that? Like he wants to peel me apart and consume the pieces of my soul.

"We should go find Vale," Nadir says, pulling away, and I don't know why that disappoints me. What did I want him to do in this room full of people? He's already told me he's ready whenever I am, but I'm leaning off the edge of a cliff and trying not to look down.

He tugs on my hand again, moving us through the crowd. I snatch a cocktail from a passing server and take a sip of the dark, earthy liquid. It's garnished with a floating cinnamon stick and a slice of orange. The alcohol warms my insides and helps to dull the electricity of my fraying emotions.

Nadir takes us to an area lined with overstuffed leather couches where a High Fae sits. His face is lined like the king's, marking him as slightly older, though he still could pass for little more than forty in human years.

"Vale," Nadir says, his voice strangely warm as the male stands up and embraces him. He's got dark auburn hair clipped neatly around his pointed ears and is wearing an impeccable emerald suit. After greeting Nadir, his bright blue eyes land on me.

"Who do we have here?"

"This is my friend," Nadir says, clearly declining to give my name. Vale doesn't hesitate to take my hand and press his mouth to the back of it with a smile far more approving than the king's.

"Well, aren't you a lovely little thing?" He leans closer, as though to whisper in my ear. "If the prince is boring you, I can assure you I'd show you all kinds of fun."

Nadir growls low in his throat, his hand coming to Vale's chest and pushing him back with a bit more force than is probably necessary. "Don't make me banish you to the ozziller pits, Vale." His tone is light, but the threat is obvious. Vale's tanned skin pales a fraction, and then he breaks into a grin.

"You know I'm just having a little fun, my boy." He claps a large hand on Nadir's shoulder, and Nadir's eyes darken as he glares at Vale. Zerra, neither of us seems capable of controlling our emotions tonight. Don't we make quite a pair.

"Nadir, don't be so rude. You were just telling me what a great spinner of tales Vale is, and I want to hear something...entertaining," I say, making my voice light and playful. If we're going to get any information out of this Fae, we need to get on his good side.

"Of course," Nadir says tightly, catching my drift. "May we join you?"

"That would be wonderful," Vale says, gesturing to the empty space on the sofa. Nadir places himself very deliberately between the two of us as we settle into the soft leather.

A server stops, lowering her tray and offering us a drink. I exchange my empty glass for a small tumbler of ruby red wine. Vale reaches for a whisky, and Nadir declines a drink. His arm slides along the back of the couch, wrapping around my shoulders. I know what he's doing and Vale doesn't miss it either, his eyes dropping to my legs that are now bare thanks to the opening in my skirt. I wonder how I can use this to my advantage without sending Nadir off into an annoying, possessive Fae tirade.

"What have you been up to lately?" Nadir asks casually, his gaze sweeping over the room.

"I'm opening a new club up in the Crimson District. Very exciting stuff," Vale says, rubbing his hands together. "You'll have to come see it when it opens," he says to me, his eyes overtly dipping to my cleavage. What a pig.

"I don't think so," Nadir says, glowering at Vale. For someone he claims to like, Nadir is behaving about as pleasantly as if he's sitting on a flaming porcupine right now. Is this because of me? I don't know why he thinks I'm not visiting Vale's club, but I plan to remind him later he's not the arbiter of what I can and can't do. Perhaps I'll go just to annoy Nadir.

Vale continues talking, rambling about this venture and that investment, and Nadir is getting visibly frustrated. Neither of us can get a word in. As I'm trying to decide how to steer the conversation in a new direction, a low fae servant emerges through the crowd. She has grey skin and a fall of long green hair, along with shimmery scales running across her cheekbones. She bows to Nadir.

"Pardon me, Your Highness, but the king asked me to retrieve you."

Nadir sighs and runs a hand down his face. "I better go." His eyes flick to me. "Will you be okay for a few minutes?"

"Of course." I nod. "Go on."

Nadir pauses, his mouth opening and then closing again, before he lifts himself up. He gives me one more lingering look before he follows the servant through the crowd. The moment he's out of eyesight, Vale slides closer, his arm easing against the back of the couch.

"I thought he'd never leave," Vale says and winks. I offer him a loose smile, even though every bone in my body wants to resist.

"How about another drink?" I ask, holding up my empty glass.

"I like the sound of that," he says, gesturing to a server who delivers us two more whiskies. Vale takes a deep sip of his and lets out a sigh, his head dropping back. I clutch mine in my hands, leaving it untouched. I need to slow down. I don't want another repeat of my first night here, and I need to keep my wits coherent.

"Ah, I always miss this when I'm traveling. Nothing tops the vintage they make in the Amber District. No one in Ouranos even comes close."

I peer into my glass and take a tiny sip. It slides down my throat with a mixture of cinnamon and honey, warming my stomach. "It's lovely, yes."

Vale takes another long draught and then gestures to a server for another. "More?" he asks, and I hold up my still-full glass.

"I'm good for now, thank you."

Vale shrugs and accepts another drink. His posture is getting looser, and I'm starting to wonder just how many of those he's had.

"Where have you been traveling?" I ask, trying to infuse my voice with wonder and naivety. Here I am, a poor silly human who's never ventured further than the borders of The Aurora. Too bad that's mostly true.

A smile flickers across Vale's lips, and he leans back, surveying the crowded room. I resist the urge to roll my eyes at his smugness.

"Have you traveled much?" he asks.

"I haven't had the opportunity."

Vale leans closer, his body pressing against mine now, and I swallow the tension in my shoulders. My dark past comes back to rear its head, and how many times must I do this to get what I want? Is *this* what it comes back to every time? I hold completely still, gripping my glass tightly.

"I've been on a mission of sorts," Vale says, his green eyes sparkling.

"A mission? That sounds fascinating," I reply, figuring flattery can't hurt.

"Indeed," Vale says. "I've been tasked with finding a very special object for the king."

My breath seizes in my chest.

"What kind of object?" I carefully make my voice neutral, widening my eyes, continuing my charade of the dazed ingenue.

Vale smiles, pressing in closer. He's finished his drink and deposits the glass on the table in front of him. His hand lands on my knee, and I inhale a sharp breath that I hope he mistakes for interest instead of the cold slither of dread that slides down my back.

"A very rare and powerful one," he replies in a low voice that I suppose is meant to be seductive. Bile climbs up my throat, but I think he's about to reveal something important, and this might be my chance.

"What is it?" I ask, dropping my own voice to a breathy whisper. *He's the most fascinating man you've ever met*, I tell myself over and over. *Just lean into this.*

"Oh, you've probably never heard of it." His tone drips with condescension. "The Ark is one of the rarest objects to ever exist. It hasn't been seen in centuries." He taps the side of his nose as I frown.

"The what?"

His hand slides higher, his fingers stopping short of the fabric of my dress. They twitch against my skin as if he's holding every part of himself back. I take in a shaky breath, covering it with a sip of whisky.

"It's—"

Suddenly, Vale is jerked away, knocking the glass from my hand, the contents spilling on the thick rug at my feet, splashing onto my bare shins. Nadir has Vale by the collar, fury and thunder in his expression. He cocks his arm and punches Vale so hard I hear the crunch of his nose collapsing as his head flings back. The entire room gasps as every single eye falls on us.

My cheeks burn with anger, with embarrassment, with the vile, uncomfortable encounter I just allowed to happen. Again, I had to use my body to get what I want, and I'm fucking sick of it. And I didn't even get anything. He isn't searching for the Crown at all.

"What the fuck, Nadir," I hiss, jumping up from the sofa. I'm not entirely sure what I'm mad at. Me for letting this happen. Him for overreacting. Everything for leading us to yet another dead end.

I don't give him the chance to reply, instead spinning on my heel and storming away. The crowd parts for me, all of them gawping. I don't look anyone in the eye as I head for the exit, my skin hot and itching, my dress suddenly too tight.

Finally, I get to the door and storm through it, taking a deep breath.

"Lor!" Nadir catches up to me. "Wait."

"What the fuck was that?" I spin around and point back to the room.

"He was touching you," Nadir snarls, his face a mask of fury.

"So what? I was prying information from him since you weren't getting anywhere."

"You're mine. No one touches you without my permission," Nadir says, his voice dropping. His hand circles my upper arm, his touch hot and electric. My magic snaps towards him, but I pull it away.

I don't want this. I don't want him. This cannot happen. The Torch already warned me, and I'd be the greatest fool in the world to fall for any of this again.

"I'm not yours," I hiss.

"I can still taste you, Inmate," he purrs, low and deadly.

"It's just sex. That's what you said. I'm the one who says who can touch me, not you!"

"Lor—"

I hold up a hand. "No. Stop. This is over." I gesture between us. "This was a terrible idea to begin with. We've failed at our task, and I don't want to see you ever again. I'll do this on my own."

"Fine," Nadir snarls, his entire demeanor shifting. "Go back to Vale. Spread your legs for him."

I stare at him, my mouth dropping open. Despite what I just said, those words tear an open gash through my soul.

"How *dare* you?" I take a step back, needing space.

"Is that what you did for Atlas, too?"

I shake my head and wrap my arms around myself. I can't believe he's saying these things to me.

"I hate you," I say, the words as bitter as poison.

"I know." His eyes are a maelstrom of rage and desire, and I have to push my emotions down, burying them where all of my demons live. Where I'll lock them away because I have far more important things to do than worry about my tangled feelings for this asshole.

He's my enemy.

He's *always* been the enemy. The reminder and symbol of everything I lost.

How could I have forgotten that?

"Fuck you," I whisper. "Find somewhere else to sleep tonight. I don't want you anywhere near me."

With that, I spin on my heel and storm away.

Chapter Thirty-five

Nadir

I watch her go with my breath twisted tight and my fists clenching so hard they ache. I'm going to pay for what I just did to Vale, but when I saw the way he was touching her, and how uncomfortable she was, I lost it.

What the fuck is wrong with me? *Why* do I care so much?

She's a challenge, that's all. She hates me so much that I want to keep pushing her. Push her to admit she wants me. But if that's all it is, then why do I want to claim her as mine? I shake my head and run a hand through my hair, gripping it tight just for something to hang on to. I'll never see her again once this is all over, I reason. If any of us lives through this, maybe at the occasional formal affair once she takes her throne. Then I can move on with my life and get her out of my head.

But I'm not stupid enough to really believe any of that is true.

I take a deep breath, trying to force myself to relax. I should go and apologize. She can take care of herself, and I should have let her deal with it. She's proven that enough times already.

But I didn't want to. She's mine. I don't know why I believe it with such conviction, but deep in my bones, I know she belongs to me. And I'll die before anyone else touches her.

Zerra, I can't believe I said those things to her. I'd deserve it if she never speaks to me again. I'll give her some space to calm down and then go smooth things over. Whatever it takes, I'll do anything to make it up to her.

I spin around, not really sure where I should go. Not back to the party and not to my room. I suck in a sharp breath when I see my father watching me, his hands in his pockets and his posture loose.

"That was quite the performance," he drawls as he saunters over, his voice glacial.

I shrug, feigning a nonchalance I certainly don't feel. Fuck, I've never been so wound up in my entire life.

"You know how women can be," I say, knowing I've already played my hand by attacking Vale. I should know better than to lose control with my father around. I'm no better than Lor at keeping my emotions in check. I've failed her in so many ways tonight.

"Where did you find her?" the king asks, peering at me with a strange light in his eyes.

"At the Scarlett Flower," I say, plucking the name of a brothel in the Crimson District from thin air. "She was an especially enthusiastic... purchase," I add, trying to keep my voice smooth.

"Oh? I wasn't aware you were a patron."

My mouth tips up into a half smile. "Why wouldn't I be?"

"What did you just call her? Lor, was it?"

"A stage name," I say, something sharp clawing up the back of my scalp.

"Of course," Rion says, scratching his chin. "Are you coming back to the party? Vale is nursing his jaw, but he should know better than to get too friendly with something that clearly belonged to you. Bygones, I'm sure."

"Yes. I'll be there in a minute. I was about to find Jessamine to discuss the labor bill, as you requested."

That's me. The ever-dutiful son, carrying out his father's wishes in the end.

"Good." He says it with a slow nod, his gaze sweeping over me with assessment. "Perhaps you'll finally be worthy of this role and see this is for the best, Nadir."

With those biting remarks, the king turns and heads to the ballroom as I try to burn holes into his skin with the heat of my hatred.

I watch as he greets the head of the Fuchsia District and her bonded partner who fawn over him like the cloying sycophants they are.

But as soon as my father disappears through the crowd, I turn and run.

He knows.

With my heart thundering in my chest, I blast through the Keep, my legs pumping. When I reach my wing, I order my guards not to let anyone through, especially the king's men.

After slamming through the door of my bedroom, panic rolls over my back when I find it empty.

"Lor!"

Storming into the room, I notice the dress she was wearing hanging off the back of the sofa. I spin around. I can't think straight. Where is she?

"Lor!"

I find her in the bathroom, scrubbing her makeup off, refusing to look at me.

"I told you to find somewh—"

"He knows," I interrupt.

She stops, her dark eyes spreading wide. "Knows what?"

"He knows who you are."

The color drains from her face as she clutches the cloth to her chest.

"That little stunt you pulled—"

"That I pulled! You're the one who caused a scene!"

There isn't time to argue about this.

"He knows. He didn't say it, but I could tell. He fucking knows."

I turn on my heel and send a blast of magic towards the door, erecting a barricade against anyone trying to break it down before I go to dig into the closet. Lor follows me, her eyes wild with panic.

"Get dressed in as many warm clothes as you can. We're leaving. Now."

Zerra, I want to kill my father. I want to shove his head into a hole filled with scorpions and watch him choke on his own tongue. I want to rip him apart with my bare hands and bathe in his blood.

But first, I have to get Lor out of here.

For once, she doesn't argue, her face ashen and her hands trembling. She stuffs her feet into her boots and pulls a thick sweater over her head. She's refusing to look at me, because I've fucked this entire thing up.

Even now, with the threat of Rion over our heads, I can't get past how beautiful she is. How she makes me feel every time she's in the room and maybe, more importantly, how she makes me feel when she isn't.

I'm worried she'll never let me touch her again. Tonight was going to be so perfect, and I ruined it. Gods, how I want to explore her. To have her in ways I've never had anyone.

I dress rapidly, forcing myself to take a deep breath and listen with one ear trained on the door. Has the king realized I know? Will he send his guards now or later? Fuck. How could I have been so careless? I'm supposed to protect her.

She digs into the chest at the foot of the bed, pulling out gloves and a scarf and a thick furry hat. My gaze constantly darts to the door, waiting for it to burst open. But I'm not sorry that I clocked Vale. The fucker deserved it for putting his hands on her.

When Lor is bundled up, I flick my head towards the balcony. That's when my bedroom door shudders, the shield of my magic rippling against the assault. We both look at it and then each other.

"Come on."

Defiance and anger flicker in her eyes. She hates me more than she ever has, but she's not stupid. She does as I ask, scurrying for the balcony.

"I'll need to carry you." I'm not sure why that's so hard to say. Lor tips up her chin, her brown eyes flashing as another loud bang rattles the door, the barrier holding on for now.

"Fine." The word is clipped at the end, and the sound slices out a piece of my heart. I ignore the stab of pain as I scoop her into my arms. For a moment, I can't breathe with our noses almost touching and our breath fogging in the cool air. I want to tell her I'll protect her. That I'll do anything to keep her safe, and that I fucked up tonight. But I can't make the words come out.

"Ready?" I ask her instead, because I'm nothing but a fucking coward.

She nods. "Ready."

I leap onto the guardrail, my magic erupting around us in a jumble of ribbons before they form into a pair of wide wings. With one last glance over my shoulder, I groan at the thought of how this night was *supposed* to end. When I turn back to Lor, her expression is blank, her lips pressed into a hard line.

The door shudders again, bowing out under the weight of the force on the other side, the wood beginning to splinter. We're officially out of time. I drop from the balcony, and Lor's grip tightens as we plunge for several feet before my wings beat. Then we lift into the air, disappearing into the night.

CHAPTER THIRTY-SIX

LOR

N adir's magic closes over us as we shoot through the sky. My arms snake around his neck as the cold air presses against me. I'm still furious with him, but right now, his closeness is comforting because my heart is wedged in my throat. The king knows. He figured it out. What does that mean for me? How hard will he try to find me?

We fly for a few minutes before Nadir descends to earth. We're deep in the Void now, the crenellations of the Keep looming far in the distance.

"Lor," he says, his voice rough, a sheen of sweat on his brow. "We need to keep moving. I just need a minute."

I nod and try to push my fear down, trying to get my hands to stop shaking.

"Are you okay?" I ask.

"Yes." He presses a fist to his chest and lets out a deep breath. "That was too close. I'm not sure I've ever been so scared."

"How much danger am I really in? He still thinks I'm powerless. He hasn't believed I'm the Primary in years."

The look on Nadir's face is full of regret. "He knows I was lying to him. That I brought you to the Keep for a reason he's currently trying to puzzle out. If he hasn't already, he's going to realize he made a mistake. There was no reason to hide you, otherwise."

As he's talking, I understand he's right. Why couldn't I have kept my mouth shut?

"I messed this up," I say, feeling the weight of everyone I've let down.

Nadir comes closer. "You didn't do anything wrong. It was my fault. He heard me say your name, and there was always a risk he'd figure it out." He scans the sky, which is flecked with stars and the striations of the Borealis overhead. Tonight, they hold no beauty for me. Tonight, they're the reminder of twelve miserable years of captivity. Of the deaths of my parents and everyone who's suffered at the hands of the Aurora King.

"We should go." I nod, casting a glance back towards the Keep, wondering if the king is about to burst through the trees.

"You're angry. Please, look at me."

"Is this really the time?"

Of course I'm angry. He acted like a possessive asshole and then insulted me to my face. I don't need him fighting my battles. I knew this was a mistake from the start, and tonight proved it once and for all. The Torch already warned me and now Nadir swiftly hammered that final nail through my heart.

His jaw hardens as he scans the sky again.

"Let's go." He holds out his hand and I take it, thankful my hands are covered with thick gloves. Though it doesn't seem to matter, my traitorous heart still skips a beat when he squeezes my fingers.

He picks me up again, and though I want to resist, I don't fight him. Distancing ourselves from the Keep is the priority right now. We can deal with this thing between us later. Or this thing that's now over between us, because I'm not doing this anymore.

His magic swirls around us again, and I can't help but think about what he promised to show me before we left for the party tonight. Nadir looks down at me, but I turn away, not wanting him to read anything I'm thinking.

It's freezing out here, and I bury into him, trying to get warm. A few moments later, the same flow of magic he used the day we rode through the forest envelops me in a warm cocoon.

We're both silent as he shoots through the air, keeping as low to the trees as possible. He seems like he wants to say something, but he remains quiet before he looks forward into the darkness. I don't know how much time passes before I recognize a familiar sight.

"No," I say as he swerves and drops us into the front courtyard of the manor house before he sets me down.

"No?"

"We're not bringing the king to where Willow and Tristan are. This is too dangerous. You need to take me somewhere else. If something happens to them, I'll never forgive you."

His hands land on my shoulders, and he turns me to face him. I'm freaking out for a thousand different reasons.

"Lor. Calm down. My father doesn't know this place exists. It's hidden from anyone I choose to hide it from. He won't find them here. Or you. I promise."

"You swear?"

"I'm not going to let anything happen to you or your family."

I don't know why I still believe him after everything that's happened, but I do.

"Okay," I say, looking towards the house that sits mostly dark, with only a few dim lights flickering in the windows.

Nadir leads me inside, closing the door softly behind us. There is no movement in the foyer, but we hear the sounds of chatter coming from the library. I round the corner to find my brother and sister with Mael and Hylene.

"Lor!" Willow shouts, jumping up from her seat and embracing me in a tight hug. "What are you doing here?"

Nadir marches into the room and pours himself a large glass of wine from the decanter on the table. "He knows," he says, and the entire room goes still against the crackling of the fire in the hearth. "We blew it." He looks at me. "I blew it," he corrects himself.

"No, I screwed up, too. I couldn't stop myself. Every time I saw him, I wanted to—" I cut off, trembling from the depth of my fury.

And then I start to cry. It comes over me like a hundred-foot tidal wave crashing into me without warning. I've been holding so much pain and so many memories and tonight was one test too many. Willow pulls me down into her chair, and I bury my face into her shoulder, my body wracked with sobs.

"It's okay," Willow whispers. "Everything will be okay. We'll figure this out."

I nod, but I don't believe her. The king will never let me go. And now he knows. Or if he doesn't know the complete truth, he suspects something now. Nadir is right. There was no reason to keep my presence a secret otherwise. We took a chance on infiltrating the Keep, and we lost the game with what I'm sure will be disastrous consequences.

That's when the door swings open, and Amya strides into the room. She's dressed in her party clothes, her cheeks flushed and her usually perfect hair loose and disheveled. "What happened! Why did you run out of there and why did father send his guards to your wing?"

She presses her hand to her chest, breathing heavily. We fill her in on what's just occurred as her shoulders drop further and further.

"No," she says softly, something broken in the sound.

"What are we going to do now?" Tristan asks, addressing everyone in the room. "You still haven't found the Crown, I take it?"

"No," Nadir says, shaking his head. "But we have enough reason to believe it's not in the Keep."

"Then where is it?"

Nadir pushes himself up from the chair and approaches me where I sit with Willow, his face hardened into grim resolve. Something tells me he's bracing for what he's about to say next.

"What?" I ask, sitting up and wiping the tears from my cheeks. "What is it?"

I push myself up slowly so I can look him in the eye as he tips his chin down to me.

"I know where we need to look."

His words are as heavy as a ceiling of marble. The air in the room grows thick, like the pressure before an impending storm, but there is no rain or thunder or lightning, only an ostensible sense that everything is about to change, yet again.

"I'm taking you to Heart, Inmate. It's time to go home."

CHAPTER THIRTY-SEVEN

"I'm not going anywhere with you," are the first words out of my mouth.

"Well, you're not going there without me. It's too dangerous."

We stare at one another, the argument from the party sitting between us, but we're surrounded by too many people, and this isn't a conversation I want to continue with an audience.

"Nadir," I say, my voice low.

"Lor," he growls, "you're going with me or you're not going. You can't get there on your own, and no one else can get you there as quickly as I can. Besides, if my father does come for you, I'm in the best position to protect you."

I look at my siblings. "What about them? It's their home, too."

"When this is over, when you get the Crown and take your queendom back, you can all go home." Nadir inhales a deep breath. "I promised I'd help you, and I intend to follow through."

"Even now?" I ask, lifting my chin, both of us knowing what I mean. Now that I've told him sex is off the table, is he still going to help me?

"Yes," he says without hesitation. "*That* was never a condition and you know it."

"What's this about?" Tristan asks, coming to stand next to me, ever my protector. "What condition?"

"Nothing Tris. It's fine." My focus returns to Nadir. "I still don't understand why you want to help me." I'm trying to see his angle. The ground is swaying under me, and I can't find my footing. "Surely you can find a way to get rid of your father without me."

"No, I cannot," Nadir says in a way that clogs the back of my throat.

"And when we find the Crown and take back my queendom?"

Nadir frowns. "What do you mean?"

"What will you do then? Come back here?" My stomach twists with the implications of what I'm asking. I told him I didn't want to see him ever again an hour ago, but it seems we're stuck with each other for a little while longer. But then what? Does he intend to let me rule in peace? Knowing what I might be capable of?

"No," Nadir says, "I mean, yes. I mean, I don't know. It all depends."

"On?"

"What happens," he says.

"On what happens when you take the Crown from me?" I ask, trying to force him to bend to whatever truths he's hiding.

"No." He shakes his head. "I don't want the Crown from you. I didn't before. I don't now. The Crown doesn't matter to me, not in the way you're implying. I only care that you're safe." There's a pained thread in his tone that forces me to drop my guard, my shoulders slumping.

"I don't know how to be safe," I whisper. "I've never been safe."

His expression darkens. "You'll be safer with me than without me. I promise I'll protect you."

"Lor," Tristan says, wrapping his hand around my elbow. He turns me to face him. "You should go with him."

I blink in surprise. "I should?"

"This has all been set in motion now. You can't go back anymore. The Aurora King knows, or at least must suspect, what you are. He nearly killed you trying to prove you were the Primary already, and he won't stop now that he has you in his sights again. The only way to get to the end is to go through."

Tristan gestures to Mael. "Tell her."

"Tell me what?"

Mael looks at Nadir, a question in his expression. Nadir nods.

"The king has been rounding up all the women in the Heart settlements and testing them."

The weight of those words nearly crushes me, threatening to cut off my air. "He's looking for the Primary," I say.

"That's what we think," Nadir adds. "But he's probably realizing he really did have you under his nose all along."

"You knew?" I accuse. "And you didn't tell me? Is he hurting them? Is he killing them?"

My voice is rising with the horror of knowing what these women might be suffering because I've been hiding.

"I didn't think you needed that added burden on your shoulders."

"He's testing women because he's looking for me! And I've been swanning about the Keep going to fucking parties for the past two weeks. You had no right to keep that from me!"

"What good would it have done? You are powerless without that Crown. And even then, we don't know if that's the key to unlocking your magic."

My entire body sags, knowing he's right, but I'm hurt that he kept this from me all the same. "You still should have told me."

He presses his mouth together. "Maybe I should have, but it's proof that my father won't stop at anything to get his hands on you, and the longer you stand here arguing with me, the more danger you're in."

Now Willow joins Tristan. "Go home, Lor," she says softly, and suddenly I'm seized with longing for a place I've never seen except in my head.

Home.

A place I only know from the stories I've pieced together in my imagination. Not even our mother lived there. She couldn't fill in those gaps for us, either. All we had were tales and rumors whispered on the wind. Nothing concrete. Nothing we could hold on to.

"We'll wait here for you. You have to do this. Tristan is right. There is no going back anymore. The moment you were taken to Aphelion, it set into action a course of destiny that can no longer be undone. We believe in you. I'm sure this is how Zerra always meant for it to happen."

It's then I finally break, the crushing weight of the last two weeks nearly folding me in two. The memories that have churned to the surface from being in the presence of the Aurora King. The terror I felt when I walked those dark hallways deep beneath the Keep. The way Nadir has turned me inside out until I don't know what I feel anymore.

My brother and sister wrap me in their embrace, and for a moment, we're transported back to Nostraza. On one of those days, when one of us was feeling particularly melancholy. On one of those days when we didn't need words to convey the infinite depths of our loss and heartache. When all we needed was to hold on to each other because our love was the only thing we had left.

"I can do this," I whisper, trying to believe it's true, but I've never been less sure of anything in my life. Willow takes my face in her hands and stretches onto her tiptoes before placing a kiss on my forehead.

"You've always been so brave, my baby sister. It's okay to be scared. This is the biggest thing we could have ever asked for. It's scary, but if there was ever anyone who can face this, it's you."

"You know siblings are supposed to be meaner to each other," I say with a half sob and half laugh. "Give each other a hard time like these two." I gesture to Amya and Nadir, who are watching us intently. They blink when I point at them before they look at each other with a smile.

Willow's answering grin is crooked. "I don't think that counts when you grow up in prison together."

I choke out another sob. "Gods, that's really fucking depressing."

That statement breaks the tension in the room, and everyone laughs before Willow hugs me again.

I look at Nadir over my shoulder. "Okay, prince of The Aurora. You aren't the ally I expected to have and I'm still not entirely sure I trust you, but you're all I've got."

Nadir's smile is wry as he tips his head. "You really know how to flatter a prince. We'll leave at first light. It's too risky to travel at night—my wings are too visible. Try to get a few hours of sleep."

I wipe my eyes and pull away from Willow as she takes my hand.

"Are you hungry?" she asks.

I shake my head.

"Your room is still made up," Amya says. "I'll just make sure everything is in order."

Willow leaves with Amya, Tristan trailing after, followed by Mael and Hylene.

After everyone clears the room, Nadir turns back to me. "Do you think they all did that on purpose? Left us alone?"

"Very subtle."

"About tonight, with Vale. I'm sorry."

"For what?"

"Not for punching the jackass, if that's what you want to hear. I'm sorry it upset you, though. And I didn't mean those things I said."

I let out a deep sigh, my irritation from earlier flaring.

"Then why did you say them?"

"Because I'm an imperfect asshole." He pauses. "But it isn't how I feel. Your sister is right, you are brave and strong and have come through fire, and I have a feeling you'll still have to face a much bigger inferno before this is done. I want to help you. I am in awe of your courage and resilience."

The edges of my anger soften a little at those words, but ultimately, they change nothing.

"Nadir, I meant what I said earlier. This thing between us is over. I can't allow myself to get distracted anymore. I'm not too stubborn to understand that I need your help if you're willing to offer it, but I need to learn to protect myself, and I'm *not* yours."

Nadir sucks in a sharp breath and it's obvious he wants to argue. His jaw flexes, and his eyes flash with sparks of crimson.

"No, but you will be," he says, and there is a solemn oath hidden in those words. The expression on his face tells me this is far from the last I've heard of this, but I must stay strong.

He will not have my heart.

I don't respond to that statement, instead straightening my shoulders and holding him with a look that I hope tells him I am resolute in my decision.

"I'll see you in the morning."

Nadir takes a step towards me, and I feel this moment for what it is. It's a reckoning, and somewhere along the way, I'm going to have to deal with the consequences of everything that's already happened between us.

"Goodnight, Heart Queen."

CHAPTER THIRTY-EIGHT

I barely sleep. Instead, I toss and turn, my mind racing with horrific visions of what's happening to those women at the hands of the Aurora King. I can practically hear their screams from across Ouranos.

He used his magic to bend and nearly break me. He dug into my skin and into my organs and tried to shred the wall of my magic. But it held. Through everything, I held out. And now that same strength is working against me, and those women are being tortured, and I have to find a way to break through my own walls. I have to find that Crown and pray it's the answer I'm seeking.

I see Nadir's face, too. The way he looked at me when I told him I wasn't his and the way he answered. Why is he so certain of this? Why does he even care?

He's a prince. A man with his pick of any woman he could ever want. Why does he keep coming back to me? I'm just a prison rat with nothing but the ephemeral promise of a future I'm unlikely to survive. It's confusing. Frustrating. And honestly, I don't have time for this right now. I have to find that Crown. And somehow, I have to stop the Aurora King. I'm more sure than ever his intentions for me are similar to what Atlas wanted.

I know I should be scared, but I'm well beyond that now. This has become about something so much bigger than me.

Eventually, I cave to a restless version of sleep, my body never fully relaxing. It's far too soon when The Aurora sky lightens from silky black to a strangely comforting grey. To think how much I once loathed its endless dreariness. When did it start to feel more like a warm blanket? Probably around the same time I kissed Nadir.

Fuck. No. That's over.

Eventually, I drag myself from bed and dress in clothing suitable for travel. Amya had already delivered some options before I went to sleep last night.

What's waiting for me in the ruined Queendom of Heart? What's left of the empire that once existed?

I don a pair of soft suede pants in dark grey and a thin black sweater before I scoop my hair into a high ponytail. I put on a pair of sturdy boots and grab the coat, mittens, and scarf I arrived with last night.

My stomach rumbles, so I go in search of breakfast. First, I need to see Willow and Tristan and say goodbye to them yet again. Hopefully, this will be the last time, but every time I leave them, I'm less and less certain I'm ever coming back.

I knock on Willow's door, hoping she's awake already.

There is a shuffle on the other side. "Who is it?"

"It's me," I say.

"Oh." She sounds uncertain and a moment later, the door cracks open. She's wearing a nightgown, her hair mussed from sleep.

There's a movement behind Willow. Amya stands behind her, also dressed in her nightgown and robe, looking rather uncertain.

"Hi, sorry. Am I interrupting?"

"No, not at all," Willow says. "We were just about to have breakfast." She opens the door wider and gestures me inside. "Come join us. There's plenty."

"Okay," I say, entering the room, feeling increasingly awkward. Why is Amya wearing her nightgown in my sister's bedroom?

Seriously, Lor. What the hell do you think she's doing here?

"Come sit," Willow says, pulling me down next to her. "Tea?"

"What's going on here?" I ask, and both of them wince. "Are you two...together?"

"Uh," Willow says, her cheeks going red. "We're...getting to know one another."

"I see." I accept the tea Willow holds out to me, cradling the mug between my hands and looking at Amya. "You know she's never been with anyone that way before?"

"Lor!" Willow cries, her face turning bright red. "Stop it!"

I glare at Willow and then back at Amya, who's sitting in the chair across from me.

"Willow has told me everything of her past," Amya says softly. "I know that already."

"So you know to be careful with her."

"Lor! I swear to the gods," Willow exclaims, dropping her face into her hands. "You're worse than Tristan. Not that it's any of your business, but we haven't done anything other than talk. We're friends."

I raise a skeptical eyebrow. "In your bed? In your nightclothes?"

Willow's eyebrows draw together. "I have dreams, Lor. Nightmares. They keep me awake. Amya's presence helps. I'm not used to sleeping in this big room alone." Her voice is a pained whisper, and I immediately feel guilty for what I've said.

Of course, I understand what she means. I felt the same way when I first woke up in Aphelion. But I'd also been too overwhelmed by the Trials to truly process everything. Waiting here for me, Willow and Tristan haven't had the luxury of those same distractions.

Amya sits forward in her seat, her eyes never leaving me. "Your sister is the kindest, most selfless person I've ever met. She's absolutely beautiful on the inside and out and as she said, we're just getting to know one another. I understand why you're protective of her, but I swear I only have her best interests at heart."

"Amya, you don't have to do this," Willow says, throwing me a glare. "This is none of Lor's business."

"It's okay," Amya says. "I know what it's like to care about you."

Willow throws up her hands and sits back. "Well, I suppose I'll just let you both talk about me then, like I'm not even here."

I can't help the smile that creeps to my face at that. Amya follows with one of her own and our gazes meet as a tentative understanding falls between us.

"Fine. I'll stay out of it." I finally take a sip of my tea, savoring the heat as it slides down my throat and then stick Amya with a glare. "But understand this, princess of The Aurora, if you hurt her, I'll kill you."

Amya's nod is grave. "Understood, Heart Queen."

"Good. Now pass me one of those pastries."

Willow grabs the basket and holds it away from me.

"Not before we have a chat about you and the prince." Her look is pointed and after what I just said, I totally deserve it.

"Yeah, we are not talking about that." I leap up and snatch the basket from her, grabbing a golden glazed pastry and stuffing it into my mouth.

Both Amya and Willow laugh. It's then I'm rescued by a knock at the door. Tristan enters without waiting for a reply.

"Tristan! You can't just walk into my room!" Willow exclaims. "Between you and Lor, I'm going to have to find somewhere else to stay."

Tristan's brow furrows. "Why, what did Lor do?"

"Nothing," I say. "Come and eat with us."

Tristan shrugs and drops into the other chair. He doesn't seem at all surprised by Amya's presence in Willow's room, and I suppose this must have been going on for at least a little while.

I'm hardly one to talk anyway, and my cheeks heat when I think about everything I've already done with Nadir.

Before long, we're joined by Mael and the prince, who also does a double-take at finding Amya here in her nightclothes. He says nothing, though.

"We should leave soon," Nadir says to me. "I don't want to linger here any longer than we need to."

"You said your father didn't know about this place, and they're safe here." I gesture to my brother and sister.

"They are," he says, gritting his teeth. "But it's still safer for you to keep moving."

"Fine, I'm ready when you are."

"How long will it take?" Tristan asks.

"A few hours," Nadir says. "I'm a bit slower when I'm carrying someone, but we can still get there before the sun sets."

"Where exactly are you going?" Willow asks. "What's left there?"

My brother and sister have all the same questions I do. I wish they could come and see it as well. It seems wrong to go there for the first time without them.

"It's basically a black hole of nothing," Mael says, leaning back in his chair. "Dead forest and swampland for miles interspersed with the ruins of the city that once existed."

"What about the people who died?" I ask. It's a morbid question, but I need to know.

Mael shrugs. "All long gone. It's been centuries."

I swallow, my throat suddenly tight.

"What about the settlements? Who lives there?"

"The people who got out alive," Nadir says. "They're waiting..."

"Waiting for...me."

He tips his head. "Waiting for their queen."

I take a deep breath and stand up, smoothing down the front of my sweater.

"Then I guess we shouldn't keep them any longer."

Willow takes my hand and stands up, wrapping me in a hug.

"Come back to us soon, Lor."

I nod against her and hope that's a promise I can keep.

CHAPTER THIRTY-NINE

A short while later, we've all gathered in the main foyer to say goodbye. Nadir traipses from the direction of the kitchen with a giant pack on his back.

"What's all that?"

"Food, provisions, a tent," he replies.

"Where's mine?"

"It's all here. I've got enough for both of us."

"I can carry my own things."

He narrows his gaze. "I can carry them. It's fine."

I roll my eyes. "Okay then, I'll keep my hands free for the important work."

He smirks and then turns to his sister. "The wards will hold while I'm gone. Father is going to be looking for me, but I think you should return to the Keep for a few days to avoid suspicion.

You too, Mael. He's going to assume you know where I am, but you'll be able to feign ignorance if you're also at the Keep. Hopefully, he's still occupied with the labor bill and his attention is divided."

They both nod and then he turns to me. "Come. We should go."

I nod and turn to give Tristan and Willow one more hug. "I love you," I say to them both, trying not to make it sound like I'm saying goodbye. "I'll be back."

"I know you will," Tristan says, his voice hard.

"Okay, I'm ready," I say to Nadir, and we step outside. The wind has picked up since yesterday and I shiver. Nadir holds out a hand to me.

"Are you going to carry me again?"

"That is the easiest way to do this."

"Can't I go on your back or something?" I don't like the way he makes me feel when he carries me like I'm his bride. It feels like too much.

"I have the pack," he says, his eyes lighting with mischief, and I can't help but wonder if he planned it this way. I want to keep arguing, but we're wasting time and this is ridiculous.

"Fine." I take his hand and give him a look that tells him not to try anything. His expression is one of mock innocence, and I think of the final words he said to me last night. That I would become his, eventually.

He pulls me close, my front pressing to his. As I glance up, our gazes lock in place for a few heartbeats, his irises swirling with violet. He doesn't affect me at all. Sure, let's go with that.

"Time to go, Inmate," he whispers with a deadly caress before he scoops me into his arms and we're surrounded by the ribbons of his magic. A moment later, we launch into the sky as his warm shield slides over my skin.

For hours, we move over the landscape as it changes beneath us, morphing from the cold mountains and endless black Void of The Aurora before giving way to lush green hills and forest. The steady movement of flight lulls me into peaceful relaxation, and it's all I can do to resist sleep after my restless night, my head bobbing with the weight of holding it up.

"Put your head down," he says to me, finally. "It's fine. I won't bite."

"You must be getting tired. We've been at this for hours."

"I'm okay for now," he replies. "We'll stop for a break soon."

I hesitate, but my eyelids are heavy, and I ignore the voice reminding me that was the first time in the past two weeks I'd slept without Nadir at my side. Giving up, I lay my head against him, my forehead pressing to his throat, wondering if I imagine his responding shiver.

When I wake up, it's to the sound of crackling logs and the smell of smoke. The sky is blue, no longer grey, and it takes me a moment to adjust. For a long minute, I lie still and listen to the sounds of my own breathing, the rushing of water, and the wind in the trees. I sit up, my head woozy.

"Hey," I mumble.

Nadir is staring at me with an intense look that makes me flush. "How are you doing?"

Pushing my hair from my face, I take in my surroundings, something catching in my throat.

"What's wrong?" Nadir asks, clearly reading my emotions.

I shake my head. "This reminds me of where we grew up before..."

"Before my father came and slaughtered your parents and threw you in prison?"

I shoot him a dark look, but there is none of the usual hardness in his face. Instead, I see something else. Not pity. But something close to that.

"Yah. That."

"We're in the northern forests of what was once part of Heart. It belongs to The Aurora for now."

I don't miss the "for now" in that statement.

He holds out a canteen to me and I take it, drinking a long gulp of cool water.

"How much farther do we have to go?"

"Not far."

"What's the plan when we get there?" I ask, taking another sip of water and accepting the piece of bread he hands me.

"We'll have to avoid the settlements. I was hoping to get a look at what's going on myself, but if any of my father's soldiers see me, there's little chance it won't get back to him. We'll comb the castle. In and out as quickly as possible."

I sit up straighter. "We have to help those women. We can't leave them like that at his mercy. What if he kills them? Or worse?"

He shakes his head. "There's nothing we can do. If they catch us, then we're...*you're* done."

"We can't leave them. I need to know he isn't hurting them."

Nadir lets out a sigh and runs a hand down his face. "Let's find the Crown first—" He raises a hand when I'm about to protest. "Let's find the Crown and then I promise we'll find a way to rescue them. You are no use like this, and you'll be even less so if my father gets his hands on you."

I snap my mouth shut. Of course, what he's saying makes perfect sense. "You swear it?"

"I promise."

It's not enough, but I understand it's the best I can hope for right now. I hate how powerless I am. How powerless I've always been.

We sit in silence for a while longer, the crackle of the fire and the sounds of the forest soothing my tired nerves. I used to love the forest when I was a child. Willow, Tristan, and I would spend hours lost in the trees, foraging for berries and building forts from fallen branches.

I smile to myself when I remember the time Tristan dumped a beehive on Willow and me while we were having a picnic. We were so mad at him, but he just laughed until we got him back later when we shoved him off a rope bridge into the river. I don't have many memories of our time before the king took us, but I cling to those happy ones like they can keep me safe from everything that's coming.

When all this is over, maybe we can spend time in the forest again. I think about Willow and Tristan and the future I hope I can finally give them. Maybe they'll fall in love and have families of their own.

"We should get going soon," Nadir says, peering at the sky. "I don't want to still be flying when the sun sets."

I nod in understanding. "I'm ready whenever you are."

He packs up our things, and I watch him while trying to pretend I'm not staring. Like a moth to a flame, I'm drawn to the chiseled lines of his face and those flashing eyes that see straight through me. I can still feel the warmth of his skin under my hands. The curve and dip of those muscles and the way he tasted in my mouth. The sounds that I drew from him that day.

My magic kicks under my skin. It's angry that I'm denying it his presence and his touch. I'm sure of that, but I'm not giving in.

Once he's done, he holds out his hand, and reluctantly I take it. Without a word, he scoops me up and we're off into the sky, the world below smearing into a green blur. After we've flown for a while, his arms tighten around me and I look up, wondering what has set him off.

That's when I see it. Ahead of us stretches a black blot. Like a bottle of ink tipped over a patch of freshly grown grass. The jagged remains of a land that was once whole and prosperous. In the center, a group of towers rises, blackened and broken, like twisted fingers pleading for help that never came.

My breath stutters, and a strangled whimper exhales from my chest. In all my dreams and in all my nightmares, I never imagined I would find myself here some day.

It's there, in all its decaying glory.

A story of sadness and loss. Of ego and mistakes and the consequences of wanting too much.

A shadow of the legacy that has haunted me every single day of my life.

The Queendom of Heart.

CHAPTER FORTY

SERCE

I t took three weeks to make arrangements for the visit back to Heart.

First, Serce sent a message to Rion, alerting him of their plans—or at least the ones she meant for him to know about. Wolf readied his soldiers because she had no intention of entering Heart without reinforcements. His army wasn't quite as large as her mother's, but she hoped she would have the element of surprise on her hands. She also hoped this visit wouldn't come to a physical altercation, but it was best to always be prepared.

Rumors said the Sun King had pulled Aphelion's support after Serce had refused to bond with Atlas. Now Heart lay without allies, save Alluvion and Tor, while further reports said Celestria had claimed neutrality. Their position in the furthest reaches of the north, where only the Sky Fae could survive for more than a few days, meant they rarely dirtied their hands with the sticky affairs of political maneuvering.

Cloris had been putting up a fuss since they'd locked her in her room, threatening them with every curse under Zerra. It was a mark to their advantage the priestess lived alone and kept mostly to herself. Serce was counting on it being a while before anyone noticed she was missing.

They'd suppressed her magic with a pair of arcturite cuffs forged in the smiths of Tor, so she couldn't do much harm, but the incessant screaming and wailing was giving Serce a pounding headache. More than once, she'd considered having the priestess's tongue cut out just to shut her the fuck up.

The only thing currently staying her hand was the fact they'd need Cloris to perform the binding ritual. For now, Cloris could shriek to her heart's content, but her fate was sealed.

Finally, it was the morning of their departure.

Serce stood in front of the mirror in Wolf's bedroom, her tunic pulled up to study the swell of her stomach, which was just starting to show. She'd already had to get her leggings taken out so the waistband would stop pinching her skin.

"Gods, you're beautiful," Wolf said, entering from the bathroom. "You're glowing. Pregnancy suits you."

Her answering grin was crooked. At first, she'd been worried about what a baby would do to her body. Would Wolf still love her when she looked like she'd swallowed a melon? But she swore he fell more in love with her every day.

He came over to where she stood, wrapping his arms around her and sliding his hands along her bare stomach. She shivered at his warm touch before leaning into him, tipping her head back so he could press his mouth to the side of her throat.

He moaned in approval, drawing her closer, grinding his already-hard cock against her ass. She loved that they could never get enough of each other.

He bit her earlobe gently. "You look so fucking gorgeous right now it would be a shame not to do something about it."

He pulled up and looked into her eyes in the mirror, running the backs of his fingers over her cheek, lust reflecting in both their eyes. Tipping her face back, he kissed her, his tongue probing her mouth, before she spun around, her arms slipping up his neck.

"We have no time," she whispered. "We have to go."

"We have time," he replied smoothly as he directed her hand under the waistband of his breeches. Her fingers curled around his thick cock, and he groaned as she gripped him, pumping her hand slowly.

"Fuck, Serce. You undo me. You are my star, my moon, my heart. I want to love you and fuck you and cherish you for every day of my life. And even when I'm wandering the Evanescence, I'll still long for the taste of your mouth and your sweet pussy."

"Wolf," she moaned as his hand slid between her legs, his palm grinding against her as he directed her towards a table.

"Turn around," he ordered. He shoved down her waistband with one hand, the other gripping the back of her neck as he bent her forward, pushing her cheek to the wood. She felt him moving behind her and then the wide head of his cock pressing against her soaked and aching core.

He gave her no warning as he thrust inside roughly. She cried out, gripping the table as shocks of pleasure sparked through her blood. Her palms squeaked against the surface as he fucked her, his strong fingers digging into her hips so firmly it would leave bruises later.

She was already getting close, her body clenching around him before she pressed back, wanting more. Wanting all of him. He responded by pulling all the way out and then shoving back in to the hilt, her cries echoing in the room every time his body collided with hers.

"You're never going to leave me," he grunted, thrusting into her, his cock filling her inch by glorious inch.

"Never, Wolf. I'm yours forever."

"I'll never let you go," he groaned, pounding with a force that bordered on violent.

"Always, Wolf. No matter what happens. From now until the Evanescence claims us."

He fisted her hair and pulled her upright so her back was flush to his chest before he sunk his teeth into her throat. The sharp sting of pain caused her stomach to tighten. He thrust again as she teetered on the edge, his hand reaching around to stroke her clit before she came apart with a blinding gasp. Wolf followed close behind with a deep moan that shuddered straight through her limbs.

"I told you we had enough time," he said, pulling up her leggings and then tucking himself back in. With a wink, he grabbed her hand. "Let's go. They'll be waiting for us."

It would take them about five to six weeks to get to Heart with the whole of Wolf's army in tow. She wished they could move things along faster, but they couldn't arrive empty-handed. She had no idea what her mother had planned and Serce would not go into this battle unprepared.

The journey from Heart was mostly smooth and uneventful, though travel was slower than they had anticipated thanks to patches of boggy ground through the Cinta Wilds. But when the walls of Heart came into view, Serce felt a familiar stirring in her chest. She'd never been away from home for this long and never felt quite right unless she was within its walls.

They left the bulk of Wolf's army on the outskirts of the queendom. While she did want her mother to appreciate their show of strength, even Serce understood that getting what she wanted would mean a rockier path if she arrived as the aggressor.

"She's going to want to make sure you're still under her control," Wolf said from his horse as it walked next to hers. "That you aren't planning to turn on her."

She nodded as she stared at the Heart Castle that stretched into the sky. The sight of it would never fail to move her. It was her spirit and her soul. Made of snowy white stone, the spires were cloaked in thick luxurious twists of vines garlanded with bursts of scarlet roses, making it look like a bouquet. The scent of flowers lingered in the air, the gentle perfume enveloping her in its familiar embrace.

She let out a deep sigh and rubbed her stomach that grew rounder with each passing day. The other night, they'd felt the baby kick and Wolf had been so moved he'd broken down into tears of joy.

She still wasn't entirely sure if motherhood would suit her, but she was becoming more confident. With Wolf at her side, hopefully they could pass for adequate parents. She hadn't benefited from an ideal role model, but she vowed to do better.

As if sensing her apprehension, Wolf reached over and held out his hand. She reached back, squeezing it and exhaling another leaded sigh.

They approached the city walls, also made of white stone, where more rose vines clamored over the surface. Serce noticed the permanent line between Wolf's eyebrows and wondered what was concerning him the most. Her mother? The baby?

Cloris was back with the army, locked in a wagon. She'd screeched for days on end, demanding to be released until they'd finally gagged her. Serce wasn't sure why they hadn't just done so from the beginning.

Wolf carried the Woodlands Staff on his saddle, cleverly disguised to look like a bow. Hidden in plain sight, he'd said, and it made sense to keep it secret for now. Her mother would be immediately suspicious if she noticed they'd arrived with the Staff in tow.

Thankfully, it blended in more easily than many of the Artefacts. Imagine having to cart around Aphelion's giant Mirror? The Stone of Tor was at least twice her height and buried deep in the surface of a mountain.

They trotted through the gates, no one barring their way as they progressed to the city. The citizens recognized her instantly, their heads bending low to honor her arrival. Serce tipped her chin in response, and before long, they approached the castle gates. Guards flanked each side, but no one made any move to impede their progress. Serce hoped this meant her mother's temperament was somewhat amicable.

A large fountain sat in the center of the courtyard, cascades of water flowing over the white stone. She'd loved playing in it when she was a child, much to the horror of her governess. She rubbed her stomach again, picturing her own children kicking up water with their tiny bare feet. No matter what kind of mother she was, she wouldn't be the sort that prevented them from having fun. All she'd ever been told was "no, that isn't fitting behavior for a princess." As if princesses couldn't be children, too.

Wolf was watching her as they made their way across the courtyard. She offered him a reassuring, if tight, smile to let him know she was okay.

They brought their horses to a halt at the entrance and Serce slid off her saddle. She wondered how much longer she'd be able to do so with the same ease before her stomach made it too cumbersome.

She arranged her cloak around her shoulders to hide the bump just visible through her tunic. She wanted to save this news until she understood what they were up against. Wolf had also dismounted, along with the rest of their small retinue.

The queen's chief advisor waited at the castle entrance, her thin hands clasped at her waist. Hemanthes wore a fine gown of pale green, her hair pulled to the top of her head where it sat coiled in a nest of tight braids. Her thin lips pressed together as she regarded Serce. They'd never seen eye to eye on anything, and Serce couldn't wait to replace her someday. A fact they both knew.

"Your Highness," Hemanthes said with a dip of her chin, the honorific uttered in a tone that bordered on insolent.

"Hemanthes," Serce replied, keeping her posture erect and refusing to reciprocate the gesture. Serce would always outrank Hemanthes, and this they both knew, too.

Hemanthes then turned to Wolf. "Your Majesty. What an honor it is to have you both back with us. Heart hasn't been the same without you here, Serce."

Serce arched an eyebrow, interpreting the hidden meaning in those words. "You're too kind, Hemanthes. Where is my mother?"

"She's currently indisposed," Hemanthes said, her tone gleeful, as though she was relishing the chance to make Serce wait.

"I'd like to see her. Now."

"That won't be possible. Perhaps you can clean up first, and she'll be available later this evening."

Another smug smile accompanied a feigned deferential tip of her head before she turned to Wolf. "I'll have someone show you to your chambers."

"He's staying with me," she said before Wolf could reply. "In my wing."

Hemanthes lifted her chin, peering down her nose.

"Petulance isn't a good look for you, Hemanthes. You all need to get over it. Wolf is my mate, and no one can come between us."

At that, Hemanthes's eyes widened, her gaze passing between Serce and Wolf. Serce smirked, enjoying the triumph of catching her off-guard. They'd already decided they would tell her mother to head off any further discussion regarding the alliance with Atlas. Not even the Queen of Heart could overrule a mate bond.

"Is it true?" she asked, now a little breathless. "A real mate?"

"Yes, we realized it shortly after we arrived in The Woodlands."

Wolf was watching her, his expression a mix of pride and barely concealed desire. Maybe going to their room for a few hours wasn't the worst idea. All these weeks on the road, surrounded by soldiers and his advisors, had put a serious damper on their alone time. But she had things to accomplish first.

"I want to see the queen now," Serce said, finally losing her patience. She didn't wait for Hemanthes to reply, grabbing Wolf's hand and skirting past her. They stormed down the wide central hallway towards the queen's private council chamber.

"Serce!" Hemanthes called after them. "Come back here!"

Serce stopped, sucking in an angry breath, and whipped around, pinning Hemanthes with a glare.

"It's Your Highness, Hemanthes. You *will* address me as my station demands, or risk finding yourself comfortable with the rats in the dungeons."

Hemanthes's features pinched together, and her throat bobbed sharply as she swallowed her indignation.

"Your Highness," she ground out, but Serce ignored her, turning away and continuing her quest to locate her mother.

Wolf marched next to Serce, tossing her a grin. "Do you know how beautiful you are when you're ferocious?" he asked in a low, rumbling voice. "Perhaps we *should* visit your rooms for a few hours first?" She smiled at the echo of her own thoughts, gripping his hand tighter.

"There will be time for that later. I promise," she said, and he smiled.

They arrived at the doors to her mother's wing, and Serce ignored the stationed guards, passing by without a glance. Though she was glad she didn't have to kill them for blocking her way, they really should be tossed into the stocks for allowing her to enter unchallenged.

She swung open the door as a dozen surprised faces turned her way.

"Serce," Daedra said grimly, clearly not surprised by her daughter's intrusion or arrival. "It's nice to see you."

"I'd like to speak with you," Serce said.

"Of course." The queen pressed her hands to the table before she rose. Her shoulders were tight and her eyes drooped. Serce imagined the queen hadn't slept much since she'd disrupted her plans, and a twinge of guilt threaded through her chest.

Nevertheless, her mother was still regal in a long white dress that flowed to the floor. The Heart Crown adorned her head, matching the large ruby necklace at her throat, marking her as queen of this territory. Serce wondered briefly if the queen had chosen these symbols for her benefit. Had she known they were coming today?

As Serce stepped forward, a tall Fae with short grey hair and a hawkish nose stood, a note of annoyance in her tone. "Serce, when will you learn you can't just barge in here and demand to see your mother?"

"Never." She shrugged. "Everyone out. This is a family matter."

A few muttered under their breaths as they obeyed her order, and Hemanthes, who followed in their wake, was the last to leave, shooting Serce a look of pure unfiltered hatred. Serce didn't care. Soon, she'd be queen of this place and get rid of them all.

"Serce," her mother said, turning her way after everyone had left. The queen looked at Wolf and tipped her chin. "Wolf. Welcome back. What can I do for you both?"

She appeared so calm that Serce wondered if the last months had even happened, but Serce also understood her mother was very good at playing games.

"What can you do for us?" Serce asked, her tone cold. "Rumors have reached me that you no longer intend to descend as we'd planned."

Her mother clasped her hands and flattened her mouth. "Is that why you've arrived on my doorstep with an entire army?"

"You don't deny it?"

"I don't deny or confirm anything. But there was no need to bring these soldiers into our home."

Serce stepped closer, trailing her fingers along the smooth wood of the council table.

"They can be sent back to The Woodlands when I have your reassurances that my crown is no longer under threat."

"You still refuse to bond with Atlas?"

Serce resisted every urge to roll her eyes. "Mother, please move past it. Wolf is my mate. The union with Atlas was doomed from the start."

The queen's jaw dropped, her eyes widening. It was the exact reaction Serce had been hoping for. "Your mate? You're sure?"

"Of course I'm sure, Mother. If you'd experienced it, you would understand it's not a feeling you can mistake."

It was a low blow. To find a true mate was as rare as unearthing a polished diamond. She was incredibly fortunate to have been bestowed with this gift from Zerra, and she should give it all the reverence it was due.

The queen's eyebrows drew together. "I'm happy for you, my daughter." There was only sincerity in her voice, which took Serce by surprise.

"You are?"

"Of course I am. To find a true mate is a rare gift. I only want you to be happy, Serce. Despite everything, I'm still your mother and I only want the best for you."

"Okay," she said, as Wolf came to stand behind her.

Daedra turned to him then. "I suppose a welcome to the family is in order. I'm sorry we got off on the wrong foot."

Wolf, ever the idealist with a warrior's heart of gold, grinned wide and swept the queen in his arms, swinging her around in a big hug. Daedra let out an undignified screech, and Serce covered her giggle with her hand.

"Put me down!" the queen demanded with laughter as she pounded her fists against his shoulders. Wolf obeyed with a grin that warmed the entire room, and the queen pushed him with a good-natured shove.

"I suppose I can see what drew you to this one," she said with a roll of her eyes.

"He's something," Serce agreed before Wolf looked at her with such love in his expression it took her breath away.

The queen smoothed down her hair and dress, trying to regain her composure. "We still need to convince Aphelion to offer their armies, but I suppose we'll now have to discuss other methods in earnest."

"That *is* what I was saying all along," Serce replied carefully, wondering if this was a trap. This seemed too easy. She noticed her mother still hadn't denied the question of her descension. Serce would let it lie for now, but vowed to bring it up later.

"Yes. I see that now. I'll send a letter to the Sun Palace. Perhaps Kyros is willing to meet again." Daedra's eyes narrowed, her gaze falling on Wolf. "What about your sister?"

"My sister?"

"She's unbonded, is she not?"

"She is. She's been in Alluvion for the past year, studying at Maris Academy."

"With The Woodlands now firmly aligned with Heart, perhaps the Sun King can be persuaded that a match with your sister would be nearly as advantageous. In fact, he'll get two realms instead of just one."

"It's an idea," Serce said, looping her arm through Wolf's, cautious about how quickly this plan had materialized. His expression was thoughtful as he nodded. She wanted to warn him not to agree to anything, but he was smarter than that.

"It could work," he said. "We can consider it. I'd need to send her a message and see how she'd feel about it."

"Wonderful." Her mother clapped her hands. "Then I'll send word to Aphelion immediately. While we wait, we can get to know one another properly. You must be tired from traveling. Why don't you rest for a few hours and we'll have dinner together?"

"Okay," Serce said. "Thank you, Mother."

Daedra smiled. "Of course. I'm so glad you're home."

They said their goodbyes and exited the chamber, heading towards Serce's wing of the castle. Once they were out of earshot, she turned to her mate.

"That seemed too easy."

"It did," Wolf agreed. "What are you thinking?"

"Send word to your army to retreat. Just enough that my mother thinks they've left. They'll need to hide somewhere."

"I'll do that right away."

"She can't know about Cloris. She must remain hidden."

Wolf took her hand, pressing his mouth to the center of her palm. "Don't worry. Our plans are still in motion. This changes nothing, and my sister isn't a pawn to be used in your mother's games."

"No, she's not," she agreed. "But we'll play my mother's games if that's what she wants. We'll just have to make sure we're playing them smarter."

CHAPTER FORTY-ONE

LOR

PRESENT DAY: QUEENDOM OF HEART

N adir lands us gently on the ground, the landscape barren, a scar scratched into the earth. There's nothing but decay and the shattered remains of the place that should have been my home. It spreads in every direction. The colorless void of heartbreak. My chest wrenches tight, the air thick and sluggish. I'm not sure I'm ready for this.

What made me think I could just walk in here and not feel *everything* with the crushing weight of being buried under a mountain?

"Are you okay?" Nadir asks, his voice gruff.

I nod, unable to find the words to speak. I'm not, but we're here now, and I have to see this through. Not just for myself, but for Tristan and Willow and every person in the settlements waiting for their lives to begin again.

I didn't start this, but I have to be the one who ends it. Somehow.

Attempting to calm the racing beat of my heart, I take stock of my surroundings. We're standing near what once was a city wall, crumbled stones littering the ground. It curves gently, disappearing into the distance.

It's colder than I expected and my breath fogs in the air. It's like we've stepped into another world that is literally frozen in time. I flex my fingers, attempting to rouse the flow of my blood when the invisible blanket of Nadir's magic wraps around me, warming my chilled limbs.

"Thank you," I whisper, and he nods before approaching me.

"I know this must feel big and terrifying, but I want to help you. I won't let you come to any harm."

"I'm scared," I say, deciding there's no point in denying it. I don't know if I've ever been more afraid in my life.

"You're allowed to be scared. No one expects you to be strong all the time. I think maybe you believe you have to."

Those earnest words catch me off-guard, and I hesitate, studying him carefully. It's like he can see straight through to the darkest parts of my soul. Like he can read all of my thoughts. Everything shifts and my magic lurches towards him with such force it nearly knocks me over. I roll my neck, willing it to behave. It will not have him.

Peering into the distance, my gaze follows a line of jagged spires shrouded in mist.

"Are you ready to go?" Nadir asks, and I allow him to take my hand and lead me into what's left of the city. Broken-down buildings surround us, the cobbles that once lined the streets shattered, impeding our steps. As I kick a chunk of stone, it goes skittering across the ground, the echo so loud it seems to make the very atmosphere shiver.

We both stop moving, our breaths held as though we're both expecting something to leap out from the shadows. It feels like eyes are watching us, though there is no sign of life. Our gazes meet and then pull away before we silently agree to keep moving. Still holding on to my hand, Nadir leads me closer to the castle.

As we approach, the weight on my shoulders sits heavier and heavier. Based on what's left of the structure, I surmise it must have been a sight to behold.

"Were you ever here when it was whole?" I ask softly.

"No. I was only a baby when everything happened."

I try to imagine what this fierce Fae prince must've been like as a small boy. It's hard to imagine he was ever full of smiles and giggles. But when I think of what he told me about his father, I decide there probably wasn't much for him to smile about.

"How old are you, anyway?"

He looks back at me with an eyebrow arched. "Two hundred and eighty-six. Practically a baby by Fae standards."

I huff out a laugh, appreciating his attempt at a joke. Tristan and I have discussed the implications if I can't shift back into my High Fae body. We don't know enough about the magic to understand if I'd be bound to a human lifespan or that of a Fae. It's just another reason I need to find that Crown.

"It must have been beautiful," I say as we approach the wall that surrounds the castle.

"It must have been," he agrees.

We pause at the wall, surveying the castle, rising up like a specter. From the corner of my eye, I notice a flash of color amidst the dull gloom. A bright red rose blooms on a green vine growing up the side of the wall.

It seems to call me, and I walk over with Nadir keeping close behind. As I stare at it, a strange tingling creeps over my scalp.

"Why is this here?" I look down the wall, noting more bursts of color where other flowers bloom. "How can anything be growing here?"

Nadir takes in a deep breath. "It just started happening."

"How do you know that?"

"Because I've come here before. Everything has been dead and gone for as long as I can remember. But a few months ago, I sent Mael to scout things out to ensure everything was still quiet, and he brought me back the head of a single red rose."

My brows draw together. "A few months ago?"

"Right around the time you were taken from Nostraza."

I sit with the implication of those words.

"Is that how you knew? Who I was?"

"I was starting to put things together and when Mael brought the rose, something in me just *knew*. He thought I was crazy. So did Amya. But they humored me into facilitating your...release."

"Kidnapping," I amend dryly.

"Semantics," Nadir counters. "Anyway, they agreed to go along with my hunch until we could prove who you were either way."

"And if I'd turned out to be just a human woman from Nostraza?"

Nadir rolls his neck and then bites his bottom lip.

"You would have killed me," I say.

"If you'd been nobody, then you would have been a loose end I had to take care of."

I spit out a derisive laugh. "You always know how to make me feel special, Nadir."

He lets out a low growl and steps towards me so quickly my back hits the wall. He presses a hand next to my head and leans in, his face just inches from mine.

"I knew you were special, Lor. I felt it the moment I met you at the Sun Queen ball. You know, when you threw yourself at me."

My mouth drops open, and I make a sound of indignation. "I didn't *throw* myself at you. I got in your way because I had a Trial to win, and you were a means to an end. Don't flatter yourself."

He smirks and pulls away. "Keep telling yourself that, Heart Queen. Your hands were all over me."

"In your dreams."

He smiles and plucks the rose from the wall, handing it to me.

I take it, rubbing the petals between my thumb and finger, its texture like velvet. I press it to my nose and inhale its delicate scent. Roses. The memory of the soap that Jude stole from me all those months ago surfaces. The same bar of soap that landed me in the Hollow. I'd been so desperate for that small bit of luxury, I'd lost control of myself.

"What do they mean?" I ask Nadir, lifting the flower in my hand.

He presses his lips together. "I think it means your legacy is waiting for you."

I cast my gaze to the ruined castle and then back to him. "You really think that?"

"It has to mean something they decided to bloom the day you were freed from Nostraza."

"This feels like a lot of pressure."

He nods sagely. "That's a feeling I understand. At least somewhat."

We cross the length of the ruined courtyard, passing a large fountain, the basin cracked and dry. I try to imagine what it might have looked like flowing with water and surrounded by the denizens of this castle. Or what my grandmother looked like striding this very path.

The doors to the castle are long gone, and the entrance sits open, the dark opening reminding me of a missing tooth in a smile. The stone is a soft grey that might have been white at some point in its history. Here, more green vines snake up, twining with ropes of deadened brown tendrils that must've once grown in abundance. Bright red roses dot their length and maybe Nadir is right, because I swear I can hear their whispers on the wind welcoming me home.

We cross the doorway, passing down a dim hallway, our steps kicking up dust and small bits of stone. The only sound is the echo of our footsteps against dulled patterned tiles that would have been glorious in their day. Up ahead, a large archway leads to a room bright with sunlight. We head towards it and step through, finding ourselves in a massive room, the ceiling soaring high above our heads.

Blood-red roses trail from floor to ceiling, crawling up the stone walls. Here the blooms are bursting in a thick carpet of velvety red, and I see the shock on Nadir's face before he turns to look at me, his gaze sweeping me from head to toe as if he's seeing me for the first time. The air is sweet and fresh, and I inhale deeply, overcome with an emotion for which I have no name.

Suddenly I feel robbed of so many things. I've tried to never mourn the existence that was taken from us, knowing it would do no good to dwell on a past I couldn't change. But right now, that knowledge squats on my chest like an anvil.

"We were happy," I say, unable to hold the words inside. "Living in the forest, the five of us. We were always happy, and our lives would have been fine. I never truly longed for any of this. It wasn't until my parents were taken, and the three of us were forced to grow up in ways none of us were ready for that I began to yearn for any of it."

Nadir is watching me as I talk. I'm not really saying these things to him, but I need the words to exist, even if no one else ever hears them.

"I'm sorry," Nadir says. "I couldn't have stopped it, even if I'd known, but I'm sorry this was the hand you were dealt. Your grandmother let you down, and my father ruined your life for his own ends."

I say nothing as I take a step deeper into the room with the rose clutched to my chest. At the far end is a raised dais with a pair of thrones made of black stone. An empty hole sits in the back of each one.

It's then I notice it. My magic is a constant swirl under my skin, and its presence has become as natural as breathing, especially when Nadir is around. But now it's edged in something different, giving it a sharpness and clarity like a sliver of splintered crystal.

I spin around, taking in every corner of the room and the ceiling that opens to the sky.

"What is it?" Nadir asks, also casting his gaze about the room, his stance ready as if waiting for an attack. "Is someone here?"

I shake my head. "No. I don't think so."

"Then what is it?"

"I think...I can feel it."

"Feel it?"

"The Crown. I think I can feel the Crown."

CHAPTER FORTY-TWO

"Where?" he asks, coming closer and scanning the room as though it might suddenly appear hovering in the air.

"I'm not sure," I say, spinning around again, trying to discern if it's leading me in a specific direction. "It just feels like it's everywhere."

"Well, that's better than nothing, I suppose." He looks at me. "What do you feel?"

"It's hard to describe, but it's like there's another layer of magic alongside the one I usually feel."

His nostrils flare as he looks around the room again. "Then we better start searching."

"This place is huge."

"It is," he agrees. "And I don't know how much time we have before my father decides this is where you've run to."

"Fuck," I say, just needing to expel the pressure building in my chest. Nadir chuckles softly next to me, his hand landing gently on the small of my back. I jerk away at his touch, and his features harden before he smooths them down.

"Sorry."

"It's fine. I meant what I said about us."

"So you've made clear." He turns away and starts walking, his long strides carrying him across the room.

"Where are you going?"

"We won't find the Crown standing here, will we, Inmate?"

I let out a low growl.

"Don't call me that," I say, hurrying after him.

We spend the next few hours wandering the crumbling corridors of the Heart Castle, stepping over detritus, broken furniture, and crumbling mortar and stones. Most of the windows are long gone, letting in the cool breeze. We wander past enormous bedrooms, finding shattered beds and moldy sheets, so rotted they crumble at the barest touch. There are black scorch marks along the walls, ceilings, and floors, and I swallow down a sting of pain, imagining the violence of the force that must have caused them.

We step through a wide opening that must have been a set of double doors once. Large arched windows and broken shelves line a library where the remnants of rotting and torn books are heaped into haphazard piles. I enter slowly, walking the perimeter, running my hands along the dry wood. I wonder what it would have been like to grow up with a library like this instead of making do with Nostraza's single rickety shelf, where I'd have to hope something worth reading would appear.

My breath catches as I turn to find two massive portraits hanging on either side of the doorway running nearly the height of the wall. The colors are faded and their bottom halves scorched black, but their faces are clear enough to make out the male and female High Fae depicted in each. I approach the one nearest to me. The female wears a long red dress with her shoulders left bare. Her black hair is swept up on her head, the ends cascading in a fall of thick curls down her back. She wears a silver crown with a single red jewel set in the center.

Instinctively, my hand goes to the locket around my neck and the sliver of stone nestled inside.

"She looks just like Willow," I say. "They could be twins."

"She was beautiful," Nadir says.

"She was." I study my grandmother—the woman who is responsible for everything.

Nadir is standing behind me, so close we're nearly touching, and I look up at him for a brief second before I walk past to the second portrait, which must be my grandfather.

He's incredibly handsome, with long brown hair braided and pulled back from his face. Even with the faded paint, I make out the intensity of his dark green eyes.

"Wolf, the king of The Woodlands," I say, softly. I wonder what kind of grandparents they would have been. His eyes are kind though, and I imagine being wrapped in his arms as a little girl. "I wish I could have met them."

"I'm sure they wish the same," Nadir says, staring at the portrait of my grandfather.

"We should keep looking." I head for the exit, suddenly not wanting to be in here anymore. This is all too much.

"Are you okay?" Nadir asks, catching up to me.

"Yes. I'm fine. We haven't looked down here yet."

He doesn't pressure me any further, and for that, I'm grateful as we continue searching. I keep checking in with that same feeling that I'm sure is pulling me towards the Crown, but it never changes. I was hoping it would become more intense or noticeable when we were nearer to the Artefact, but it remains frustratingly consistent.

As night descends, Nadir aids our search with a ball of yellow light he casts over our heads that illuminates the darkening castle.

"I don't get it," I say after we've finished searching another wing. "It never wavers. It's just the same buzz."

"Maybe it isn't the Crown you're feeling."

The thought had occurred to me, too. Maybe I've just convinced myself I feel something because I want it to be true so much.

He approaches me and raises a hand to touch my cheek, his hand snapping together into a fist at the last moment before he lets it drop. I try to ignore my twinge of disappointment. He's honoring my wishes, and I should be happy about that. My stomach rumbles, and I look outside, noticing the sun has set.

"We've been at this for hours," Nadir says, following my gaze. "Let's get something to eat."

I nod and follow him back to the center of the castle where we first entered. Nadir finds the pack he left there and starts unloading it. He has a small tent and two sleeping bags set up before long.

"I hope this is okay. I only had room for one tent," he says.

"We've been sharing a bed for weeks. I think we'll be fine."

"This is a little more...confined."

I look at the tiny tent and then at him. His broad shoulders will probably take up most of the space. Anticipation runs down my spine, but I dismiss it. I'm done with him.

"What's for dinner?" I ask, wanting to change the subject. We'll deal with the matter of the tiny tent later.

"Let's get a fire going. You think your ancestors will mind if we use the floor in here?"

I look around, wondering if their ghosts are watching over us right now. "Technically, I'm queen of this dump, and I'll allow it."

Nadir smiles and then winks. "Then let's go find some wood."

We head into the forest, and an hour later we have a merrily crackling fire surrounded by a ring of stones. Nadir puts together a stew with thick, rich gravy, fresh tender peas, and chunks of venison.

"You can cook," I say.

"Is that a statement or a question?"

I shrug. "I didn't think princes did things like cook for themselves."

Nadir smirks and takes a bite of his stew. "When you're in the army, everyone has to chip in. You learn pretty quickly how to keep up, lest you be ostracized."

"Don't tell me you've ever cared what anyone thought about you."

He arches a dark brow. "When they sleep next to you, it's best to keep on their good side. Otherwise, you end up with a missing bedroll, your eyebrows shaved, or all your clothes tossed in the river."

I snort and cover my mouth, laughing. "Okay, that makes sense." I take a sip from the canteen we're sharing and wipe my mouth. "When were you in the army?"

"Do you know about the wars your grandmother started?"

A knot twists in my stomach, and I nod. "A little. My mother said it went on for a long time."

"The first lasted only a few years," Nadir says. "The fall of Heart left a vacancy of power that everyone leaped to snatch for themselves, especially when magic was no longer a part of the equation. In a strange way, it leveled the playing field, leaving a bloody and brutal battle where no one knew how to win."

"Then what?"

"Then a couple of decades later, when everyone's magic started returning, the fighting broke out again. This one went on for years. It was slower, but equally destructive. The problem has always been that the realm itself seems to resist any attempts at being conquered."

I frown. "What does that mean?"

He shakes his head. "It's hard to explain. But every time one side would gain an advantage, it was like Zerra herself stepped in to take it away."

He stops, as though considering his words for a moment. "By the time the second war started, I was a fully grown Fae and had no choice but to join the front lines next to my father. In the end, there truly were no victors. No one could maintain the upper hand for long enough for it to matter, and finally, we called a truce, abandoning this place and agreeing to let it lie forever."

"Until your father found us and thought he could use me. And then Atlas tried to do the same." I shake my head, realizing how much of a pawn I've been in their schemes.

"Yes," Nadir says. "Forever is a long time, I guess."

"Was it terrible? The war?"

"Of course. It was a war. The things I saw. The numbers of Fae, both High and low, and humans who died, were countless. So many we lost track. We all did things we aren't proud of."

I stare into my bowl, gripping it between my hands. "Why did she do it? My grandmother. Why did she cause all this?"

Nadir shakes his head. "I don't know that. I'm not sure she could have known the true extent of the fallout her actions would cause."

"I suppose not."

The sky is fully dark now as we sit in the flicker of the campfire flames.

"Sometimes I worry that I'm going to mess this up, too." I'm not sure why I'm allowing myself to be vulnerable with Nadir, but something about his presence always gives me the freedom to just let go. Like no matter what dark secret I tell him, he will never judge me for it.

"I can understand that," comes his reply. He shifts and his arm presses against mine. As he's about to move again, I grab his elbow and hold him in place.

"It's okay."

His shoulders drop, and his face relaxes. "I think all you can do is to be aware of the choices you're making," he says. "I can't know what was in your grandmother's head or what caused her fall, but the fact that you're even thinking about it means you have the chance to do better."

I consider that, grateful he isn't telling me not to worry or that it won't happen.

"I'm not sure what better even means." I sweep a hand out to encompass the destruction surrounding us. "Why do I think this even needs to happen? Ouranos is operating just fine without Heart. What if the very act of my being here spoils everything? What if this is how things should remain and I'm just going to upset the balance in favor of even more ruin?"

Ruin.

The words from the Aurora Torch flit through my head, but when it said "ruin" it had been referring specifically to Nadir. Right?

He angles his body towards me.

"I don't think it's actually a decision you get to make. All this was set in motion when Atlas stole you from my father. Hell, it started when my father took you from the woods all those years ago. Power can only grow in a vacuum and while Heart has sat here quietly for more than two centuries, eventually someone would come here and claim it.

"The Mirror told you to find the Crown. It did that for a reason. It must understand something yet to be revealed." He then looks away, his gaze wandering towards the open forest beyond the city walls. "And you still have people who are waiting. Many who were alive when this was their home, and some who weren't who've never truly had one. You're not just doing this for yourself, you're doing it for them, too."

He stares at me with such ferocious intensity the inside of my stomach twists.

"Thank you. I needed to hear that."

The corner of his mouth quirks up. "Anytime, Heart Queen." He moves to stand. "We should get some sleep. We have a lot more ground to cover."

We both stare at the small tent, an awkwardness blooming between us. We've already crossed so many barriers of intimacy, but I drew a line in the sand when we left The Aurora, and it's tipped everything on its side.

"I'll sleep out here. It's been a while since I've enjoyed the sight of the stars."

He doesn't give me a chance to respond before he stalks over to the tent and drags his bedroll and sleeping bag out. I drop to my hands and knees and crawl into the small structure, lying on my back and staring at the canvas ceiling. I hear Nadir shifting outside, getting himself set up, and a few moments later, silence settles in the air. Everything is much too quiet, and suddenly, I've never felt so alone in my entire life.

Not giving myself a chance to second-guess this decision, I get up and drag my own bedroll out of the tent, placing it next to Nadir's. He watches me, one hand tucked behind his head, the other resting on the ground at his side. I settle onto my pillow and look up at the hole in the ceiling, marveling at the sparkling blanket of stars in the sky.

"It's so beautiful," I whisper.

"It is," he confirms. Then, I *do* second-guess myself. I shouldn't have come out here. I'm sending him mixed signals, but my own head is so mixed up I don't know how to do it any other way.

"We should get some sleep," I say, but it sounds like a feeble kind of protest. "I have a hard time sleeping alone," I add, feeling the need to explain my presence at his side. "I slept for so many years surrounded by people, and I don't know how to do it alone. I hated it in Aphelion."

"I understand. Go to sleep, Lor."

His eyes flicker in the darkness, swirling with violet and green, and I don't know what makes me do it, but I reach out and touch his hand. There is no hesitation before he moves his own and threads his fingers through mine before we drift off to sleep.

Chapter Forty-three

We spend the next day searching every room and hallway and nook of the castle. That constant buzz, that incessant feeling, remains as steady as the moment we arrived. I'm ready to tear my hair out in frustration.

"I don't know," I finally cry out after we've cleared yet another wing. We're back in the throne room, the fire burning. I pace while Nadir warms up the leftover soup from yesterday. "It never changes. Maybe I'm wrong and this means something else. Maybe it was always there, and I just convinced myself it was different."

"We'll keep searching tomorrow," Nadir says. "There are still places to look."

"And if we still don't find it? How much longer can we stay here before your father finds us?"

"If we still don't find it, we move to the next idea."

"And that is?" I ask, raising my brows.

He stirs the pot, testing the heat of the stew. "I haven't quite figured that out yet."

I huff and lean against the pillar, crossing my arms.

"Where else could it be? Who might know?"

Nadir ladles soup into a bowl and passes it to me, our fingers brushing. We haven't acknowledged the fact that I left the tent to sleep next to him last night after telling him I wanted to keep my distance. The touch sends sparks up my arm, making my heart thump too hard in my chest. I need to get away from him. His nearness is overwhelming, and I feel like I'm going to crack at any moment. He spoons out his own bowl, and I walk over to sit down next to him.

"What about the Woodlands Staff?" he asks. "If the Mirror and Torch both spoke to you, then maybe the Staff would, too. You have Woodlands blood flowing in your veins as well."

"But we can't just waltz up to Cedar and ask for it. Then that's another person who knows what we're trying to do."

"Did he know you had magic? I wonder if he knew you were the Primary."

I shake my head. "I have no idea. I don't know what relationship my parents had with him. As far as I know, he never interfered beyond seeing my mother to safety as a baby. I'm not sure if he even knew that my siblings and I existed."

"He's your family. It might be safe to tell him."

I scoff at that. "Right, because family can always be trusted."

Nadir's look is grim. "Fair enough."

We both fall silent as we eat our meal, each of us lost in our thoughts. When I'm done, I set the bowl down and stand up, striding over to the two thrones on the dais. I stare at them, trying to piece together the broken fragments of my thoughts. Being here feels like we're at the beginning of something, and I can't help but think that I'm already letting everyone down.

"Go and sit in it," Nadir says, walking up next to me, his voice soft.

"I couldn't," I say.

"It belongs to you, Heart Queen."

"Not yet, it doesn't."

He moves closer, and I resist the urge to lean into his pull. "You don't need the Crown to know this is your rightful inheritance. Sit down and see what it will feel like. Remind yourself what you're fighting for."

I look up at him, the irises of his eyes swirling with violet. They're so mesmerizing. So beautiful, I just want to stare at them all day. I want to stare at *him* all day.

"Alright." I ascend the steps and stop in front of the throne and then turn around and sink into the seat. The fabric cover has all but rotted away and yet, even in this empty room, I feel a shift. I imagine a future where this castle is restored to its former glory. I imagine Tristan and Willow here with me, each taking their place at my side. While the Crown might be mine, I won't rule this queendom without their guidance. This is their legacy as much as it's mine.

Nadir walks forward and bends on his knee, his head bowing.

"What are you doing?"

He looks up with a smirk. "Kneeling for the queen."

"Stop that," I say, something awkward bursting in my chest.

He grins and tips his head. "You look glorious up there."

Enjoying his admiration way more than I should, my cheeks burn at the compliment.

"Na—" I break off and my eyes go wide.

"What is it?" he asks.

"It changed."

He stands up and comes closer. "It did?"

I jump up from the seat and circle around the back to a stone wall covered with roses and vines. The buzzing in my veins has shifted, the drone pitching lower. I press my hands to the wall, and there's a tug from the center of my stomach, a hook dragging me forward.

"Here. I think it's here." I press on the wall, but of course, it's solid and nothing happens.

Nadir is already running his hands over the stone. "Is there a door? A latch or a lever?"

We both search the wall, looking for a chink or a crack or something that might open it. After a few minutes, we come up empty-handed.

"We have to knock it down," Nadir says, stepping back.

"How? It's a solid stone wall."

He tosses me a cocky grin.

"You're traveling with the Aurora Prince, Inmate. Back up."

I do as he says as ribbons of colorful light whip from his fingertips, swirling into a tornado. The effect is hypnotizing as the colors move and slide and twist against each other. Nadir takes a few steps back, pulling the lights towards him, forming them into a massive ball. It pulses and flickers like his own personal sun. He then lifts his hands over his head and hurls them forward, the ball crashing into the wall and splitting apart like a drop of water hitting the ground. Ribbons of light blast out and a crash shreds the air. I cover my head against a shower of stone and dust.

The roar of the cracking stone is deafening as the ground shudders. After a few seconds, everything falls silent. I cough, dust coating my mouth. Suspended in the air, it covers my clothes and my hands and my hair.

"Are you okay?" Nadir asks, his hair and clothes also dusted in a fine layer of white.

"I think so." In a wry voice, I add, "That was a little dramatic."

"I like to act with style." He holds out his hand, and I take it. "Let's go see what's there."

We step over the debris, kicking away the stones and rocks, climbing over the largest pieces. Behind the mess sits a round chamber, the walls made of the same white stone as the rest of the castle. But it's instantly obvious it's completely empty.

"There's nothing here."

Nadir presses his mouth together. "Do you still feel the change?"

I nod. "Yes, it's pulling me in."

"Then there has to be something here."

We enter the room, performing the same set of moves we did on the first wall, searching for a hidden latch or door.

"Agh!" I cry out, banging my fists against the stone. "Every time we take one step forward, we come up on another dead end. Where is it!"

"It's here," Nadir says, circling the room. "It has to be." He's so full of confidence that I want to believe him, but the longer we remain in this empty chamber, the more hopeless I become.

My gaze drifts upward to an opening carved into the ceiling, letting in a shaft of moonlight that reaches the ground, forming a small bright spot. Blowing out my cheeks, I cross the floor and spin around, searching for the clue I've missed. When I pass under the beam of light, my knees buckle. The buzzing under my skin sparks, ricocheting through every cell and nerve. "Nadir," I gasp, as the sensation flares again, causing my stomach to pull tight. "I feel something."

He's next to me in an instant, his arm wrapping around my waist to hold me up. He pulls me back, and we both stare at the column of light. "But there's nothing there," I say, running my hand through it and sucking in a breath at another sharp pull in my chest. "But *something* is there."

Nadir frowns, circling the beam slowly. He casts out a crimson ribbon of magic, followed by another one of emerald and then of violet. They hit the beam of light and bend around it, curving to accommodate an invisible barrier. He sends out more magic, more ribbons curling, until it's formed a cylinder that spins slowly in the center of the room.

"What is it?" I whisper, staring up at it.

"It's magic," he says. "Mine can't get through it." He lifts his arm and calls all his ribbons of color back, leaving an empty space again.

"I don't understand."

Nadir presses his mouth into a line and gives me a look that suggests he's about to tell me something I don't want to hear.

"I suspect it can only be touched by Heart magic and that it's protecting something very important."

"The Crown," I breathe, staring at the empty spot.

"The Crown. Whoever or whatever created this, must have done so to ensure only a true member of Heart could get at it."

"So we'll go get Tristan. Maybe he has enough magic to unlock this."

Nadir is shaking his head. "I'd also guess it's only the magic of the Primary that will do it. Who else would be the rightful finder of the Heart Crown? Besides, we don't have time. My father is searching for us."

"But I can't," I say, my chest crumpling in disappointment. "I can't unlock this without the Crown, and I can't get the Crown without unlocking this." I place my hand over my heart, feeling the surge of magic and that infuriating wall that's keeping me from it.

"You can," Nadir says, coming closer, his hand circling my elbow. "I'll help you."

"But you tried, and you couldn't."

"So we'll try again. Try harder. It isn't magic you need to get at your power, Lor. It's you. The only one preventing you from accessing it is you."

"That's not true," I hiss, tearing my arm away. "I want this more than anyone."

He steps in closer, his hand tipping up my chin. "I know you do, but you're so scared of your past. Of what will happen if anyone sees what you're capable of, that you're locking yourself away."

"Because of what your father did!" I scream, once again tearing from his grasp. "I had to lock it away. I nearly killed myself burying it so deep so I could protect myself and my family. He did this to me!"

"He did," Nadir growls, moving towards me, not leaving me room to escape. "He did that, and for that, he will fucking pay. I swear it to you, Lor. With my every last dying breath, I will make him pay for everything he did. But you're not a little girl anymore and he can't hurt you. I won't let him hurt you again."

"You can't promise that."

"I can and I do," he growls. "You're mine, Lor. You might not believe it yet, but you are, and I'm not going to let that monster touch you ever again."

I inhale a deep breath. "I'm not sure I know how." Tears sting the backs of my eyes, hoping that at least part of what he's saying is true.

He takes my hand and pulls me towards him before turning me to face the shaft of moonlight in the center of the room. He places an arm across my collarbone and a hand on my stomach, pulling me tight against him.

"Breathe," he whispers, his mouth brushing my ear. My magic flares under my skin, and today his presence doesn't soothe it. Today it's wild and feral, like it wants to reach out and snatch him, lock him up and keep him forever. I do as he says, sensation flickering across the surface of my body as my head tips back against his shoulder.

A moment later, bands of Nadir's magic wrap around my legs and my hips. It slides higher, around my waist and my chest, while my magic stretches for his.

"Do you feel it?"

I nod, my eyes closing as he reaches inside me again and he grunts.

"It's there, Lor. It's trying to play with me." There is amusement in his voice and a note of pride. I revel in it, feeling his magic twin with mine, their cadence thrumming together like a perfectly tuned symphony.

"We're going to do this together. We're going to grab hold of that wall and pull. When you feel it crack, you need to be ready. We may only get a moment. But when it opens, concentrate on casting whatever is in there out towards that pillar."

He tightens his hold. "Can you do that, Heart Queen?"

"I don't know." I lift my head and stare at the empty space in front of me.

"Can you do it, Heart Queen?" he repeats, his voice low and rumbling.

"I can do it," I say, trying to mimic his confidence.

"Yes, you can. You're going to do this because you are the strongest fucking woman I've ever met. Because you're a queen without her crown and it's time to take it back. Do you hear me?"

I nod, a strange feeling twisting in my chest at his words. "I hear you."

He says nothing else as his magic braids through mine. Both threads are a strange puzzle that fits together but doesn't quite match. His magic is round and soft and languid, while mine is jagged and crisp, full of hard edges. Yet there's a harmony they find together, like they understand one another.

"Concentrate," he says as our magic delves into that cavity in my chest where my locked power is trapped.

We pry at the edges that are fused together, but for a hairline crack that's so close to freedom I can almost taste it. I groan as we dig deeper. It doesn't hurt exactly, but it feels like something is rummaging around in the meat of my organs. A pressure or a presence that's going to split me open.

"Are you okay?" Nadir whispers, his face pressed to my ear, his grip on me tight.

I nod. "Yes. Keep going."

We work together, pulling and pulling, and then I feel it. The barest shift, so slight I might have missed it if I weren't concentrating with every ounce of my will.

"It's working," I say. We keep going, pulling and pressing, trying to coax slivers of movement. Again, there's the barest shift and I gasp, gritting my teeth so hard I feel it to the back of my skull.

A little more, and another shift, and then it happens.

A crack. An opening splits and pain shoots through my body as I cry out, but I don't let go, plunging into that cavity, pushing through it until suddenly a web of red lightning shoots from my fingers and slams into the empty beam of light. It flashes, turning into a pulsating column of fiery crimson.

Then it's there.

The Heart Crown.

It hovers in the center, spinning slowly, the blood-red stone winking in the light.

"Ah!" I cry out before the opening inside my chest slams shut, the lightning stuttering and the column of light flashing out.

"No!" I scream and lunge for the Crown, worried we're about to lose it. But the Crown is still there, plunging to the ground. I leap, but I'm too slow. Nadir goes for it, faster than an arrow, and snatches it from the air.

He holds it up, his eyes wide and his mouth open. I stare as he hands it to me, both of us breathing heavily. Tears slide down my cheeks as I take it in my hands, twisting it and examining it from every angle.

"We did it," I say.

"You did it, Heart Queen."

Nadir's looking at me, not the Crown, with a mixture of emotions that feel too complicated to name.

"Try it on," he says, and I shake my head.

"Not without Willow and Tristan. I can't do this without them."

"Of course. We'll head back to the manor first thing in the morning."

I look back at the Crown, marveling at its sheer presence. It seems to vibrate with life. I never, ever thought I would be here holding this in my hands with the remnants of its power running through my blood.

"I felt my magic. It was there!"

"You did. How do you feel?"

"I...feel amazing. I could do this again. Right?"

"Of course you can."

"Thank you," I say. "I couldn't have done that without you."

The brilliant smile he gives me then flicks on a bright light that I've been trying to drown in darkness since the day we met, blinding me with its force.

Without thinking about it, I stride forward, grab him behind the neck and pull his face towards mine, kissing him fiercely. He grunts and wraps his arms around my waist, meeting my kiss, our mouths sliding together. With the Crown gripped in my hand, I loop my arms around his neck, and he kisses me harder, his tongue driving into my mouth before he pulls away, his eyes wild and his breath shallow.

"What was that for?"

"I just...needed to kiss you."

He tips his head with a hopeful gleam in his eyes. "Do you need to do it again?"

"Yes."

Nadir groans, his hand coming to the back of my head as he bends me back and kisses me again so deep, I feel it throb *everywhere*.

"Does what you said still stand? That you're ready, any time I am?" I ask.

"Fuck, yes. Of course it does."

"I need you. I want you." My voice is a strained whisper.

"I thought you said this was done," he replies, his intense gaze searing into me.

"Fuck what I said."

"Oh, thank gods."

Then he kisses me again.

CHAPTER FORTY-FOUR

NADIR

"Let's get out of here," I say, tugging on Lor's hand. We step over the shattered remains of the wall, and as soon as we clear the worst of it, I pull her towards me, gripping the back of her neck, trying to bring her closer.

"Gods, you make me crazy, Lor. I'm going to fuck you until you have to beg me to stop."

I hoist her up, wrapping her legs around my waist. Zerra, she feels so perfect against me. I carry her down the dais and press her against the pillar next to where we slept last night, my mouth burning hot kisses down her neck. I slide my hands into the opening of her sweater, preparing to tear it off her, when she tenses.

"Don't," she cries out. "That's the only one I packed."

I give her a wicked smile, dropping her to the ground before I yank up the hem, and toss it away.

"Fine, this time, I'll take it off properly, but next time I'm tearing every last stitch off you."

I don't give her the chance to respond as I capture her mouth with mine. She tugs at the hem of my tunic, and I lift my arms, desperate to feel her hands on me. I was so worried I'd fucked this up forever. That she was going to hold to what she said about this never happening again. Should I stop and make sure she knows what she's doing? Fuck, I want this so much. I can't. She's mine, and this was always inevitable. I will never, ever let her go.

She tosses my shirt in a pile with her sweater and then I grab her waist, lifting her up again so I can back her against the pillar before I grind my cock into her stomach. I'm so hard it's painful, but it's the most delicious sort of ache.

She lets out a breathy moan as my hips thrust against hers, and I suck on her neck. She tastes so fucking good I want to devour her. My hands slide up her ribs and then cup her breasts. They fit in my hands like they were meant for me. I knead them and pinch her nipples hard enough to make her gasp, the sound shooting straight to my cock.

"I'm going to fuck you, Heart Queen. You're going to ride me until you come so hard you see stars."

"Yes," she whispers. "Oh gods, yes."

She peers up at me with those dark brown eyes that always pull me under before I lift her away from the pillar, gripping her ass in my hands. Carrying her over to our haphazard pile of sleeping bags, I lay her down and stretch over her before I kiss her hard and deep, hoping she understands the message I'm trying to lay at her feet like a trail of rose petals.

My tongue drives into her mouth as I rub my cock between her thighs. I can smell how wet she is, and it's driving me to the edge of control already.

"Nadir," she begs. "Please."

Fuck, I love it when she says my name like that.

"What do you want?"

My hand slides down her throat and chest, between her breasts and down her stomach as I reach for the button on her leggings. I flick them open and slide my hand past the fabric, stopping just short of her pussy. "What do you want?"

"Touch me," she says. "Do everything you promised."

I want to shout out a thank-you to Zerra. Attempting to control the tremble in my limbs, I smirk and then slide my hand lower, my gaze pinned with hers. When I find the slick wetness of her pussy, I groan. "Gods, you're so wet."

She closes her eyes, her thighs falling open while she grips my wrist, urging me on. As if she'd ever need to ask for anything from now until the day I die. I slide my finger against her smooth wet skin, my senses exploding at the thought of getting my tongue on her again. I can't wait to taste her and lap up every last drop.

"Zerra," I say, breathing against her throat. I'm doing everything I can to hold myself back. I want this to last forever. Until the sun burns out and the mountains crumble to dust. She moans with pleasure, and the sound is fucking music to my ears.

"Beg me, Lor, beg me to touch you."

"Please," she whimpers. "Touch me, please."

A growl rumbles in the depths of my chest as I slide a finger into her. Fuck, she's so hot and tight. My cock throbs in anticipation.

"Yes," she cries out, her hips lifting to meet my hand as I circle her clit with my thumb. How I love watching her come undone for me like this.

"That's it," I whisper. "Fuck my hand, Lor."

Her back arches, her breasts thrusting up. But I need her to be naked. I need to see all of her. After pulling my hand out, I get on my knees and hook my fingers into her waistband. "Are these your only pair, too?" I ask, pissed off at her lack of clothing.

"Yes!"

"Next time, pack more clothes."

"We were in a hurry," she snaps, and I grin.

"I love it when you're angry with me."

Her nostrils flare in irritation, and she has no idea how irresistible she is when she's like this. I snarl and tug on her pants, dragging them down her legs with jerky movements. My hands won't work right because I'm so wound up. I pull off her boots and toss everything away, and then I sit back and stare at her. I can't get enough air. Pushing my hair out of my face, I let out a ragged breath.

"You are so fucking beautiful."

Her open gaze is raw with an emotion I want to claim as my own. The scars that mark her body fire an acute rage for everyone who's ever hurt her, but they also prove just how unbelievably brave she is.

I run a hand up the side of her calf and then her thigh, tracing every line and curve with the reverence of a holy disciple. I'm hungry and wild for her. She grabs my wrist and tugs me to her.

"I need you inside me. Now."

Those are the best words I've ever heard in my life. I crack into a devilish smile, but I have no intention of giving her what she wants just yet. Instead, I press my hands to the insides of her thighs.

"Beg me, Lor. You kept shutting me out. Now it's time to earn it."

"Asshole. I hate you," she says, and I smile.

"Fuck, I get so hard when you say that."

"I can keep calling you names if that's what you prefer," she says with a challenge in her eyes. That, too, makes my blood simmer like I've been dropped in boiling oil.

"Call me whatever you want, *Inmate*."

"Nadir," she growls with impatience and gods, I'm enjoying this. I pick up her foot, kissing the inside of her ankle.

"*That* is actually my name, sweetheart."

Her eyes flash and she might be one second from leaping up and biting out a chunk of me, which has my dick growing even harder.

"The thing is," I say, making conversation like she's not lying before me naked and waiting like a buffet. I kiss her calf, sucking on her soft skin. She trembles and I watch with satisfaction as her mouth pops open. After a glance at her wet pussy, I resist the urge to smother her with my mouth. "I can't decide if I want to fuck you hard and fast, or take my time and draw this out as long as possible." She whimpers and I meet her gaze with a mischievous smile. "Either way, we're not leaving here until I've done both. Multiple times."

I kiss the inside of her knee, propping her ankle on my shoulder and sliding my hand down the outside of her thigh. Her head falls back with a moan that sounds like part desperate plea and part surrender.

"Tell me you're mine," I say, and her head snaps up. I can't read what's in her expression, but she has to understand what I'm beginning to suspect. Lor didn't just drop into my life by chance. None of this is a coincidence. It's destiny. We were made for each other. What we have goes deeper than lust. Deeper than love.

"Never," she counters, and my heart seizes. "This is just sex, remember?"

My hand tightens around her ankle, the other one sliding up the inside of her thigh as she shivers under my touch. I know she feels this, too. She *has* to.

I lean over her. "Trust me. You're mine. Say it."

But something cracks.

Her eyes darken and she shakes her head, her lips rolling together. Her ankle jerks, but I hang on, desperate to cling to whatever I sense is about to crumble away.

"Let go of me." There's no playfulness in her expression anymore.

"Lor—"

"No. Stop. This was a mistake."

Those words slice deep, my heart carving into ribbons as I finally release my hold. Now she's getting up, retrieving her clothing and stuffing her feet back into her leggings.

"What's the matter?" I ask with bewilderment, but she refuses to look at me. "What did I do?"

She picks up her discarded tunic and tosses my shirt at me. "Put that back on."

"Lor!" I grab her arm, but she yanks it away.

"I'm not yours! I am *mine*!" She's shaking, her entire body glistening with a sheen of sweat.

Gods, what have I done? I pushed her too hard. I was too fucking impatient. She has a lifetime of shit to work through, and I need to back off.

"I won't be anyone's ever again. Do you understand me? I don't want this. I shouldn't have kissed you. I'm sorry. That was a mistake." She yanks her tunic over her head and then drops to her knees, rearranging the blankets. She still won't look at me. "It won't happen again. I got carried away with my magic and the Crown..."

"It's okay," I say.

Her gaze flicks up to me for a fraction of a second before she looks away again and nods. She scrubs a tear from her cheek with the sleeve of her arm and then lies down on her bedroll, curling up, so her back is towards me.

I stand there with my shirt still balled in my fist, staring at her. She looks so small and scared right now, only a shadow of the ferocious woman I know she is. *I* did this to her.

Is this over? Does she just need space and time? Whatever it is, I won't push her again. Or at least I'll try.

She sniffs and rubs her cheek again, but still doesn't turn my way.

Finally, I pull my shirt over my head and then stretch on to my own bedroll. I stare at her back, wishing she would just talk to me. Or hold my hand like she did last night. That would be more than enough right now.

"Lor?" I venture, but she doesn't answer. She just hugs her arms tighter and curls into herself even further. Holding in my sigh of dejection, I vow to give her the space she needs. I've waited this long for her to come into my life, and I'll wait for her forever if that's what it takes.

Turning on to my back, I tuck an arm under my head and stare at the starry sky as I listen to Lor's soft breaths and sniffles, desperately wishing I could ease her pain.

She's the only thing that's ever made me feel any sort of true happiness. Somehow, she's cracked the hard-worn shell built by my father, and forced me to *feel* something other than an eternal need for revenge.

Lor is mine. I've never been so sure about anything in my life. I just need to be patient. Still, I rub at my chest, wondering how I'm not bleeding out on the floor thanks to the gaping wound in my heart.

I awake to the chirp of birds, their tweets nipping at my troubled dreams. I blink, the sunlight stinging my eyes, and then my brow furrows. In all the years I've been coming here, I've never seen or heard evidence of anything alive inside Heart, much less a cheerful bird.

I look at Lor, knowing she's the reason for this. Her queendom is calling her home. It's waking up in her presence. My chest tightens at the thought. When the truth is revealed, it's going to throw off the entire balance of Ouranos. She might not realize it yet, but she's going to have to battle against more than just my father for what's hers. But I vow to be there with her every step of the way.

Even if she never lets me touch her again.

She's rolled over in sleep and is facing me now. She was having nightmares last night, and I wanted so badly to hold her, but knew she wouldn't welcome that. A line dents the spot between her brows even now, her memories haunting her.

Her dark hair spills over her shoulders, and I resist the urge to pick up a lock to hold between my fingers. I look up at the sky that's just starting to lighten. We should get going, but I hate to disturb her. I could lie here forever staring at her, something I'd never get away with if she were awake.

She lets out a sleepy moan and shifts before her eyes slowly peel open. When she sees me, her gaze holds mine for several long seconds, the exchange heavy with meaning.

Even if she stopped me last night, those few minutes that I kissed her and touched her were like surfacing from the bottom of an ocean trench with stones tied to my ankles. I'll never forget the sounds she made or the way she felt against me.

Patience, I remind myself again. I'll wait forever if I have to. She can fight me all she wants. She can keep pretending she doesn't feel it, too, but eventually she'll understand.

"Good morning, Heart Queen," I say, and she blinks as she pushes herself up and runs a hand down her face.

"Nadir, about last night—"

"It's fine," I say, cutting her off. "You don't need to apologize."

She tugs on her lip with her teeth and then nods before she stands up and starts packing away her bedroll, once again refusing to look at me. I follow her lead, taking down the tent we never used and packing up the rest of our things. She picks up the Crown, holding it in her hands, blinking back tears.

"Thank you for helping me last night," she says, still averting her gaze. "With my magic." She finally looks at me. "I couldn't have done that without you. All those years, I thought it was gone forever. Your father took it from me, and you gave it back."

Then she turns away again, and I want to comfort her so badly my skin burns.

"Could you do it again? Right now?" I ask instead, and she shakes her head.

"No, but at least now I know it's possible. After we get back to my brother and sister, we'll figure out what comes next."

I blow out a breath. "Right. We should get going."

She gives me a serious look and dips her chin in acknowledgment. We continue packing up the rest of our belongings. Lor wraps the Crown in a blanket and carefully nestles it into my pack before I sling it over my shoulders.

Now she's biting the inside of her cheek, something else clearly on her mind.

"What is it?" I ask.

"I want to go check on the women."

I was afraid of this.

"Lor, no. We can't. If anyone sees us, my father will know where we are within hours."

"I need to know they're okay," she says, her eyes shining. "It's my fault they're in your father's hands."

I run a hand through my hair and stride over. Her eyes are on the ground, and I tip up her chin. She doesn't flinch at my touch, only meeting my gaze with that fierce determination that makes my knees go weak every single time.

"It is not your fault. None of this is your doing. My father is the one who took you from your family. He's the one who forced you to hide your magic, and he's the one who's taken those women. And now that he must suspect who you are, he won't have any more reasons to test them. He'll let them go."

"Don't patronize me."

My mouth flattens with the grim truth. He might stop testing them, but he won't simply let them walk free, either.

"I need to know they're okay," she whispers, and the sound spreads hairline fissures through my chest.

I think of Heart's desecrated settlements. Even after all these years, they bear no name. They're both permanent and fleeting. Made up of people who've lived on the edge of nothing for centuries. Waiting for their queen. Waiting for Lor.

How can I deny her this?

I'm about to agree to this wholly terrible idea when the scuttle of a stone catches my attention. I turn around. Someone's here. Lor must hear it too, because she's looking in the same direction. Our gazes meet and I reach for her, spinning my magic to form my wings as a prickle of dread creeps down my spine.

She allows me to scoop her up into my arms and then I look up and what I see makes my blood run cold. A ring of soldiers wearing the uniforms of The Aurora stand at the edge of the opening, a dozen crossbows aimed straight at us.

"Fuck," I say. "We need to run."

But I already know we can't come back the way we came in. The thud of boot steps is drawing nearer. They have us cornered, and they're not even trying to be quiet.

"They found us."

Lor sucks in a sharp breath, and I place her back on her feet before I take her hand. "Let's go."

We both dash for the opposite end of the throne room, and I catch a fleeting glimpse of my father's guards as they burst into the room. We just barely manage to evade a blast of Aurora light that spears past, hitting the far wall with a resounding explosion.

There's no question it's my father's magic, and he's here, coming for us. Coming for Lor.

We make our way to a staircase and start pounding up the steps that wind up in circles. Lor takes them two at a time and I keep close behind, the pack I'm still wearing on my back bouncing.

An ominous rumble follows us up, the sounds of my father's guards in pursuit.

"Faster," I say. "Faster." She doesn't look back as she picks up her pace, keeping one hand on the wall as we spiral higher and higher. From all of our searching, I know this staircase leads to a flat section of the roof. If we're fast enough, maybe we can escape from there.

Lor stumbles, crying out as she misses a step. Her knees slam against the stone and she grunts, clearly holding in a scream of pain. Nearly tripping over her, I stop to help her up. She's already struggling to stand, and it's then I realize how hard she's shaking. I can't blame her. If my father gets his hands on her, then it's over for both of us.

I shove my hands under her armpits and lift her back on her feet, keeping one arm around her waist as we hobble up the stairs while I half carry, half drag her up. The fabric of her leggings is ripped, exposing a pair of scraped, bloody knees, but she doesn't complain as she trudges forward, breathing heavily.

The sounds behind us are growing louder, the closer they get.

Finally, we reach the top of the staircase and shove open the rotted door. Any locks or handles are long gone, giving us no way to bar the exit. Not that it would be any use against the king.

"Come on!" I yell, taking her hand, once again whirling out my magic into my wings so we can try to escape. But just as I'm about to pick her up, a rope of blue light wraps around my legs and I trip, careening forward and catching myself at the last minute.

"Nadir!" comes a voice that sends a shudder through my limbs. I spin around to find my father, surrounded by a contingent of his guards. "Stop. You can't run from me. Just hand her over, and we can be done with this."

"Get behind me," I say to Lor, my eyes never leaving the king. She does as I ask, shielding herself, one of her hands gripping my upper arm.

"You can't have her!" I shout across the roof, and my father smirks. Gods, I want to walk over there and rip out his heart, but my first priority is getting Lor the fuck out of here.

He saunters forward, one slow, arrogant step after another. "Who will it be, then? This *girl* or your mother? Or perhaps your sister?"

"You wouldn't dare touch Amya," I snarl. He wouldn't. I have to believe that. He's been using my mother's safety to control me my entire life, and it's always worked. What I have to understand is that at some point, he's going to force me to make a choice I know will haunt me through eternity.

"But what if I already have?" he asks, tipping his head. I can practically feel Lor reacting behind me, her body stiffening and her fingers tightening on my arm. I know she's worried about her siblings.

"You're lying," I say.

Gods, I hope he's lying. He's just trying to get to me. He can't have found them.

"Are you willing to take that chance?"

He takes another step, and I hold up my hand. "Don't come any closer."

The wind is picking up, the sky darkening as thunderclouds roll overhead. I have to take the chance because of who Lor is and what I think she's capable of. If she ends up in my father's hands, I fear for the future of everything and everyone.

I shuffle back and Lor moves with me, her hand still clutched to my arm so tight her nails dig in.

That's when my father raises a hand and a spear of emerald green light explodes in our direction. She ducks as I counter his magic with a red blast that spreads out, forming a shield. My father's magic dissipates against it, but before I have the chance to go on the offensive, he sends out another blast of light. I notice then his guards are closing in, corralling us towards the edge of the roof and the perilous drop below, their crossbows aimed with deadly precision.

The king continues firing off more strings of magic, and I deflect them, but just barely. His magic is stronger than mine, and I will only be able to resist for so long. I can tell he's holding back because he wants to remind me he can best me without having to tap into the depths of his power. But I hang on.

For Lor and her family. For my mother and for Amya. For everyone in Ouranos who has no idea they're counting on me right now.

"Nadir," my father grits out, clearly starting to lose his patience. "Enough of this!"

That's when he strikes with the full force of his power. Thick bands of light shoot out, burning through my shield and then surrounding me. He closes his fist, and his magic tightens, strangling me like I'm wrapped in iron chains. I struggle against it, but it's no use.

"Lor," I choke out. "You have to run."

There's nowhere for her to go, though, and we all know it. My legs buckle as my father's magic continues to squeeze, my arms pinned uselessly to my sides.

"Lor," I whisper as I fall to my knees. My father lifts his other hand, and it's then I know it's over. The entire future I've been constructing in my head is gone before it even started. I can't bear to think about what he's going to do when he gets his hands on her. I want to scream and lash out at the injustice of it.

I just found her, and now she's being taken far too soon.

There's another squeeze of pain, my lungs compressing on the verge of collapse, before a blinding red flash streaks across my vision. I suck in a breath, waiting for the inevitable strike of death, but then lightning—red and crackling and humming with electricity—forks down from the sky and slams into the stone floor.

It tears the roof apart, sending my father and his soldiers flying. The magic caging me in releases, and I wait on my hands and knees, sucking in deep breaths, coughing and choking as my lungs fill with air.

When I look up, I'm too surprised to speak at the sight before me. My father and his guards are now surrounded by a massive dome made of sparking crimson lightning. I turn to look at Lor, who's staring at her hands before she looks up at me.

"I don't know what happened," she says with awe as I struggle to my feet.

"That's my girl," I whisper.

"Nadir!" comes my father's voice and I turn back.

He sends out a blast of magic against Lor's barrier, but all it does is ricochet off the inside, arrowing right into the chest of one of his guards, who collapses in a heap. My father's expression turns to thunder, his fist clenching like he wants to punch a wall through it.

"Don't do this!" he shouts, his voice cracking. The sound of it wills me into temporary stillness. It's the only time in my life

I've ever heard him be anything less than one hundred percent in control of himself. "You don't understand what she is!"

"Nadir!" Lor says. "I don't know how long that's going to hold. I think we should go."

I nod slowly as my gaze hooks into my father's. Neither of us moves, and it's at that moment I know I can never go back. While I've openly rebelled against the king my entire life, he's always believed I was ultimately on his side. He thinks he knows exactly how to bring me to heel, and I've always used this blind spot to my advantage.

But as he stares at me now, I see the understanding that settles in his eyes.

Finally, he knows that I've *never* been on his side. That everything I've worked for has been with the goal to destroy him. Today, a battle line has just been drawn. He will hunt me now to the ends of the earth. Do whatever he can to crush me before I can get to him.

The corner of my mouth quirks up in a dry smile because I have the Heart Queen and she's on *my* side. No matter how much she might hate me, she will always hate him more. Then I lift up my hand and touch my fingers to my forehead, offering my father a mock salute before I spin on my heel and race for Lor.

Without breaking my stride, I scoop her up, cradling her against me as my wings erupt. I launch us into the air and, with a burst of speed, send us tearing across the sky.

Chapter Forty-five

LOR

Burying my face into his chest, I tremble as Nadir wraps his arms around me. That was too close. I can't stop replaying what the king said about Amya. Did he find the manor? Are they all dead or worse? I sense Nadir is having similar thoughts because we say nothing as he holds on to me tight and we make our way back to the manor.

As we fly through the sky, I wonder where all of this ends.

It's only now I truly comprehend the overwhelming enormity of what I'm trying to accomplish. There is nothing left of the home I don't even know. Of this figment of my mind that existed only in a dream. It was a story my mother told us as she tucked us in at night. I can barely remember her face anymore, her features blurred and distorted.

The only true memory I have is that our parents loved us. That I know for sure. But nothing else was real. They tried to give us a safe and happy home, but it was only an illusion with all the permanence of wet tissue. A thin cloak draped over the fear that chased them every day of their lives. Their days were always limited, and it was only a matter of time before someone, be it the Aurora King or another ruler in Ouranos, came knocking.

As we hurtle through the air, I barely register our surroundings. It doesn't feel like much time passes before I catch sight of the Void and the majestic range of mountains that border the northern edge of The Aurora looming far in the distance.

Nadir's face is drawn with his lips pressed together, a conflict of emotions brimming in his eyes. They swirl with pink and violet and green, and I sense there are so many things he needs to say. He doesn't voice them, though, instead turning back to stare out over the horizon.

I'm not sure how we'll ever get past what happened last night. After he'd helped me with my magic, I was so alive. So powerful. My blood was on fire, and he'd never looked more beautiful. I wanted him. Every part of me had wanted him.

But then he had to try to claim me as his, and I can't allow that. He can talk about his possessive Fae nature all he wants, but I'm not a prize for him to stake his flag. I already belonged to the Aurora King for twelve long years. And then Atlas tried to cage me, too.

I will never belong to anyone ever again.

He will never have my heart.

Before long, we're within view of the manor house. Nadir descends into the Void, depositing us onto a path worn into the forest floor. He's breathing heavily, and he leans against a tree, his eyes closing and his head falling against it.

"Are you okay?" I venture, approaching him, resisting the urge to touch him, always fighting the need. Eventually, this twisted tangle of feelings for him will fade. "Nadir?"

He opens his eyes and looks at me, nodding his head. "I'm fine. Just tired."

"You didn't stop this time. You should have taken a rest."

"We don't have time for that. We have to keep moving," he says, pushing himself away from the tree and stalking past me. "Come on."

Without another word, we head down the path and wind our way through the trees.

"What about your father?" I ask, breaking the silence.

A shadow falls over Nadir's expression. "It doesn't change anything. He already knew we were hiding something."

"Do you really think he found them? Should we have come back here?"

He shakes his head and pins me with a fierce look. He doesn't say what I'm sure we're both thinking. That we have to know if they're all okay before we move on.

"No. I'm sure he was bluffing." The words are confident, but they sound forced. Pushing a slow breath through my nose, I nod my head.

A moment later, there's a howl in the distance and two white blurs burst from the foliage. Morana and Khione streak towards us, barking loudly. Nadir drops into a crouch and wraps an arm around each of their necks, nuzzling his face into their thick fur.

"I missed you girls, too," he says fondly, and the warmth in his voice burns in my chest.

Surely if the dogs are here, then everyone else is okay? Or are they trying to warn us?

When he's done, he stands and the dogs make their way over, circling my legs and trotting alongside as we continue our way back to the manor.

After we traverse a few more bends, the top of the house comes into view. Everything appears fine, the manor intact, and I whisper a prayer to Zerra on my lips. Please let them all be okay.

When we arrive at the gate, he unlocks it and holds it open. I stand before the doorway, the moment resting heavy on my shoulders.

"Ready?" Nadir asks, and I shake my head.

"Not really."

His mouth forms a grim line before he opens the door, and we step into the quiet hallway. I'm about to call out when I hear a screech, and Willow comes flying down the stairs.

"Lor! You're okay!" She crashes into me and wraps me in her arms. "Zerra, we've been so worried."

"Oh gods," I say, squeezing her tight and willing my legs not to crumple under me.

Amya, Mael, Hylene, and Tristan also enter the foyer, the rest approaching from another room. They're all here and alive and it's right then, the tight band of worry cinching my ribs loosens. They're okay. The king was lying.

I meet my brother's gaze.

"Did you find it?" he asks with no small amount of hope in his voice. With the Crown tucked inside Nadir's pack, I suddenly become aware that the time has come. Tristan and Willow are safe, and there are no more excuses left. I clasp the necklace at my throat, feeling the pulse that beats within it.

"We found it."

Tristan's eyes shine as he strides over and envelops me in a hug. "What was it like?" he whispers into my hair.

"It was...home, Tris. It's a mess, and it's all in ruins, but it was home, and I can't wait to show it to you."

He squeezes me tighter, and we stay that way for a few more moments until someone snaps their fingers in my ear.

"This is very touching," Mael drawls. "But can we get on with this? You do remember you have a murderous king searching for you?"

Tristan pulls away and snarls at Mael. "Fuck off, asshole."

"He found us," Nadir says grimly, and as we all make our way towards the large living room at the back of the house, he fills them all in on our encounter, including the way my magic reacted when the king attacked. When he's done, Mael eyes me from head to toe.

"So any chance the king thought he might be mistaken about who you are is now gone."

"I think so."

Nadir drops the pack from his shoulders, and I immediately dig into it, pulling out the Crown. There is a collective hush through the room as I unwrap it and hold it up. Everyone moves closer, as if drawn to its center of gravity.

"It's chipped," Mael says, frowning. "The stone there. Does that mean it's broken?"

The back side of the large stone indeed has a piece cut out, almost as though someone tried to hide it. My siblings and I share a look, knowing the time has also come to reveal the final hand we have left to play.

"It's okay. Lor has the rest of it in that locket," Nadir says, and I whirl on him. He stands against the wall, arms crossed and one ankle over the other, a smug gleam in his eyes.

"How did you know that?"

"You're constantly touching that necklace." He unfolds himself and strides over, lowering his mouth to my ear, so only I can hear him. "You can't keep secrets from me, Inmate. I see you."

I pin him with a furious glare and crack open the locket, revealing the small red jewel inside.

"How did you manage to hang on to it all these years?" Amya asks, her eyes wide.

"We had to get creative," I say. "This thing has passed through both me and Willow more times than I can count."

"Disgusting," Mael says, wrinkling his nose, and I offer him a bleak look.

"We did what we had to," Willow says, taking it from my hand. "There were so many times we came close to losing it. When Lor disappeared, I thought it was gone forever."

Willow tries to hand it back to me, but I look at Tristan. "You do it," I say to him. "Neither of us would have survived this long without you."

"Lor—"

"Please. I want you to. I may be the Primary and this Crown may sit on my head, but there will never be a day that you and Willow aren't just as important to Heart. You are its keepers, too. You've held this dream even longer than I have."

Tristan nods and takes it from Willow. With the Crown still in my hands, he presses it to the larger red stone. The silver band warms, glowing brightly before it dims, the jewel pieces now fused together as though it was always whole.

"Do you think mother knew what it really was when she told us to protect it?" Willow asks, and Tristan and I both shake our heads.

I feel Nadir's gaze on me, and I look back at him. He tips his head, his eyes swirling with color as the corner of his mouth lifts.

"It's time, Heart Queen. Let's unleash hell on my father."

Everyone is silent as I place the Crown on my head. It's heavier than I thought it would be, maybe weighed down with centuries of expectation.

I close my eyes, waiting to feel its power. Waiting for it to speak to me like the Torch and Mirror.

"Reach for your magic," Nadir says, and I try to mimic what we did in the castle.

Nothing happens.

My eyes open to find six sets of curious eyes watching me. "I don't feel anything," I say, panic edging my voice. "I don't feel anything."

Nadir's hands circle my shoulders from behind. "It's okay. Be calm. Try again."

I nod and take a deep breath, trying to quiet my pulsing heart. I do as he asks, reaching for that distant power I can't quite grasp. In my head, I'm screaming at the Crown to wake up. To hear me.

Please, help me. Please.

But there's nothing. It may as well be a useless hunk of metal.

With a cry of rage, I pull it off my head. "It's not working!"

I look at the faces watching me, and it's clear no one else knows what to make of this.

"Nadir, what do we do?"

"Fuck," he says, running a hand along the back of his neck. "I don't know. I was so sure this would work."

"But you always have a plan," I say, feeling everything slipping away.

"I don't, this time." His expression is bleak, and I sink into the nearest chair, dropping my face into my hands, tears already streaming down my face.

"What are we going to do?" This time I look at my brother, who seems equally perplexed.

"Try again," he says. "Maybe you just need one more try. You did it earlier with the king."

"He's right," Nadir says. "What happened there?"

"I don't know. I just saw what he was doing to you and I reacted..." I trail off.

When the king was hurting Nadir, I'd never felt such visceral rage in my life. I've always wanted to kill that monster, but right then, my hate and my loathing fossilized into something that burned like acid poured over an open wound. I would have done anything at that moment to protect Nadir, and that thought settles uncomfortably over my shoulders.

The mood around the room is solemn.

"There has to be something we can do," Amya says, pacing with her hands on her hips. "There must be some way to unlock your magic."

"What do you suggest?" Mael says, his voice tight. "We're putting a lot of faith in an object that no one has seen in hundreds of years. What if it's...dead?"

I turn it in my hands. "It's not. I can feel it. It's how I found it in the Heart Castle. It's alive. Maybe it's just asleep."

"It needs your magic," Nadir says. "It needs *you* to wake it up."

I shoot him a look. "It only worked because I was desperate. We can't rely on that. I can't beat your father if I can't control it."

Everyone in the room falls silent, lost in their own thoughts. I get up and wander to the window with the Crown clutched in my hand. The room faces south, towards the rest of Ouranos. Evening has fallen, and the sky is turning black, faint shimmers of colors streaking across the sky.

South. Of course.

How could I have forgotten?

"The Mirror." I spin around as everyone turns to me. "The Mirror said when I found the Crown, I should come back, and it would have a gift for me. What if this is it?"

They all exchange wary glances. I'd never considered *how* I would get back to the Mirror, only that I had to.

"It said that? You never told me," Nadir says. I give him a look that suggests now is really not the time to discuss what I have and haven't kept from him.

He moves past it, rubbing his chin with a hand. "It's possible."

I let out a long, slow breath. "Then that's it. We have to go back to the Sun Palace."

"How are you going to do that?" Mael asks. "Atlas is still hunting for you." He points to Nadir. "And he banned you from Aphelion. You can't just waltz in there and ask to visit his throne room."

"We'll go," Tristan says, and Willow nods her agreement.

"And me, too," Amya adds. "I've always been on Atlas's good side."

Nadir growls. "That's because he wants to fuck you."

Amya rolls her eyes. "I can handle myself, big brother."

"It has to be me," I say. "The Mirror said it had a gift for *me*." I look at everyone, daring them to argue. This is my fight, and no one is leaving me behind.

"Then I'm going, too," Nadir says.

"So we're all sneaking in," Mael says, running a hand down his face. "This is going to be a disaster."

"Not if we have a plan," I snap.

"Do you have one?"

"No. Not yet. But we'll figure something out. We have to."

Again, we share a round of wary looks.

"Maybe we can get Gabriel to help us," I muse, and Nadir snorts. "What? Why is that funny?"

"Gabriel can't help you, Lor."

"He tried to. Sort of," I say, somewhat defensive of my old warder who wasn't exactly my friend but felt like he could have been, had our circumstances been different.

"Lor, Gabriel is essentially a slave. He can't disobey Atlas even if he wanted to."

I frown. "What do you mean?"

"The wings. Those aren't natural. The warders are bred specifically for the purpose of serving the king. They're bound to him for life and have little autonomy of their own."

It's monstrous, but I realize this explains Gabriel's erratic behaviour. "That's why he was nice to me one moment and..."

"A complete ass the second?" Nadir asks. "Well, part of that is just his sparkling personality, but yes, his primary duty is to protect his king, and nothing can stand in the way of that."

"He's bound for life?"

Nadir nods. "Unless Atlas chooses to release him, but he would never do that. He's far too obsessed with his own sense of self-worth and his meager grasp of power. The Sun Court has never been the same since your grandmother nearly destroyed Ouranos." I ponder Nadir's words, feeling a strange melancholy for Gabriel. "At any rate, we can't rely on him."

"I have friends there."

"Former Tributes," Mael says. "Nope. They're too closely watched."

Everyone goes quiet again and Nadir sighs. "I don't want to linger here much longer. There's still my father to consider, and sooner or later, he's going to find this place too. Heading south would at least buy us some time. It could take a while for him to think to look for us there."

"You don't have to come," I say. "This isn't your responsibility anymore. You helped me get the Crown. We can take it from here."

Nadir strides over to me, his expression dark. His hands curl at his sides, and I get the sense he wants to touch me but holds himself back. Instead, he stops so close that I have to look up to meet his gaze. "What have I told you? I'm with you until the end. You're not going anywhere without me."

My chin rising, I give him a sharp nod. "Okay, then."

I try not to show my relief. I have no idea how I'll do any of this without his help.

"So we're just winging this?" Mael asks, skepticism dripping from those words.

Nadir looks at his friend, his expression serious. "So it would seem."

"We'll plan on our way there," Amya adds hopefully, though we can all hear the doubt in her tone.

"We broke her out of there," Mael says, gesturing with both hands to his left, as if we all don't know that, before he swings his hands to the other side. "And now you want to bring her back? With a target on both your backs?"

Nadir tugs on the bottom of his jacket. "It would seem that's the measure of it. You in? We're going to need you."

Mael tips his head and grins, his dark eyes alight with glee. "You know I'd never miss the chance to stir shit up. Especially when Atlas is involved."

Nadir gives him a crooked smile and then looks back at me. "You're sure about this? It's going to be exceedingly dangerous."

I swallow a knot in my throat. I'm terrified, but this is the only way. "Of course I'm sure. You think I haven't handled worse? Besides, you just said you don't have any other ideas."

Nadir tips his head in a gesture of concession, and then he turns to address the rest of the room.

"Then everyone get some sleep. Tomorrow we head back to Aphelion. Zerra help us all."

CHAPTER FORTY-SIX

SERCE

Cloris kneeled bent over in her cage, her silver hair ragged and limp. She'd been refusing any food or water, throwing it at the guards while screaming to be let out. Serce was sure the priestess was losing her foothold on reality, especially since she'd also stopped using the latrine, choosing instead to defile the floor of her cell. Serce stood over her and wrinkled her nose at the pathetic sight as Cloris lifted her head and snarled.

"If you think this is going to make me let you go, you're mistaken," Serce said, wrapping her hands around the bars. She leaned forward, but then snapped back as her eyes watered from the stench. They'd been in Heart for two months now, trying to get Cloris to cooperate. They needed her to perform the ritual to bond Serce and Wolf, but her patience was wearing thin.

The only advantage was it had given her time to sidle back into the queen's good graces. They had been playing nice ever since Daedra had learned she was to become a grandmother. Word had been sent to Aphelion regarding the proposed bonding with Wolf's sister, and their armies were headed north. His sister would accept the bond once she was done with her studies at Maris Academy in eighteen months.

It was all a lie, of course.

Once Serce got her hands on the Crown, she wanted nothing to do with Atlas or Aphelion. She would have no need of them. Her goal now was to conquer, not ally. She just needed to ascend and bond with Wolf. Then all of Aphelion's army would fall to their knees.

Cloris bared her teeth at Serce, peering through a ragged curtain of grey, tangled hair. Wolf hadn't allowed Serce to resort to torture, but this situation was becoming untenable. She was tired of waiting, and she needed to forge ahead with her plans before the Sun King arrived. Cloris hissed again, and Serce wondered how she'd slipped so far into this impression of a wild animal. Perhaps Cloris had never been playing with a full set of marbles.

Serce rolled her eyes and snapped her fingers, attempting to draw Cloris back. She wouldn't be much use in this state. A sharp pain jabbed her ribs and Serce clutched her stomach, now rounded with their child. The way Wolf's face lit up at night when they lay in bed was enough for her to endure this insufferable discomfort. She would be more than ready to see the end of this, though.

Cloris opened her mouth, moaning with a high-pitched wail as she scraped her nails down her face, leaving a set of deep gouges. Gods, Serce wished she'd just shut up. She rubbed her temple, pain building behind her eyes. No matter how much progress she'd made with her mother, she still hadn't gotten confirmation of when Daedra would finally descend. It was wearing at every last one of Serce's nerves.

Spinning on her heel, she made her way to the large tent sitting in the middle of the clearing. Wolf's forces had been hiding out here since they'd arrived, and this, too, was becoming more and more dangerous. Hiding a group this large was no easy feat. Wolf's forest magic was doing the heavy lifting to keep them hidden, but eventually something had to give.

Serce pushed through the flap where Wolf was conversing with his generals. As always, he took her breath away, his deep brown hair flowing down his back and his green tunic stretching over his formidable frame. His wings were folded behind him, and his eyes lit up as he turned to greet her. She ran a hand over her stomach and stepped inside.

"Ready for dinner?"

Wolf nodded, exchanged a few more words with his generals, and then strode over to clasp her hand. They headed back outside and stopped when shouts rose in the distance. A scout came bounding through the trees, her cheeks red and her chest puffing out.

"Your Majesty," she said, dropping to her knee, gasping. "The Aurora. They're marching this way."

"What?" Serce asked. "You're sure?"

The messenger nodded. "Positive."

"How many?" Wolf asked.

"At least several battalions that I could see. Thousands upon thousands."

"How far away are they?"

The messenger, finally catching her breath, shook her head. "A day, at most. Probably less."

"How did you not see them earlier?" Serce demanded. "How can an army that size just creep up on you?"

"I don't know, Your Highness. One minute there was no sign of them, and then suddenly there they were."

Serce glowered at the messenger, her lips thinning. Rion had clearly used some kind of magic to conceal his army. That's when they heard a wild cackle from Cloris's cage. She sat on her knees, her hands gripping the bars and her face pressed between them. She was laughing maniacally.

"He knows. The king. He knooooows," she said, and then she cackled again.

Serce stormed over. "What did you just say?"

Wolf came up behind her, and Cloris looked up at them both, her smile manic and her eyes rolling.

"He knooows," she repeated with her fingers pressed to her lips.

"She's been working with Rion," Wolf said, his expression tight.

The pain behind Serce's eye gave a stabbing throb.

"Fuck!" she screamed, balling her fists.

Now Rion and Kyros were compressing them from both sides and she still didn't have that Crown. There was no question in her mind Rion wasn't here to join with her. He'd played her, and she'd fallen for it. Would Aphelion choose to ally with Heart if they saw The Aurora was now part of the equation? Would they retreat or attempt to smother her, too? Serce couldn't hold them both off at once, no matter how strong she was.

"Chain her up," Serce ordered, pointing to Cloris. "She's coming with us. We do this tonight. There's no more time."

A sharp pain shot through Serce's back and she groaned, pressing her hand to it and sucking in several breaths before she straightened.

"Are you okay?" Wolf asked, but she waved him off.

"I'm fine."

A guard unlocked Cloris's cage before two more took her by each arm and dragged her to her feet. She refused to walk, her body remaining limp.

"Gag her," Serce said and then turned around and stalked back to their horses. They were due to have supper with her parents, and Serce had planned to again bring up the subject of the queen's descension, but the time had come for more drastic measures.

With Cloris and Wolf's soldiers in tow, they made their way back to the city, drawing more attention to themselves than Serce would have liked. Did her mother know about Rion yet? Had her scouts missed his approach, too?

They headed for the castle and made their way towards the private dining room where Serce's parents waited. Her back was aching now, her stomach tight. Gods, how she couldn't wait to get this baby out of her.

She stopped and whirled around. "We need to hide her until the time is right," Serce said, pointing to Cloris. "Take her to my wing for now." The two soldiers who held the priestess by each arm nodded and then dragged her away.

"Let's go," Serce said, taking Wolf's hand as two more of his guards followed closely behind.

They found the room where her parents were already seated, and Serce did her best to affect a mask of calm. She didn't want her mother to sense anything amiss.

"Serce!" her mother exclaimed, coming over to embrace her daughter. "Are you okay? You look pale!"

Serce inhaled a deep breath as her back spasmed again. "Oof," she said as she bent over. "Yes. My back is just hurting today."

"Come and sit," her father said, helping her into a chair.

Servants swarmed around them as they brought out the meal, but Serce had no appetite, either from the pregnancy or stress, she wasn't sure. Whatever the case, she could practically hear the drone of Rion's forces marching closer, making her queasy. She would rip that bastard apart for double-crossing her. She picked at her food, feeling both tense and listless at the same time.

"Serce? Are you okay?" her mother asked. "You've been so quiet during dinner."

Serce grimaced. "I'm fine. Just tired. The baby."

"Of course. You should stay off your feet until she comes."

Serce blinked. "She?"

Her mother smiled. "The Crown confirmed it last night. You're carrying a girl, and she will be the next Primary. It predicted she would have an important destiny to fulfil. One that would shape the very fabric of Ouranos."

Warmth bloomed in Serce's chest at those words. Yes. This was her duty. Everything she'd fought for and worked for. Wolf grabbed her hand and squeezed it, and she smiled at him.

She groaned as pain gripped her midsection, bending over before she felt the strangest sensation release below her waist.

"Your water!" Daedra cried. "The baby is coming!"

Sure enough, Serce's dress was now soaked, fluid collecting at her feet. *No.* Not now. She had to finish this first.

"Call the midwife!" the queen shouted, and a flurry of servants burst into action. Serce moaned as another wave of pain hit her.

"Your Majesty!" One of the Heart Queen's soldiers came striding in next. "The Aurora has been seen marching on Heart. They are nearly at our border."

Serce watched as her mother's face went ashen. "What? Why? Now?" The Heart soldier confirmed all the same facts Wolf's scout had.

Somehow, Rion had snuck up on all of them. That fucking bastard.

The midwife had also arrived, along with a wet nurse, and was moving Serce to the settee in the corner of the room. Serce dropped into it and found her mother standing over her. Wolf knelt at her side, his hands clasped around one of her own.

"What did you do?" Daedra asked, her voice low with accusation. "Why is Rion here with an army?"

"What I had to," Serce said, wincing in pain. "Let me have the Crown, Mother. You know it's the only way to stop him."

Her mother's face was hard, her eyes blazing. "You allied with our enemy?"

"You gave me no choice!"

Daedra swallowed, her throat bobbing. "I would have let you have it."

"When, Mother? You've been dancing around it ever since I spurned Atlas. I've waited long enough."

"I didn't think you were ready, and this proves I was right."

Serce groaned as another contraction wracked her body. "He'll kill us all if you don't descend."

"Sit back," the midwife said, her wary glance darting between mother and daughter. "I need to check your dilation."

Serce did as she was asked, her skin slicked with sweat. Another contraction hit her, and she squeezed Wolf's hand. He leaned up and kissed her forehead. "It's okay. I'm right here." Serce nodded and touched his face as she winced.

Serce watched from the far end of the room as her mother paced, guards and advisors coming in and out to speak with her before they left to carry out her orders.

For the next few hours, Serce labored as night fell on the city. Word had spread that The Aurora was marching on Heart.

Their army was smaller, and Aphelion was still days away—they might not arrive in time to provide aid. If they were even willing. They could just as easily turn around and march in the other direction, abandoning Heart to its fate, perhaps returning later to pick through the pieces.

Serce lay on the sofa, stripped down to a robe and wearing a thin nightgown now as Wolf dabbed her head with a cold compress.

"We're almost there," the midwife declared, checking on Serce again.

Outside, torches could be seen flickering in the distance as The Aurora drew nearer and nearer. The city was preparing for attack, but everyone waiting in this room knew they couldn't hold off the Aurora King for long.

"What were you thinking?" Daedra finally said, her temper exploding. She'd been pacing for hours, a dark cloud hanging over her head.

"Daedra," the king said. "This isn't the time."

"It is the time! He's practically on our doorstep! What was she thinking?!"

"Give me the Crown, Mother. I'll bond to Wolf and then we can beat him. I can beat him."

Daedra's eyes filled with tears as she looked at her daughter, disappointment and regret obvious in her expression. Unwittingly, Serce had backed them all into this corner. Sure, it hadn't gone exactly as she planned, but there was always more than one way to skin a cat.

"You need to start pushing!" the midwife declared then, and Serce wanted to scream at her for interrupting. But a wave of pain wracked her body, and she squeezed her eyes closed as she let out a moan.

"It's coming!" the midwife said. "Push!"

Serce did as the midwife asked while Wolf held her hand and murmured encouragement. Daedra sat on her other side and did the same. Their feud was forgotten for this brief moment as they brought the next generation—the next Primary—into the world.

"Push! Push!"

Serce groaned, and she pushed as hard as she could, when the pressure finally released.

"It's a girl!"

Tears ran down her face as her head fell back, and she let out a burst of triumphant laughter.

"Serce, you are the most incredible woman to walk this earth," Wolf said softly, peppering her face with kisses. The baby was bundled up and handed to Serce, who then passed her to Wolf, her body spent. He looked on the baby with so much love Serce thought her heart would explode.

But there would be time to enjoy this later, because shouts drew their attention outside, and Serce could see that Rion's army was much too close for comfort now. She struggled to sit up.

"Get Cloris," she told Wolf. "We need her."

He nodded and headed for the door with the baby in his arms, opening it and speaking to his soldiers, who waited outside. He returned to her side, his eyes glued to the little girl who stared up at him with a pair of big, dark eyes.

"She looks just like you," he said, kissing Serce again. They both admired the baby, and Serce felt something shift in her heart she hadn't expected. She loved this child already and would do anything to protect her. Finally, for the first time, she felt like she could be a mother.

The door banged open and Wolf's soldiers came in, dragging Cloris between them. She was hissing and wailing, the last bit of her sanity in tatters. They let her fall to the ground, where she slammed to her knees. She wrapped her arms around herself and rocked back and forth, her eyes glassy.

"What's going on?" Daedra asked. "Who's this?"

"Meet Cloris," Serce said, waving a weak hand. "She's going to perform the binding."

The queen glanced at the feral, half-crazed priestess with a dubious look. "Are you sure about that?"

A blast outside drew everyone's attention, their heads swiveling towards the window. A giant ball of colorful light hung suspended in the air. It was a message and a warning. Rion wouldn't wait long to enter the city.

"You need to get the baby out of here," Daedra said, not addressing Serce, but speaking to Wolf. "If they break down the gates—"

Her words sliced off with an ominous ring, but they knew what she was implying. Wolf's eyes darkened as he peered out the window at the ball of magic hovering in the sky. Whatever happened tonight, things would get messy before the dust settled.

Serce and Wolf looked at each other, and she nodded. She saw something break in his eyes as he nodded, too. Serce would get him back to his child. She would make sure of it. It was the only thing he'd ever asked of her.

"Call in your soldiers," Daedra said, opening the door and gesturing them inside. "No one will notice one or two of them leaving the city. You must do this if the Primary is to survive. The wet nurse should travel with them."

Wolf bent down so Serce could say goodbye. She touched the baby's forehead and placed a kiss on her cheek, tears leaking from the corners of her eyes. Was it possible to love someone this much when she'd only just met them?

Reluctantly, Wolf handed the swaddled child over to the wet nurse, who then clutched the baby to her chest. Tears ran down his face, too.

"We'll come for you soon, little one," he whispered, and kissed her head before addressing his soldiers. "Take her to my brother. Tell him to keep her safe until we come for her."

"Yes, Your Majesty," one of them replied.

"As quickly as you can," Wolf said, casting another glance over his shoulder.

They were about to leave when Daedra said, "Wait!" She walked over and undid the chain hanging around her neck. A gold necklace with a red stone hanging from it. "Something to remember me by, in case we don't make it."

The soldiers tipped their heads and then they left the room, the baby and the nurse between them. After they'd left, Daedra turned to her daughter. The atmosphere was tense with sorrow and fear, and so many things yet to come.

Serce pushed herself to stand, ignoring the pain in her body. She walked over to her mother. "It's time."

"No," Daedra said. "You've lost your way, Serce. I can't leave Heart in your hands."

"You will give it to me," Serce snarled. "I don't care if I have to take it from you."

"You know it won't work," her mother whispered. "You'll lose everything."

"You confirmed our daughter is the next Primary, Mother. The Crown is already mine."

Daedra's eyes filled with fear as she looked at her daughter. "I'd hoped you were better than all of this. I wasn't perfect as a mother or a queen, but I always tried to do my best. And now you've brought this destruction on us."

Serce let out a deep breath, her patience stretching thinner than gossamer.

"Bring Cloris," she said to Wolf. "And the Staff."

She heard him move as he retrieved the bow he'd arrived with, snapping it out of the casing that concealed it. Serce noticed he moved more slowly than usual, like he was floating through sap. She would get him back to his daughter if it was the last thing she did.

Daedra's eyes swung to the Woodlands Staff and widened. "You planned this from the very beginning. This is madness. This won't work."

"Of course I did, Mother." She ignored the rest of her mother's comment as she stalked towards the queen, who retreated until the backs of her thighs hit the dining table. Fear, true fear, had entered the queen's eyes, but Serce was blind to all of it. She snatched the Crown from her mother's head, swelling with the certainty that soon its power would be hers.

"Hold them," Serce ordered the group of Wolf's soldiers, who waited near the door.

While everything had been happening, they'd been surreptitiously instructed to remove Heart's forces from the room.

Now only The Woodlands army remained. Serce watched the surprised looks on her parents' faces as they were bound in the same type of arcturite cuffs they'd used on Cloris, before either of them could react.

"Serce!" her mother said. "You would do this to us?"

Serce turned away as Wolf picked Cloris up by the scruff and dragged her over. She crumpled at their feet in a babbling mess.

Gods, this entire thing had been pointless. Cloris was useless. Serce was going to have to do this herself. She fumbled around in Cloris's pocket, retrieving the book the priestess had been allowed to keep. The priestess continued to babble, her eyes rolling to show the whites.

Then Serce placed the Crown on her head. The silver felt warm against her skin, and her throat thickened with emotion.

Finally. After all this time.

Daedra shook her head as a tear slid down her cheek. "Don't do this," she said in a raw whisper. "You'll doom us all."

"Remember, it was you who refused to descend."

The lights in the room dimmed, pitching them into darkness. Rion's ball of magic hovered outside, casting them in shadows and the reflections of violet, emerald, and crimson.

She turned to Wolf, who held the Staff, his expression fierce.

"Are you ready?" she asked, flipping the book open.

Wolf nodded. "Of course, my queen."

He approached her, and she peered up at him, love bursting in her chest. No one would ever keep them apart, and together, they'd rule over Ouranos.

He cupped the back of her head with his hand and kissed her. "Let's do this so we can kick Rion's ass and get back to our daughter."

Serce found herself grinning. Their daughter. They hadn't even had the chance to name her. It would be the first thing they'd do when they were all reunited.

"For our daughter," she whispered, and he touched her forehead to hers.

"For all of us, Serce."

She looked down at Cloris, who was still babbling to herself. "We'll have to do this ourselves."

A large bang came from outside, shaking the entire castle. They'd broken through the gates. Shouts and screams rose as Serce watched from above while The Aurora army flowed into the city like a stain of ink.

"Hurry," Wolf said.

Serce flipped to the incantation Cloris had referenced when she'd still been sane.

"It says we need to repeat it three times while we hold each Artefact."

She held his hand as she read through the lines one by one:

Forge a bond of sea and sky

That Zerra cannot deny

When their fates are woven and spun

Take these hearts and make them one

The Crown on her head grew warm, crimson lightning sparking up her arms. Wolf's staff glowed brightly as green ribbons of smoke swirled around him. Their eyes met, and she'd never felt stronger or more connected to anyone in her life.

As she read the lines again, red and green met and twinned together, forming a single line of magic that glowed more brightly than the sun. As her lightning sparked, green smoke coalesced around them, converging into a show of their immense power.

It was the most beautiful thing she'd ever seen.

Another blast rocked the room, nearly throwing them off balance as the sounds of battle grew outside. They were coming.

The Aurora King was coming and Serce knew he'd come for *her* first.

She read the incantation for a third time.

Forge a bond of sea and sky.

Her power grew, swelling in her chest and her limbs.

That Zerra cannot deny.

Crimson bolts flashed through the room, spearing from the ceiling to the floor.

When their fates are woven and spun.

Green smoke swirled around them as her power swelled and swelled. Wolf's eyes sparkled like emeralds twirling in fire. He looked upon her with wonder and awe as his wings stretched out behind him.

She had never felt so strong. Magic coursed through her. Rivers of it. Waves of it. Oceans of it. She was stronger than anyone would ever be.

She closed her eyes and tipped her head up, inhaling a deep breath before she looked back at Wolf and their eyes locked.

Power. Strength. Destiny. *Mates.*

Yes, this is what she'd been waiting for all along.

She began the fourth line just as the castle shuddered again, the windows cracking and smashing apart in a shower of glass.

"Take these hearts and..."

The magic kept filling her as she said each word, one by one, wanting to prolong this moment for just another second. The moment when she'd finally take everything she'd ever wanted. She gripped Wolf's hand with all of her strength and said the last three words.

"...make...them...one."

As her voice fell silent, white noise flashed in her ears, a high-pitched whine that spiraled up and up just as a bright bolt of crimson lightning struck the ground between them, hurling them back and then...

The world shattered, and there was nothing but darkness.

ACKNOWLEDGMENTS

This whole writing thing has been such an adventure and I can't even begin to express how fortunate I feel to be on it.

Melissa, my writing spouse, I don't know what I'd do without your enthusiasm and your humour and just your wild and lovely spirit.

Bria, you've become one of the first people I go to when I've got another book done.

Shaylin, I feel like I found a writing soulmate in you. You're so talented and brilliant, and I can't thank you enough for putting your mark on this manuscript and all the rest.

Ashyle, thank you for your insight and wisdom—you have such a keen eye for everything.

Emily, thank you for being my sounding board and daily companion.

To Alexis and Alex, thank you for your unending support. The past three years would have been impossible without you.

To Priscilla and Elayna—thanks for being my last eyes on this book and for joining me on this journey. I look forward to publishing so many books next to you in the years to come. And thanks to Rae for your help with the incantation at the end!

Thank you to the slew of beta readers that helped me make this book everything it could be: Raidah, Elyssa, Nefer, Suzy, Ashley, Alexis, Catina, Emma, Rachel, Chelsea, Stacy, Holly, Elaine, Rebecca, and Kelsie.

To the reading community on BookTok and Bookstagram, thank you for being so enthusiastic and supportive of a brand new author who still had to prove herself. You're honestly the ones who made this all possible.

To my mom who was the one who always read books and looked at me and said "couldn't you write this?" Yah, I guess I finally did.

To my kids, Alice and Nicky, you are a never ending source of joy in my life, even when you're driving me crazy. It's a good thing you're cute. Thanks for being patient with me when I get distracted writing stories in my head when you talk to me sometimes.

And of course, to my husband Matthew, who's support and belief in me has never wavered a single day since we met all those years ago. Thank you for giving me the space and the freedom to pursue this and for allowing me to be the dramatic one. I'm not exaggerating when I say I couldn't do this if I didn't have a partner who gets it.

extras

orbitbooks.net

about the author

Nisha J. Tuli has always been obsessed with worlds she cannot see. From Florin to Prythian, give her a feisty heroine, a windswept castle, and true love's kiss, and she'll be lost in the pages forever. Bonus points for protagonists slaying dragons in kick-ass outfits.

When Nisha isn't writing, it's usually because one of her two kids needs something (she loves them anyway). After they're finally in bed, she'll usually be found with her e-reader or knitting sweaters and scarves, perfect for surviving a Canadian winter.

Find out more about Nisha J. Tuli and other Orbit authors by registering for the free monthly newsletter at orbitbooks.net.

if you enjoyed

RULE OF THE AURORA KING

look out for

THE JASMINE THRONE

by

Tasha Suri

One is a vengeful princess seeking to depose her brother from his throne. The other is a priestess searching for her family. Together, they will change the fate of an empire.

Imprisoned by her dictator brother, Malini spends her days in isolation in the Hirana: an ancient temple that was once the source of powerful magic — but is now little more than a decaying ruin.

Priya is a maidservant, one of several who make the treacherous journey to the top of the Hirana every night to attend Malini's chambers. She is happy to be an anonymous drudge, as long as it keeps anyone from guessing the dangerous secret she hides. But when Malini accidentally bears witness to Priya's true nature, their destinies become irrevocably tangled . . .

1

PRIYA

Someone important must have been killed in the night.

Priya was sure of it the minute she heard the thud of hooves on the road behind her. She stepped to the roadside as a group of guards clad in Parijati white and gold raced past her on their horses, their sabers clinking against their embossed belts. She drew her pallu over her face—partly because they would expect such a gesture of respect from a common woman, and partly to avoid the risk that one of them would recognize her—and watched them through the gap between her fingers and the cloth.

When they were out of sight, she didn't run. But she did start walking very, very fast. The sky was already transforming from milky gray to the pearly blue of dawn, and she still had a long way to go.

The Old Bazaar was on the outskirts of the city. It was far enough from the regent's mahal that Priya had a vague hope it wouldn't have been shut yet. And today, she was lucky. As she arrived, breathless, sweat dampening the back of her blouse, she could see that the streets were still seething with people: parents tugging along small children; traders carrying large sacks of flour or rice on their heads; gaunt beggars, skirting the edges of the market with their alms bowls in hand; and women like Priya, plain ordinary women in even plainer saris, stubbornly shoving their way through the crowd in search of stalls with fresh vegetables and reasonable prices.

If anything, there seemed to be even *more* people at the bazaar than usual—and there was a distinct sour note of panic in the air. News of the patrols had clearly passed from household to household with its usual speed.

People were afraid.

Three months ago, an important Parijati merchant had been murdered in his bed, his throat slit, his body dumped in front of the temple of the mothers of flame just before the dawn prayers. For an entire two weeks after that, the regent's men had patrolled the streets on foot and on horseback, beating or arresting Ahiranyi suspected of rebellious activity and destroying any market stalls that had tried to remain open in defiance of the regent's strict orders.

The Parijatdvipan merchants had refused to supply Hiranaprastha with rice and grain in the weeks that followed. Ahiranyi had starved.

Now it looked as though it was happening again. It was natural for people to remember and fear; remember, and scramble to buy what supplies they could before the markets were forcibly closed once more.

Priya wondered who had been murdered this time, listening for any names as she dove into the mass of people, toward the green banner on staves in the distance that marked the apothecary's stall. She passed tables groaning under stacks of vegetables and sweet fruit, bolts of silky cloth and gracefully carved idols of the yaksa for family shrines, vats of golden oil and ghee. Even in the faint early-morning light, the market was vibrant with color and noise.

The press of people grew more painful.

She was nearly to the stall, caught in a sea of heaving, sweating bodies, when a man behind her cursed and pushed her out of the way. He shoved her hard with his full body weight, his palm heavy on her arm, unbalancing her entirely. Three people around her were knocked back. In the sudden release of pressure, she tumbled down onto the ground, feet skidding in the wet soil.

The bazaar was open to the air, and the dirt had been churned into a froth by feet and carts and the night's monsoon rainfall. She felt the wetness seep in through her sari, from hem to thigh, soaking through draped cotton to the petticoat underneath. The man who had shoved her stumbled into her; if she hadn't snatched her calf swiftly back, the pressure of his boot on her leg would have been agonizing. He glanced down at her—blank, dismissive, a faint sneer to his mouth—and looked away again.

Her mind went quiet.

In the silence, a single voice whispered, *You could make him regret that.*

There were gaps in Priya's childhood memories, spaces big enough to stick a fist through. But whenever pain was inflicted on her—the humiliation of a blow, a man's careless shove, a fellow servant's cruel laughter—she felt the knowledge of how to cause equal suffering unfurl in her mind. Ghostly whispers, in her brother's patient voice.

This is how you pinch a nerve hard enough to break a handhold. This is how you snap a bone. This is how you gouge an eye. Watch carefully, Priya. Just like this.

This is how you stab someone through the heart.

She carried a knife at her waist. It was a very good knife, practical, with a plain sheath and hilt, and she kept its edge finely honed for kitchen work. With nothing but her little knife and a careful slide of her finger and thumb, she could leave the insides of anything—vegetables, unskinned meat, fruits newly harvested from the regent's orchard—swiftly bared, the outer rind a smooth, coiled husk in her palm.

She looked back up at the man and carefully let the thought of her knife drift away. She unclenched her trembling fingers.

You're lucky, she thought, *that I am not what I was raised to be.*

The crowd behind her and in front of her was growing thicker. Priya couldn't even see the green banner of the apothecary's stall any longer. She rocked back on the balls of her feet, then rose swiftly. Without looking at the man again, she angled herself and slipped between two strangers in front of her, putting her small stature to good use and shoving her way to the front of the throng. A judicious application of her elbows and knees and some wriggling finally brought her near enough to the stall to see the apothecary's face, puckered with sweat and irritation.

The stall was a mess, vials turned on their sides, clay pots upended. The apothecary was packing away his wares as fast as he could. Behind her, around her, she could hear the rumbling noise of the crowd grow more tense.

"Please," she said loudly. "Uncle, *please*. If you've got any beads of sacred wood to spare, I'll buy them from you."

A stranger to her left snorted audibly. "You think he's got any left? Brother, if you do, I'll pay double whatever she offers."

"My grandmother's sick," a girl shouted, three people deep behind them. "So if you could help me out, uncle—"

Priya felt the wood of the stall begin to peel beneath the hard pressure of her nails.

"Please," she said, her voice pitched low to cut across the din.

But the apothecary's attention was raised toward the back of the crowd. Priya didn't have to turn her own head to know he'd caught sight of the white-and-gold uniforms of the regent's men, finally here to close the bazaar.

"I'm closed up," he shouted out. "There's nothing more for any of you. Get lost!" He slammed his hand down, then shoved the last of his wares away with a shake of his head.

The crowd began to disperse slowly. A few people stayed, still pleading for the apothecary's aid, but Priya didn't join them. She knew she would get nothing here.

She turned and threaded her way back out of the crowd, stopping only to buy a small bag of kachoris from a tired-eyed vendor. Her sodden petticoat stuck heavily to her legs. She plucked the cloth, pulling it from her thighs, and strode in the opposite direction of the soldiers.

On the farthest edge of the market, where the last of the stalls and well-trod ground met the main road leading to open farmland

and scattered villages beyond, was a dumping ground. The locals had built a brick wall around it, but that did nothing to contain the stench of it. Food sellers threw their stale oil and decayed produce here, and sometimes discarded any cooked food that couldn't be sold.

When Priya had been much younger she'd known this place well. She'd known exactly the nausea and euphoria that finding something near rotten but *edible* could send spiraling through a starving body. Even now, her stomach lurched strangely at the sight of the heap, the familiar, thick stench of it rising around her.

Today, there were six figures huddled against its walls in the meager shade. Five young boys and a girl of about fifteen—older than the rest.

Knowledge was shared between the children who lived alone in the city, the ones who drifted from market to market, sleeping on the verandas of kinder households. They whispered to each other the best spots for begging for alms or collecting scraps. They passed word of which stallholders would give them food out of pity, and which would beat them with a stick sooner than offer even an ounce of charity.

They told each other about Priya, too.

If you go to the Old Bazaar on the first morning after rest day, a maid will come and give you sacred wood, if you need it. She won't ask you for coin or favors. She'll just help. No, she really will. She won't ask for anything at all.

The girl looked up at Priya. Her left eyelid was speckled with faint motes of green, like algae on still water. She wore a thread around her throat, a single bead of wood strung upon it.

"Soldiers are out," the girl said by way of greeting. A few of the boys shifted restlessly, looking over her shoulder at the tumult of the market. Some wore shawls to hide the rot on their necks and arms—the veins of green, the budding of new roots under skin.

"They are. All over the city," Priya agreed.

"Did a merchant get his head chopped off again?"

Priya shook her head. "I know as much as you do."

The girl looked from Priya's face down to Priya's muddied sari, her hands empty apart from the sack of kachoris. There was a question in her gaze.

"I couldn't get any beads today," Priya confirmed. She watched the girl's expression crumple, though she valiantly tried to control it. Sympathy would do her no good, so Priya offered the pastries out instead. "You should go now. You don't want to get caught by the guards."

The children snatched the kachoris up, a few muttering their thanks, and scattered. The girl rubbed the bead at her throat with her knuckles as she went. Priya knew it would be cold under her hand—empty of magic.

If the girl didn't get hold of more sacred wood soon, then the next time Priya saw her, the left side of her face would likely be as green-dusted as her eyelid.

You can't save them all, she reminded herself. *You're no one. This is all you can do. This, and no more.*

Priya turned back to leave—and saw that one boy had hung back, waiting patiently for her to notice him. He was the kind of small that suggested malnourishment; his bones too sharp, his head too large for a body that hadn't yet grown to match it. He had his shawl over his hair, but she could still see his dark curls, and the deep green leaves growing between them. He'd wrapped his hands up in cloth.

"Do you really have nothing, ma'am?" he asked hesitantly.

"Really," Priya said. "If I had any sacred wood, I'd have given it to you."

"I thought maybe you lied," he said. "I thought, maybe you haven't got enough for more than one person, and you didn't want to make anyone feel bad. But there's only me now. So you can help me."

"I really am sorry," Priya said. She could hear yelling and footsteps echoing from the market, the crash of wood as stalls were closed up.

The boy looked like he was mustering up his courage. And sure enough, after a moment, he squared his shoulders and said, "If you can't get me any sacred wood, then can you get me a job?"

She blinked at him, surprised.

"I—I'm just a maidservant," she said. "I'm sorry, little brother, but—"

"You must work in a nice house, if you can help strays like us," he said quickly. "A big house with money to spare. Maybe your masters need a boy who works hard and doesn't make much trouble? That could be me."

"Most households won't take a boy who has the rot, no matter how hardworking he is," she pointed out gently, trying to lessen the blow of her words.

"I know," he said. His jaw was set, stubborn. "But I'm still asking."

Smart boy. She couldn't blame him for taking the chance. She was clearly soft enough to spend her own coin on sacred wood to help the rot-riven. Why wouldn't he push her for more?

"I'll do anything anyone needs me to do," he insisted. "Ma'am, I can clean latrines. I can cut wood. I can work land. My family is—they were—farmers. I'm not afraid of hard work."

"You haven't got anyone?" she asked. "None of the others look out for you?" She gestured in the vague direction the other children had vanished.

"I'm alone," he said simply. Then: "*Please.*"

A few people drifted past them, carefully skirting the boy. His wrapped hands, the shawl over his head—both revealed his rot-riven status just as well as anything they hid would have.

"Call me Priya," she said. "Not ma'am."

"Priya," he repeated obediently.

"You say you can work," she said. She looked at his hands. "How bad are they?"

"Not that bad."

"Show me," she said. "Give me your wrist."

"You don't mind touching me?" he asked. There was a slight waver of hesitation in his voice.

"Rot can't pass between people," she said. "Unless I pluck one of those leaves from your hair and eat it, I think I'll be fine."

That brought a smile to his face. There for a blink, like a flash of sun through parting clouds, then gone. He deftly unwrapped one of his hands. She took hold of his wrist and raised it up to the light.

There was a little bud, growing up under the skin.

It was pressing against the flesh of his fingertip, his finger a too-small shell for the thing trying to unfurl. She looked at the tracery of green visible through the thin skin at the back of his hand, the fine lace of it. The bud had deep roots.

She swallowed. Ah. Deep roots, deep rot. If he already had leaves in his hair, green spidering through his blood, she couldn't imagine that he had long left.

"Come with me," she said, and tugged him by the wrist, making him follow her. She walked along the road, eventually joining the flow of the crowd leaving the market behind.

"Where are we going?" he asked. He didn't try to pull away from her.

"I'm going to get you some sacred wood," she said determinedly, putting all thoughts of murders and soldiers and the work she needed to do out of her mind. She released him and strode ahead. He ran to keep up with her, dragging his dirty shawl tight around his thin frame. "And after that, we'll see what to do with you."

The grandest of the city's pleasure houses lined the edges of the river. It was early enough in the day that they were utterly quiet, their pink lanterns unlit. But they would be busy later. The brothels were always left well alone by the regent's men. Even in the height of the last boiling summer, before the monsoon had cracked the heat in two, when the rebel sympathizers had been singing anti-imperialist songs and a noble lord's chariot had been cornered and burned on the street directly outside his own haveli—the brothels had kept their lamps lit.

Too many of the pleasure houses belonged to highborn nobles for the regent to close them. Too many were patronized by visiting merchants and nobility from Parijatdvipa's other city-states—a source of income no one seemed to want to do without.

To the rest of Parijatdvipa, Ahiranya was a den of vice, good for pleasure and little else. It carried its bitter history, its status as the losing side of an ancient war, like a yoke. They called it a backward place, rife with political violence, and, in more recent years, with the rot: the strange disease that twisted plants and crops and infected the men and women who worked the fields and forests with flowers that sprouted through the skin and leaves that pushed through their eyes. As the rot grew, other sources of income in Ahiranya had dwindled. And unrest had surged and swelled until Priya feared it too would crack, with all the fury of a storm.

As Priya and the boy walked on, the pleasure houses grew less grand. Soon, there were no pleasure houses at all. Around her were cramped homes, small shops. Ahead of her lay the edge of the forest. Even in the morning light, it was shadowed, the trees a silent barrier of green.

Priya had never met anyone born and raised outside Ahiranya who was not disturbed by the quiet of the forest. She'd known maids raised in Alor or even neighboring Srugna who avoided the place entirely. "There should be noise," they'd mutter. "Birdsong. Or insects. It isn't natural."

But the heavy quiet was comforting to Priya. She was Ahiranyi to the bone. She liked the silence of it, broken only by the scuff of her own feet against the ground.

"Wait for me here," she told the boy. "I won't be long."

He nodded without saying a word. He was staring out at the forest when she left him, a faint breeze rustling the leaves of his hair.

Priya slipped down a narrow street where the ground was uneven with hidden tree roots, the dirt rising and falling in mounds beneath her feet. Ahead of her was a single dwelling. Beneath its pillared veranda crouched an older man.

He raised his head as she approached. At first he seemed to look right through her, as though he'd been expecting someone else entirely. Then his gaze focused. His eyes narrowed in recognition.

"You," he said.

"Gautam." She tilted her head in a gesture of respect. "How are you?"

"Busy," he said shortly. "Why are you here?"

"I need sacred wood. Just one bead."

"Should have gone to the bazaar, then," he said evenly. "I've supplied plenty of apothecaries. They can deal with you."

"I tried the Old Bazaar. No one has anything."

"If they don't, why do you think I will?"

Oh, come on now, she thought, irritated. But she said nothing. She waited until his nostrils flared as he huffed and rose up from the veranda, turning to the beaded curtain of the doorway. Tucked in the back of his tunic was a heavy hand sickle.

"Fine. Come in, then. The sooner we do this, the sooner you leave."

She drew the purse from her blouse before climbing up the steps and entering after him.

He led her to his workroom and bid her to stand by the table at its center. Cloth sacks lined the corners of the room. Small stoppered bottles—innumerable salves and tinctures and herbs harvested from the forest itself—sat in tidy rows on shelves. The air smelled of earth and damp.

He took her entire purse from her, opened the drawstring, and adjusted its weight in his palm. Then he clucked, tongue against teeth, and dropped it onto the table.

"This isn't enough."

"You—of course it's enough," Priya said. "That's all the money I have."

"That doesn't magically make it enough."

"That's what it cost me at the bazaar last time—"

"But you couldn't get anything at the bazaar," said Gautam. "And had you been able to, he would have charged you more. Supply is low, demand is high." He frowned at her sourly. "You think it's easy harvesting sacred wood?"

"Not at all," Priya said. *Be pleasant*, she reminded herself. *You need his help.*

"Last month I sent in four woodcutters. They came out after two days, thinking they'd been in there *two hours*. Between—that," he said, gesturing in the direction of the forest, "and the regent flinging his thugs all over the fucking city for who knows what reason, you think it's easy work?"

"No," Priya said. "I'm sorry."

But he wasn't done quite yet.

"I'm still waiting for the men I sent this week to come back," he went on. His fingers were tapping on the table's surface—a fast, irritated rhythm. "Who knows when that will be? I have plenty of reason to get the best price for the supplies I have. So I'll have a proper payment from you, girl, or you'll get nothing."

Before he could continue, she lifted her hand. She had a few bracelets on her wrists. Two were good-quality metal. She slipped them off, placing them on the table before him, alongside the purse.

"The money and these," she said. "That's all I have."

She thought he'd refuse her, just out of spite. But instead, he scooped up the bangles and the coin and pocketed them.

"That'll do. Now watch," he said. "I'll show you a trick."

He threw a cloth package down on the table. It was tied with a rope. He drew it open with one swift tug, letting the cloth fall to the sides.

Priya flinched back.

Inside lay the severed branch of a young tree. The bark had split, pale wood opening up into a red-brown wound. The sap that oozed from its surface was the color and consistency of blood.

"This came from the path leading to the grove my men usually harvest," he said. "They wanted to show me why they couldn't fulfill the regular quota. Rot as far as the eye could see, they told me." His own eyes were hooded. "You can look closer if you want."

"No, thank you," Priya said tightly.

"Sure?"

"You should burn it," she said. She was doing her best not to breathe the scent of it in too deeply. It had a stench like meat.

He snorted. "It has its uses." He walked away from her, rooting through his shelves. After a moment, he returned with another cloth-wrapped item, this one only as large as a fingertip. He unwrapped it, careful to keep from touching what it held. Priya could feel the heat rising from the wood within: a strange, pulsing warmth that rolled off its surface with the steadiness of a sunbeam.

Sacred wood.

She watched as Gautam held the shard close to the rot-struck branch, as the lesion on the branch paled, the redness fading. The stench of it eased a little, and Priya breathed gratefully.

"There," he said. "Now you know it is fresh. You'll get plenty of use from it."

"Thank you. That was a useful demonstration." She tried not to let her impatience show. What did he want—awe? Tears of gratitude? She had no time for any of it. "You should still burn the branch. If you touch it by mistake..."

"I know how to handle the rot. I send men into the forest every day," he said dismissively. "And what do you do? Sweep floors? I don't need your advice."

He thrust the shard of sacred wood out to her. "Take this. And leave."

She bit her tongue and held out her hand, the long end of her sari drawn over her palm. She rewrapped the sliver of wood up carefully, once, twice, tightening the fabric, tying it off with a neat knot. Gautam watched her.

"Whoever you're buying this for, the rot is still going to kill them," he said, when she was done. "This branch will die even if I wrap it in a whole shell of sacred wood. It will just die slower. My professional opinion for you, at no extra cost." He threw the cloth back over the infected branch with one careless flick of his fingers. "So don't come back here and waste your money again. I'll show you out."

He shepherded her to the door. She pushed through the beaded curtain, greedily inhaling the clean air, untainted by the smell of decay.

At the edge of the veranda there was a shrine alcove carved into the wall. Inside it were three idols sculpted from plain wood, with lustrous black eyes and hair of vines. Before them were three tiny clay lamps lit with cloth wicks set in pools of oil. Sacred numbers.

She remembered how perfectly she'd once been able to fit her whole body into that alcove. She'd slept in it one night, curled up tight. She'd been as small as the orphan boy, once.

"Do you still let beggars shelter on your veranda when it rains?" Priya asked, turning to look at Gautam where he stood, barring the entryway.

"Beggars are bad for business," he said. "And the ones I see these days don't have brothers I owe favors to. Are you leaving or not?"

Just the threat of pain can break someone. She briefly met Gautam's eyes. Something impatient and malicious lurked there. *A knife, used right, never has to draw blood.*

But ah, Priya didn't have it in her to even threaten this old bully. She stepped back.

What a big void there was, between the knowledge within her and the person she appeared to be, bowing her head in respect to a petty man who still saw her as a street beggar who'd risen too far, and hated her for it.

"Thank you, Gautam," she said. "I'll try not to trouble you again."

She'd have to carve the wood herself. She couldn't give the shard as it was to the boy. A whole shard of sacred wood held against skin—it would burn. But better that it burn her. She had no gloves, so she would have to work carefully, with her little knife and a piece of cloth to hold the worst of the pain at bay. Even now, she could feel the heat of the shard against her skin, soaking through the fabric that bound it.

The boy was waiting where she'd left him. He looked even smaller in the shadow of the forest, even more alone. He turned to watch her as she approached, his eyes wary, and a touch uncertain, as if he hadn't been sure of her return.

Her heart twisted a little. Meeting Gautam had brought her closer to the bones of her past than she'd been in a long, long time. She felt the tug of her frayed memories like a physical ache.

Her brother. Pain. The smell of smoke.

Don't look, Pri. Don't look. Just show me the way.

Show me—

No. There was no point remembering that.

It was only sensible, she told herself, to help him. She didn't want the image of him, standing before her, to haunt her. She didn't want to remember a starving child, abandoned and alone, roots growing through his hands, and think, *I left him to die. He asked me for help, and I left him.*

"You're in luck," she said lightly. "I work in the regent's mahal. And his wife has a very gentle heart when it comes to orphans. I should know. She took me in. She'll let you work for her if I ask nicely. I'm sure of it."

His eyes went wide, so much hope in his face that it was almost painful to look at him. So Priya made a point of looking away. The sky was bright, the air overly warm. She needed to get back.

"What's your name?" she asked.

"Rukh," he said. "My name is Rukh."